MONSIEUR PAMPLEMOUSSE
OMNIBUS

VOLUME 3

Monsieur Pamplemousse Omnibus

Volume 3

Michael Bond

a&b

This edition published
in Great Britain in 1999 by
Allison & Busby Limited
114 New Cavendish Street
London W1M 7FD
http://www.allisonandbusby.ltd.uk

Monsieur Pamplemousse Stands Firm
first published 1992 by Headline Book Publishing PLC

Monsieur Pamplemousse on Location
first published 1992 by Headline Book Publishing PLC

Monsieur Pamplemousse Takes the Train
first published 1993 by Headline Book Publishing PLC

A catalogue record for this book is available
from the British Library

ISBN 0 7490 0442 8

Design and cover illustration by Pepe Moll

Printed and bound by Biddles Limited,
Guildford, Surrey.

Contents

Monsieur Pamplemousse Stands Firm

Contents

1
OPERATION BALLPOINT

The scene would have appealed to Monet; and, given his eye for a pretty form and his unquenchable appetite for the good things in life, without doubt it would have inspired him to reach for the nearest palette and brushes with all possible speed, his beard quivering with barely suppressed excitement. It had all the ingredients for a masterpiece.

The occasion was the annual staff party given by Monsieur Henri Leclercq, Director of *Le Guide,* France's oldest and most respected gastronomic bible. The setting was his summer residence near Deauville; the date, 15 July. It was a date which marked the start of the Season; a season of international bridge, theatre, golf tournaments, jazz concerts at the casino, and above all as far as the Director was concerned, six weeks of horse racing.

The party was an event much looked forward to by the staff, not so much for the delights of Deauville itself – but because the Director was a generous host and they knew that the food and the wine would be beyond reproach; the surroundings and the ambience such as would have assured it a top rating of three Stock Pots in their own publication had it been eligible. In short, it was a chance for everyone to indulge themselves at someone else's expense.

The majority of the office staff had arrived in a specially chartered coach; by and large those who spent their days 'on the road' came by car as a matter of course; a few, like

Monsieur and Madame Pamplemousse, had opted for the relative luxury of travelling by train.

The Director's summer residence was inland from the sea, in a wooded area halfway between Deauville and Pont l'Evêque; convenient both for the airport and the *autoroute* to Paris, which could be reached in under two hours. Nestling in a pocket in the hills, the house was scarcely visible from the winding country lane which provided the one artery connecting it with the outside world. It was a veritable paradise: an immaculately kept garden of Eden contained within a few hectares of land.

Any tourists, having visited the fourteenth-century Romanesque church in the nearby village, and still preoccupied by the sight of its ancient stained-glass windows and collection of canvases by Jean Restout, might easily have missed the house altogether as they went on their way, *en route*, perhaps, to one of the local cheese factories. But had they chanced to spy it through a gap in the hedge as they drove past, they could have been forgiven for assuming they had stumbled across a film company on location, or a freshly assembled kit of parts arranged for the benefit of a photographer working on the country issue of a glossy ideal home magazine.

The gravelled drive, entered via a pair of ornate, remotely controlled wrought-iron gates standing a little way back from the road, having wound its way down the hillside past weeping willows and a scattering of beech trees set in immaculately tonsured lawns, ended up as a large circular parking area outside a picturesque black and white half-timbered house of the sort normally encountered only in dreams or in house agents' advertisements found in out-of-date magazines in dentists' waiting-rooms. Bearing the inscription 'price on application', they had always 'only

12

just been taken off the market' should anyone be bold enough to make further inquiries.

Between the house and an equally charming stable block of generous dimensions which served as a garage, there was a large patio dotted with garden furniture, the whiteness of which was offset by splashes of red from the mass of *Danse du Feu* roses climbing the wall behind.

As it made its way down the hill the drive passed a large brick and stone Norman dovecot to one side and on the other a stream with a white wooden bridge which led nowhere, but looked as if it might. The stream, in turn, cascaded over a waterfall and into a large pond on the surface of which there floated a variety of ducks. (Guilot, who for some reason knew about ducks, had a theory they had been bought by the architect via a mail-order catalogue; they were almost too perfect a collection to have arrived where they were simply by chance.

Perfectionist that he was, the only change Monet might have made would have been to divert the stream away from the pond in order to provide suitably tranquil conditions for his beloved water lilies. Although he was probably aware, more than most people, that even in Paradise, one cannot have everything.

Clad in a white apron to protect his green corduroy trousers and tweed jacket from the splashes of recalcitrant fat, and sporting a tall chef's togue on his head, the Director had been busy for most of the late morning and early afternoon dispensing hot *saucisses*, *andouilles* and *boudin noir* from an enormous barbecue in the centre of the patio.

Brushed with melted butter and served with caramelised slices of apple, the grilled *boudin* had been most popular of all and he had been hard put to keep pace with the demand.

There had been pieces of leg of lamb on skewers too; *pré-salé* lamb from the sea-washed marshes of Mont St Michel.

The meal had started simply enough with freshly boiled shrimps – and for those whose preference ran towards a cold collation, to follow there had been a choice between lobster mayonnaise or thick slices of local ham baked in cider, accompanied by tomato salad and marinated cucumber, served with local bread and wedges of rich, yellow, Normandy butter.

There were those, and it has to be said they formed the majority, who were unable to make up their mind and found themselves accepting both offerings of the cold collation and then followed that with a selection from the griddle.

After a suitable gap there was Camembert, Livarot and Pont l'Evêque cheese: all in a perfect state of ripeness – the Camembert, an unpasteurised version from a local farm; the Livarot, orange-coloured and served from its package of banded marsh grass; the Pont l'Evêque, soft and smooth in its golden rind.

And now, to complete the pastoral scene, a bevy of local girls, rosy-cheeked and dressed in traditional costume, appeared as if by magic carrying enormous earthenware platters, some piled high with freshly cooked *bourdelots* – apple dumplings wrapped in butter pastry – others with mounds of strawberries, and still more with bowls of thick cream the colour of ivory.

Cider – *bon bére*, the true Norman cider which remains still until poured, when it sparkles, frothless and pure as a mountain stream – had flowed freely throughout, although there was wine in variety available for those who preferred it to the fermented juice of the *pommes*. The Director was not one to stint his guests.

It had been a splendid feast. And now the after-effects were beginning to show. All available chairs on the patio were occupied, some clearly for the rest of the afternoon. Bernard was already fast asleep under a tree. Those who had gone so far as to bring tennis rackets, having mentally ear-marked the two courts at the rear of the house for an afternoon's sport, were having second thoughts. A half-hearted game of croquet was in progress. Glandier, never one to let an opportunity slip by, was chatting to one of the serving girls. Any moment now he would be asking her if she would like to see one of his conjuring tricks. Madame Grante, swaying slightly from a surfeit of cider, watched disapprovingly from a distance. Others were setting off up the drive to explore the village.

Monsieur Pamplemousse decided it was a good thing the usual group photograph had been taken before lunch.

He looked for Doucette, but she was some distance away, engaged in animated conversation with the Director's wife. Pommes Frites was busy clearing up behind the barbecue.

The Director, fresh from his ablutions, emerged from the kitchen, peered round the garden, then beckoned.

'I wonder if I might have a word with you, Aristide?'

As he followed his host into the house, Monsieur Pamplemousse couldn't help but reflect that it was a rhetorical question. He could hardly have declined, and certainly the Director hadn't left him any time to say 'no' even if he had wanted to.

He wondered idly what was in the wind. It struck him that his boss was wearing a slightly furtive air. His suspicion was confirmed a moment later when the Director, having led him into the drawing-room, excused himself for a moment while he went off to make certain as he put it 'that they wouldn't be disturbed'.

Monsieur Pamplemousse glanced around the room. The works of several minor Impressionists adorned the walls, the balanced composition of antique furniture, silverware and other artefacts reflected the quiet good taste of its owners: taste which was not only quiet but expensive too, if he was any judge. Loudier, who had been with *Le Guide* longer than most, was undoubtedly right in his theory that the Director had married into money. It was hard not to feel a touch of envy; and he would have been less than honest if he had said otherwise.

On the other hand he couldn't picture living there himself. The Director moved easily in such surroundings. He was in his element. But had Monsieur Pamplemousse been asked which he would really prefer, his own or the Director's way of life, he knew in his heart which he would choose.

He crossed the room and looked out of the window. The rich pile of the Aubusson carpet beneath his feet felt as soft as had the freshly manicured lawn outside; a lawn which he noted was rapidly emptying of guests.

He caught sight of Doucette on the far side, still walking with the Director's wife, and he was about to open the French windows and call out when he heard a door open behind him.

The Director entered the room and as he came up behind Monsieur Pamplemousse and followed the direction of his gaze immediately withdrew into shadow, signalling his guest to do likewise.

'I suggested to Chantal that she take Madame Pample- mousse to see the dovecot,' he said, closing one of the curtains slightly. 'It should keep them busy for a while. The history of the Norman dovecot dates back to Roman times.'

Catching Monsieur Pamplemousse's eye, the Director made haste to justify his last remark.

'Please don't think for one moment that I wish to say something I would rather my wife didn't overhear . . .'

Monsieur Pamplemousse pricked up his ears still further. As an opening gambit the Director had assured himself of an audience. Guy de Maupassant could not have wished for a more riveting start to one of his stories.

'What of Madame Pamplemousse, *Monsieur?*' he enquired innocently. 'Would she be interested were I to repeat what you have to say?'

'You must answer that question yourself after I have told you, Pamplemousse,' said the Director crossly. 'I really cannot make these decisions for you. Speaking personally, I would err on the side of caution.'

Monsieur Pamplemousse glanced out of the window again, but Doucette and the Director's wife had already disappeared. Pommes Frites looked as though he was up to no good with the Director's Borzoi behind some nearby bushes. One of his senses having been satisfied, he appeared to be more than ready to round things off by assuaging a second. Monsieur Pamplemousse was on the point of wondering if he should mention it when the matter was decided for him.

'Pamplemousse, are you listening to me? I fear I do not have your undivided attention.' Clearly, the Director was in no mood to be diverted from whatever it was he had on his mind.

'I was about to say, Aristide, that we live in changing times. Only the other day I saw a young girl driving an *autobus* through the streets of Paris, and a very good job she was making of it, too.'

Monsieur Pamplemousse waited patiently. Clearly there was more to come. The Director would hardly have brought him indoors in order to discuss the merits or otherwise of female bus drivers.

'It is getting harder and harder to differentiate between the sexes.'

Monsieur Pamplemousse nodded his agreement. 'It is most apparent, *Monsieur*, in the area of *les toilettes*. I often have to study the pictures on the doors most carefully. Then, more often than not when you go inside you discover they are all one and the same anyway.'

The Director grunted impatiently. 'That is not quite what I meant, Pamplemousse.

'I meant that increasingly one finds women doing work which in the past has always been regarded as man's province.'

'Like coal mining, *Monsieur*?'

'No, Pamplemousse, I do not mean coal mining, although doubtless in some parts of the world – Russia, *par exemple*, it is already an established fact. I am thinking of nearer home.'

Monsieur Pamplemousse considered the matter. 'But we already have a good record in that respect, *Monsieur*. Old Rambaud on the gate was grumbling about it only the other day. Things have gone to the other extreme. According to him even the office cat is female. At a rough guess I would say the female staff in the offices of *Le Guide* already outweigh the males by some ten to one.'

'Ah, Pamplemousse,' the Director looked at him triumphantly, glad to have got his point over at last. 'In the offices that is so, but what of those on the road – the Inspectors? Is it not time we had a female Inspector?'

Monsieur Pamplemousse looked dubious. 'What of the others, *Monsieur*? How will they feel about it?' He couldn't picture Truffert taking kindly to the idea for a start.

It was rumoured that he'd only become an Inspector in order to escape from his wife. *Le Guide* was one of the last bastions of male chauvinism – at least as far as the Inspectors were concerned. In many ways it was the nearest equivalent in France to an Englishman's club.

Crossing the room, the Director began nervously to rearrange some flowers in an enormous bowl standing on a table in front of the fireplace. 'For the time being, Aristide, there is no need for the others to know.'

'I fail to see the point, *Monsieur.* Surely they will have to be told sooner or later.'

'Not necessarily, Pamplemousse.'

'Comment?'

Flowers were rearranged yet again. The Director looked as though he was beginning to wish he hadn't started on them.

'That, Aristide, is where you come in.'

'I, *Monsieur?'*

'There is really no point in my telling the others, if at the end of her attachment the lady in question fails to make the grade. They will all have been upset for nothing.'

Monsieur Pamplemousse began to look even more dubious. 'But supposing, *Monsieur* . . . just supposing, she does make the grade . . . and there is no reason why she shouldn't. The number of women chefs in France is growing . . .' Despite his initial misgivings, he found himself warming to the thought of there being a female Inspector. It would certainly add a bit of sparkle to the annual group photograph.

'Why should she fail, *Monsieur?'*

'Because, Pamplemousse, at the end of her attachment you will make absolutely certain that she does.'

'1, *Monsieur?* Why me?'

The Director glared at him. 'I do wish you wouldn't keep saying "I, *Monsieur?*" *It* not only makes you sound like a parrot, but one singularly bereft of a working vocabulary.

'I say *you*, Pamplemousse, because it is *you* to whom she will be attached – figuratively speaking, of course.'

Monsieur Pamplemousse stiffened and turned to leave. There was a point where lines had to be drawn and this was it. 'No, *Monsieur. Pardonnez-moi . . . mais . . .*'

'*Asseyez-vous*, Aristide. *Asseyez-vous*, there's a good chap.'

Motioning Monsieur Pamplemousse towards a deep leather armchair, the Director reached for a decanter and poured a generous helping of golden brown liquid into a glass. It was dark with age.

'Try some of this. I am not normally much of a one for Calvados, but when in Normandy . . . It is a *Les "Aieux" L'Aigle Millésimé* 1947. I think you will like it.' He filled a second glass and downed it in a single swallow.

'I have a particular reason for asking. I know that in view of your past reputation I may be playing with fire, but I need someone of discretion . . . a man of the world. A man who will understand the problem and act accordingly.'

'I understand the problem, *Monsieur*. I can see the addition of a *femme* to what has always been a domain *masculin* will pose many problems, but as you said earlier, times change, and they need not be insurmountable. In any case, I have to say that to prejudge a poor innocent girl in this way would be grossly unfair.'

'Life is often grossly unfair, Pamplemousse. Life, for many people, is unfair from the moment they are born. As for the person concerned being "innocent" I doubt if she knows the meaning of the word. You might say that in many respects Elsie has little cause to feel hard done by, but

20

when it comes to the allocation of "innocence" she may well feel she was given short measure.'

'Elsie?' repeated Monsieur Pamplemousse. A warning bell began to sound in the deep recesses of his mind.

'Did you say her name is Elsie, *Monsieur?*'

The Director nodded unhappily.

'Not,' continued Monsieur Pamplemousse relentlessly, 'the same Elsie who for a brief period was in your employ? The English *au pair* who cooked *boeuf rôti* the night Doucette and I came to dinner? *Boeuf rôti* with a pudding known as Yorkshire?'

The Director looked even more ill at ease. He replenished his glass. 'You remember her?'

'I could hardly forget her, *Monsieur.* She cooked like a dream, but she was also the stuff that dreams are made of.'

'An unlikely, but devastating combination, eh, Aristide?'

Oui, Monsieur. And I have to tell you straight away that the answer is *non.'*

To say that Monsieur Pamplemousse remembered Elsie was the understatement of the year. After their brief encounter he had lain awake for the rest of the week thinking of very little else. Freudian dreams involving Elsie had filled his sleep. Elsie dressed in the uniform of a water Inspector; Elsie dressed as a swimming Instructor, Elsie in oilskins rescuing him from drowning . . .

The Director took a precautionary look into the garden. When he next spoke it was with a lowered voice.

'Aristide, that girl is totally without scruples. Why she should suddenly evince a desire to become an Inspector heaven alone knows. But she is determined to get her way, and if she doesn't my life here will not bear thinking about . . .' With a wave of his hand which embraced that part of

21

his estate which could be seen through the French windows he downed his second glass of Calvados.

'She is threatening you, *Monsieur*?'

'Not in so many words. She has simply intimated that if there is a problem in granting her request perhaps she should visit me here so that we can discuss the matter in more detail. Can you picture it?

'You have no idea what life in a small village is like. Everyone knows everyone else's business. In Paris you can be anonymous. In the country, traffic through the kitchen is often worse than the Champs Elysées on a Friday evening. Then there is the Curé to be considered. *Monsieur le Curé* is one of the old school, steeped in the ways of a bygone age. The world with its changing mores and behaviour patterns has passed him by.'

The Director gave a shudder. 'I can hear the sound of her high heels on the cobblestones as she goes to see him.'

Monsieur Pamplemousse had a sudden thought. 'Could you not return to Paris for a few days, *Monsieur*? You could deal with the matter there.'

'And miss the start of the season? It is short enough as it is.'

'There must be other beaches, *Monsieur*. Le Touquet . . .'

The Director gave him a glassy stare. 'One does not come to Deauville in order to disport oneself on the beach, Pamplemousse.'

Although he didn't actually physically recoil at the idea, clearly he was distancing himself from it as far as he possibly could.

Monsieur Pamplemousse had spoken without thinking. On further consideration he doubted if the Director had ever been on a beach in his life. He certainly couldn't picture him with his trousers rolled up to the knees making sand-castles. Paddling as a form of pleasure would have by-passed him. Nor would he take kindly to Pommes Frites shaking himself over all and sundry after returning from a swim. He decided to change the subject.

'May I ask what happened with Elsie, *Monsieur?*'

'Nothing, Aristide. I swear on my copy of *Le Guide* that nothing untoward took place. What was intended merely as an encouraging pat while she went about her work, an avuncular gesture as she applied her feather duster to the chandelier in the hall, was grossly misconstrued. Or, to put it in another way, I suspect Elsie chose, for her own good reasons, to misconstrue it, filing the incident away in her mind for future use should the occasion demand. That occasion has arrived. Elsie wishes to be an Inspector.'

'But surely, *Monsieur*, if she brings the matter up, then it will simply be a matter of her word against yours.'

'Exactly, Pamplemousse. There, in your inimitable way, you have put your finger on the nub of the problem.'

Monsieur Pamplemousse fell silent.

'I have learned over the years, Aristide, that when it comes to a husband's word against that of another woman – whatever her age or circumstances or disposition, then it is the latter's word the wife invariably believes. When it involves a girl like Elsie, the dice are loaded from the very beginning. Nature has endowed her with qualities which give rise to immediate suspicion on the distaff side.'

Monsieur Pamplemousse couldn't help but be aware of a certain fellow feeling. 'But why me, *Monsieur?* Why not someone else? Bernard – or Glandier. Either of them would probably jump at the chance. Glandier especially.'

'Exactly, Aristide. And in so doing they would undoubtedly fall for Elsie hook line and sinker. Her little finger would be the least she would twist them around. They might even come up with a recommendation for her permanent employment. I agree that in normal circumstances pairing her with you would not be the happiest combination, but these are not normal circumstances.'

'What shall I tell my wife, *Monsieur?*' He couldn't picture Doucette taking kindly to the news that he had a female attached to him, and if she ever discovered it was Elsie she would be down on him like a pile of bricks.

'Have no fear, Aristide, I have thought of that.' Sensing victory at last the Director reached for his wallet, opened it, and withdrew a somewhat dog-eared photograph. 'This is a picture of the daughter of a cousin of mine. As you can see she was not exactly in the front row when looks were given out. You can take it as an insurance policy. Should any enquiries be made *chez* Pamplemousse you can say this is your attachment.'

Monsieur Pamplemousse examined the picture. The Director was right. 'Barrels must have been scraped, *Monsieur.*'

'*Exactement.* If you must tell Madame Pamplemousse, I suggest you choose a suitable moment and then arrange for her to come across the photograph by "accident". I'm sure I need hardly tell an old hand like yourself how to play your cards.'

While the Director was talking, Monsieur Pamplemousse took out his pen. The photograph was printed on matt paper and it was a simple matter to add a few spots in strategic places. In a matter of moments what had been merely unattractive became positively repellent. Trigaux in the art department would have been proud of him. He felt sorely tempted to add the beginnings of a moustache, but decided it might be overdoing things.

The Director rubbed his hands together briskly. 'Excellent, Pamplemousse. Excellent. You have missed your vocation.

'I can't tell you how relieved I am. I knew you wouldn't let me down. I must say that in some ways I envy you the task.'

Monsieur Pamplemousse brightened. 'You are welcome to go in my place, *Monsieur*,' he said, clutching at straws. 'In fact, it might be a very good idea. Then no one can accuse you of partiality.'

'*Impossible*, Aristide. *Impossible!* It is the first of the season's important race meetings tomorrow. Elsie arrives at Bordeaux airport on the afternoon flight You will need to be there by sixteen-thirty and as you know it is a long drive from Paris.'

'Bordeaux!' Monsieur Pamplemousse couldn't remember when he had last visited the west coast of France. 'It is a long time since I tasted the delights of Michel Guérard at Eugénie les Bains, *Monsieur*. They say he has gone from strength to strength.'

The Director gave a grunt. 'I am afraid, Pamplemousse, you will have to rely on the opinion of others for the time being. Les Prés d'Eugénie is not on your itinerary.'

Monsieur Pamplemousse tried to conceal his disappointment 'Ah, perhaps *Monsieur is* thinking of Au Bon Coin at Mimizan. Mimizan itself is like an abandoned film set, but the lake beside which the restaurant stands is very beautiful and I am told that the small island which adjoins the hotel has now been laid out as a garden . . . as for the food . . .'

'No, Pamplemousse, I do not have Au Bon Coin in mind either. Or rather, Elsie does not. Her initial demands, I have to say, are surprisingly modest.

'She has expressed a desire to explore the coastal area around Arcachon. Quite why she wishes to go there I do not know, I suspect an ulterior motive, but who am I to deny her wish? It has the advantage of being relatively unspoiled.'

'It has the corresponding disadvantage, *Monsieur*, of being relatively unencumbered with restaurants of note. As I recall, Stock Pots are minimal.'

'All the more reason to go there, Pamplemousse. It will be a challenge for you; something to get your teeth into.'

It struck Monsieur Pamplemousse that in the circumstances the last phrase was singularly inappropriate. Offhand, he could think of many other places he would stand more chance of finding something worth while to sink his teeth into.

'Elsie has even given me the name of an hotel near Arcachon where she wishes to stay – the Hôtel des Dunes. Unfortunately it doesn't appear to be listed in our records, or in any other guide come to that, so I am unable to tell you much about it. However, accommodation has been arranged. You can use it as a base for a week while you explore the area. I told Elsie she could have that amount of time in which to prove herself and she seemed reasonably satisfied. The rest is in your hands.'

Recognising defeat, Monsieur Pamplemousse rose from his chair. 'I will do my best, *Monsieur*, insofar as my conscience will allow. I cannot guarantee the result, but in the meantime I will of course report back to you on a regular basis.'

'No, no! Pamplemousse.' The Director looked agitated. 'I have gone to great pains to make certain Chantal knows nothing whatsoever about my plans. As far as she is concerned Elsie went back to *la Grande Bretagne* for good. It must remain that way. Absolute secrecy is the order of the day.'

'But, *Monsieur* . . .'

The Director held up his hand. *'Discrétion absolue,* Pamplemousse!'

'I understand what you are saying, *Monsieur,* but supposing . . . just supposing something goes wrong. I may need to telephone for further instructions.'

'Things must not go wrong, Pamplemousse. As for telephoning me here, that is out of the question. It is quite within the bounds of possibility that either by accident or design Chantal could pick up an extension receiver and overhear our conversation, then where would I be? Her suspicions would be aroused on the instant.'

Monsieur Pamplemousse considered the matter for a moment or two. The Director was right in his last remark. He wouldn't normally have any reason for telephoning. The Director's wife would smell a rat straight away if she caught them talking.

'In that case, *Monsieur,'* he said, tapping his teeth with the pen, 'we must think up a reason. Perhaps I could leave something behind when we go today. Something precious . . .'

The Director clapped his hands together. 'Good thinking, Aristide. You have it right there in your hand!'

Monsieur Pamplemousse gave a start. 'But that is my favourite Cross pen, *Monsieur.* I shall be lost without it. Besides, it will be a bad omen I am sure.'

'Nonsense, Aristide. In a week's time you shall have it back. If all goes well you can have a dozen pens.'

Now that the idea had been suggested, the Director entered into the scheme of things with all his old enthusiasm. Without waiting for a reply he took the pen from

Monsieur Pamplemousse and stuffed it down the side of the chair.

'No one will find it there unless they are looking specially.

'We must find a code-word. What is the English word for *stylo*? Ballpoint; we will call the whole thing Operation Ballpoint. Should you run into trouble all you need do is say the word and I shall be on the *qui-vive* immediately.'

Without further ado the Director picked up a small antique hand-bell. 'I will ring for some tea. No doubt you and your wife will be wanting to get back to Paris and have a reasonably early night in view of your journey tomorrow. After tea I will arrange for a car to take you to the train.'

'It's a lovely evening,' said Doucette, as they disembarked outside the *gare* in Deauville. 'Why don't we go for a walk and catch a later train?'

Monsieur Pamplemousse looked at his wife in surprise. It was a long time since she had suggested such a thing. Normally, she would have been only too anxious to get home.

Pommes Frites decided matters for them. Pommes Frites could smell the sea, and in Pommes Frites' opinion anyone who went to the sea-side and didn't go on the beach needed their head examined. Without further ado he set off in the general direction of the harbour.

The tide was in when they reached the yacht basin. On the Trouville side of the Touques estuary they could see boats of the fishing fleet being made ready for the night's work. In less than twelve hours' time they would be back again and the little fish market alongside the *quai* would be bustling with activity.

Monsieur Pamplemousse wished he'd thought to bring his camera with him. It was easy to see why the light had attracted the early Impressionists, although what they would have made of the hideous new high-rise apartments which blocked the view of the sea on the Deauville side was anybody's guess.

Crossing the little pedestrian walkway which spanned the harbour entrance gates, they skirted the port until they reached the Promenade des Planches – the boardwalk made famous in the film *Un Hormme et une Femme*.

Pommes Frites galloped on ahead, blissfully unaware of notices reminding owners of dogs that anything untoward must happen below that area which would be covered by the incoming tide. It didn't leave him much room for manoeuvre.

'Aristide, is there anything going on between you and *Monsieur le Directeur?*'

Lost in his own thoughts, Monsieur Pamplemousse gave a start. 'Why do you ask, *chérie?*'

'Apparently he has been acting very strangely over the past few days. Besides, he made it perfectly obvious he wanted to get together with you on his own. Chantal knows even less about dovecots than I do.' The fact that Doucette was suddenly on Christian-name terms with the Director's wife did not escape Monsieur Pamplemousse.

'I gather it has to do with a letter which arrived from England, earlier in the week. Chantal found bits of it down the waste disposal the next morning. There was a picture of the queen on one of the stamps.'

Monsieur Pamplemousse gave his wife a side-long glance. 'What else did Madame Leclercq have to talk about?'

'Oh, this and that.'

They strolled along the boardwalk in silence for a while. A burst of screeching from a flock of sea-gulls wheeling in the sky above the harbour marked the passage of a fishing boat. Pommes Frites found a large stick on the sand and brought it for his master, wagging his tail in anticipation. Monsieur Pamplemousse absentmindedly obliged and had it returned to him in a flash.

'There have been phone calls,' said Doucette. 'And once, when Chantal pressed the re-dial button, she got an English number. '

'Did she find out who it was?'

'No. The person hung up immediately they heard her voice.'

Monsieur Pamplemousse breathed an inward sigh of relief.

Cars were starting to draw up outside the Casino, disgorging occupants in evening dress. From where they were walking he could see the lighted chandeliers within. The gaming-room itself would be closed to the outside world. There would be a room full of one-armed bandits of course – a sign of the times – but, apart from the cars and posters heralding a visit by Lionel Hampton and Dave Brubeck, he doubted if the scene was very different to the days when Marcel Proust used to go there regularly in order to gamble and dance the night away.

As they drew near, without either of them saying a word, they turned off the boardwalk and away from the sea.

'The fact is . . .' began Monsieur Pamplemousse, 'I have been entrusted with a very delicate mission. The Director told me in strictest confidence, but I know you won't say anything.'

As they headed back towards the town he gave Doucette a brief run-down of the Director's plans, omitting both Elsie's name and his own instructions; neither of which would go down well – it was hard to say which would be worse. Of the two, he infinitely preferred to argue his way out of the latter.

'If that's all there is, then if you ask me he's making a mountain out of a molehill. Anyway, I don't see why it has to be an English girl. There must be plenty of French girls more than capable of doing the job.'

Monsieur Pamplemousse gave a shrug as much as to say who am I to comment?

Halfway back to the station they stopped at a café. He suddenly felt unusually dry and in need of a long glass of something cold and thirst-quenching. He decided to stay with cider. Doucette chose a *citron pressé*.

When they had finished, Monsieur Pamplemousse called for *l'addition* and in opening his wallet, allowed the Director's photograph to fall on the table.

'It is so that I shall recognise her at the airport,' he said carelessly.

Doucette glanced at it. 'She doesn't look at all as one might expect. She looks in need of care and protection. Perhaps I should come with you for once?'

'Now, now, Couscous. You know how I feel about mixing work with pleasure.' It was hard to tell whether the question had been asked in innocence or not.

'Poor thing. Just look at her face. I've never seen so many spots.' Holding the photograph up to the light, Madame Pamplemousse subjected it to a closer inspection.

Monsieur Pamplemousse's heart missed a beat. Stamped across the back in large letters was the name of a well-known French processing company. But he needn't have worried. His wife had other things on her mind.

'How very strange.' She dipped her finger in a glass of water and applied it to the surface. 'Someone must have been defacing it. Look – the ink comes away. What can it mean?'

Monsieur Pamplemousse shifted uneasily in his seat. 'I think you have been married too long to an ex-detective, *chérie*. It has made you suspicious.'

'But don't you think it is strange?' Doucette wasn't to be diverted that easily. 'Why should anyone wish to do that? It isn't even well done.'

'I really don't know, Couscous,' said Monsieur Pamplemousse testily. 'People do the oddest things. I'm sure there is a simple explanation.

'All I know is it couldn't have been me.' He opened his jacket and pointed to the inside pocket. 'I have lost my pen. The one you gave me years ago. When we get to the *gare* I must telephone the Director in case I left it there.'

'Ah! That reminds me. I can save you the trouble.' Doucette reached for her handbag. 'I have some good news for you. Chantal found it tucked away in the side of a chair. She gave it to me just before we left. You must have dropped it when you and the Director were having your chat. I told her how upset you would have been.'

Monsieur Pamplemousse was hardly listening; his mind was racing in different directions. Warning bells began to sound again, only much louder this time; a whole carillon. If Chantal had found his pen she must have been giving the room a fine going-over. And why had she given it to Doucette and not to him? It sounded distinctly fishy. It was imperative that he get in touch with the Director as soon as possible and warn him.

'Are you sure it is mine?'

'It has your initials on the side.'

They caught the 19.21 stopping train to Lisieux and changed there for the Paris express. It arrived at the Gare St Lazare at 22.01 precisely and they were home by half past ten.

While Doucette bustled about doing things in the kitchen, Monsieur Pamplemousse slipped into the bedroom. Keeping his fingers crossed in the hope that Doucette wouldn't catch him in the act, he dialled the Director's number. A problem shared was a problem halved.

'*Monsieur.*'

There was a pause. 'I am sorry.' The Director sounded sleepy. He must have gone to bed early, doubtless worn out by his exertions over a hot barbecue.

'I am afraid you have the wrong number. There is no one here of that name.' His voice had a muffled quality to it, as though he had his head under the bedclothes.

'Ballpoint, *Monsieur!*'

There was a certain vicarious pleasure to be derived from saying the word. The Director was right; it did have a much better ring to it than *stylo*.

For reasons he couldn't quite put his finger on, Monsieur Pamplemousse had an uneasy feeling in the back of his mind that he was about to be plunged into deep waters: waters that were not only deep, but black, with hidden undercurrents. As he replaced the receiver he took comfort in the knowledge that he was no longer the only one likely to lie awake that night wondering what the morrow would bring. A problem shared was a problem halved.

2
OMENS GALORE

Propping up the counter of Le Rendezvous bar at Mérignac airport, Monsieur Pamplemousse ordered his third Kir of the day. The first had been at an *autoroute café* south of Tours on the journey down from Paris, where they had stopped for lunch; the second when he arrived in Bordeaux, hot, tired and thirsty. It had hardly touched his lips. Now he was ready for the third, to be sipped in a more leisurely fashion while he kept a watchful eye on the exit doors leading from the Arrivals area.

It had been a long drive. Even using the *autoroute* all the way, it had taken over seven hours; eight if you included the stops. His *deux chevaux* was never designed to break the world speed record. Not, according to the barman, that there had been any great need to hurry; the summer schedules were in operation – the holiday season was about to begin – need one say more, *Monsieur? As* if that wasn't enough to contend with, there were the usual seasonal problems with Air Traffic Control.

Having poured the drink, he seemed pleased to have someone to talk to as he set about polishing the glasses.

Monsieur Pamplemousse listened with only half an ear. After being cooped up in the car for so long he needed time to unwind. Pommes Frites looked as though he was feeling the effects too; padding up and down the hall like a caged lion while he awaited his master's bidding, occasionally pricking up his ears as he caught the sound of an aircraft taking off or landing.

The Kir was better than expected, perhaps because he was in wine country. It was also unusually generous.

He eyed a row of telephones on a nearby wall, wondering if he should try ringing the Director. Then he remembered there was a race meeting in Deauville that day. Resisting the temptation to make a fictitious call so as to get a moment or two of peace, he inquired about the hotel.

'The Hôtel des Dunes? Funny you should ask that.' The barman gave one of the glasses an extra polish and then studied it as he held it up to the light. 'I hadn't even heard of it until the other day, and now you're the second person wanting to know where it is in less than a week. It's on the other side of Arcachon. Head for the town, then when you get to the other side, make for Pyla-sur-Mer and hug the coast road. Watch out for the sign – it's easy to miss.

'I'll tell you something else about it . . .'

But he had lost his audience. Seeing a flurry of activity further down the hall, Monsieur Pamplemousse downed the rest of his drink and made his way to join the welcoming throng at the bottom of a ramp leading from the Arrivals hall. He glanced up at a board as he went. It showed the AF1859 from London had landed five minutes ago.

Behind a glass partition passengers were already scurrying around looking for trolleys, stationing themselves optimistically in strategic positions alongside an empty carousel while they waited for something to happen.

A second carousel started up on the other side of the hall and everyone began moving again. It was like watching a television repeat of the opening scene in *Monsieur Hulot's Holiday*. Somehow people were always at their most vulnerable when travelling; sheeplike in their behaviour as they allowed themselves to be herded from pillar to post, anxious for reassurance and obeying every command which came from on high.

He caught sight of Elsie at the back of the hall. She was accompanied by an older man pushing an empty trolley. A moment later they disappeared from view. Elsie probably never went anywhere without people dancing attendance on her, a supply of willing hands ready to reach out and offer help at the slightest hint of a problem.

A few seasoned travellers carrying hand luggage emerged through customs. The first was an obvious Englishman wearing a tropical suit and a panama hat. Clutching a small leather attaché case and a pair of Bush and Meissener field-glasses, he disappeared with a purposeful stride; probably heading for one of the local bird sanctuaries.

Close on his heels came a sprinkling of businessmen; dark-suited, over-weight and perspiring slightly. He guessed they were in the wine trade on a late *en primeur* buying spree. Good reports were coming in about the previous year's vintage and some owners had been holding back in the hope of getting a better price.

Elsie was one of the last out. Her travelling companion had deserted her and she was making heavy weather of the trolley. Monsieur Pamplemousse's heart sank as the automatic doors parted and he caught sight of all the luggage. It looked as though she had come prepared for a long stay. If Elsie had aspirations to work for *Le Guide* he would have to spell out lesson number one: never carry anything which wasn't entirely necessary. That would be yet another problem if they started employing female staff; a man could happily go on wearing the same suit day in day out. Elsie would have brought a different outfit for every meal.

Only too well aware of glances being cast in his direction, Monsieur Pamplemousse went forward to greet his protégée as she gathered speed coming down the ramp.

'Elsie! *Bonjour! Comment allez-vous?*'

'Oooh, am I glad to see you. I thought I was never going to get 'ere.' Elsie looked Monsieur Pamplemousse up and down as she skidded to a halt. 'You 'aven't changed much, I must say.'

'Neither have you.' Monsieur Pamplemousse essayed an attempt at gallantry. 'A little younger, perhaps.' He gave a sigh. 'Ah, how well I remember your Yorkshire puddings.'

'Saucebox!' A playful blow to the chest took him by surprise and sent him reeling.

Pommes Frites reacted with commendable speed. One moment Elsie was patting her blonde hair into place, the next moment she found herself pinned to a nearby pillar.

'Ere what's going on? What sort of a welcome is that? Go away! Shoo! You reek of garlic.'

'*Assieds-toi!*' Monsieur Pamplemousse leapt to her assistance. With ill-concealed reluctance Pommes Frites obeyed his master's command. Releasing his captive, he retreated a pace or two, at the same time keeping a watchful eye on Elsie's heaving bosoms: a self-appointed task in which he was obviously not alone.

'I trust you are not hurt?' Monsieur Pamplemousse also viewed her appendages with some concern.

'Nothing that a little bit of a rub in the right place won't put right,' said Elsie cheerfully. As she spoke she pulled back one shoulder of her dress, offering up an expanse of flesh for closer inspection.

'Can't see anything wrong with it, can you?'

Monsieur Pamplemousse shook his head. Patently the starboard *doudoune*, unencumbered by any man-made means of support, was as nature had intended it to be; large, firm and in pristine condition. He mopped his brow. Elsie's *balcons* were as he remembered them.

Out of the corner of his eye he saw the barman miss the top of a glass by several centimetres as he poured himself a drink.

'Allow me.' Reaching past Elsie he fed five francs into a *Péage* machine, waited for a ticket to emerge, then took charge of the trolley.

'Do not forget, *Monsieur. Embrassez le côte!* If you hug the coast you will have no trouble.'

Monsieur Pamplemousse treated the barman's aside as they passed his counter with the contempt it deserved. He led the way out of the hall and across a service road towards the car park.

His 2CV, still hot from the journey, had become hotter still through standing in the afternoon sun.

'Phew!' Elsie fanned herself with a magazine as she settled down in the front seat. 'It ain't half hot! I'm all of a fluster. What with your dog and everything.'

'Pommes Frites is very protective,' said Monsieur Pamplemousse as he climbed in beside her and started the engine. 'Also, I am afraid we had *saucisson à l'ail* on the journey down. It is made with pork, plus a little brandy and a touch of saltpetre. It was a local variation and it was unusually powerful. I think there may have been a little too much garlic.'

'You're telling me,' said Elsie, waving the magazine with renewed vigour. She winced as Pommes Frites breathed out heavily from the back seat.

Taking the hint, Monsieur Pamplemousse set about unrolling the roof canopy.

Once outside the airport he took the first right at a roundabout on to a minor road, then right again on to the

D106. As they settled down to a steady fifty k.p.h. he glanced across at Elsie. She was feeling around in the area above the windscreen.

'You will find a map in the door compartment.'

'Do *what?*'

Monsieur Pamplemousse tried rephrasing the remark. 'The map. It is in the compartment of the door.'

'I thought that's what you said.'

'I assumed you were wishing to navigate.'

'Navigate? I was looking for a mirror wunn I. A girl's got to think of her appearance. You never know. My mum always says that if you got yer make-up on and a pair of clean knickers it doesn't matter what 'appens to you. Don't tell me we're lost already?'

'I am not familiar with the area,' said Monsieur Pamplemousse. 'According to the barman we need to hug the coast. I think perhaps we should take a left soon.'

'Well,' said Elsie, with a note of finality, 'that's as may be, but for your information I don't drive, so I've not never 'ad to navigate.'

Monsieur Pamplemousse experienced a feeling of relief. The ability to drive a car was an essential requirement for anyone wishing to work as an Inspector for *Le Guide*. The Director would be pleased when he heard the news. If Elsie had to take driving lessons it could prolong the problem indefinitely.

'I was hoping that since you chose to stay at the Hôtel des Dunes you might know where it is.'

Elsie gave a hollow laugh. 'You'll be lucky. Some people say I don't know my left titty from my right titty.' She announced the fact with a touch of pride. 'But as I always say, if you follow your instincts who needs a map?'

Monsieur Pamplemousse concentrated on the road ahead for a minute or two while he considered the last remark.

'Vanity mirrors are an optional extra,' he said at last, pleased with his command of the English language. It was not the kind of thing one would necessarily find in a phrase book. Most phrase books dealt only in negatives. 'This car has no vanity mirror.' 'The vanity mirror has fallen off.' The people who wrote them must lead extraordinarily unsatisfactory lives, forever losing their wallets or worse.

'Had I known that one day you would be a passenger I would certainly have asked for one,' he added.

Elsie pursed her lips as though about to utter the word 'saucebox' again, but had second thoughts. Pommes Frites was watching her every movement from the back seat.

'If there's no mirror,' she said, 'you'll just 'ave to take me as I am.'

'I am more than happy to, Elsie,' said Monsieur Pamplemousse. 'And please call me Aristide.'

It was Elsie's turn to look thoughtful as they drove along in silence for a while.

Monsieur Pamplemousse spent the time racking his brains as he tried to recall snippets of information culled from a brief reading of *Le Guide* during his stop on the way down.

It was hard to tell what Elsie was thinking. Her face registered very little in the way of emotion as she gazed out at the passing scene. It might have been a moonscape, albeit one which was dotted with signs advertising cherries for sale and peppered with little groups of cyclists limbering up for the coming season.

The fact that Sarah Bernhardt had spent the latter part of her life in nearby Andemos, riding around town in a little invalid cart after her leg was amputated, would probably leave Elsie unmoved.

He wondered if he should tell her about the time in 1927 when 80,000 metric tons of pit props had been exported by sea from Cap Ferret to *Grande Bretagne,* but he doubted his ability to strike the right note for someone who was patently neither a miner nor a wood merchant. He was right.

'Are you trying to make me wet myself with excitement or summock?' said Elsie, when he essayed an attempt.

Monsieur Pamplemousse decided to make one last effort. It was a case of nothing ventured, nothing gained. 'Did you know it was near here that a certain Monsieur Allègre built the first steam trawlers in the world? He called them *Le Turbot* and *La Sole.*'

'The trouble with you French,' said Elsie, 'is you bring sex into everything. I can't get on with all these "le's" and "la's". You don't know where you stand. I don't see no sense in it.'

'The French,' said Monsieur Pamplemousse defensively, 'are known for their logic.'

'Try telling that to a female turbot,' said Elsie.

Signs pointing towards the ornithological park at Le Teich passed without comment; the storks, the bluethroats, the bearded tits and the stilt birds could rest easy in their nests as far as Elsie was concerned; the mullet and the bream in the ponds and lakes were free to carry on catching flies with impunity; the ducks and geese would be able to continue their swimming undisturbed.

The nearer they got to their destination the quieter Elsie became. Monsieur Pamplemousse wondered if it was nerves. She didn't look the nervous type. If that were the case he was in for a fraught week.

On the other side of Arcachon Monsieur Pamplemousse followed the barman's instructions and took the coast road. Pyla-sur-Mer came and went and suddenly the whole of the basin was spread out before them. Away in the distance he could see a long line of white-capped rollers marking the point where the Atlantic ocean met calmer waters at the narrow entrance to the bay.

They passed some people having a picnic and he felt hunger pangs. Pommes Frites saw them too and peered out of the back window as they drove on.

The Dune du Pilat – the first and largest of the great dunes which formed a backdrop to the Côte d'Argent – loomed into view.

'"Pilat" means a "pile of sand",' said Monsieur Pamplemousse, as he executed a sharp turn to the left and the road began to wind uphill.

Elsie eyed the scene with a distinct lack of enthusiasm. 'They must be expecting to do a lot of building, that's all I can say.'

A moment later – just as the barman had said – they came across a sign for the hotel, half hidden behind some trees. If he hadn't been forewarned and consequently not had his wits about him he would have driven straight past. Braking sharply, he turned off the road. The driver of a car following behind gave a blast on his horn.

But Monsieur Pamplemousse had his own problems. Pressing even harder on the brake pedal, he skidded to a halt, just in time to avoid colliding with two police cars coming the other way. The occupants stared out at them. An officer in the passenger seat of the second car saluted Elsie. A colleague in the back passed a remark and the others laughed. The driver removed one hand from the wheel and gave the shaking of a limp wrist signal. There was renewed laughter.

Monsieur Pamplemousse could have written the dialogue.

He wondered briefly why there had been two cars. There were a dozen reasons for there being one; two carrying a total of eight officers suggested something more serious.

Moving off, he drove a short distance down a gravelled lane lined on either side with pine trees. It was no wonder the barman had been so emphatic. The hotel itself must be completely hidden from the road. Monsieur Pample-mousse's heart sank as a building came into view. The entrance to it was devoid of any recommendations whatso-ever. There was not a single plaque to be seen; even the Camping Club de France had failed to bestow any kind of award.

Climbing out of the car, he automatically took stock of his surroundings as he went round to open the other door for Elsie. They were not auspicious. The obligatory menu pinned to the inside of a glass case was hand-written and looked as though it had been there for a very long time. From a distance it was impossible to tell what colour the ink might have been originally.

There was a sprinkling of cars with foreign number plates parked to one side of the ill-kept driveway. One with English number plates, a German registered Mercedes, a Renault 25 with a Paris number, a Peugeot with a Hertz label on the inside of the windscreen, plus a couple of others which looked as though they might belong to the hotel.

Pommes Frites jumped out through the roof of the car and hurried round the back of the building on a tour of inspection. He returned a moment or two later looking gloomy. Clearly the smells from the kitchen area hadn't rung any gastronomic bells as far as he was concerned; rather the reverse.

Entering the hotel, Monsieur Pamplemousse brightened momentarily as he spotted a large fish tank just inside the door. Anticipation was short-lived. The water looked murky, and there was a dead *langouste* lying on the bottom.

There was no sign of a lift. The only area of wall where one might have been was occupied by a large oil painting of a woman on a horse. It looked as though it had recently been cleaned, which was rather more than could be said for the rest of the room.

A pile of well-thumbed brochures spread out across a counter partly concealed a bellpush. They looked as though they might have been put there for that very purpose. He pushed them to one side and tried pressing the button. Somewhat to his surprise there was an answering ring from somewhere nearby.

An ageless person of saturnine appearance emerged through an opening behind the reception desk and eyed them without enthusiasm. Welcoming smiles were conspicuous by their absence.

'There are no rooms.' Bending down, he produced a COMPLET notice and placed it firmly on the counter.

Monsieur Pamplemousse felt in his pocket for a card.

'We have reservations,' he said firmly. 'Confirmed reservations for two rooms with bath. I do not wish to be difficult, but . . .'

With a decided show of ill grace the man consulted a list under the counter, then turned to a board behind him and removed two keys. 'Eleven and twenty-one. They are on different floors.' He seemed to derive a vicarious satisfaction at the thought.

'*Chiens* are twenty francs a night extra. Fifteen if you share.'

Monsieur Pamplemousse gained equal satisfaction as he returned one of the keys. 'You will find *Mademoiselle's* baggage on the back seat of my car. There are six pieces. '

He turned away from the desk. 'If eleven is not to your liking, Elsie, let me know.'

Seeing that Elsie seemed preoccupied with the painting on the wall, Monsieur Pamplemousse repeated his remark.

'Eleven!' Elsie turned to face him. 'What do you mean, eleven? I'm supposed to be 'aving twenty-one. It was all arranged.'

Monsieur Pamplemousse took a deep breath. Initially his sole reason for letting Elsie have the room on the first floor was because there would be fewer stairs for her to climb. However, there was no accounting for the workings of the female mind, and if she was going to be difficult then so be it. Two could play at that game. There were moments in life when authority had to be established; parameters laid down. To his way of thinking this was one of them. If he didn't do it now he never would.

'I am afraid,' he said, 'I have already taken it.'

He decided to leave Elsie to it. She was well able to take care of herself. Already he could sense the other man was battling against his instincts over the matter of the luggage, and he knew which side would win. Elsie's pout at being thwarted had already been replaced by her 'little girl lost' look.

Signalling Pommes Frites to follow, Monsieur Pample-mousse made his way up the stairs. As he reached the first landing he came face to face with another picture. It had obviously replaced a larger painting at some time. A lighter patch on the wallpaper showed clearly where the previous one had hung In the style of the Impressionists, the painting was of a canal in summer time. The poppies in the

45

foreground contrasted strangely with a vase of dead flowers standing on a table further along the corridor.

Mounting a second flight of stairs he was aware of a familiar smell. It was a smell he had encountered many times in other small hotels: a mixture of heat, dust, and stale air.

His first impulse on entering his room was to fling open the window. He immediately wished he hadn't. Although there was only a slight breeze blowing, he could feel the sand stinging his face. Any view there might have been was almost entirely blocked by an enormous dune. It answered the question as to why everywhere felt so airless.

He closed the window and glanced around the room. Flowered paper covered the walls. The furniture was basic from a pre-war hotelier's catalogue. He ran his finger along the top of a chest of drawers. As he expected, it was covered with a layer of fine sand; it must have got everywhere during the previous winter's bad storms.

On the wall behind the bed there was yet another picture. This time it was in the style of an early Van Dyck. At least someone in the hotel must be making an effort. Whoever it was certainly had catholic tastes. The bedside light worked and there was also a telephone. The bed itself was firm to the touch and the linen looked crisp enough. In one comer there was the ubiquitous refrigerator with a list of its contents and the corresponding prices stuck to the outside. It must be a godsend after a day climbing about on the dunes. It was probably where the hotel got most of its profit as well.

The bathroom contained no surprises.

Monsieur Pamplemousse unpacked his bag, then looked at his watch. It was past six o'clock.

As he started to undress he fell to wondering what had made Elsie choose such an out-of-the-way hotel to begin her apprenticeship. Perhaps, despite her outward air of confidence, she was intimidated by large, glossy establishments, just as he had been when he was her age. Except that things were different now. Elsie's generation took everything in their stride, behaving as if the world owed them a living.

He wondered what she would make of the plumbing. Was she, even now, standing in the bath on the floor below him trying to operate the shower? If so, he hoped she was having better luck than he was. It took him a good five minutes of fiddling to fathom out the workings; another five to empty the bath, which in the meantime had become almost full to overflowing. The whole thing wasn't helped when in the middle of it all he heard someone trying his door handle. By the time he'd got out of the bath, wrapped himself in a dressing gown and reached the door, whoever it was had disappeared.

Monsieur Pamplemousse returned to the shower. Somewhere in France there must be a man with a grudge against society; a man who took enormous pleasure in designing bathroom fittings which effectively concealed their means of operation.

The occupants of the adjoining room seemed to be having similar problems. Snatches of German filtered through the wall; first a woman's voice raised in anger, then a man's. It was some minutes before the argument subsided, gradually merging with the sound of running water.

Although it was only a few minutes past seven when Monsieur Pamplemousse finally left his room, bathed, shaved, and wearing a change of clothing, the sun had already disappeared and the corridor was in semi-darkness.

The dune must effectively advance lighting-up time in the hotel by a good hour or more.

As he fiddled with the key in the lock he felt rather than saw a momentary flash of light coming from somewhere behind him. For a split second he took it to be a flash of lightning. It was sultry enough for a thunderstorm. Then, as he reached the stairs and looked down, he saw Elsie disappearing towards her room. She was carrying a Polaroid camera.

Mentally Monsieur Pamplemousse awarded her bonus points. If she was already at work taking pictures of the inside of the hotel she must be serious about wanting to be an Inspector. It made up for her earlier behaviour. All entries in *Le Guide* were accompanied by a photograph. In the filing room back at Headquarters there was a whole library of references – several million of them – painstakingly built up over the years. He made a mental note to let Elsie have a go with his issue Leica. It might inspire her.

Monsieur Pamplemousse paused on his way down the stairs and took a longer look at the picture of the canal. Interestingly, someone had bothered to install a security alarm. Whoever it was had done a good job; the wire was barely perceptible to the naked eye. He couldn't help reflecting that if the picture was that special the owners might have chosen a better place to hang it; one where it would be possible to view it by something other than the light from a *minutenrie*. Perhaps the simple explanation was that its predecessor had been stolen and the new one was simply a cheap replacement.

As he reached the entrance hall he glanced at the fish tank. The *langouste* was nowhere to be seen. An elderly battlescarred lobster with bandaged claws had taken its place. It eyed him mournfully through the glass as though realising it might be next on the list.

For no good reason save that it was a matter of contrasts, it reminded Monsieur Pamplemousse of an incident which had occurred on the journey down from Paris. Returning to his car after lunching at an *autoroute* restaurant, he had encountered two men in white coats pushing a trolley. He'd naturally assumed they were delivering fresh supplies. It wasn't until he drew level with the trolley that he realised the truth. Lying beneath a sheet was a little old lady. Presumably she was being transported between two hospitals and didn't want to miss her *déjeuner*. She had smiled at him as they passed.

At the time he had found the brief episode immensely cheering; a sign of the indomitable spirit of human beings. Truly, a reversal of the saying that in the midst of life we are in death; a good omen in fact. Now, with the memory of the lobster fresh in his mind, its days clearly numbered, he wasn't quite so sure.

3
POMMES FRITES
SPRINGS A SURPRISE

On entering the dining-room Monsieur Pamplemousse found the atmosphere was, to say the least, morgue-like.

'M'sieur' dame.' Taking his seat at a table near the window he gave a courteous nod to an English couple and two young children sitting nearby. The wife pretended not to have noticed. The man was eyeing a *langouste* with disfavour. Monsieur Pamplemousse wondered if it was the one which was missing from the tank. Time would tell.

The woman glared at Pommes Frites as he took his place alongside Monsieur Pamplemousse. It was yet another example of popular misconceptions. The English were supposed to be fond of animals and yet they wouldn't dream of sharing a meal with their pets, preferring to leave them outside in their car and risk possible asphyxiation.

In the far corner of the room a group of three men were seated round a table poring over a map. From the way they were dressed and the cut of their clothes, he guessed they were Americans.

There was no sign of the German couple who had been having a row in the next room. Perhaps they were still making it up under the shower. He hoped the hot water lasted out.

In another corner a solitary diner – he guessed it might be a passing rep – sat turning the pages of a book in a desultory fashion. He had already consumed the contents of a bread basket and the best part of a bottle of red wine, and was no further advanced with his meal.

The rest of the diners looked as though they had been there for so long they were part of the furniture and fittings.

It struck him that apart from the English family, who had probably come down early because of the children, the one thing the guests all had in common was that none of them was eating.

He glanced around the room, automatically registering the decor. Wood-panelled walls – much too dark in the circumstances. More paintings. They looked as though they'd been hung without any rhyme or reason. Although having said that, he'd seen worse in many an art gallery. There was a still life near the door – a bowl of fruit alongside a vase of flowers – which particularly caught his eye and he longed to straighten it. The flowers certainly looked in better shape than the plastic ones on his table, which resembled no known species he had ever come across. He blew on them and a small cloud of fine sand rose into the air.

Unlike the bed linen, the table cloth felt soft to the touch. He suspected it had been there for some time. On the other hand – he picked up the salt cellar – the cruet was solid silver.

Monsieur Pamplemousse's musings were brought to an abrupt halt by the arrival of Elsie.

His own entrance had elicited no more than the usual covert glances and the kind of whispered remarks that any group of people make when they spy a stranger in their midst; their prior arrival having given them a certain proprietorial interest in the comings and goings of others who had yet to learn the ropes.

Elsie's appearance, however, produced a kind of stunned silence.

In marked contrast to the other guests, whose garb was not only casual, but in the case of the Americans verging on the *al fresco,* she was wearing a transparent off-the-shoulder evening dress which somehow managed to reveal far more than it concealed. Her progress across the room was punctuated by a series of *'Pardonnez-moi*'s', 'Please don't move,' and 'Oh, dear – silly me – I should have gone the other way – I do 'ope it comes off,' as she squeezed her way in and out of the tables.

In his role of waiter, the receptionist, revealing himself to be a man of many parts, followed closely behind, only darting on ahead at the last moment to ensure her seat was properly in place when she reached the table.

Menus and the wine list arrived with a flourish. Their order was taken; the wine – a Sancerre – arrived with embarassing speed. Monsieur Pamplemousse tested it and nodded his approval. It had a characteristic 'gunflint' aroma and at least it was suitably chilled.

'Maurice is ever so nice really,' said Elsie, as the waiter departed. 'He helped me with the bath taps. I got in such a tizwaz with the shower, you wouldn't believe.'

Monsieur Pamplemousse surreptitiously felt below the tablecloth.

'Ere, what are you up to?' asked Elsie in a loud voice.

'I wish to make notes about the wine,' he whispered, reaching for his pen.

'That's your story,' said Elsie. 'Pull the other one – it's got bells on. I've met your sort before.'

'Comment?'

'Tell me what you're really up to.'

'I have a secret compartment in my right trouser leg,' hissed Monsieur Pamplemousse. 'It is where I keep my notebook.'

'If I get a job as an Inspector,' said Elsie, 'I could keep a notebook up my knickers. 'Cept I don't always wear any and even if I did it might fall out, if you know what I mean.'

Monsieur Pamplemousse was conscious of a lull in the conversation around him. The English family were staring in his direction; the man twirled his moustache thoughtfully as he eyed the back of Elsie's dress. His wife was telling the children to eat up and not ask questions.

The smaller of the two asked why not. The mother asked why it kept on asking questions. The child asked why she wanted to know.

It was a no-win situation for the mother.

He caught the word 'disgusting' as a platter of oysters resting on a bed of fresh ice and seaweed arrived at their table. He wasn't sure whether it applied to the food, to him personally, or the hotel in general.

'One of the chief rules an Inspector working for *Le Guide* has to obey,' said Monsieur Pamplemousse, 'is that of anonymity. Total and absolute anonymity.'

'What, no free meals?' exclaimed Elsie.

'No free meals,' said Monsieur Pamplemousse firmly, 'on pain of instant dismissal.' He made an entry in his notebook.

'What you writing?'

'I was making a comment on the *huîtres*. I think seven out of ten for presentation, don't you agree?'

Elsie helped herself to one. 'I'll tell you something for nothing. I wouldn't give them much for "you know what". Anyone what was expecting them to do the trick would 'ave another think coming. I don't feel a bit randy, do you?'

Monsieur Pamplemousse couldn't help but be aware that the rest of the dining-room was hanging on his answer. Even Pommes Frites looked interested.

'They are not at their best at this time of the year,' he said. 'It is the breeding season and they have a certain milkiness.'

'They're no more *fines de claires* than what I am,' continued Elsie, warming to her subject. 'I bet if they 'ad a "sell by" date stamped on their shells you wouldn't be eating them. I only 'ope they didn't come out of the same tank as that dead *langouste*.'

Out of the comer of his eye, Monsieur Pamplemousse saw the man at the next table stiffen, his fork poised halfway to his mouth.

'To give them the benefit of the doubt,' he said, 'they are old enough and large enough to be called *huîtres raptures*. They would have been better roasted and served with a little garlic butter and lots of bread.'

'My mum,' said Elsie, 'used to simmer them in their own juice, wrap them in bacon, grill them, then serve them on toast – "Angels on Horseback"'.

'Funny things, oysters,' she continued dreamily. 'I wonder what it's like changing sex every now and again?'

'Confusing, I would imagine,' said Monsieur Pamplemousse.

'It wouldn't 'alf give some people a shock if you picked the right moment to do it.'

They sat in silence for a while, each busy with their own thoughts. Monsieur Pamplemousse found it hard to picture Elsie as being anything other than what she was, although from some of the tales he'd heard from Loudier about the nightly goings on in the Bois de Boulogne anything was possible. Loudier was near to retirement and did the Paris area.

'You have oysters in *Angleterre* then?' he remarked politely as the waiter removed the dish. 'I thought you mostly ate fish and chips wrapped in newspaper.'

'Do we ever. Mind you, it's not like it was. According to my old dad, Royal Whitstable natives bred on London clay used to be the best in the world. Where I was brought up there was whelks and cockles and mussels every Saturday evening as well. I used to eat them out of a paper bag on the way 'ome from the flicks.' Elsie was clearly her old self again. Her enthusiasm was infectious, and Monsieur Pamplemousse found himself discoursing on the many and varied habits of crustacea, large and small.

While they were talking the waiter arrived with their second course. Monsieur Pamplemousse gazed at the plate as it was put before him.

'The annual consumption of oysters in France is over eighty thousand tons,' he continued.

'I expect that accounts for a lot of things,' said Elsie darkly. She paused and looked across the table at him. 'Is everything all right?'

'*Non!*' Monsieur Pamplemousse glared down at his plate. '*Non.* It is far from all right.'

He signalled for the waiter. Since they were by the sea it had seemed a good idea to choose *turbot sauce messine*. Dreams of a freshly caught turbot reposing in a dish of milk and water whilst being baked in a slow oven, then served with a sauce made from melted butter and flour, eggs, cream and mustard, gently stirred the while as leaves from a sprig or two of tarragon, parsley, chervil and chives were added, disappeared.

He prodded the contents of the dish with a knife. A smell of stale fish filled the air. The flesh didn't simply come away from the bone, it positively fell off as though it couldn't wait to escape. Pommes Frites took one look at it and then made for the exit.

'I see what you mean,' said Elsie. 'I could do better than that with one 'and tied behind my back.'

Monsieur Pamplemousse braced himself as the waiter drew near. 'Will you kindly return this dish to the kitchen,' he exclaimed. 'Pay my respects to the chef and tell him it is so grossly over-cooked even its own mother wouldn't recognise it.'

'And while you're at it you can tell 'im the plate's colder than an Eskimo's bum,' added Elsie.

'I am afraid that will not be possible,' said the waiter.

'Not possible?' Monsieur Pamplemousse felt his hackles begin to rise. Once again he reached for his pen – this time in deadly earnest.

'The *patron* has disappeared. He went out two days ago to buy some cigarettes and he hasn't been seen since. Madame Bouet has taken to her bed. And as Monsieur Bouet is also the chef . . .'

'I am sorry to hear that,' Monsieur Pamplemousse looked slightly less aggrieved. 'But what about the *brigade*? Can they not take over?'

The waiter raised his eyes to heaven. 'There is no *brigade, Monsieur.* There is only old Pierre. He is doing his best, but in the twenty-five years he has been here he has never once been allowed near the stove.'

'He wasn't joking when he said they 'ad problems,' said Elsie as the man disappeared again. 'I'll tell you something else. There's someone got their eyes on you. They keep giving you funny looks.'

Monsieur Pamplemousse grunted. He felt like saying that ever since Elsie entered the room people had been giving him funny looks. If the rest of the diners had anything else in common, other than a lack of food, it was that they were all taking an inordinate interest in everything he said or did and he was suddenly filled with an overwhelming desire to escape.

'Shall we take café elsewhere?'

'What and miss the sweet trolley?'

'Another very good reason,' said Monsieur Pamplemousse. It wasn't always easy to tell whether or not Elsie was being serious.

Elsewhere resolved itself into a small room which was clearly reserved for breakfast. There were six tables covered with red and white checked cloths. The walls were lined with matchboard, painted brown, and there was an old dresser which seemed to be a repository for a collection of equally ancient magazines. On one of the walls there was a painting of a beach scene. At least it was an improvement on the dining-room where, apart from the still-life, most of the pictures had been of an ecclesiastical nature.

Elsie picked up one of a pair of bronze figures on a shelf and turned it over.

'You like them?' asked Monsieur Pamplemousse.

'You don't 'ave to like them,' said Elsie. 'They're by Jaquet.' Without waiting for an answer, if indeed there was one, she picked up a pack of cards.

'Know any tricks to pass the time?'

Monsieur Pamplemousse thought for a moment. 'There is *Cherchez la femme.* If you like I will show you.'

Removing the ace of spades, the ace of diamonds and the queen of hearts from the pack, he laid them face downwards in a row on one of the tables, making sure the queen was in the middle.

57

'Tell me where the queen is.'

'It looks a bit like what we call "Find the Lady",' said Elsie, pointing to one of the outside cards.

'Oh, Glandier, where are you now?' thought Monsieur Pamplemousse, as he turned it over to reveal one of the aces. By sheer coincidence he'd watched his colleague demonstrate the three-card trick at the Director's party and the mechanics of it were still fresh in his mind.

'Shall we try again?' he asked. 'This time, I want you to watch my hands very carefully.'

Picking up an ace with his left hand, he showed it to Elsie, then he gathered up the other two cards with his right hand, making sure that she could see the queen was underneath the second ace.

Slowly and carefully he laid the cards face down again, placing the queen on his right.

'I think it's that one,' said Elsie, pointing to the middle card.

'Non.' Monsieur Pamplemousse tried hard to keep the note of irritation from his voice. The whole object of the preliminary exercise was to make the punter feel over-confident. He could hardly do that if Elsie kept getting it wrong.

'Ooh, you are clever,' said Elsie, after she had failed to get it right for the fifth time running. 'Can we do it properly now? Like me putting a little something on it?'

Monsieur Pamplemousse shook his head. 'I would not dream of taking your money.'

'Oh, go on – be a sport.' Elsie touched his jacket lapel lightly with her hand. 'Let's 'ave a bit of fun.'

Faced with Elsie's round blue eyes gazing imploring into his, Monsieur Pamplemousse felt himself weakening.

'If you really wish to . . .'

'Yes, please,' said Elsie. She looked round. 'Oh, dear. Silly me! I've left my bag upstairs. Would you mind lending me a hundred francs?'

'A hundred?'

'It's not worth playing for matchsticks,' said Elsie.

Monsieur Pamplemousse hesitated, then reached for his wallet. 'On one condition . . .' Despite Glandier's theory that there was one born every minute so why not make good use of the fact, it hardly seemed right to take advantage of such childlike innocence. 'If you win you may keep it. If you lose then you need only give me my hundred francs back.'

'Sounds fair enough,' said Elsie.

Monsieur Pamplemousse went through his routine again, picking up one of the aces with his left hand, gathering up the queen and the other ace with his right. This time when he threw the cards on to the table he arranged for the queen to end up on his left. It hardly seemed worth bothering with the subtlety of relying on quickness of the hand to deceive the eye and dealing the top rather than the bottom card first.

'I think it's that one,' said Elsie, pointing to the card on his left.

'I bet you thought I was going to choose the one in the middle,' she said cheerfully. 'Oh dear, now I've been and gone and taken your money.'

Monsieur Pamplemousse watched his note disappear into the dark recesses of Elsie's cleavage. He resolved to ring Glandier in the morning.

'You could try winning it back,' said Elsie. 'I think I'm getting the hang of it now.'

'I think,' said Monsieur Pamplemousse, 'I may take Pommes Frites for a walk.'

He was about to leave the hotel when he heard his name being called.

'Monsieur Pamplemousse. Monsieur Pamplemousse. *Le téléphone.*'

Monsieur Pamplemousse hesitated, then signalled Pommes Frites to go on ahead. 'I will take it in my room.' He had a feeling in the back of his mind that it might be the Director, a feeling that was confirmed a few minutes later when, breathing heavily from having taken the last few stairs at the double, he picked up his bedside receiver.

'Pamplemousse!' The Director sounded equally short of breath. 'Where on earth have you been?'

'I am sorry, *Monsieur. I* came as quickly as I could. Is anything the matter? Are you all right?'

'No, I am not all right.' There was a muffled cough from the other end of the line. 'I cannot keep my head under the bedclothes for very much longer.'

Monsieur Pamplemousse looked at his watch It was barely twenty-thirty. '*Monsieur* is in bed?'

'Pamplemousse, I would hardly have my head under the bedclothes were I sitting outside on the lawn.'

Monsieur Pamplemousse stood rebuked. 'No, *Monsieur,* but . . .'

'I am in bed,' continued the Director, obviously choosing his words with care, 'because I am extremely tired. And before you ask me why I am extremely tired, I will tell you.

'I received your message last night, Pamplemousse. It came through loud and clear, despite my having to hold the receiver under the duvet.'

'I trust it did not cause you problems, *Monsieur.*'

'It might have done, had it not been for the fact that on the spur of the moment I made up a story about an itinerant *plume* salesman. One has to think on one's feet, Pamplemousse.'

'Or even lying down, *Monsieur.*'

The Director ignored the remark. 'Unfortunately, Chantal chose not to believe me. She has, I fear, a suspicious nature. She spent practically the whole of the night questioning me. As fast as I nodded off she woke me again. Today has been even worse. She hasn't let me get anywhere near a telephone.'

'Women, *Monsieur.*' Monsieur Pamplemousse sometimes envied the Director's happy knack of convincing himself of the veracity of his own stories. He couldn't help but wonder if he would have felt even more outraged had he been telling the truth.

'I trust you have settled in, Aristide?' The Director sounded slightly mollified. 'I did ask that you be given a good room – one facing *la mer* Elsie, I understand, had already stated her preference.'

'Without consulting a compass, *Monsieur*, it is hard to tell whether my room is facing the sea or not. The highest sand dune in Europe happens to be standing immediately outside my window. The only point in its favour is that at least I am protected from the worst of the elements. Although, having said that, it is the only hotel I have stayed in where it is necessary to empty the sand out of one's shoes *before* going on to the beach.'

'Not worth a detour, Aristide?'

'Even if one happened to be within a hundred metres, *Monsieur*, it would not be worth making a detour.'

'How strange. Elsie was most adamant that she wished to stay there. By the way, how is Elsie?' Monsieur Pamplemousse thought he detected a note of nervousness in the Director's voice.

'Earlier this evening she was talking of changing her sex. Apart from that she is well.'

'That shows remarkable dedication. Would there were more in our organisation prepared to make such a sacrifice.'

'I do not think it had anything to do with her wish to be an Inspector, *Monsieur.*'

'Nothing you have done, Pamplemousse, I trust?' said the Director anxiously.

'Certainly not, *Monsieur.*'

'Irrespective of the surgical problems involved – and in Elsie's case I would say they are considerable – it would not be good news. An added complication . . .'

'You were about to say, *Monsieur . . .*' Monsieur Pample-mousse broke in quickly before the Director indulged in yet another flight of fancy.

'Ah, yes, thank you for reminding me, Aristide. Chantal will be back from the bathroom at any moment. I grant you she spends an inordinate amount of time in there – what she does I have no idea, but there are limits to the amount of time even she can spend in front of a mirror – I rang to warn you . . . Don't, on any account . . .'

Whatever else the Director had been about to say was lost in a rustle of bedclothes. His voice suddenly came through loud and clear.

'Good. Good. It was kind of you to ring. In that case I will order six kilos of *framboises* . . . If you have any prob-lems, let me know at once. Make sure they are in perfect condition. We have important guests . . .'

Monsieur Pamplemousse replaced the receiver. The Director had obviously added an itinerant raspberry-seller to his list of callers. It was to be hoped it would meet with more success than his previous effort. If it didn't he could be in for another sleepless night.

Sitting on the edge of his bed mulling over the conversa-tion, Monsieur Pamplemousse wondered what on earth it was he mustn't do. He was so lost in thought it was a moment or two before he realised someone was knocking on his door. It sounded urgent.

He opened the door and Elsie entered clutching her Polaroid camera.

''Ere, you know your dog . . .'

'Pommes Frites? Of course I know him. Why do you ask?'

'Because he's just gone past my window and 'e 'ad a whatjemecallit in his mouth . . . You know, a *jambon*.'

'A *jambon*? But I doubt if there is a *boucherie* within several kilometres of here.' Monsieur Pamplemousse considered the other possibilities. 'Unless, of course, he has discovered an out-of-town *Super-Marché*.'

'It wasn't,' said Elsie meaningly, 'the kind of *jambon* you'd find in a supermarket – not even a French one.' She handed him a print. 'Just you wait till you see what's on that.'

4
ENCORE

Monsieur Pamplemousse took the print from Elsie and held it up to the light. The faint image he'd spotted when she first entered his room was already forming itself into a picture.

'*Sacré' bleu!*' He saw what she meant. It was a good likeness of Pommes Frites. Although he wasn't actually smiling at the lens, the camera had caught a certain self-satisfied expression on his face as it recorded him hurrying past some bushes outside the hotel. Fresh details were emerging with every passing moment. Traces of yellow sand were clearly visible on the end of his nose; the colour of his coat – the rich blacks, the reddish tints and the fawns – were all there, along with the green of the foliage in the background. It was a tribute to Dr Edwin Land's invention which, making use of a sandwich of chemicals and a couple of rollers, enabled a photograph to manifest itself before one's very eyes in a matter of moments.

All the same, it was not the kind of picture even one of Pommes Frites' most ardent admirers would have singled out for pasting in the family album. Still less would they have awarded it a place of honour on the mantelpiece, and Monsieur Pamplemousse gave the principal subject hardly more than a passing glance. He concentrated instead on the object Pommes Frites was carrying. In particular his attention was directed towards an ominous red trickle which disappeared out of the bottom left corner of the picture.

There was no denying that Elsie was correct in identifying the object as a *jambon*, but it was a judgement which would have won her no prizes in a photographic competition; tickets for a holiday for two in the Algarve would not have come winging her way. Even the rawest recruit to the world of *boucherie*, an apprentice butcher learning his trade or a sausage-maker fresh from a school of *charcuterie*, would have had little difficulty in deducing the fact that whatever its origins, the *jambon* in question had never been an integral part of either beast or fowl; comparisons with wall charts would have been a waste of the instructor's time.

Any lingering doubts as to possible alternatives would have been instantly dispelled by the fact that a good four-fifths of the object was covered, not in caterer's muslin, but in the tattered remains of some thicker, white material, from the far end of which there protruded a foot. A foot which, in turn, was encased in an old-fashioned wooden *sabot* of the kind favoured by some older members of the catering trade whose work entailed their spending long hours slaving over a hot stove.

It was no wonder Pommes Frites was looking pleased with himself. Had he still been a member of the elite *Division Chiens* of the Paris Sûreté he might well have been in line for a commendation.

'Queer, innit,' said Elsie soberly. 'Gave me quite a shock when I saw 'im go past with it sticking out of 'is mouth.'

'We must find him immediately.' Removing a flashlight from his bag, Monsieur Pamplemousse reached for the door handle. He had a sudden mental picture of Pommes Frites entering the hotel and running round the dining-room, anxious to show off his prize to all and sundry. It didn't bear thinking about. An even worse possibility was if he happened to bump into Madame Bouet, freshly risen from her bed. It might send her back there, never to rise again.

Although the evidence was purely circumstantial, the conclusion that the object in Pommes Frites' mouth had once belonged to the missing patron of the Hôtel des Dunes seemed inescapable. Monsieur Pamplemousse's policeman's instincts were roused; the scent of the chase was in his nostrils.

Flinging open the bedroom door, he was about to rush into the corridor when he stopped dead in his tracks.

'*Merde!*'

He felt an enveloping warmth as Elsie cannoned into him from behind. 'What's up?'

'*C'est impossible!*'

Impossible was hardly the word for it. *Merde* upon *merde!* He could scarcely believe his ill fortune. Coming towards him – halfway between his room and the stairs, were two people he recognised. Not only did they come from Paris – that would have been bad enough; but they lived two floors above him in the same apartment block. Recent arrivals, to be sure, but he had met them in the lift on a number of occasions.

'It's them,' hissed Elsie. 'The ones I was telling you about. The ones what was staring at you downstairs.'

Monsieur Pamplemousse signalled for her to go back into the room.

He gave an inward groan. It was too late for him to follow suit. The couple were bearing inexorably down on him, the man already had his hand outstretched in greeting.

'Monsieur Pamplemousse.'

Monsieur Pamplemousse shook his head. Desperate situations demanded desperate measures. On the spur of the moment he decided to brazen it out

'*Oui.* However, I do not think we have ever met.'

The man looked taken aback. 'You are not Monsieur Aristide Pamplemousse from the *septième é'tage?*'

'*Non.*'

The couple gazed at him in disbelief. All too well aware of the woman straining to look over his shoulder, Monsieur Pamplemousse glanced round. Elsie was bending over the bed, whiling away the time by smoothing down the cover where he had been sitting. She had her back to them.

Pulling the door shut behind him, he decided that attack was the best form of defence. In any case he had burned his boats. Retreat was now totally out of the question.

'You are from Paris?' he inquired.

'*Oui. Naturellement.* Monsieur Blanche . . . from the ninth floor. My wife . . .'

'Then I fear you must be mistaking me for my twin brother.' Monsieur Pamplemousse cut short the introductions. 'My surname is Pamplemousse, certainly. But my first name is Albert.'

It worked. Disbelief gave way to incredulity, to be followed moments later by a grudging acceptance of the fact that truth was sometimes stranger than fiction.

Though he said it himself, it had to be one of his better essays into the craft of acting. The Director was not the only one capable of thinking on his feet. The only shame was that he couldn't be there to witness it for himself.

Monsieur Blanche raised his hands. '*Mon Dieu!* It is an incredible likeness.'

'In looks only, I fear,' said Monsieur Pamplemousse. 'Deep down we are very different.'

'A thousand pardons, *Monsieur*. I had no idea.'

Monsieur Pamplemousse allowed himself a faint smile of forgiveness. He raised his right hand as though in absolution.

'A not unnatural mistake. It is not the first time. Although I have to admit it is one which hasn't happened for a number of years.

'Aristide and I went our separate ways soon after we left school. He was always the do-gooder, the studious one – his nose for ever buried in a book. Whereas I, I found it impossibly hard to live up to the example he had set. When he was only six he could recite the whole of the Lord's Prayer – backwards.'

'Poor Aristide.' Monsieur Pamplemousse found himself warming to his part. 'Is he still doing good works? He should have become a priest, that one. Do you not agree?'

'Not from all I have heard,' said Madame Blanche grimly. Her lips were set in a straight line. They bore an uncanny resemblance to those of Madame Grante in accounts when she was dealing with a particularly problematical P39.

'Oh, really?' Monsieur Pamplemousse stopped in his tracks, curiosity overcoming a desire to make himself scarce as quickly as possible. 'What have you heard?'

'Nothing that bears repeating,' said Madame Blanche firmly. Denied a view of his room, eyeing the torch in his right hand with disfavour, she was doing her best to get a closer look at the polaroid photograph in his other hand. Monsieur Pamplemousse hastily turned it round so that the back was towards her.

'Well, do please remember me to Aristide when you are back in Paris. On second thoughts . . .' Fearing that in his enthusiasm he might have been overdoing things, he had a sudden flash of inspiration. 'Perhaps it is better if you say nothing at all about our meeting, not even to his wife Doucine . . .'

'Doucette,' said Madame Blanche. 'I know her well. We often meet in the launderette.'

'Do you now?' said Monsieur Pamplemousse thoughtfully. He looked Madame Blanche straight in the eye. 'Well, from all I remember of Doucette, she would be most upset. She made Aristide swear never to mention my name again. It will only reopen old wounds.

'And now, *à bientôt.*'

Feeling behind him he made contact with something infinitely softer and more yielding than a doorknob.

'Oooh!' said Elsie. 'You are a one.'

'*Pardon.*' Monsieur Pamplemousse realised all too late that the door to his room had swung open again.

'I was hoping you'd help me with my bra,' said Elsie in her best voice. 'It's been and gone and got itself all twisted. Can't think how it happened.'

Monsieur Pamplemousse found himself hoping the Blanches' command of colloquial English was less than perfect. But at that point fate intervened on his behalf. It manifested itself in the shape of the three Americans he had seen in the restaurant earlier in the evening. They arrived upstairs in a bunch and squeezed their way past without so much as a '*pardon*' or an '*excusez-moi*', leaving in their wake a trail of whiskey fumes and the smell of stale cigars. At close quarters he wouldn't have trusted any one of them more than he could have thrown them – which wouldn't have been very far – and he found himself instinctively checking for his wallet. Doubtless they had fared no better than anyone else in the restaurant, but that didn't excuse bad manners.

He gazed after them as they disappeared round a corner at the far end of the corridor. They were an odd collection.

He couldn't help but wonder what strange machinations of fate had brought them to that part of France. They must all have been in their late sixties. Successful in whatever it was they did for a living if the combined weight of gold bracelets and other adornments was anything to go by.

Away from the dining-room they looked even more like fish out of water; they would have been more at home in a night club than in an out of the way sea-side resort: the Negresco in Nice rather than the Hôtel des Dunes in the Landes. Perhaps they had been taken for a ride by their travel agent. If that were the case he wouldn't like to be in the man's shoes when they returned home.

At least the diversion had solved his problem. When he looked round Monsieur and Madame Blanche were heading back along the corridor towards their room. Madame Blanche with scarcely a backward glance, Monsieur Blanche with as many as he could decently get away with.

'What was all that about?' asked Elsie.

'A slight case of mistaken identity, that is all. I thought they would never go.'

'I could tell that,' said Elsie. 'That's why I thought I'd come out and 'elp.'

Monsieur Pamplemousse put the photograph on the table beside his bed for safe keeping, then as soon as the coast was clear he ushered Elsie out of the room and locked the door behind him.

'Quick . . . before they come out again.' The Blanches looked the sort of people who would most likely take a stroll before going to bed. The less he saw of them from now on the better.

He paused on the first landing as a sudden thought struck him.

'Tell me, when did you first notice them?'

Elsie thought for a moment. 'I dunno. They came in halfway through the meal . . . just after Pommes Frites went out.'

'Aah.' Monsieur Pamplemousse breathed a sigh of relief.

He might just get away with pretending to be his own twin brother, but suggesting Pommes Frites was anyone other than Pommes Frites would be pushing things; two pairs of identical twins could be carrying probability to extremes.

It was even more imperative that they find Pommes Frites as soon as possible. If they were seen together his cover would be blown and no two ways about it. From the expression on Madame Blanche's face he might just as well ring Doucette himself and get it over with.

Taking the stairs two at a time, he rushed out into the night leaving Elsie to follow on behind as best she could.

Blissfully unaware of the interest his earlier perambulations had caused, totally uncognisant of the deep waters his master had got himself into, Pommes Frites stirred into action the moment he heard the front door of the hotel open and he recognised the sound of familiar footsteps.

Apart from one brief return trip to the dune, he had been waiting patiently behind a bush for some considerable time, and he was anxious for a spot of action.

For the first half hour or so after leaving the hotel he had been in his element. As far as he was concerned the previous day's outing on the beach at Deauville had been a mere warming-up, a preliminary canter to get the limbs moving. Pleasant enough in its way, and certainly not to be sneezed at, but as nothing compared to the joys of gallivanting about on the Dune du Pilat in the dark.

Finding the *'jambon'* had been an unexpected bonus. Pommes Frites' immediate reaction had been to rush back to his master bearing the evidence of his discovery. Unable to shout 'Eureka! I've found it!' as Archimedes had done when he stepped into an overflowing bath and hit on the principle of buoyancy, he had contented himself with a muffled bark or two.

But that had been over half an hour ago. Since then reaction had set in, and during the time at his disposal Pommes Frites had been doing a lot of thinking.

Whilst a long way from being able to claim a laser-sharp mind when it came to working out problems, Pommes Frites was nevertheless blessed with more than his fair share of common sense.

During his time with Monsieur Pamplemousse they had stayed at a great many hotels: some good, some bad. There had been establishments where dogs were treated as welcome guests and others where they were barely tolerated. In most hotels they were able to share a room, but on other occasions such an arrangement had been frowned upon. However, not since the time when they had stayed at an hostelry belonging to an aunt of the Director had the food been quite so abysmally bad. It was not simply abysmally bad; in Pommes Frites' experience it was uniquely abysmally bad.

Since his master was clearly intending to stay for more than one night – Pommes Frites recognised the signs – the unpacking of the bags, the hanging up of clothes – there was only one possible explanation, and Monsieur Pamplemousse's appearing at dinner without a tie confirmed it; they were there for reasons unconnected with work.

Pleased with his deductions, Pommes Frites had rested his brain for a while, at the same time keeping a watchful eye through the window on goings on in the dining-room in case he was missing anything. He saw Monsieur and Madame Blanche arrive. He saw his master and Elsie get up and leave. Soon after that he saw Monsieur and Madame Blanche do likewise.

The rest had done Pommes Frites good. Almost as soon as he returned to his thinking he came up with the answer. If they were not there for reasons connected with work, then they must be there for pleasure. In other words they must be on holiday. Normally if they were on holiday his master would have brought Madame Pamplemousse, but that was a minor point. Pommes Frites decided it was not for him to reason why.

The important fact was that, food apart, they were there to enjoy themselves. It was a time to relax. For the nonce work was a dirty word. Games would be the order of the day, and Pommes Frites decided it should be kept that way.

Pommes Frites knew his master better than most. Give his master a problem and he was liable to retire into himself for days on end with scarcely a word to anyone.

It was his, Pommes Frites' duty, to ensure that didn't happen. Having reached that conclusion he made his second excursion of the evening to the Dune du Pilat.

So it came about that when Monsieur Pamplemousse rushed out of the hotel shouting '*va chercher . . . va chercher . . .* fetch . . . fetch', and then, realising the remaining occupants of the dining-room, having little better to do, were watching his every move with more than a passing interest, did a double take and almost immediately began shouting '*cache-le . . . cache-le . . .* hide . . . hide', Pommes Frites scarcely batted an eyelid.

Clearly it was all part of a new game his master had invented; a variation on hide and seek.

Entering into the spirit of things, Pommes Frites disappeared into the night leaving his master and Elsie to follow on as best they could. Racing up the dune, he steered a course which took him away from the spot where he had first found the *jambon*, whilst at the same time avoiding by a long way the spot where he had reburied it.

Pommes Frites reappeared several times during the following quarter of hour or so, each time hovering a tantalisingly few metres ahead of his pursuers, before racing on again, leading them higher and higher and further and further away from the hotel.

Monsieur Pamplemousse was the first to crack.

'I think,' he gasped as they paused for breath, 'Pommes Frites is of the opinion that he is, how shall I say? . . . playing a game.'

'I don't know 'ow you say it,' gasped Elsie. 'I think he's being bleeding difficult. If anyone 'ad told me when I left 'ome that I'd find myself chasing a dog up a bloody great 'eap of sand in the dark I'd 'ave told them to get their 'ead seen to. Or, better still, have 'ad mine examined.'

'Life is full of surprises,' said Monsieur Pamplemousse.

'Yeah? Well, I've got one for you,' said Elsie crossly. 'If there's one thing I can't stand about the sea-side it's the bleeding sand. It gets everywhere. It's not my scene. How they stand it in the Foreign Legion I don't know.'

Monsieur Pamplemousse considered the last remark for a moment. The possibility of joining the Foreign Legion to be beside the sea had never occurred to him. He doubted if it had to many of those who had actually taken the plunge and signed along the dotted line.

'I have heard tell that it drives some men mad,' he ventured.

'I'm not surprised,' said Elsie. 'Talk about bleedin' Beau Geste.'

Not for the first time Monsieur Pamplemousse found himself wondering why Elsie had picked on the Hôtel des Dunes for her baptism of fire. A mattress beneath a parasol on the private beach reserved for patrons of the Carlton Hotel in Cannes would have been more up her street. From all the Director had said she could have taken her choice from anywhere in France.

On the other hand he had to agree with her. Running up and down the Dune du Pilat was not his idea of a fun way to spend an evening either. *Montée assez difficile* was how Michelin, with their flair for understatement bordering on pedantry, described it. Monsieur Pamplemousse could have thought up many other alternatives. It would take him a week to get rid of the sand. There was sand in his shoes. There was sand in his hair. There was sand where in the normal scheme of things no sand should ever be allowed to enter.

For a brief moment he would have swapped places with the Director. The Director would have had his portable telephone with him. Assuming the buttons had not been jammed with grit, he would have lost no time in summoning help. Helicopters would have been taking off from Mérignac.

He cast his eyes around. They must be at the highest point of the dune, some hundred metres or so above sea level. The wind had dropped – perhaps because it was now high tide – and the sky was clear. At any other time, and in any other circumstances, it would have merited one of *Le Guide's* Easels – the symbol for an outstanding view. He could see lights twinkling like a giant necklace of pearls strung round the bay as far as Cap Ferret. Behind them lay the Médoc and the vineyards which lined the left bank of the Gironde – the vineyards of St Estephe, Pauillac and St Julien, whose names went around the world.

Between the lighthouse at the end of the peninsula and where they were standing he could dimly make out the darker shape of the Ile aux Oiseaux in the centre of the bay. Fig trees grew there, and tamarisk and sea heliotropes.

He wondered what Brémontier, the architect of the whole scheme, would have thought of it had he still been alive. In carrying out the government's order to stop further erosion from the sea by fixing the soil with low-growing plants, he could hardly have dreamed that in such a short space of time there would be so much change. The Atlantic winds had done more than their share of creating a natural monument to his achievement: two hundred kilometres of fine golden beach now lined the west coast of France.

He caught the sound of a motor boat – probably a local fisherman – and glancing down he thought he saw a glimmer of light from somewhere far below, then it disappeared.

Of Pommes Frites there was neither sight nor sound. He had either given up the game or he was biding his time for a fresh assault.

The dunes rolled away into the distance, unfolding along the seashore as far as the eye could see, and behind them lay the vast forest of the Landes, the largest in Europe, dark and brooding. It was hard to believe that a hundred years ago it hadn't even existed; a wilderness of scrubland and shifting sands and marshes, where the inhabitants walked about on stilts as they tended their flocks of sheep. Now there were over three and half million acres of pine trees. He gave a sigh.

'It is very romantic.'

Elsie took immediate precautions.

'That's as may be,' she said meaningly, 'but I've got a headache.'

Monsieur Pamplemousse was reminded of a remark the Director had made shortly after he'd first introduced Elsie. 'A nice girl, but she suffers a great deal from *mal de tête*.'

At the time he suspected it might have been a case of the Director covering his tracks, but now he wasn't so sure. Elsie was what some of his coarser colleagues would have called a prick-teaser.

'What do you think 'e's done with it?' asked Elsie, breaking into his thoughts.

Monsieur Pamplemousse shrugged. In the excitement he had almost forgotten the reason for their being there. Perhaps he should have rung the local *gendarmerie* in the first place. At the time it had seemed sensible to find Pommes Frites first. Now he wasn't so sure.

'Tell you something, if 'e's buried it anywhere round 'ere we'll never find it in a month of Sundays – not unless 'e wants us to.'

Monsieur Pamplemousse had to agree. He knew Pommes Frites of old. Once he had his mind set on something he was not easily diverted.

'What we need,' said Elsie, 'is a late-night butcher's.'

'*Comment?*'

'I've been thinking. If you was to buy a leg of lamb – well, it doesn't 'ave to be lamb, of course – it could be anything. But if you was to do that and give it to 'im it's just possible he might go and bury it in the same place.'

Monsieur Pamplemousse's first inclination was to dismiss the idea as impractical. The possibility of finding anything, let alone a *boucherie* open at that time of night seemed highly unlikely. On the other hand it was better than doing nothing.

Playing for time while he made up his mind he removed a dog whistle from an inside pocket and blew into it.

'Shouldn't think that'll do much good,' said Elsie.

'It is not meant to make a noise,' said Monsieur Pamplemousse. 'It is a silent one.'

'If 'e doesn't come,' said Elsie, 'you'll never know whether it's working or not. You could 'ave got sand in it.'

In the face of feminine logic, Monsieur Pamplemousse gave in. Employing similar thought processes to the ones that Pommes Frites had used earlier, he decided that perhaps Elsie was right. They needed to play him at his own game. They couldn't stay where they were for ever, and Pommes Frites was more than capable of finding his own way back to the hotel.

Given the fact that even as he spoke, Pommes Frites, having also heard the sound of the boat, was making his way slowly and silently down the dune towards the sea, it was a wise decision.

All good things come to an end, and even though it had been one of the best games he had played for ages, a sixth sense told him that it was time to get back to work again. Good resolutions arrived at on his master's behalf disappeared like magic. Nostrils open to catch any scent which might be in the air, his long ears – normally hanging loose in deep folds about his head – alert to every stray sound, slowly and with infinite patience Pommes Frites edged closer and closer to his target.

Patience was a commodity thin on the ground on the other side of the dune. Having not surprisingly drawn a blank in his search for a *boucherie,* or indeed a purveyor of any known form of comestibles, Monsieur Pamplemousse was reading from a menu posted up on the glass door of a small building they had stumbled across.

'*Lundi: laitue, timbale Milanaise, fromage blanc, biscuits.*

'*Mardi: carottes râpées, rôti de boeuf, riz au beurre, glaces.*

'*Jeudi: tomate ou concombre, filets de dinde braisés, peetits pois et carottes, Camembert, fruits . . .*'

'Do you 'ave to?' groaned Elsie. 'I'm starving.'

Monsieur Pamplemousse shone his torch through the glass. Picasso-like paintings adorned the walls. A large, brightly coloured wooden railway engine occupied the centre of an uncarpeted room. There was a row of coat hooks fixed to the near side of the engine's boiler. They looked surprisingly close to the ground. He ran his torch along the row and beyond until he reached a row of tiny desks.

'*Alors on a compris*' – the penny had dropped. They were standing outside an infants' school. He looked at the menu again. It was for the week prior to the summer *vacances*.

'I should think they'd bloody need a holiday after all that,' said Elsie, when he told her. 'Poor little buggers. My 'eart bleeds for them, I don't think. It wasn't like it in my day, I can tell you.'

'Nor mine,' agreed Monsieur Pamplemousse. 'And that was much longer ago. Taste classes are now on the National Curriculum.'

When they got back to the hotel he made for his car and felt underneath the driver's seat. Removing a neatly folded sheet of plastic, he attached a small cylinder to a protruding nozzle and pressed a button.

'Blimey!' Elsie watched open-eyed as a kennel began to take shape. 'Whatever will they think of next?'

'It is the only one of its kind,' said Monsieur Pamplemousse proudly. 'I had it specially made.' He took it round to the side of the hotel and found a suitably level piece of ground beneath his room window.

'I think if and when Pommes Frites takes it upon himself to return he should do a bit of guard duty. As for myself . . . I am of the opinion that it is time for bed.'

It also occurred to him that in the circumstances it might be as well to distance himself from Pommes Frites for a while. With luck, Monsieur and Madame Blanche might think he belonged to the hotel.

'Tell you what,' said Elsie. 'How about 'aving a little snack in my room first?'

'You have food?' said Monsieur Pamplemousse. 'In your room?'

'Always look after number one,' said Elsie. 'That's my motto. No one else is going to. It's everyone for theirselves in this world.

'And there's some champagne in the 'fridge. I checked.'

Monsieur Pamplemousse needed no more convincing.

The champagne was a pleasant surprise. It was a half bottle of Billecart-Salmon *rosé:* light, fruity and extremely elegant. After the time spent on the dune it tasted like nectar.

'I daresay we can put it on expenses,' said Elsie.

'Have you met Madame Grante?' asked Monsieur Pamplemousse.

'Who's she when she's at 'ome?' said Elsie.

'The problem is not when she is at home,' said Monsieur Pamplemousse. 'It is when she is in the office. I think perhaps I had better help you with your P39.'

The thought of Elsie doing battle with Madame Grante was an interesting one – he wasn't at all sure who would emerge the victor; the only certainty was that if Madame Grante lost she wouldn't forget. In the end it was he who would be made to suffer.

Elsie opened the fridge door again and removed two packets. The first packet was labelled 'chocolate fingers'. The second, which was covered in translucent plastic material, contained what looked like a selection of small white ceiling tiles edged with brown.

'Good thing I came prepared, innit.' She took a knife and a third packet from the dressing-table drawer.

Monsieur Pamplemousse watched while Elsie spread some butter over one of the tiles.

'What is it?' he asked. 'And where did you find it?'

'It's bread. I brought it with me, dinna I? And am I glad I did!'

Monsieur Pamplemousse wasn't sure whether the last remark was a question or a statement. The English habit of putting an inflection at the end of a sentence, going down in tone rather than up was hard to get used to. Not that Elsie was as big an offender as most. On the whole her voice tended to be on one level. He decided she had made a statement.

'You mean, it is not of today's baking?'

Elsie gave a hollow laugh. 'Today's? Blimey! I doubt if it's last week's. English sliced loaf lasts for ever – just so long as you remember to scrape the green off. That's its strong point.'

'There are others?' inquired Monsieur Pamplemousse. It reminded him of a television documentary he had once seen on the phenomenon of English bread. There had been shots of men squeezing loaves, then standing stop-watch in hand, timing how long it took them to regain their original shape. Taste had not figured largely in the findings.

'It takes all sorts,' said Elsie. 'Just 'cause you don't like sliced loaf don't mean to say it's wrong.

'When I was small,' she continued, 'I used to like granulated sugar on bread and butter. I suppose you get more sophisticated as you grow older.'

Monsieur Pamplemousse couldn't help thinking that despite Elsie's prowess in the kitchen and her undoubted knowledge of certain areas relating to matters of food, she was not Inspector material. No one could possibly like sliced bread coated with *sucre*. He watched while she took one of the chocolate fingers from the packet, laid it on a slice of buttered bread, then rolled it up to form a baton. It was hard to imagine what kind of symbol they might use in *Le Guide* to denote a restaurant specialising in such things. If it looked at all like the one Elsie was holding, the chances were it might give potential customers the wrong idea.

'Does it have a name?' he asked politely.

'It's a chocolate-finger sandwich, innit,' said Elsie. 'I mean, what else would you call it?'

'It looks very sustaining,' said Monsieur Pamplemousse. He took a tentative bite. Although he was loth to admit the fact, it tasted much nicer than he had expected. The second bite was even nicer.

'When I was small I used to enjoy eating raw *croissant* mixture dipped in *confture.*'

'There you are,' said Elsie. She handed him a third baton.

'I think perhaps I will take it back to my room for later,' said Monsieur Pamplemousse.

'You're a poppet,' said Elsie unexpectedly. As he stood up to leave she planted a large, wet kiss on his forehead. 'Nightie, night, sweet repose. All the pillow, all the clothes. See you in the morning.'

Outside in the corridor, clasping the chocolate-finger roll like a weapon in his hand, the inevitable happened. He heard voices in the hall. His timing couldn't have been worse if he'd tried. A moment later Monsieur and Madame Blanche came into view, returning from their walk. Monsieur Pamplemousse gave them a good-night wave with his free hand as they followed him up the stairs.

It occurred to him that he had ways of making Madame Blanche sniff.

Back in his room he gazed at his reflection in the mirror. He had chocolate round his mouth and lipstick on his forehead.

Hearing more voices outside and the sound of a door slamming he crossed to the window and looked out. He was just in time to see what must be old Pierre – the newly incumbent chef – leaving the hotel. His back was bent and he was walking slowly, lurching slightly from side to side as though in a dream. As he mounted his bicycle and wobbled off into the night he looked a broken man.

Monsieur Pamplemousse closed the shutters. Worn out by the combined effect of the long drive from Paris and by the evening's exertions, he decided to leave telephoning the police until the morning. He wasn't sure what he was going to tell them anyway and he simply couldn't face the thought of long explanations.

But despite feeling tired, sleep eluded him – he had far too many things on his mind; Elsie . . . Pommes Frites' strange behaviour . . . the Director's warning, cut off in mid-sentence . . . his own new identity . . .

He wondered how he and Elsie would spend the rest of the week . . . tomorrow they could drive into Arcachon . . . he would have to go there anyway to report Pommes Frites' find . . .

Once, when he had almost dozed off, he was nudged awake again by the sound of a car back-firing in the distance – a sudden sharp crack like a gun going off.

It took him a while to settle down again. He wondered if Madame Blanche would say anything to Doucette. If she had half a chance she would. He would meet that problem when it happened. In the meantime he had to admit there was a certain attraction about his new role.

It was perhaps half an hour or so later that he heard a car arrive at the hotel. He groped for the torch and checked the time on his watch. It was a little after one o'clock. Doors slammed, followed shortly afterwards by footsteps on the stairs. He guessed it must be the Americans returning from a night out.

They paused outside his door and he heard whispering. He was beginning to wish he'd let Elsie have his room after all. For some reason the top floor of the hotel far outweighed the first in the popularity stakes. Perhaps everyone was hoping for a view of the sea.

Monsieur Pamplemousse couldn't have put a time to when he finally fell asleep, but it seemed only a matter of moments before he was woken yet again, this time with a vague feeling of unease. It took him a moment or two to force himself properly awake. He switched on the light. A quick glance at his watch showed him it was now two-twenty. He was about to sink back on to his pillow when he heard a whining noise from somewhere outside his window.

Jumping out of bed, he flung open the shutters intending to remonstrate in no uncertain terms about dogs who stayed out late without their master's permission, when he paused. The moon was hidden behind some trees, but even in the shadow there was something familiar about the way Pommes Frites was standing.

Returning a moment later with his torch, Monsieur Pamplemousse trained it on the area below his window and pressed the switch. As he did so he caught his breath.

It was, in many respects, a duplicate of the scene Elsie had captured earlier in the evening; a scene which he had already irreverently labelled in his mind as 'Pommes Frites with *jambon*'.

Bidding Pommes Frites to remain exactly where he was, Monsieur Pamplemousse disappeared from the window. He returned a moment later with Elsie's photograph. It needed only a simple comparison between Pommes Frites' latest find and that shown in the picture to confirm his worst suspicions.

In all but one respect the salient features of the *jambon* were remarkably similar, in size, shape, and by virtue of being encased in a white, cotton material. However, unless Monsieur Bouet had been a singularly careless dresser, or had by some unfortunate quirk of nature been endowed with two right feet, then the inescapable conclusion was that Pommes Frites had discovered yet another *jambon*, for the end of his latest find was encased not in a wooden sabot, but in a rope-soled canvas pump.

5
THE SEVENTH DWARF

'Cheer up,' said Elsie. 'It may never happen.'

Monsieur Pamplemousse broke off a morsel of bread from a slice of *baguette* and eyed it through eyes weary from lack of sleep. There was a certain lack of crispness in the crust which summed up his own state of mind.

'I'm afraid it already has. You can hardly call finding two dead bodies in one night a non-event.'

'They weren't your actual bodies,' said Elsie. She leaned across the table and patted him consolingly. 'Only bits and pieces like, and you haven't even got those any more. Well, not until Pommes Frites finds them again. *If* he ever does. No wonder he looks gloomy. He's worse than you are.'

'Pommes Frites often looks gloomy,' said Monsieur Pamplemousse defensively, 'but that doesn't mean to say he is unhappy. Although he may well be so at the moment. I think he is suffering from a sense of failure.'

'I'm not surprised,' said Elsie. 'Fancy not being able to find his *jambons*. Fine bloodhound 'e is.'

'It is hardly his fault that a wind sprang up during the night,' said Monsieur Pamplemousse. 'Any trails there might have been disappeared in the sand. I defy anyone to find them. Also, he is probably unhappy because he thinks I have been avoiding him and he is at a loss to understand why.'

'And have you?'

'In a way, yes. But only because I think the less we are seen together the better. I doubt if Madame Blanche would accept that my twin brother also owns an identical blood-hound. Several times I have had to send Pommes Frites on his way in case I got caught with him. This morning, when I heard the Blanches approaching, I had to push him out of the window before he had finished his *croissant*. He was most upset. I should have taken *petit déjeuner* in my room.'

'I'm glad I'm not married if that's the way you 'ave to carry on,' said Elsie. 'It sounds to me as though you're up the creek without a paddle.'

'That is one way of putting it,' said Monsieur Pample-mousse. 'In France we say *"être dans le pétrin"*.'

It had not been the happiest of nights. No sooner had he got back to bed than he'd heard a scream coming from Elsie's room. Others had heard it too, but he had reached her first – rather to his regret. Clearly the worst of interpretations had been placed, not only on his presence, but on what he appeared to be doing. Disentangling high-heeled shoes which had become deeply enmeshed in the seat of a wicker-work chair was no easy task – particularly at three o'clock in the morning. It was a wonder Elsie hadn't gone straight through and done herself permanent damage.

He glanced across at her. She must have a thing about standing on chairs. It was curious how someone who was able to take the earlier events in her stride should go into a state of collapse at the sight of a spider. That was her story anyway.

In the end he had done the decent thing and let her have his room for the remainder of the night.

It had not been the happiest of days either. The Police had been less than grateful when he bid them *adieu* that afternoon. A day spent tramping up and down the dunes had left no one in the best of tempers, least of all the contingent of 'volunteers' from the local *gendarmerie.* Their hearts had never been in it, and viewing the Dune du Pilat by daylight and at close quarters it was easy to see why. Pommes Frites had not been high in their popularity stakes. The fact that other dogs brought in from Bordeaux had fared no better counted for nothing. Scepticism had been rife among the rank and file; their plastic bags had gone back to Headquarters unopened. Only Elsie's polaroid picture saved them from total ignominy, providing as it did the one shred of evidence that the whole thing had not been part of a bad dream on Monsieur Pamplemousse's part.

The fact that it also provided the Police with the first positive clue as to the fate of what must by now be regarded as the late Monsieur Bouet, counted for nothing. That it had been a genuine part of him was confirmed in no uncertain manner by Madame Bouet, whose decline when she saw the photograph and identified the sabot reached a new low and was audible far beyond the confines of her apartment adjoining the Hôtel des Dunes.

Circumstantial evidence provided by Monsieur Pamplemousse himself pointed to Pommes Frites' second find as being an equally essential part of Monsieur Bouet's underling, Pierre. Really, the Police had no cause to grumble at receiving such an unexpected bonus, but that hadn't stopped them. Congratulations on a job well done were not forthcoming. Murmurs of appreciation for Monsieur Pamplemousse's public spiritedness in volunteering the information were muted to the point of inaudibility.

He was also having doubts about the wisdom of not revealing his true identity. On the spur of the moment, seeing a glint of recognition in the eyes of the *officier* in charge of the investigation at the name Pamplemousse, it had seemed a good idea to take advantage of his newly acquired identity. Warming to the idea, he'd tended to over-embroider the part of a twin brother rather than play it down. Signing the statement had set the seal on his folly. There was no going back. In the old days, if their positions been reversed and the truth had come to light, he would have thrown the book at the other party.

'You could take him to a dog parlour and 'ave him dyed black,' said Elsie, breaking into his thoughts. 'That'd kill two birds with one stone. The Blanches wouldn't recognise 'im and he'd really 'ave something to look gloomy about then.'

'Bloodhounds always look morose,' said Monsieur Pamplemousse. 'In repose it is their natural expression. It simply happens to be worse than usual at the moment.'

As if to reinforce his statement, a deep sigh issued from beneath the table. It was Pommes Frites' way of pointing out that a), in an ideal world conversation ought to take place after a meal rather than before it, and b), in his humble opinion too much emphasis was being placed on eating in restaurants where fish predominated.

'Gives me the creeps,' said Elsie. 'I wouldn't like to be shipwrecked on a desert island with 'im, I must say. 'E'd be a right bundle of laughs, I don't think.'

They ate in silence for a while. Elsie's mind was clearly elsewhere. He fell to wondering about her and what sort of life she led back in England. It was hard to envisage. Outwardly she was confident and well organised, frighteningly so at times. It was hard to picture her at home doing the dusting. On the other hand, the snack in her room the previous evening had revealed a totally different side to her character. It had made him warm towards her, as though he had been let in on a guilty secret, which in a way he supposed he had.

Elsie was dressed rather more discreetly than had been the case then. The off-the-shoulder number must have suffered on the dunes. By comparison, her latest outfit, in plain, unadorned black wool, wouldn't have looked out of place on a nun about to take her final exams. Even so, her habit of leaning across the table whenever she had something important to say would have brought a worried frown to even the most broad-minded of Mother Superiors overseeing her practicals, as would the accompanying waft of quietly expensive perfume. Someone, somewhere, must be keeping Elsie in the style to which she had clearly become accustomed.

Her presence certainly didn't go unnoticed by the other occupants of the restaurant where they were dining. At the Paris Lido it would have been eye-catching; in Arcachon it was little short of sensational.

Monsieur Pamplemousse wasn't at all sorry the owners, in ploughing much of their profit back into the business in the form of designer vegetation, had also been fortunate enough to engage the services of someone with green fingers. Ivy formed a screen around their table; passion flowers grew rampant; tradescantia trailed where others failed to grow. From time to time he was aware of eyes peering through gaps in the foliage. It was worse than dining in some South American jungle surrounded by hostile natives who had never seen a white woman before. He regretted not bringing a can of fly spray. Had he done so, he would have been sorely tempted to use it.

The Restaurant Joséphine was as unlike the Hôtel des Dunes as it was possible to be. In fairness, they had a head start; at the current rate of scoring, two heads. The *patron* was hard at work in the kitchen – every so often he caught sight of a man in a white hat peering round a corner to see how things were going out front. Madame Joséphine, despite Elsie's disparaging 'mutton dressed as lamb', was ever-present and solicitous.

They ordered *paté de foie gras*. It came with a glass of chilled *demi-sec* Vouvray – a perfect accompaniment. To follow, they chose grilled sea bass. It was presented on a bed of dried fennel. A waiter arrived clasping an amber bottle. Flamed in Cognac, the stalks of the fennel imparted a scent which flavoured the whole dish. Inspired by the first course, Monsieur Pamplemousse consulted the *carte des vins* again and changed his order from a Muscadet to an older Vouvray. There was only a token mention of Burgundy.

The dessert was a toss-up between *Iles flotantes, Crème brûlée, Tarte maison* and *Mousse au chocolat à l'orange*. They both chose the mousse. It came with a separate bowl of cream which was left on the table. The chocolate was satisfactorily dark and bitter, and the faint taste of orange gave it a certain distinction, lifting it above the norm.

'How would you rate the meal?' asked Monsieur Pamplemousse as Elsie licked her spoon clean.

'The *pâté* was all right,' said Elsie. 'But it was round. I reckon it came from a tin. The sea bass was great, but then, there's no reason why it shouldn't have been. The olive oil on the salad was too cold – probably straight out of the fridge. If it had been warmer it would have brought out the flavour more. I reckon a Wrought-Iron Table and Chair – plus.'

Monsieur Pamplemousse nodded his approval. It tallied with the current entry in *Le Guide*. It was a cut above a Bar

Stool – the symbol for a good place to stop *en route*. He wondered if Elsie had checked it herself before they came out. Then he dismissed the idea. She had left the booking to him.

'Some of my favourite restaurants are in that category. They are the backbone of French cuisine.

'I have never eaten here before, but the owner is in his late fifties – a few years older than *Madame*. I would guess they have been here most of their lives. The menu has probably hardly changed since they began. They get their fish practically straight out of the ocean. You are right . . . the *patron* has probably cooked sea bass so many times he could do it with his eyes shut.'

'No Stock Pot?'

'*Non.*' Monsieur Pamplemousse shook his head. 'The menu is too limited for that. Besides, to award a Stock Pot to a restaurant such as this would do the patron a grave disservice. Here he is, happy in what he does, wanting no more than to earn an honest living. He has his faithful band of regulars. They come here because they know what to expect and would doubtless go elsewhere if they didn't get their *soupe de poisson* on Thursdays or their lobster *cassoulet* on Saturday evening. If he had a Stock Pot his costs would treble or even quadruple overnight. He would have to take on more staff, particularly in the kitchen. People from outside the town, from Paris, from other parts of the world, would seek him out. He would need to appoint at least one assistant chef and train him in his ways, otherwise he could never afford to be ill or take a day off. He would have to find accommodation for them. Then he would need to invest heavily in wine. The present list is much too short and parochial. Life would never be the same. And once having been awarded a Stock Pot, he would live in fear of losing it.

'In the case of a three-Stock-Pot restaurant the problem is much worse. It is one of the reasons why so many chefs branch out into other areas – to make the whole thing pay. I know chefs who would sooner not have the award. Success in life is a mixed blessing. Often you find you have mounted a treadmill from which there is no escape.'

Elsie looked at him curiously. 'What made you become an Inspector?'

Monsieur Pamplemousse shrugged. 'Fate. I resigned from my previous post and quite by chance, on the very day that I left, with no idea of what I was going to do – or even *could* do – I happened to bump into the Director.'

'Funny thing, fate,' said Elsie. 'I mean – like us being here this evening. In fact, everyone being here come to that.'

'It is the same with the hotel,' said Monsieur Pamplemousse. 'I often wonder what brings people to a certain spot at one particular moment in time.'

'Yeah. Well . . . like I said, it's fate. I suppose . . .' Elsie looked for a moment as though she was about to develop her thesis, but then Madame Joséphine arrived with the coffee and a plate of *tuiles dentelles*.

Monsieur Pamplemousse waited until she had departed before continuing the conversation.

'What do you think of it? The hotel, I mean. You will need to make out a report. It will be difficult in the circumstances, but it will be a good exercise. I will go through the form with you tomorrow. There are categories for everything, from the car-parking facilities to the quality of the bed linen, from ease of access for those who are incapacitated to the view from the room. It is several hours' work.'

'I know one thing,' said Elsie. 'The hotel's not like what it said in the brochure.'

'They often aren't,' said Monsieur Pamplemousse drily. 'A wide-angle lens and a good imagination can work wonders.'

''Alf a kilometre to the sea,' said Elsie bitterly. 'They didn't say nuffin' about there being a bleedin' great pile of sand in the way. You can't see it even if you stand on a chair.'

'An unfortunate oversight,' said Monsieur Pamplemousse. 'Why did you choose this hotel? I'm surprised they even have a brochure.'

'It was Reginald's idea,' said Elsie.

'Reginald?'

'My boy friend. He'd heard it was interesting down 'ere. Only he couldn't come 'isself.'

'He is a food Inspector?'

'Reginald?' Elsie gave a hollow laugh. 'He wouldn't know one end of a sausage from the other.'

She looked around the restaurant as though anxious to change the subject. 'I wouldn't mind being in this business.'

Memories of the one meal Elsie had cooked the night he and Doucette had dined with the Director came flooding back. It had definitely been Stock Pot material.

'I am sure you would be very good at it.' Monsieur Pamplemousse helped himself to a *tuile*. 'I'm sure you'd do better than these. They are much too soft to the touch. Another reason for not recommending a Stock Pot.'

'They were probably made this morning,' said Elsie. 'Can't say as I blame him. You can't do everything at once. That's the trouble. If Reginald and me opened a restaurant I'd be stuck in the kitchen all day long, slaving over a hot stove while 'e did the chatting up. I can picture it all.'

'Does he have any particular interests?'

'Interests? Reginald's interested in anything that makes money. Buying and selling mostly. Import and export. This, that and the other.'

'What sort of things?' Monsieur Pamplemousse found himself growing more and more intrigued. It was like playing some kind of guessing game.

'Well . . . let's say he's got 'is finger on what people want and he knows where to get it. But not in the kind of way your Paris friend would be interested in.'

'My Paris friend?'

'You know. That art dealer you was spinning a yarn to yesterday evening.'

'Monsieur Blanche? How do you know he is an art dealer?'

'Well – whatever. He was standing in front of that painting on the landing this morning making notes. And he 'ad his camera and a magnifying glass with him. I reckon he's got 'is eye on it.'

'Do you now?'

''Course, it's not like dealing in jewels. Reginald always says that jewels combine the maximum wealth in the smallest possible space.'

'Madame Chanel said much the same thing,' said Monsieur Pamplemousse drily.

'Well, she would, wouldn't she? It's all right for some. She probably didn't 'ave much trouble going through customs.

'That's where jewels have the advantage. There's all sorts of places you can stick them so as other people won't see – not unless they're poking their nose into places where they shouldn't be, if you know what I mean. Not like a painting, unless it's a miniature of course.'

Monsieur Pamplemousse was beginning to feel a little out of his depth. A sudden thought struck him.

'Monsieur Blanche is not the only one to have taken a photograph of the picture.'

The blue in Elsie's eyes took on a metallic tint; momentarily more cobalt than azure. 'Well, it's nice innit.' Helping herself to another *tuile*, she bent it almost double between her fingers and thumb. 'I see what you mean. Still, the coffee's all right. I always think there's nothing worse than a bad cup of coffee at the end of a meal. Spoils the whole evening.'

Taking the hint, Monsieur Pamplemousse withdrew his notepad and took the opportunity to jot down a few notes.

'So where did you get your know-how from?' asked Elsie.

'I have always been interested in food. I was lucky enough to have a mother who was a born cook. Then I spent some time attached to the Paris food fraud squad while I was with the Sûreté. It gave me an insight into what can be done if you are that way inclined. Putting margarine into *croissants au beurre;* using walnut juice to dye Moroccan white sand truffles black and then passing them off as the real thing; butchers fiddling their scales and selling short weight . . .'

Monsieur Pamplemousse broke off and looked across the table with some concern as Elsie started to choke. 'Let me get you some water.'

'While you were doing what?' gasped Elsie.

'Did *Monsieur le Directeur* not tell you? I was with the Paris Sûreté for many years. I joined them soon after I left school.'

'You're not still with them, are you?' demanded Elsie. 'I mean . . . like . . . attached as it were.'

Monsieur Pamplemousse shook his head. 'After I resigned I severed all my connections.' It was the short answer and the simplest.

Elsie looked relieved.

96

'What made you do it? Resign, I mean.'

'I had a little trouble with some girls at the Folies . . .'

'You mean there was more than one?'

'Fifteen,' said Monsieur Pamplemousse.

'Blimey!' Elsie looked at him with renewed interest and something akin to respect. 'I can't wait to 'ear more.'

'There is nothing much to hear,' said Monsieur Pamplemousse. 'It was literally a case of my being caught with my trousers down. Someone gave me a knock-out drop and left me locked in a cupboard above the chorus girls' dressing room. When I came round my clothes had been stolen and there was a cine camera . . . with some exposed film . . . someone had bored a hole through the ceiling. It was what is known as a "put-up job".'

'Of course,' said Elsie.

'You do not have to believe me,' said Monsieur Pamplemousse stiffly.

'I believe you,' said Elsie simply.

'*Merci.* No one else did at the time, and I had little recourse but to resign. That is how Pommes Frites and I met – he had just been made redundant following a cut-back and they gave him to me as a farewell present.'

For years the ignominy had followed him around. 'Doing a Pamplemousse' had become a synonym in the force for scandalous behaviour. For a time he had even thought of changing his name. It was one of the reasons for his prevarication at the *gendarmerie* that morning; the certain knowledge that revealing his true identity would have given rise to nudges and winks and barely suppressed guffaws.

'I thought you French were supposed to be broad-minded.'

'It is true that we are perhaps less hypocritical about these things than some.' Monsieur Pamplemousse avoided the phrase 'two-faced'. 'But there was another factor. One of the girls had been got at and was prepared, if necessary, to swear that certain acts of a bizarre nature had taken place. I wished to spare my wife that.'

'Dear, oh dear,' said Elsie. 'Well, I never. I don't know what Reginald will say when I tell him. It's a bit "them and us" as far as 'e's concerned.'

'Is it necessary that he should know?' asked Monsieur Pamplemousse.

'I suppose not,' said Elsie dubiously. 'It's just that Reginald's a dab hand at getting things out of me and he gets upset if I don't tell 'im everything.'

'And he would consider me one of "them"?'

'Once a copper – always a copper – that's what Reginald says.'

Monsieur Pamplemousse refrained from replying that in his opinion the reverse was also true. Instead he called for the bill.

All the same, he had to admit there was a certain amount of truth in the saying. As they left the restaurant and began walking down the street towards the boulevard de la Plage where he had left his car, he found himself automatically looking around with a policeman's eye, making a mental note of shop windows, the way people walked and dressed, vehicle registrations.

The white exterior of the Casino de la Plage came into view and he pointed to a car parked just inside the gates. It had a Hertz sign stuck to the windscreen.

'We are not the only ones in Arcachon from the hotel. The Americans are also here.'

'Ooh, can we go in too?' Elsie slipped her arm into his and gave it a squeeze. 'Please. I don't know when I last 'ad a flutter.'

Monsieur Pamplemousse hesitated. *Chiens* would not be admitted. There was no doubt in his mind that he would incur further opprobrium from Pommes Frites if he consigned him to the car for the rest of the evening. His emergency biscuits were back at the hotel, and leaving the radio on would be no compensation. On the other hand . . . He wondered if Elsie had the ability to change the colour of her eyes at will. They were now the lightest of blue: as light as the touch of her thigh against his.

Avoiding Pommes Frites' gaze, Monsieur Pamplemousse opened the car door and ushered him into the back seat.

The interior of the Casino was a duplicate of all casinos everywhere. He could have described it without going inside. The marble staircase, the thick carpet, the chandeliers, the staff who looked as though they spent their entire lives in evening dress.

Having registered, he waited while Elsie went through the formality of producing her passport. As soon as she had received an entrance card she disappeared into the *toilette* to put on her 'war paint'. When she came out he noticed she was wearing a thin gold chain round her neck with a single diamond set in a horseshoe-shaped mounting. She also had on a pair of matching earrings.

Entering the gaming room was like taking a step back into the thirties. Dark corners were non-existent. Doubtless there were hidden television cameras monitoring their every movement – the 'eye-in-the-sky'. Video recorders would be in operation. He caught the familiar sound of the ivory ball against the spinning roulette wheel, punctuated every so often by the sharp riffling of cards. In the restaurant he'd been the only one with a tie and he'd felt out of place, now he was glad he had worn one. Less chic than Deauville – where the Director was probably ensconced at that very moment and where jackets and ties would be *de rigueur* – it was still a place where people dressed as for an occasion.

As he escorted Elsie towards the bar Monsieur Pamplemousse glanced around the room. Most of the tables were already crowded. There were several small groups of Japanese men present, their faces as expressionless as those belonging to the card dealers themselves. He wondered where they went to in the day-time – he couldn't remember seeing any parties of Japanese when he and Elsie had driven through Arcachon the day before.

He pulled up two stools. 'What will you have?'

'Adam's Ale,' said Elsie.

'Qu'est-ce que c'est?'

'Aqua pure Water. I want to keep a straight 'ead. Back in a minute.'

Reflecting that Elsie was full of surprises, Monsieur Pamplemousse ordered a Badoit. It cost more than his vin *rouge*. Come to think of it, she hadn't drunk much at dinner either.

Wondering if she had planned to visit the casino all along, he watched as she strolled over to one of the *vingt-et-un* tables where the Americans were playing. They were concentrating on the game. Although it was too early for any really high play, it looked serious. They had obviously come prepared, for they were all in evening dress. Short, thick-set, hair close cropped, they could have been taken for extras in a pre-war gangster movie.

After a while Elsie left the table and went across to a *caisse* at the far end of the room. She returned clutching a handful of plastic chips. From where he was sitting Monsieur Pamplemousse couldn't see their value.

The Americans parted to let her in as she rejoined their table and for a while she was lost from view. For someone who hadn't visited a casino in a long time she seemed very much at home.

Monsieur Pamplemousse sipped his drink and turned his attention to the rest of the room.

There was a certain fascination in watching the speed at which the croupiers worked, just as there was in watching anyone who was highly skilled and professional. Their rakes moved faster than a serpent's tongue as they cleared the tables after each turn of the wheel, tossing counters back into the appropriate squares with uncanny accuracy.

Once a copper – always a copper. It was a fact that trouble seemed to follow him around, but it was equally true to say that over the years he had developed a nose for it. Perhaps the reverse applied; it was he who attracted the trouble.

Sitting at the end of each roulette table were two men – the *Chef de partie* and his assistant. Dark-suited, anonymous, unsmiling and completely interchangeable, watching every movement of the play: those of the croupiers as well as the punters. It would be hard to get away with anything. One whiff of suspicion and next time you would be politely but firmly refused admission. The odds were always on the house.

It was also a fact that when he first joined the force he had found himself isolated from many of his old friends. True, he had made new ones, but he had realised very quickly that it would always be a case of 'us' and 'them' – of his being on the other side of the fence in many people's eyes.

Draining his glass as Elsie rejoined him, he pointed to hers. 'You won't change your mind?'

'No, thanks, ta ever so.' Elsie took a swig of her Badoit and then felt in her handbag. 'Take this. It'll pay for the meal.'

Monsieur Pamplemousse looked at the pile of notes on the bar counter and shook his head. *'Le Guide* will be paying. Provided we make out a report I will claim it on expenses. That is why we are here.'

'Go on,' said Elsie. 'There'll be plenty more where that came from before the night's out. I'm on to a winning streak.'

'You are staying? Wouldn't it be better to leave while you are ahead? Winning streaks don't last for ever. It is a battle between you and the casino and they always win in the end.' He tried not to make it sound too holier-than-thou.

'Reginald wouldn't agree. He says gambling is a battle between you and yourself.'

Monsieur Pamplemousse sighed. He was beginning to feel that if anyone ever published a book of the sayings of Reginald, he ought to be in line for an autographed copy.

'Why don't you go on back?' said Elsie. 'I'll be all right. I can get a taxi.' She snapped her handbag shut and held up the back of her right hand to be kissed. 'Be good. And if you can't be good – be careful.'

'I was about to give you the same advice,' said Monsieur Pamplemousse. 'If you need any help, you know where I am.'

'A bientôt, as they say.' Elsie fluttered her eyelashes and kissed him lightly in return.

Not unaware that he probably had lipstick on his brow, but hesitant about removing it with his handkerchief in case he forgot about it later, Monsieur Pamplemousse made his way out of the casino and back to the car. He felt curiously deflated. There was no reason why Elsie should wish to spend the evening with him, and yet he couldn't rid himself of the feeling that in some way he had been used.

Apart from a few pockets of light from out-of-town restaurants, he drove through darkness most of the way back to the Hôtel des Dunes. Arcachon went to bed early.

His mood was not improved by Pommes Frites, who showed his disapproval of the whole evening by pointedly shifting his weight around whenever they turned a corner, going with the tilt of the car rather than against it, so that on several occasions they nearly turned over.

The hotel car park looked deserted. The English family had left early that morning. The Blanches' Renault was there and so was the Mercedes belonging to the German couple.

The lights were on in the foyer, but there was no other sign of life. Maurice, the general dogsbody, was conspicuous by his absence. Having been up since before dawn attending to the *petit déjeuner* he'd probably gone to bed early. At least he hadn't locked up.

Monsieur Pamplemousse went behind the desk and removed his key from a row of hooks on the wall behind it. In a cubbyhole beneath it there was a slip of paper with a message to telephone the Director as soon as possible.

On the way up the stairs he paused halfway and took a long look at the painting. He was no expert, but it did have a certain 'something'. It could be a copy of an early Impressionist – a Sisley perhaps. It really needed to be seen in daylight and from a distance to get the full effect. He wished now he'd brought a flash attachment for his camera.

Back in his room he closed the shutters, picked up the telephone and dialled the Director's number. It was answered on the first ring.

'Pamplemousse! Where have you been? I have been trying to reach you all the evening.' Once again the Director's voice had a muffled sound.

'I have been out for a meal, *Monsieur*. Then Elsie expressed a desire to visit the casino.'

'She is with you now, I trust?'

'*Monsieur, I* am in my room. What are you suggesting?'

'No, no, Pamplemousse. You misunderstand me. I am merely asking you if she is at the hotel.'

'I left her at the casino, *Monsieur.*'

There was a sharp intake of breath from the other end.

'Alone? That is not good news.'

'But, *Monsieur*, I am hardly her keeper . . .'

'Aristide . . . yesterday I received a telephone call from *Angleterre*. I was trying to tell you about it last night when we were interrupted. Whoever it was refused to give a name, but there were strange noises going on in the background – shouts, and what sounded like someone drawing a stick across some bars. All the voice said was "Look after Else . . . or else". It was most confusing. When I asked which Else he meant, the caller hung up. Frankly, I am worried. What do you think it can mean?'

'I have no idea, *Monsieur.*' The thought of there being two Elsies was not one he wished to entertain for the moment.

'I charge you with her safety, Aristide.'

'But, *Monsieur*, she is a big girl . . . well able to look after herself . . .' The *débâcle* with the card trick came back to him.

'I know she is a big girl, Pamplemousse . . .' The Director paused for a moment, clearly drawing on his store of memories. 'I am also well aware that in the normal course of events she is more than able to look after herself. All I am saying . . .' There was a click followed by the dialling tone.

Monsieur Pamplemousse gazed at the receiver in his hand for a moment or two before replacing it in its cradle.

Pommes Frites looked at him inquiringly. Ever sensitive to the moods of others, he could tell that something was exercising his master's mind. Not one to harbour rancour for any length of time, particularly with those he loved, he stood up and wagged his tail sympathetically.

Monsieur Pamplemousse took the hint. Pommes Frites was right. It was time for a walk. In times of stress there was nothing like a good walk to clear the mind.

The wind which had got up during the previous night had dropped again and the air on top of the dunes was as clear as it was possible to be. The tide was neither in nor out. From where he stood he could see the waves shimmering in the moonlight as they broke gently along the line of the beach, but they were too far away for the sound to reach him.

He sat down on the sand for a while, going over in his mind the conversation he'd had with the Director. Despite Elsie's grumbles, he couldn't help liking her. No one could possibly accuse her of being negative or standoffish. He had to admit he missed her company. Mentally tossing a coin, he wondered if he ought to go back into Arcachon and make sure she was all right. It came down tails. She would hardly thank him if he did turn up at the casino. Clearly she had wanted to be left to her own devices, and she might well suspect the worst if he reappeared.

Suddenly aware that Pommes Frites was pricking up his ears, Monsieur Pamplemousse concentrated his attention closer to home. At first he could detect nothing, then gradually he heard the soft crunching sound of footsteps in the sand. It was accompanied by heavy breathing. Every few moments it stopped altogether as whoever was responsible paused for a rest. He caught the glimmer of a flashlight.

Signalling Pommes Frites to lie low, Monsieur Pamplemousse flattened himself against the sand. It felt surprisingly warm. He was none too soon. A moment later the bent figure of a man came into view, making heavy weather of the last few metres of the climb before he reached the summit. Head down, he passed by them some ten metres or so away, then rapidly gathered speed, slithering from side to side as he headed back down the way they had just come.

Watching the gnome-like figure as it disappeared in the direction of the hotel, Monsieur Pamplemousse was irresistibly reminded of a scene from *Snow White and the Seven Dwarfs*. The only difference being the figure wasn't wearing a miner's lamp, and the occasional gleam came not from the head of a pick, but from moonlight striking the handle of a metal detector he was carrying over his shoulder. Neither Dopey nor Sneezy, not Bashful or Doc, and certainly not Happy; Monsieur Blanche looked extremely grumpy and ready for sleep.

6
THE CAST ASSEMBLES

Monsieur Pamplemousse came out of the *gendarmerie* in Arcachon and joined Pommes Frites who had been waiting patiently on the steps. He paused to breathe in the fresh air, then glanced at his watch. It said 10.34. The sun was already above the top of the buildings on the other side of the street. The best of a glorious July morning had been wasted in the tedium of getting things down on paper. A course in speedwriting wouldn't have come amiss. If he'd had anything to do with the matter he would have had a go at the man taking notes in an attempt to wean him off pencil-licking. He suspected the *officier* in charge of the case was being deliberately slow. Several times he'd looked as though he had been on the point of saying something revealing, and each time it boiled down to going over the same old ground once again.

What was he doing in Arcachon? When had he arrived? Had he driven straight down from Paris? What was his occupation? If he lived in the Auvergne what had he been doing in Paris?

Questions, questions, questions.

The more the *officier* persisted, the more stubborn Monsieur Pamplemousse became, safe in the knowledge that they could hardly accuse him of any crime. Once again, he had conveniently forgotten his *carte d'identité*, making a great show of searching through his pockets, grimacing and 'poofing' as he went. He wouldn't get away with it a third time. The twenty-four hours' grace he had been given in which to produce it would go all too quickly, and then what? He would meet that problem when it happened.

All in all, Monsieur Pamplemousse felt the outrage of a man caught out concocting a story which he had told so well he'd come to believe in it himself. His twin brother had become so real in his mind, it seemed positively insulting to query his existence.

Ever sensitive to his master's vicissitudes, and anxious to register support and sympathy, Pommes Frites left his mark on the wheel of a police car parked outside the entrance. As he followed Monsieur along rue Georges Hameau and across rue Général Leclerc towards the railway station where the car had been left he recognised the signs of a pensive mind at work: the wandering gait, the hands in the pockets, the absentminded air of a man lost in thought.

There were two games of *boules* in progress on the sandy area between the road and the *gare*. They were probably a permanent fixture. The first was made up of a group of old hands – retired fishermen to a man if their wind-dried faces were anything to go by – and the second a bevy of younger players, among them two women. A sign of the times if ever there was one. Where would it all end? His old father would have died of shock; his mother would have said they were no better than they should be and looked the other way. Coats hung alongside scoreboards nailed to a line of trees only just beginning to sprout after their spring pollarding. The audience sitting on the red hardwood benches was mostly made up of taxi-drivers waiting for the arrival of the next train from Bordeaux.

Monsieur Pamplemousse joined them, watching first one game, then the other, but he found it hard to concentrate and after a moment or two he continued with his walk.

Something untoward was going on at the Hôtel des Dunes, that was for sure. The Super hadn't said it in so many words, but at one point – either by accident or design – he'd let slip the fact that it had been under observation prior to the murder. He didn't say why or for how long.

At the end of the parking area Monsieur Pamplemousse made his way back to the pavement and stood waiting for the traffic lights to change before crossing the road. As he did so he happened to glance across towards the far side of the busy square. To his surprise he saw Elsie coming out of the post office on the corner.

Wearing a striped Breton jersey over matching dark-blue slacks and yachting cap, she looked the picture of health. She might well have just stepped out of a commercial advertising the life-giving powers of ozone. Heads turned as she disappeared in the direction of the sea, her high heels giving her bottom a decidedly provocative wiggle.

Monsieur Pamplemousse had to admit that his feeling of relief at seeing Elsie was tinged with guilt. His first reaction when she hadn't responded to his knock at breakfast time had been one of panic that he'd done nothing to follow up the Director's telephone call and that something might have happened to her. A hurried check of the rack in the hall had shown that her room key was missing, as was a note he'd left saying he had to leave early and suggesting they meet outside the casino later that morning, so that they could inspect another restaurant at lunch time.

Elsie certainly didn't look as though she'd spent the night in debauchery; quite the reverse. Most likely she had slept late and then got a taxi into Arcachon. Either that or someone had given her a lift. As for being in the *P.T.T.*, she had probably been doing nothing more mysterious than posting a card to Reginald.

The thought reminded Monsieur Pamplemousse that he hadn't sent a card to Doucette. It was usually the first thing he did. Following Elsie down avenue Gambetta he stopped outside a *tabac* and found himself confronted by what at first sight seemed like an embarrassment of riches, but which he quickly narrowed down to a choice between shots of the dunes taken from a variety of angles, the oyster beds at high tide, the same oyster beds six hours later, a distant view of the lighthouse at Cap Ferret taken from the Arcachon side of the bay, the tapping of pine trees for their resin – the second local industry – or what looked like the same nude girl disporting herself on one of the many sheltered beaches round the bay. He decided to play safe with a montage of the first five.

While he was in the shop he bought a map and a local guide to the area in order to top up on his store of information. *Le Guide* concentrated on hotels and restaurants. Details concerning the area itself were kept as succinct as possible and there was always something new to learn.

As he waited for his change, Monsieur Pamplemousse glanced at the headlines in some of the *journaux*. Most of them accorded space on the front page to the disappearance of Monsieur Bouet, but there was no mention of foul play, nor of the possibility of there being a second body. The Police must be playing it down for all they were worth. He wondered why. Perhaps they thought it would be bad for the tourist trade just prior to the season.

After making his way through the town he stopped on the front to admire an old double-tiered carousel. The organ music cheered him up a little and he wandered on to

110

the pier to watch the local fishermen angling for their evening meal. He wished now he'd suggested meeting Elsie earlier. She was probably doing a round of the boutiques.

A yellow bulldozer went about its task of levelling the beach. A low-flying Air Force jet shot past making everyone jump.

As he left the pier a coach drew up and began disgorging a load of elderly passengers. Some set off immediately to join a queue for the nearby Aquarium, others sat down on the nearest bench, seeking the shade of the tamarisk trees which lined the promenade; the more adventurous made their way down on to the beach, the men removing their shoes and socks and rolling up their trousers as they entered the sea, the women abandoning all sense of propriety as they lifted their skirts in a way they would never have done at home.

Truffert was right. Water did something to people. He should know. Before becoming an Inspector he'd spent years in the Merchant Navy. It was such a sparkling day Monsieur Pamplemousse was almost tempted to join them. Doucette would have been in there like a shot.

Pommes Frites had no inhibitions. There were shrieks and cries of 'Ooh, la! la!' as he dashed into the water.

Monsieur Pamplemousse fitted a wide angle lens to his Leica and recorded the moment for posterity.

Looking at the scene through the view-finder it was hard to believe that only a short while before, and a bare kilometre or so away at that, those same waters had witnessed what had every appearance of being not one, but two particularly bloody murders. He wondered what the reaction would be if a leg or an arm suddenly floated into view, or if one of the fishermen hooked something unexpected. It would certainly put them off their *dîner.*

Feeling at a loose end, he worked his way along the beach, pausing every so often in order to throw a stick for Pommes Frites. Reaching some concrete steps, he climbed them slowly and found himself standing on the outer wall of a vast marina. It was a forest of masts; packed with yachts and motor craft of every shape and kind – there must be two thousand at least. To his left, at the entrance to the harbour, a statue in the shape of a giant anchor was dedicated to those lost at sea; a warning to week-end sailors who must go past it in droves during the season, although if the speed at which most of the current ones were travelling was anything to go by he doubted if many of them gave it a second glance. Time and a desire to be first in the queue took priority.

He was about to take another photograph when he heard his name being called. Panning quickly down he registered a familiar figure waving to him from the stem of a motor launch just leaving the marina.

Elsie, her blonde hair streaming in the wind, had discarded her trousers and top in favour of a minuscule black bikini. It struck Monsieur Pamplemousse that as she hadn't been carrying a beach bag she must have come prepared. He clicked the shutter before returning her wave.

As the boat swept past he recognised one of the Americans at the helm; the oldest of the three and the one who seemed to be the leader. The other two were nowhere to be seen. Perhaps they were still in the casino.

Daylight did nothing for him; sunlight even less. He would have been more at home on the lower slopes of Montmartre than here in Arcachon. Despite his expensive clothes and shoes you could see your face in, he was surprised Elsie didn't see him for what he was – a *voyou* – a hoodlum. There was no accounting for tastes.

Rapidly changing to a narrow angle lens, Monsieur Pamplemousse followed the boat's progress as it passed through the harbour entrance and made a turn to port. It looked as though Elsie and her new-found escort were heading towards the furthest tip of the peninsula at the entrance to the bay.

Monsieur Pamplemousse's first impulse was to ignore the whole thing. Write it off as being all part of life's rich, and sometimes most unsatisfactory pattern. What did it matter to him if Elsie had chosen to ignore his note? If she was prepared to risk chalking up a black mark that was her decision.

All the same, he couldn't help feeling intrigued.

A moment later, acting on an impulse, he made his way quickly back along the beach in the direction of the pier. He was in luck's way. The 11.30 ferry to Cap Ferret was about to leave. Signalling Pommes Frites to go first, he scrambled after him and made his way through the crowded cabin towards the open stern. They had the last two seats.

Seconds later the boat slipped its moorings and edged out from the steps. As soon as it was clear of the pier, it swung round in a wide circle between two rows of marker buoys and then quickly gathered speed.

Heading south, they hugged the coast for a while, past rows of small hotels and apartment blocks interspersed with occasional examples of baroque housing: a hotch-potch of sea-side architecture.

Pyla-sur-Mer came into view and as soon as they were clear of the oyster beds the boat swung to starboard and headed west towards the far side of the bay.

Looking back over his shoulder, Monsieur Pamplemousse had a clear view of the dune. At the Arcachon end

113

a zig-zag vertical line of enormous old wartime pill-boxes lay at drunken angles. Was it his imagination working over-time, or did they have a certain doom-laden air about them? Although they had obviously shifted their position over the years, they were so solid, nothing short of an atom bomb would ever destroy them completely. They had been built to last for ever; part of an unfulfilled plan by the Germans during the war to transform the Basin into a haven for their fleet of warships. Making use of his camera lens again he made out a helicopter landing-pad on a jetty to the town side of the beach. To its right there was a First Aid station with a red cross painted on its roof. From the look of the water level the tide must be around the halfway mark. Panning up, he searched in vain for the hotel, but it was hidden by the trees.

It was hard to picture the possibility that somewhere in that vast mass of sand lay the grizzly remains of the hotel *patron*. If it were true, then they might never be found. It was no wonder the police had given up; it was a thankless task.

Monsieur Pamplemousse gave an involuntary shiver. He couldn't have put it into words, but neither could he escape the feeling that somehow the forces of fate were beginning to take over. It was the age-old question of what made you be in a certain place at a certain time. Was it pure chance that led him to be sitting where he was at that particular moment? If he had waited until the next ferry, or spent time writing his card to Doucette, would everything from that moment on be different? He would never know the answer.

It was hard to raise any feelings for someone he hadn't met; he didn't even have the remotest idea what Monsieur Bouet had looked like. All the same, Monsieur Pample-mousse couldn't help wondering what he had done to end up the way he had. If he'd upset someone then he must have done it in a big way. Perhaps, if he had a guilty secret, he'd carried it with him to his sandy grave. And what about his assistant? Had he been a party to the same secret, or had he accidentally stumbled across something he shouldn't have?

Madame Bouet was obviously taking it badly, as well she might. Nevertheless, someone would have to run the hotel. If the first night's performance was anything to go by they would need a new chef for a start.

Not for the first time he found himself toying with the idea of looking elsewhere. The German couple had already left. Perhaps even now they were having another row in a shower further along the coast. But Elsie seemed dead set on staying put and at least his room was reasonably comfortable.

Monsieur Pamplemousse scanned the water for any sign of her boat, but the bay was busy with craft of all shapes and sizes – a mixture of yachts and motor launches, with here and there a larger boat carrying a party out for a day's fishing.

To be totally truthful he had to admit to more than a faint twinge of jealousy that Elsie had left him in the lurch, totally ignoring his note. He couldn't even console himself that it was for a younger man; that he could have well understood. It was simply someone with the means to hire a boat. And why not? Perhaps because for all Elsie's faults he'd thought better of her. She didn't have to say yes to the first man who came along. Clearly she had made a play for more than a turn of the wheel at the casino last night. He wondered what Reginald would have to say if he got to hear of it.

Monsieur Pamplemousse felt more and more aggrieved. Elsie wasn't exactly proving to be a dedicated representative of *Le Guide*. There had been no question of her asking if she could have the day off. Normally she would have been expected to explore the area, checking on other entries in *Le Guide*, making notes on any changes which might have taken place. It all had to go down.

Pulling his hat down over his face to shield it from the sun, he settled back to make himself comfortable. He should have known better. It was a signal for the boatman to throttle back. Yet more oyster beds came into view and a moment later they slid alongside the pier at Bélisaire. It was almost mid-day. The journey had taken just over twenty minutes.

Monsieur Pamplemousse hesitated outside a café at the end of the pier, but it was too early for lunch. A narrow-gauge railway track ran along the side of the road. It disappeared invitingly round a corner and into some woods, but the tiny platform by the terminus was deserted. He consulted a timetable on the wall of the booking office. The first train wasn't due to leave until the afternoon so, with Pommes Frites at his heels, he set off to explore the area on foot

Large private houses built at a time when the area was the summer haunt of wealthy burghers from Bordeaux rubbed shoulders with modern apartment blocks now occupied by lesser mortals. Cars with boat trailers proliferated.

Their walk took them back down a pedestrian precinct lined with identical eating places displaying carbon-copy menus. There was a smell of cheap cooking oil in the air. Elsie was nowhere to be seen.

Lost in thought, Monsieur Pamplemousse gave a jump as there was a sudden sharp crack from behind him. He ducked instinctively, only to see a small boy on a skateboard shoot past, weaving his way in and out of the other pedestrians before executing a complicated airborne manoeuvre which doubtless had some esoteric name – like a banana or a porcupine. There was another, louder crack as he landed heavily on the paving stones. A strange variation – half skateboard, half uni-cycle – came out of a side street. It was propelled with great aplomb by its owner. A moment later both boys disappeared down the precinct without a word being exchanged.

Monsieur Pamplemousse envied their style and self-confidence. In his time it had been roller skates – not very good ones at that – and he'd had to run the gauntlet of running comments from his contemporaries. Nowadays, communication other than by means of monosyllabic grunts seemed almost a sign of weakness.

He returned to the harbour feeling hungry after the walk. The café by the pier was beginning to fill up. He studied the menu outside, comparing it with what was on the plates of those already eating. Taste buds signalled their approval.

Finding himself one of the few remaining tables near the water's edge, he sat back to admire the view. It was easy to see why it was so popular with the purveyors of postcards.

The little harbour was surrounded by oyster beds, misshapen branches sticking vertically from the water to mark the perimeter gave them a kind of rustic charm. The layers of flat plastic mesh baskets containing the oysters in the second stage of their development piled up in long rows. When the tide came in they would disappear again. Nature, according to the guide book, ensured that their water was changed twice a day; 400 million cubic metres of it. The annual oyster production in the bay of Arcachon was between ten and twelve thousand tonnes; 37,000 acres out of a total area of 4,320,000 was given over to it.

In the face of such statistics Monsieur Pamplemousse had no choice but to order a sea-food platter and a *demi* Muscadet. Detecting a certain restiveness below the table, he asked for a *steak frites* and a *pichet* of *vin rouge* to follow.

Beyond the oyster beds he could see a few motor launches at anchor in the water, but it was impossible to tell which, if any, might be the one Elsie had been in. From a distance they all looked the same. It was quite possible her escort had tied up in one of the little harbours further along the coast at the far end of the Cap. If, indeed, they had come to that end of the peninsula at all. There were plenty of alternative places to moor.

The sea-food platter came and went, and while the paraphernalia of plate stand, dishes and other impedimenta were being removed, Monsieur Pamplemousse dipped his fingers in a bowl of water, wiped them dry with his napkin, then poured himself some more wine and settled back to await the arrival of the steak. He was beginning to feel more at peace with the world. The only cloud on an otherwise spotless horizon came in the form of a warning growl from somewhere near his feet.

Looking around, Monsieur Pamplemousse realised why. It was a question of territories. Pommes Frites was having to compete with the regulars; a motley selection of resident freelancers who obviously put in a daily appearance. In a brief survey of the surrounding tables he counted no less than nine other dogs. Apart from a Dandie Dinmont and what in a poor light might have passed for a Dogue de Bordeaux, they were a raggle-taggle selection of ambiguous pedigree and even more uncertain ancestry.

Doubtless encouraged by residents with an eye to saving on biscuits during the holiday season, they patrolled the restaurant with an expert air, sizing up the clientèle before homing in on likely looking subjects. Once a decision had been made they settled down as close as possible to their chosen target, watching every mouthful. A mangy-looking Wolfhound with unusually yellow teeth appeared to be the ring-leader. Definitely not a dog to be trifled with. Not that it appeared to bother Pommes Frites. A visiting Chihuahua belonging to a woman at the next table looked suitably grateful as yet another growl sent the animal packing.

As his second course arrived, Monsieur Pamplemousse reached for the mustard and resolutely turned his back on the scene.

The steak, lightly seared under the grill, was covered in melted butter. The *frites* arrived seconds later, piping hot on a separate platter. He tested one in his fingers. It was as he liked them, crisp and golden on the outside, yet soft and yielding within. In the end it was the simple dishes he enjoyed the most, although they were often the hardest to do. Pommes Frites stirred expectantly as he heard his master call for a green salad. It was a good sign.

It was as Monsieur Pamplemousse cut and speared the first mouthful of his steak that he happened to catch sight of another ferry arriving. He glanced at his watch. It must be the 14.30 from Arcachon. The light was perfect. Only the waves from the wake of the boat as it swung round to tie up below the end of the pier disturbed the reflections in the water. Reaching for his camera, he quickly composed a picture of the jetty with the oyster beds in the background. Foreground interest was provided by a potted shrub, one of a row standing outside the restaurant.

Having waited patiently for the *moment critique* when the passengers were halfway through disembarking, Monsieur Pamplemousse was about to press the shutter release button when he froze. To his horror, slap bang in the middle of the picture he saw Monsieur and Madame Blanche advancing down the pier. There was no possibility of escape. They were heading straight towards him. Recognition on their part was but a few short steps away.

Afterwards Monsieur Pamplemousse couldn't remember exactly what came over him. Perhaps it was simply a case of desperate situations demanding desperate but not necessarily considered measures. Whatever the reasoning, or lack of reasoning behind it, having issued a peremptory order to Pommes Frites to make himself scarce with all possible speed, he made a grab for the Chihuahua at the next table and with his other hand reached out towards his plate. The blissful expression on the creature's face as it caught sight of an approaching meal faded rapidly as its tongue, wet with anticipation, made contact with the steak.

All major events need some train of events to set them going. The atomic bomb requires its minor explosion to trigger off the horrifying chain reaction; earthquakes come about because of movement within the bowels of the earth which eventually cause them to erupt in protest. In the case of the Chihuahua it was the unexpected advent of *moutarde de Dijon* against tongue which provided the necessary catalyst.

Although he had never been lucky enough to witness a performance at the *Comédie française,* let alone the *Théâatre nationale* (even at matinée performances neither establishment exactly went out of its way to encourage the presence of *chiens),* Pommes Frites considered himself something of a connoisseur when it came to the raw material of life from which writers of plays gained their ideas.

Having stationed himself behind a convenient tree at what he judged to be a suitably safe distance from both

Monsieur Pamplemousse and the restaurant, he watched in silent awe as the drama before him unfolded with alarming speed. The aggrieved expression on his face at having been banished from the table changed to one of wonder. Everywhere he looked there was something fresh to be seen.

Waiters, who until that moment had resolutely refused to catch the eye of diners impatient for their *l'addition,* appeared as if by magic. The chef materialised brandishing a carving knife. He was followed by a bevy of lesser hands, each clutching an implement of their particular calling; oyster knives vied with glass decanters, meat pounders with butcher's cleavers. The sound effects were deafening. It was theatre in the round and no mistake.

In the centre of it all the Chihuahua, foaming at the mouth, its eyes as large as saucers and as red as the proverbial beetroot, took one terrified look at what was going on around it, then made a dive inside Monsieur Pamplemousse's jacket where it proceeded to part company with the steak, noisily and with all possible speed.

Taking full advantage of the diversion, and emboldened by the absence of Pommes Frites, the Wolfhound rallied his troops with a brief but pointed howl, then led them in clearing unwatched plates of their contents. Bellows of rage and feminine shrieks rose from all sides. In a matter of seconds the restaurant became a seething mass of snarling fur.

The owner of the Chihuahua, distraught at seeing the state its loved one was in as it emerged gasping for air from the confines of Monsieur Pamplemousse's jacket, climbed on to a chair and began crossing herself as though her own end was also nigh. Downing the last of his wine, a priest at an adjoining table hastened to provide comfort. He looked all set to perform the final rites.

If the object of the exercise had been to divert Monsieur and Madame Blanche's attention from any possible relationship between himself and Pommes Frites, Monsieur Pamplemousse had succeeded beyond his wildest dreams.

Even from a distance of some fifty paces it needed no expert in lip-reading to perceive Madame Blanche's views on the matter. The oval-shape formed by her lips said it all. It was a 'poof' to end all 'poofs'. The look of scorn on her face as she went on her way dragging Monsieur Blanche behind her was something to behold. Pommes Frites shrank back behind the tree, holding his breath until they were safely past.

When he next looked out he saw to his disappointment that the pageant was nearing its end. He was just in time to see his master disappearing down the road with the Wolfhound loping along behind. If Monsieur Pamplemousse had every appearance of making a bid for the next Olympics, the dog was behaving as though it had all the time in the world. It even paused for a moment in order to take a quick snatch from a clump of grass. Only the sight of its bared teeth and the sound of a scarcely suppressed snarl pointed to the fact that, far from being a vegetarian, it was merely working up an appetite before going in for the kill.

Pommes Frites gave a sigh as he set off after them. He was too nice a dog to spend overlong on the thought that it served his master right, but as both hunted and hunter disappeared round a corner, he couldn't help but dwell on it for a moment or two, wondering if perhaps the full moon were responsible for his master's strange behaviour over the past few days.

Thoughts of a philosophical nature were far from Monsieur Pamplemousse's mind as he raced through the town. They ranged from wondering what would happen if he took refuge in a passing gift shop – the owners were hardly likely to welcome him with open arms – to weighing up his chances of escape by plunging down a side street and into the sea. Clearly, from the way they were shying away he would get little or no help from any of the passers-by. No one would come to his rescue if the dog turned out to be a powerful swimmer.

In the end the solution rose up in front of him in the shape of a tall, white cigar-shaped building, the red top of which was surmounted by a glass enclosure.

Summoning up a final burst of speed which took even the Wolfhound by surprise, he beat it to the lighthouse by several yards.

Ignoring an elderly woman in black seated behind a desk in the entrance hall, cutting off in its prime her explanation that although there was no entrance charge, *pourboires* were at the discretion of the individual and would benefit those prepared at any time of the day or night to drop what they were doing in order to risk their lives in ensuring the safety of others – it was up to *Monsieur* – he made for the stairs, leaving her saucer of carefully arranged ten-franc coins undisturbed.

Had he paused to consult his guide, Monsieur Pample-mousse would have seen in passing that there were 258 steps to the top of the lighthouse. He didn't bother to count, but if pressed he would have put it at many more.

Emerging on to the viewing platform at long last, he collapsed against the perimeter wall, fighting to regain his breath. Focusing his gaze on the ground some fifty metres below he could see no sign of the Wolfhound. Either the brute had given up the chase or it was already on its way up. With any luck it had fallen foul of the *Madame* at the door.

Gradually he became aware that he was not alone. On the other side of the circular platform he could hear voices. Peering round the corner he saw a small group of sightseers being regaled by an ancient mariner on the splendour of the panoramic view spread out before them. If they had witnessed his ignominious progress through the town they showed no sign. Most of them seemed more interested in the local football stadium.

The man was making the most of his captive audience.

'*Oui*. There is nothing between us and the United States of America. Just five thousand or so kilometres of Atlantic Ocean.

'*Oui, oui*. In winter the storms can be very bad. Last winter they were the worst we had ever known. The whole lighthouse swayed. You see the *Limite de Prudence . . .*' he pointed to a line of white-capped rollers between the two strips of land marking the point where the sea entered the bay. 'That was one mass of boiling water. The Dune du Pilat . . .' heads turned in Monsieur Pamplemousse's direction, 'the Dune du Pilat was like the Sahara desert in the middle of a sandstorm.

'*Non*. The white tower you can see a kilometre and a half away to the west was not the original lighthouse. This,' said with some pride, 'this is the site of the original. It has always been so. The lighthouse may have been destroyed by the Germans in 1944, but in 1946 it was completely rebuilt.

'The white building is the Semaphore Tower . . . it is used by the military. That has always been there – for as long as I can remember. The new lighthouse was built on exactly the same spot as the old.'

Monsieur Pamplemousse listened with only half an ear. The other half was waiting for the sound of approaching paws.

'*Oui.*' The man turned in response to a question. 'The restaurant by the harbour is a good place to eat.'

'That is true. I have just eaten there myself.' Even as he spoke Monsieur Pamplemousse realised he had made a mistake. The warm sun combined with his marathon sprint through the town had left their mark. A malodorous smell was beginning to emanate from his person.

The keeper stared at him for a brief moment or two, then turned. The others hastily followed on behind as he moved away towards the leeward side of the building.

'From here you can see the whole of the Fôret Domaniele de Lège et Garonne . . .' But the damage was done. The attention of his audience was concentrated instead on Monsieur Pamplemousse. Mostly it was one of alarm as he followed them round the circular platform. In an effort to escape several tried to push their way past him towards the stairs, then clearly wished they hadn't as he barred their progress.

Monsieur Pamplemousse was trying to keep his options open. The worst was about to happen. His ears had picked up the sound of heavy breathing. It was getting louder with every passing second.

It was a fifty-fifty chance which way the animal went. If it turned right at the top he was done for, if it turned left it would have to push its way through the crowd and time would be on his side. To Monsieur Pamplemousse's relief he heard it turn left

Taking advantage of the sudden diversion he made a dive through the opening and disappeared down the stairs rather faster than he had come up. A moment later he set off down the road, this time taking a different direction, away from the Bay side and towards the Atlantic ocean.

Monsieur Pamplemousse's sudden flight didn't go unnoticed. Resting his chin on the parapet of the observation platform, Pommes Frites watched in amazement as act two of the drama in mime unfolded before his very eyes.

His master appeared to have gone berserk. Having overtaken a small boy on a skateboard, he suddenly stopped, turned, and entered into conversation with him. First came the crouching down and the patting of the head. Then, when that seemed to be of no avail, it was followed by the old trick of distracting attention. Monsieur Pamplemousse pointed up to an imaginary object in the sky and while the boy's back was turned he made a grab for the skateboard.

It must have been something of a desperate measure, for he only travelled a matter of a few metres before he fell off. Rising to his feet and dusting himself down, he then ran hither and thither for a while, before making a wild dash for a small train winding its way up from the beach. He appeared to be having an argument, first with the driver, then with the passengers as he clung to the side trying to force his way in to the crowded carriage.

Eventually, as the train slowed down for some traffic lights, he leapt off it and began waving at some distant figures walking away from him up the road – they were too far away for Pommes Frites to recognise them – but clearly his master knew who they were.

Then, almost as though he'd had a sudden change of mind and didn't want to see them after all, he hid behind a tree until they had disappeared down a lane leading towards the sea.

Pommes Frites shook his head sadly as he followed Monsieur Pamplemousse's progress from tree to tree until he was but a speck on the horizon. He had a friend in Paris whose owner had behaved in a similar fashion. In the end he'd had to be taken away. He didn't know what he would do if that happened.

Having decided the time had come for him to intervene, Pommes Frites made a firm mental note of the point where he had last seen his master, then set off in pursuit.

Unaware of the consternation he had been causing, Monsieur Pamplemousse relaxed for the first time since he'd fled from the café. The Wolfhound must have given up the chase for it was nowhere to be seen. But best of all he had found what he was looking for. There in the firm sand near the water's edge he'd come across two sets of footprints. One set looked as though they had been made by a pair of rope-soled boating shoes; the other had to be Elsie's. There couldn't be many people on the beach that day who were wearing high heels.

He quickened his pace. The tide was coming in fast. It wouldn't be long before all traces disappeared completely.

It wasn't until he rounded a groyne and looked up that Monsieur Pamplemousse suddenly realised he had been so busy following the footprints he had completely lost sight of his immediate surroundings. As far as the eye could see there were naked bodies stretched out on the sand: hectares and hectares of bare flesh in various shades of pink, brown and black. Several of those nearest to him were already giving him strange looks as they caught sight of his camera. There was a very definite feeling of unrest in the air. The man nearest to him reached for a portable telephone.

Monsieur Pamplemousse beat a hasty retreat and made his way up the beach in the direction of a small dune. To his relief there was no one else in sight – probably because his side of the groyne was exposed to the prevailing wind. He weighed up the pros and cons of the situation for a moment or two. The possibility that Elsie and her escort might be making for one of the many nudist beaches dotted along the Atlantic coast hadn't crossed his mind. It put him on the horns of a dilemma and no mistake.

There was only one thing for it. Crouching down, he divested himself of his clothing. Folding it into a neat pile, he placed it on a patch of dry sand well out of reach of the incoming tide. Then, pulling the brim of his hat down over his eyes, he lengthened the straps on his camera case, slung it round his front and, with the nonchalant air of one who did such things every day of his life, retraced his steps.

Keeping as close to the water's edge as possible, his only other article of adornment – a gold Capillard-Rieme wrist-watch – glinting in the afternoon sun, Monsieur Pample-mousse resumed the pursuit of his quarry, adding his not inconsiderable mite of whiteness to the general ambience.

It was some ten minutes later, having followed a course roughly identical to that of his master, that Pommes Frites arrived on the scene. It was no great feat of navigation. Indeed, it would have needed a hound with singularly insensitive nostrils not to have located where Monsieur Pamplemousse had ended up. Pommes Frites could have done it with his eyes closed.

At first his joy at finding the clothes had been unbounded, alloyed only by a faint feeling of puzzlement as to why his master wasn't inside them. Never one to harbour a grudge, ever ready to turn the other jowl, he followed the trail of footprints down the beach as far as the water's edge. There he stopped dead in his tracks, scanning the water in vain, for there wasn't a soul to be seen. Suddenly he feared the worst. On his way there he had seen a red flag flying.

Even Pommes Frites knew that a red flag meant danger. He let out a howl.

The thought that Monsieur Pamplemousse might have gone swimming for pleasure never entered his mind. In all the time he had known him he had never seen Monsieur Pamplemousse don a bathing costume let alone enter the water. There was only one interpretation to be arrived at. The answer was simple. Something had snapped and his master had decided to end it all.

Pommes Frites made his way back up the beach with a heavy heart. There was only one thing to be done. It was a case of carrying out the canine equivalent of a burial at sea. And as with a burial at sea, when the waters close inexorably over the coffin and it disappears without a trace, so, having dragged his master's clothes back down the beach and dug a suitably large hole, he paid his last respects as an extra large wave broke over the spot.

Barring an earthquake or some other act of God, Pommes Frites felt confident that Monsieur Pamplemousse's belongings would remain undisturbed until the end of time. No bone could have been better hidden, no tribute more sincere. It was a simple gesture, but in the circumstances it was the least a dog could do for his master.

7
POMMES FRITES THINKS AGAIN

Monsieur Pamplemousse gazed at the spot where he was perfectly certain he had left his clothes less than a quarter of an hour before. 'I can assure you they were here. I remember the place exactly. There is the rock . . . there is a piece of seaweed . . .'

'*Oui, Monsieur.*' The *gendarme* sounded weary.

'It is a *mystère.*'

'*Oui, Monsieur.* Perhaps they have been stolen?'

Monsieur Pamplemousse looked around the beach. There wasn't a soul in sight on their side of the groyne. He gave the sand a desultory stab with his toe. It felt soft and yielding.

'No one in their right mind would have taken them. They are covered in *chien*'s vomit.'

The *gendarme* gave a shrug. Clearly the state of Monsieur Pamplemousse's clothes was of academic interest beside the matter in hand.

'There have been a number of complaints, *Monsieur.* From those on the *plage des naturistes*, you understand?'

Monsieur Pamplemousse raised himself to his full height. 'Are you accusing me of being a voyeur?' he thundered. '*Un individu qui se rince l'oeil?* – a peeping Tom?'

Wilting beneath his gaze, the *gendarme* lowered his eyes. He contemplated Monsieur Pamplemousse's lower regions for a moment or two, then took out his notebook.

While the man was busy writing, Monsieur Pamplemousse took the opportunity to lengthen his camera strap still further.

'I am an ornithologist.'

The *gendarme* gave a sigh. 'That is what they all say, *Monsieur*. But with respect, I would suggest *Monsieur* is looking in the wrong direction. The Ile aux Oiseaux is on the other side of the peninsula. It is inside the Bassin d'Arcachon.'

'I am perfectly well aware of that,' said Monsieur Pamplemousse. 'I happen to be looking for the Banc d'Arguin which is at the entrance to the Bassin. I understand it is covered with marram grass and that it provides shelter for a large colony of seabirds. I am particularly interested in the sandwich tern.'

The *gendarme* carried on writing. 'I am pleased to see *Monsieur* has made good use of our local guide. Doubtless *Monsieur* has his camera with him because of his interest in bird watching.'

The *double entendre* did not go unnoticed by Monsieur Pamplemousse. He decided he must tread carefully and try not to lose his temper.

'May I see your *carte d'identité, Monsieur?*'

'Oh, *Mon Dieu! Mon Dieu!*' Monsieur Pamplemousse made a great play of patting himself all over, first both sides of his chest, then his hips and finally his posterior. 'I had it with me when I came out this morning. I wonder where it can possibly be?'

The truth of the matter – in fact the only ray of sunshine in the whole dismal affair- was that in anticipation of his being asked that very same question when he visited the *gendarmerie* in Arcachon he had changed into his other suit. His precious notebook in the secret compartment of

131

his right trouser leg, his Cross pen without which he always felt lost, his identity card and various other personal items he would have been sad to lose, were all safely tucked away in the hotel room.

His attempt at striking a jovial note failed miserably. Clearly it had had the opposite effect. Officialdom came into play.

'In that case, *Monsieur,* I must ask you to accompany me to the *commissariat de police.*'

'I trust you have some kind of covering in your *voiture.*' Monsieur Pamplemousse followed the *gendarme* up the beach 'A blanket perhaps? Or even a rug?'

The man gave a hollow laugh. 'This is not Paris, *Monsieur.* It is not even Bordeaux.' He pointed to a bicycle propped against a tree.

Monsieur Pamplemousse stared at it. 'You mean I am to ride that!'

'No, *Monsieur,*' said the *gendarme* patiently. 'I shall be riding the *bicyclette. You* will be walking.'

'Walking? How far is the *gendarmerie?*'

'How far?' The question gave rise to a certain amount of head scratching. 'The nearest one is at Le Petit Piquet. Nine kilometres away . . . perhaps ten. I am only on attachment for the day. It is the start of the holiday season and . . .'

'Je refuse! Absolument!'

The *gendarme* leaned over his handlebars and peered at Monsieur Pamplemousse's watch. 'There is always the *autobus* if you prefer it. If we hurry we may just catch the next one to Bordeaux.'

'No, I would not prefer it!' barked Monsieur Pample-mousse.

The *gendarme* shrugged. 'As you wish, *Monsieur.* In that case I will leave you here while I telephone for assistance.'

He cocked his head in the direction of the next beach. 'By the sound of it you will not be alone.'

Monsieur Pamplemousse gave a start. He'd been so engrossed in his own misfortunes he had failed to pay any attention to what was going on around him. Now that the gendarme mentioned it there did seem to be an inordinate amount of noise coming from the other side of the groyne. Screams, shouts, voices raised in anger, it sounded for all the world as though someone was holding a lynching party.

He essayed a quick peep over the top.

'*Sacré bleu!*'

'*Monsieur?*' The officer joined him. '*Mon dieu! Chiens!*'

Monsieur Pamplemousse sank down out of sight. If he hadn't seen it with his own eyes he wouldn't have believed it possible.

It wasn't just *chiens*, it was one particular *chien*. What Pommes Frites thought he was up to was hard to imagine. Or rather – he rephrased the question – what he was up to was clear for all to see. Why he was doing it was another matter entirely.

Not to put too fine a point on it, and for reasons best known to himself, Pommes Frites was busily engaged in running up and down the beach sniffing all and sundry as fast as he could go. As an exercise in the triggering-off of girlish screams and manly oaths it was highly successful. One touch of his wet nose on an unsuspecting *derrière* and the effect was both instantaneous and electric. But as a means of endearing himself to the population at large it ranked as a non-starter. The *plage* was in an uproar.

'Is there nowhere else we can go?' demanded Monsieur Pamplemousse. 'You cannot possibly expect me to walk nine kilometres like this.'

The *gendarme* considered the matter. 'The *Mairie* in Bélisaire is not far away,' he said dubiously.

'Then I suggest we make our way there with all possible speed,' said Monsieur Pamplemousse.

'I will take your camera, *Monsieur.*'

'Is that necessary?'

'I am afraid so, *Monsieur.*' The *gendarme* didn't actually say it might be used in evidence against him, but Monsieur Pamplemousse got the point.

'May I suggest *Monsieur* makes use of his *chapeau* instead?'

Monsieur Pamplemousse hastily swopped his hat for the camera.

The *gendarme* gave a whistle as he took it. 'An R4. This is some camera.' He fondled it with his hands. 'Lovely finish. You get what you pay for, I suppose. I don't think I'd want to take it on the beach. One grain of sand and . . .'

'You are interested in photography?'

'A little. But nothing like this. This is what I call a professional job.' He checked the number of exposures taken, then held the camera up to his eye. 'I see you are using a wide-angle lens, *Monsieur.*'

'I was just taking some general views,' said Monsieur Pamplemousse. 'To establish the geography.'

'Aaah !'

'*Merde!*' Monsieur Pamplemousse suddenly realised his other lens had been in his trouser pocket.

'There is something wrong, *Monsieur?*'

'It is nothing,' said Monsieur Pamplemousse. Nothing! Nearly four thousand francs worth of lens. Madame Grante would not be amused.

He glanced anxiously over his shoulder as more shrieks came from the next beach. The worst possible scenario would be if he was linked in any way with what was happening on the other side of the groyne. That, coming on top of everything else, would be the final straw.

There was a click. 'Nice shutter, too,' said the gendarme. 'Very easy movement. Lovely camera.'

'I do wish you wouldn't point it in my direction,' said Monsieur Pamplemousse crossly.

Glancing anxiously over his shoulder in case Pommes Frites caught sight of him walking off the beach, Monsieur Pamplemousse followed the *gendarme* along a slatted wooden walkway leading towards the main road.

He needn't have worried. Pommes Frites' mind was on other things. Sensing the moment of truth had arrived, glad to be of service at long last, he was in his element as he darted hither and thither, sniffing a bottom here, checking another one there. Not since the passing out party at the end of his course with the Paris Sûreté had he been able to give such free rein to his natural instincts without fear of repercussions from on high.

After burying his master's clothing, he had spent some time turning the whole matter over in his mind. Although blessed with lightning reactions in an emergency, Pommes Frites' thought processes were not always of the fastest. Not for him the snap decisions of a business tycoon; fax machines requiring instant replies would have had short shrift in his kennel; computer salesmen would have been shown the door.

Following a great deal of long-drawn-out reasoning, which he had carried out while exploring the hinterland of Bélisaire, he had begun to wonder if he had done the right thing. Once the seeds of doubt had been sown they had grown rapidly.

135

It struck him for a start that if Monsieur Pamplemousse had done away with himself he wouldn't have taken his camera with him. Nor would he have carried out the deed wearing a hat. Monsieur Pamplemousse was very punctilious about that sort of thing. Whichever way he looked at it, from whatever angle, Pommes Frites reached the inescapable conclusion that he'd made a boo boo. There was a distinct possibility his master might not have given up the ghost after all.

It was with such thoughts uppermost in his mind that he returned to the beach only to discover the tide had come in a long way during his rambles. It was while swimming ashore after a fruitless search of the sea bed for his burial ground that he came across the beach full of nudists and hope of finding his master alive and well was born again.

The first bad news for Monsieur Pamplemousse during his walk to the *Mairie* came in the shape of a black diesel-engined locomotive belonging to the *Tramways du Cap Ferret*. It was on top of them before he had a chance to hide. With a shriek of protesting metal, the engine rounded a bend pulling behind it three open-sided carriages packed with holiday-makers wending their way home from the beach. The driver gave a toot, and as the whole entourage ground to a halt he leaned out of his cab and exchanged a brief word with the *gendarme*. Another note was added to the latter's book.

To Monsieur Pamplemousse's horror he caught sight of Elsie and her companion sitting in the last carriage. Fortunately he spotted them first, but it was a narrow squeak. He did the only thing possible. To avoid recognition he covered his face with his hat.

As the train rattled on its way several of the passengers applauded, but by then Monsieur Pamplemousse was past caring.

Still bothered by the event, he was ill-prepared for the second encounter. It happened when they reached the shopping mall. The mother of the skate-boarding child was waiting for him. She pursued him down the road pointing an accusing finger and hurling abuse. Seeing Monsieur Pamplemousse in a state of *déshabillé* clearly confirmed her worst suspicions. Others joined in, until what had started off as a purely personal vendetta grew out of all proportion.

The very, very bad news came as they neared the *Mairie;* an unlikely modern building not far from the lighthouse. Signs outside advertised an exhibition by local artists. Either they were small in number or space was at a premium. Monsieur Pamplemousse had never seen such a small *mairie*. As he followed the *gendarme* up the drive, tempering haste to escape the throng with as much dignity as he could muster in the circumstances, he nearly collided with a couple coming out.

'*Pardon . . . excusez moi . . .* please forgive me.' Instinctively Monsieur Pamplemousse raised his hat as he stood back to let them pass.

It was a momentary lapse in concentration and he replaced the *chapeau* almost immediately, but the damage was done. Stoniness of expression on the distaff side was tempered by one of triumph as the woman looked him up and down.

'You may not remember,' said Monsieur Pamplemousse weakly, 'but we met in the hotel. I believe you know my brother, Aristide.'

Madame Blanche's wind-dried lips parted reluctantly. 'Indeed I remember meeting you in the hotel. I remember it all too well. But if that is the case, then you are not who you said you were at the time. I suspected as much.'

'I assure you, *Madame* . . .'

'You can assure me until you are blue in the face,' said Madame Blanche, her voice trembling with rage, 'but with my own eyes I have just seen proof positive of your identity. I was right all the time. You are Aristide Pamplemousse. Why you should wish to pretend you are his twin brother I do not know – although I fear the worst.'

Conscious that Madame Blanche had been addressing the crowd as much as himself, Monsieur Pamplemousse did likewise.

'It is the penalty one pays, *Madame,* for a moment of madness,' he boomed. 'Now that you have divulged our guilty secret to all and sundry, I only hope my wife is as forgiving as your husband must be, although in her case I feel she will find it harder to understand.'

For a moment he thought she was going to explode.

'Did I hear her say Aristide Pamplemousse?' asked the *gendarme* as Monsieur and Madame Blanche swept down the path and pushed their way through the crowd.

Monsieur Pamplemousse nodded as he followed the other inside.

'Not Aristide Pamplemousse, late of the Paris Sûreté?'

Monsieur Pamplemousse nodded again. 'My twin brother. The poor woman is demented. She keeps mistaking me for him.'

The *gendarme* looked at his charge with new respect. 'He is famous.'

'A very brilliant man,' said Monsieur Pamplemousse. *'Formidable.'*

'Formidable, but also flawed would you not say?'

'No,' said Monsieur Pamplemousse. 'I would not say that.'

'If it was the same Aristide Pamplemousse who was dismissed because of that affair with fifty girls at the Folies,' said the *gendarme*, 'there must be something wrong with him.'

'He was not dismissed,' said Monsieur Pamplemousse. 'He took early retirement. And it was not fifty chorus girls, it was only fifteen.'

'*Quinze.*' There was an accompanying whistle. Clearly to anyone stationed in Cap Ferret the number was immaterial. The prospect of being involved with one chorus girl must be fairly remote; fifteen beyond the wildest of dreams.

Glancing back down the road, the *gendarme* jerked his thumb in the direction of Madame Blanche. '*Monsieur* must be a glutton for punishment.'

Monsieur Pamplemousse followed the direction of the man's gaze. It was a tiny consolation that the Blanches seemed to be engaged in a violent argument about something.

'It was a very dark night,' he said.

'Pitch black I should think.'

The *gendarme* led the way past some startled art lovers who were clearly more used to seeing their life studies on canvas rather than face to face, and into a small room at the side of the building.

'I am sorry to have to treat the brother of Monsieur Aristide Pamplemousse like this.' He rewound the film, then opened the back of the Leica and removed the spool. 'But I have some checking-up to do . . . you understand? I shall not be long.'

'He would have done the same,' said Monsieur Pamplemousse gruffly, 'but while you are about it I would like to use the telephone.'

'There is one on the table by the window,' said the *gendarme*. 'I will make the necessary arrangements. I am sure when they hear who you are related to, it will be no problem. In the meantime, I must ask you to wait here.'

Monsieur Pamplemousse grunted. He could hardly do otherwise.

Left to his own devices, he gazed out of the window wondering what to do next. In the circumstances he could hardly ring Doucette. That would really let the cat out of the bag. Questions would be asked. It was Deauville or nothing. He eyed the curtains thoughtfully. They were made of some kind of netting material, but it was better than nothing.

The Director's number seemed to be permanently engaged. When he eventually got through a maid answered. *Monsieur le Directeur* was changing for dinner, but she knew he had been trying to reach Monsieur Pamplemousse.

There was another wait, then the Director himself came on the line. For a change his voice came through loud and clear.

'Why are you always so impossible to find, Pamplemousse? I have come to the conclusion that I must insist you carry some kind of bleeper. I have tried the hotel. I have tried every restaurant within twenty kilometres which is listed in *Le Guide*. I have tried the casino. I even telephoned the Police . . . I spoke to some idiot who said he knew your twin brother. I played along with it, of course. I said he must be mistaken because I happen to know your twin brother very well and he is in Italy.'

Monsieur Pamplemousse groaned inwardly. If the Director had been covering up for him he feared the worst. 'Aaah, that is bad news, *Monsieur*.'

'If it is bad news, Pamplemousse, I do not wish to hear it. I have enough bad news of my own. Today has not been a happy day on the track. My horse came in at ten to three.'

Monsieur Pamplemousse couldn't resist it. 'What time was it due in, *Monsieur?*'

There was a momentary silence at the other end of the line.

'Pamplemousse, if that was meant to be a joke, it was in very poor taste. Please be brief. Time is getting on, and . . .'

'I am in a very vulnerable position, *Monsieur.*'

'Come, come, Aristide. You are no more vulnerable than thousands of others who are making telephone calls at this very moment.'

'With respect, *Monsieur,* there is nothing to prevent passers-by seeing into the room . . .'

'Can I get this absolutely clear, Pamplemousse? Are you telling me you have no curtains? What kind of establishment is the Hôtel des Dunes?'

'I am not speaking from the Hôtel des Dunes, *Monsieur* . . . I am in the *Mairie* at Cap Ferret. There are no curtains at the window because I am wearing them. There is an art exhibition and people are coming and going all the time . . .' Even as he spoke a second coach laden with tourists drew up outside. He retreated across the room as far as the phone cord would allow. 'They are made of netting, and . . .'

'Pamplemousse . . .' The Director sounded weary.

'*Oui, Monsieur?*'

'Pamplemousse, it may be a foolish question, but why are you wearing curtains?'

'Because I have no clothes, *Monsieur.*'

'Aah!' The Director gave a long drawn-out sigh of defeat. 'I won't ask any more. But please be brief. My wife and I are getting ready to go out. Chantal is in the bathroom, but she will be with me at any moment. What is it you want? I hope this doesn't mean your car has broken down yet again. It is high time you took advantage of one of the staff vehicles. I will speak to Madame Grante in the morning.'

'*Monsieur*, there has almost certainly been a murder at the Hôtel des Dunes . . . possibly two . . . The chef and his principal assistant . . .'

'The food is that bad?' He had gained the Director's attention at long last. Having gained it, Monsieur Pamplemousse pressed home his advantage.

'I fear there may be worse to come. I am carrying out your instructions to watch over Elsie, but I am somewhat hampered at present. Elsie and I are separated, and until I get another suit and a good lawyer it will remain that way. After your last message I thought you should know that. I cannot in truth say that I am sorry. As far as I am concerned Elsie can stew in the *bouillon* from her own *pot-au-feu*. She is wholly irresponsible. As for her ever becoming an Inspector . . .'

'Pamplemousse . . .'

'*Oui, Monsieur?*'

'This is splendid news. Surely, that is the whole object of the exercise. I knew I could rely on your good offices. All I need from you now is a report to that effect. I fail to see the problem.'

'*Monsieur!* Until I am given some new clothes there will be no report. Not only have I lost almost everything I was standing up in, but I am being held in the *Mairie* at Bélisaire pending charges.'

'Charges, Pamplemousse? What charges? Surely you are not being accused of the murders?'

'No, *Monsieur,* mine are quite minor offences I assure you and I have an answer for all of them . . .'

'Pamplemousse, the reason I tried to contact you earlier was to reassure myself that all is well. Now I regret having spoken to you. Tell me the worst. A moment ago you used the word *charges.* Are you telling me there are more than one?'

Monsieur Pamplemousse did a quick count with his free hand. 'It depends, *Monsieur,* on whether or not they wish to throw the book at me. I am afraid I have run out of fingers.

'Causing a disturbance in a restaurant . . .

'Stealing a dog . . .

'Causing it unnecessary distress by force feeding it with mustard . . .

'Leaving the same restaurant without paying the bill . . .

'Then there was an unfortunate incident with a child. I was merely trying to discover where it had bought its skate-board, but its mother thought otherwise . . . my motives were misunderstood . . .

'Travelling on a vehicle belonging to the *Tramways du Cap Ferret* without the benefit of a ticket . . .

'Disturbing the peace *sur la plage* . . .

'Indecent exposure . . . possibly there will be more than one charge on that count . . . I am afraid that while I was standing on a chair in order to take down the curtains a coach party arrived . . .'

'Pamplemousse!' There was an explosion from the other end of the line. 'I do not wish to hear another word.'

'It is difficult not to expose yourself, *Monsieur,* when the only item of clothing you possess is a *chapeau.* Especially when you wish to avoid being recognised lest someone should by some misfortune link your name with *Le Guide* and telephone one of the less reputable *journaux*. And, of course, it is not just *Le Guide*. There is Elsie to think of, not to mention your own good name, *Monsieur*, and that of your wife. In the circumstances she would not be pleased.'

He knew by the silence which followed his last remark that he had scored a direct hit.

'What is it you require, Aristide? Even at this late hour I will endeavour to pull strings, but it is the very last time. Fortunately it is the height of the season. Deauville is alive with Deputies. This afternoon there were more members of Government to be seen at the race track than there were runners for the whole of the meeting . . .'

'*Monsieur* . . .'

'Yes, Pamplemousse?'

'*Monsieur*, while you are arranging for my release, I wonder if it would be possible to organise a new set of clothes? I take a size thirty-nine collar. Also some shoes and some money. And, *Monsieur* . . .'

'Yes, Pamplemousse?' A note of weariness seemed to have crept into the Director's voice again.

'If you are talking to Madame Grante, perhaps you would be kind enough to tell her I have mislaid my narrow angle lens?'

Monsieur Pamplemousse replaced the receiver. He had a satisfactory feeling he wouldn't have much longer to wait. Soon the telephone lines radiating out from Deauville would start to hum.

Drawing up the only available chair, he placed it with its back towards the window and made himself as comfortable as circumstances allowed. If he kept very still he might be mistaken for a discarded work of art.

Casting his mind back over the afternoon's events Monsieur Pamplemousse had a sudden thought. He knew there had been something odd about the Blanches. It had been hovering in his subconscious and now he remembered what it was.

Monsieur Blanche had been wearing a leather thong around his neck. Attached to it had been a miniature sextant; an antique model of the kind used by navigators when they wished to take an accurate measurement of the angle between two terrestrial bodies.

Madame Blanche had been carrying a notepad and pencil.

Furthermore, they had both been heading in the direction of the lighthouse.

8
ROBBERY WITH VIOLENCE

If Monsieur Pamplemousse had been born with a tail he would have wagged it unashamedly. The sight of Pommes Frites wagging his own appendage furiously as he drew near the harbour in Bélisaire gave rise to feelings it was impossible to describe.

Ignoring the waiters as he hurried past the waterside café Monsieur Pamplemousse greeted his friend like a long lost brother. The response was satisfyingly mutual.

Pommes Frites was overjoyed. Waiting on the quai-side had been his second brainwave of the day. His thinking had been that since they had arrived by boat, it was more than likely his master would go back that way. All the same, he could hardly believe his eyes when he saw Monsieur Pamplemousse coming down the road. Even the fact that he appeared to be wearing a suit which was several sizes too small for him failed to dampen his relief. As for the way he was walking – in a kind of mincing, crab-like motion, as though his feet were hurting – that was neither here nor there. The simple truth was there for all to see. His master was alive and well.

Patently Pommes Frites' line of reasoning more than made up for his earlier débâcle on the beach, but it had taken its toll and he felt quite worn out as they made their way on to the pier. Given a choice between exercising his grey matter and a run along the beach, Pommes Frites would have chosen the latter every time; it was much less tiring.

Ignoring the hunger pains gnawing away at his stomach – he could hardly expect to be welcomed with open arms at the restaurant – Monsieur Pamplemousse led the way along the jetty and joined a small group waiting outside the ticket office for the arrival of the last ferry to Arcachon. Already it could be seen heading their way.

Idling away the remaining few minutes before the boat arrived, he expended two francs of his change on a coin-operated telescope. To his disgust it didn't work. He slapped it several times but nothing happened. The screen remained obstinately blank. The harbour master emerged from his box and struck it once with the palm of his hand. There was a click. The trick wasn't so much how forcefully you hit it as of knowing exactly where to apply the blow.

'You have done it before?'

There was an answering grunt. 'You are the third today.' It sounded as though a fourth customer might be unlucky.

Monsieur Pamplemousse pointed the telescope in the direction of the mainland. Viewed from a distance towards the end of the day the Dune du Pilat had a vaguely menacing air about it. Despite the lateness of the hour there were still people to be seen. Magnified by the lens they appeared as so many ants, rushing hither and thither in an apparently aimless fashion. Lower down he spotted a few motor boats bobbing about in the water near the shore. He wondered if Elsie's was one of them. They might have returned to the hotel that way. He panned up and to the left, but it was impossible to make out anything amongst the trees. He panned down again. The rescue station looked as though it was about to close for the night. He was in the act of following a water skier who shot past when

147

there was a click and the screen went blank. Monsieur Pamplemousse decided not to incur the displeasure of the harbour master by risking another two francs. He wasn't at all sure what he was looking for anyway. Elsie? Hardly. It was too far away to recognise anybody.

Elsie was a problem. It was hard to watch over someone as self-willed as she was.

And yet . . . his gaze softened . . . there was something very beguiling about her – a mixture of being street-wise and yet surprisingly innocent at the same time. It must be her blue eyes. He ought really to give her one more chance. This evening he would insist they get down to writing out a report. In the circumstances they could hardly include the hotel restaurant – or even the hotel itself. They would have to seek out a typical restaurant in the area and concentrate on that. *Le Guide*'s standard form covered every aspect of dining out – nothing was left to chance. All the same, completing it was still a daunting task requiring a good deal of effort. It would be interesting to see what Elsie made of it.

One thing was certain. The chief wouldn't be too pleased if Monsieur Pamplemousse went back on what he'd said over the phone.

Monsieur Pamplemousse was still lost in thought as he clambered on board the ferry. They cast off almost immediately. Pommes Frites took up a position of honour in the bows. With the wind furrowing his brow as they gathered speed he looked for all the world like a carved figurehead, and almost as inscrutable.

Monsieur Pamplemousse bent down to remove his shoes. As he massaged his aching feet he felt a patch of soreness across his back and chest. If he wasn't careful he would suffer for it over the next day or two. It was a long time since he had exposed himself quite so much to the elements.

Getting the shoes back on was a struggle. It took him all the way to Arcachon and the rest of the passengers had already disembarked by the time he and Pommes Frites scrambled on to the steps of the pier. There were still a few fishermen to be seen. It looked as though most of them would be eating out that night. As they reached the end of the line a man standing slightly apart from the rest half turned and caught Monsieur Pamplemousse's eye.

'The chief wants to see you in his office right away.'

Monsieur Pamplemousse hesitated. Then, as the man bent down over his empty basket, he took the hint and went on his way.

'D'accord.'

All the same, it was a case of first things first. A visit to a late-night chemist for some sun-burn oil was top priority.

His search took him through the town and along past the parking area in front of the *gare*. To their left most of the cafés and restaurants were already full. It reminded him once again that it was a long time since he had eaten anything. Averting his gaze, Monsieur Pamplemousse glanced across the road and to his surprise he caught sight of Elsie standing by his car. Clearly her mind had been running along parallel lines to Pommes Frites'.

Waiting until there was a gap in the traffic, he crossed over and headed towards her. She was dressed as he had seen her earlier in the day and she was carrying a large oblong-shaped parcel wrapped in brown paper.

He felt a surge of excitement as they drew near and she waved. Resolutions about reading the riot act went out the window.

'Are you alright?' Elsie looked genuinely concerned. 'I was beginning to think the worst.'

'I could say the same about you.'

Contriteness replaced concern. 'Oh, dear. I'm sorry about this morning. It was a case of needs must.'

The translation eluded Monsieur Pamplemousse. 'Did you have a good day in Bélisaire?'

'Not so as you'd notice,' said Elsie. 'Pommes Frites chased us off the beach din 'e? Who's a naughty boy then?'

Pommes Frites looked round, unsure whether he was being addressed or not.

Monsieur Pamplemousse glanced at the parcel. 'But you were able to do some shopping?'

'Yeah.' Elsie's eyes went glazed, as they always did when something came up she didn't wish to discuss.

Having drawn a blank, Monsieur Pamplemousse decided to try another tack. 'Don't you think it is time we had a little talk?'

'I thought you might say that.' If anything, Elsie looked relieved. 'I was hoping you could give me a lift back to the hotel.'

Monsieur Pamplemousse hesitated. He had no wish to incur the displeasure of the officer in charge. And it would mean waiting even longer for dinner. But on the other hand he didn't fancy the thought of taking Elsie along to the *gendarmerie* with him. 'I am afraid that is not possible,' he said. 'I have somewhere else to go before I return.'

'Please.' Elsie snuggled up to him. It was a most disconcerting habit. 'I don't know as I want to go back there alone. Not now most of the others seem to 'ave left.'

Monsieur Pamplemousse wanted to ask what happened to her American friend. He resisted the temptation.

'All right, we'll go back.' He led the way towards his car.

'I need a change of shoes from my room,' he said gruffly. 'My feet are killing me. We can talk on the way. Pommes Frites had better stay with you at the hotel. He will make sure you come to no harm.'

Elsie settled herself in the front seat. 'Are you cross with me?'

'Me? Cross?' Monsieur Pamplemousse turned and looked at her as they drove out of the car park and joined the stream of homeward-bound traffic at the roundabout. He used the moment to choose his words with care.

'Perhaps disappointed would be a better word.'

'Don't tell me you're jealous.'

'I have no cause to be jealous.' The words came out with rather more heat than Monsieur Pamplemousse intended. 'It strikes me that you are not being particularly faithful towards your boy friend.'

'Reginald? Oh, 'e'd understand. It was 'is idea. Anyway, 'e can't be here on account of the fact that he's otherwise engaged on 'er Majesty's pleasure.'

'He is with a government department?'

Elsie gave a hollow laugh. 'Dead right. He's doing bird.'

'*Oiseau?*' Monsieur Pamplemousse looked puzzled.

'You know . . . bird-lime . . . time. It's cockney rhyming slang for "in the nick".'

'Oh, dear. I am sorry. That is unfortunate.' Monsieur Pamplemousse wasn't sure what to say. It would certainly put paid to Elsie's chances of getting a job with *Le Guide*. The Director would never countenance employing an Inspector whose credentials or those of their nearest and dearest were not entirely beyond reproach.

'I shouldn't waste any sleep,' said Elsie cheerfully. 'I told 'im that's what comes of being a naughty boy.

Besides, 'e knows how to look after number one, does Reginald. He's in what they call an "open" prison. It's ever so nice. You should see 'is cell. It's like an 'otel room. Television. Cocktail cabinet. Fax machine. He reckons it's more cost effective than an office. There are no overheads – 'cept for the odd 'andout here and there. They're a greedy lot of bastards. But apart from not getting his oats as often as 'e would like, he's doing all right. Mind you, it couldn't 'ave 'appened at a worse time. That's why I'm over 'ere.'

'You mean you are doing it for Reginald rather than for yourself?'

'That's right.' Elsie seemed relieved to have got it off her chest.

Monsieur Pamplemousse felt his mind racing as he drew into the hotel car park. It certainly explained why Elsie's mind wasn't on her job.

'But why does Reginald want you to be an Inspector? I thought you said he wasn't interested in food.'

Elsie felt in her bag. 'Look – 'e'd kill me if 'e knew I'd told you, but I'll give you a clue.' Unfolding a newspaper cutting, she handed it to him. It showed two men on sand tractors posing alongside a Sherman tank partly submerged in a sand dune.

'Guess where that picture was taken.'

'Here? In Arcachon?'

Elsie nodded. 'It wasn't on the beach at Brighton.'

Monsieur Pamplemousse glanced at the date. It was the spring of that year.

'It must have happened during the big storms.'

'Right again.'

'So your Reginald is interested in government surplus?' It was a shot in the dark.

152

'Amongst other things,' said Elsie. 'You could say that Reginald's interested in anything that's surplus. That's why 'e's got where 'e 'as.'

Monsieur Pamplemousse was still mulling over Elsie's last remark as he finally entered the *gendarmerie* in Arcachon.

The *officier* was standing by the window in his room waiting for him. He glanced pointedly at his watch and then, waving aside Monsieur Pamplemousse's apologies, motioned towards a chair opposite his desk. A lamp was half-angled towards it. It was the classic questioner with his back to the light situation.

It struck Monsieur Pamplemousse as he seated himself that the man looked a little older than when he had last seen him. He judged him to be in his early forties, but he could have been ten years older. Grey hair, close cropped: a face which had already seen better days.

It was tempting to say he knew the feeling. That he, too, in his job often had to work long hours: driving, eating rich meals – when all he wanted to do was get to bed with a glass of wine and a sandwich. But he knew what the response would be. It was almost universal whenever the subject came up. 'I should be so lucky!' The grass was always greener on the other side of the fence.

'Well, Monsieur Pamplemousse . . . late of the Paris Sûreté . . .'

'You know?'

'I'm not sure that I ever thought otherwise, but I was prepared to respect the reasons behind your desire for anonymity. Although in the beginning I was a little unhappy that you might be muscling in on our territory.

'Anyway, it wasn't difficult. Earlier today I had a strange man on the telephone who professed to know your twin brother well. Afterwards, I had only to check with your records.'

Monsieur Pamplemousse could picture it. The Director going out of his way to be circumspect, but at the same time overdoing the embroidery. He would have aroused the suspicions of the girl on the switchboard let alone a police inspector.

'*Alors* . . .' The *officier* accompanied his raised hands with a shrug. 'Let us forget the past,' his gesture said. 'Now to business.'

He went straight in.

'Have you noticed anything odd about the Hôtel des Dunes?'

'Are you asking me in my capacity as an ex-member of the Sûreté?'

'I am asking you as someone probably over-averagely observant.'

'It is bizarre. The whole place is a disaster area. The service is practically non-existent. The food is not fit to be fed to the seagulls . . .'

The *officier* tried another tack.

'What do you know about the last war? More specifically, what do you know about looting?'

Monsieur Pamplemousse felt bewildered. He had expected to be questioned about murder in the recent past, not things that had happened in his childhood.

'I was brought up in the Auvergne and in the beginning it didn't affect us as much as it did those who lived in the big cities. We were part of the unoccupied zone. Those of us who lived there were more concerned with helping our parents look after their few cows and sheep.'

'And the looting of works of art? What do you know of that?'

'On a personal level, very little at all. Mostly it is what I have heard and read since. I know that in many countries it was systematic, ruthless and on a vast scale. Not just private collections, but whole museums – national treasures. Hitler had dreams of establishing a cultural centre in Linz where he was born – it was to be the Mecca of the art world – so vast it would make the Louvre look like a small town museum. The Nazis took into "protective custody" everything they could lay their hands on.'

The *officier* opened a drawer of his desk and removed a bulky manilla folder. He opened it up and laid it out facing away from him.

'Take a look at this.'

Monsieur Pamplemousse skimmed through the first few pages. It was a familiar story. The systematic rape of Europe by Hitler. He had read it all before. It went far beyond the taking of livestock, food, arms, ammunition, rolling stock, ships, copper, zinc, lead, and raw materials of every kind. The entire gold reserves of Czechoslovakia had been annexed; the Hungarian Crown Jewels removed for 'safe keeping'.

The further east the Germans had gone the more ruthless they had become – Hitler had no great regard for their culture; the whole of Poland was plundered in less than six months; churches, museums, private collections, nothing was sacred. Later on it was the turn of Russia. Leningrad was pillaged, then Kiev and Kharkov. Nearer home, France, Holland and finally even their old allies, Italy, had been forced to yield up their treasures. One way and another the Third Reich ended up with the largest single collection of accumulated wealth in the world.

The only good thing about Hitler's ambition was that at least much that might have been destroyed for ever was saved for posterity. In just one mine near his hideaway in Berchtesgaden nearly seven thousand canvases were found; paintings by Fragonard, Watteau, Bellini, Titian, Canaletto, Rubens, Van Dyke. They were worth a fortune then; by today's prices the value would have been astronomical.

Monsieur Pamplemousse leaned back. 'A very thorough review of what went on, I'd say. I must congratulate you. Clearly, had he won the war, Hitler would have been the possessor of undreamed-of wealth.'

The *officier* rose from his desk and crossed to the window. 'Fortunately he didn't. He lost. And at the end of the war came the total collapse of Germany. During the final weeks when it became clear which way things were going, a great panic set in. Everything had to be shifted, and shifted quickly. Not just the loot, but the entire contents of German museums were packed away in crates in order to keep them safe from the Allied bombers.

'As you may know, the Bavarian salt mines became a favourite destination. In many ways they were ideal; the perfect hiding place. They were nearly always in sparsely populated areas. They had a constant temperature of between 45 and 65 degrees, and most of them contained some kind of rail system which made movement easy. The scale of it all was astronomical. In the Merkers Mine alone there was a hoard with an estimated value at that time of over $300,000,000. Any attempt at keeping a record of what came in soon went by the board. The hills, as they say, were alive to the sound of music, only it was the music of the cash register.

'There it all was – an unbelievable amount of wealth lying about in caves and tunnels – crates of books here, *objets d'art* there, tapestries, Greek sculptures, Egyptian and Roman busts, coins, gold and silver bars, currency –

U.S. dollars, Swiss francs, French francs – suits of armour alongside some of the great masterpieces of the world, much of it stolen from the great Jewish family collections whose owners had long-since perished in the gas chambers.'

'So . . .' Monsieur Pamplemousse asked the question he'd been dying to ask ever since the other had begun his dissertation. 'What has all this to do with the murder of an inn-keeper in Arcachon?'

The *officier* turned away from the window. 'Very few things in this world are entirely black and white. The Allies had their gangsters too, not to mention just plain opportunists. The American army, who were first on the scene, wasn't just made up of good people. No army ever is. In some areas corruption was rife. Small-time gangsters got big ideas.'

'Things went missing . . . *en route*?' Somewhere at the back of Monsieur Pamplemousse's mind a glimmer of light began to dawn, but he decided to say nothing for the time being.

'There was chaos everywhere. Those who had survived the war were still in a state of shock; dazed and apathetic. The railways had been destroyed. Roads were blocked by refugees pushing prams, carts, bicycles – anything with wheels they could lay their hands on. Cities and towns lay in ruins. In some areas there was a total breakdown in communication, water, power, gas – all the things one normally takes for granted. No one was going to query the movement of trucks for the simple reason they all had their own problems to do with the simple process of staying alive. People would do anything for a carton of cigarettes or a pound of butter. For anyone wanting to make a quick fortune the opportunity was handed to them on a plate.

'It wasn't so much the gold. Gold is one thing – solid bullion is heavy – each ingot weighs anything between ten and twenty kilograms – it has its problems. Also, it was mostly accounted for, counted and checked, and always – again by its very nature – it was sent under escort. Gold was to do with governments.

'But works of art were something else. Who really knows the true value of a painting? The task of cataloguing it all was monumental. A truck-load of gold bullion has a certain value. Who can say what a truck-load of paintings or other works of art is worth? Imagine being a GI detailed to take a lorry containing untold treasures to some destination you had never even heard of before – just a pin-prick on the map – five or six thousand kilometres away from home.'

Monsieur Pamplemousse broke in. 'You are saying that even now, forty-five years later, there is still a lot that is unaccounted for?'

'Of course. How could it ever be otherwise?'

'So?'

'So.' The *officier* sat down in his chair again and closed his eyes. 'Picture a night in 1945, 20 April to be precise. A lorry draws up outside the Hôtel des Dunes. It is driven by a young lieutenant in the American army. He is accompanied by three other men and his current mistress – a German girl. They ask for accommodation and they are given it. They are free with their cigarettes and their food and they clearly have plenty of money. The owner is only too willing to oblige. They stay at the hotel, mostly sleeping during the day and going out at night. Some days later, when the time comes for them to leave, the lorry is empty. The owner of the hotel – Monsieur Bouet's father – is sworn to secrecy. He hasn't seen a thing. Anyway, what is there to tell? He truly hasn't seen

158

anything. Then they drive off into the night and they are never seen again.'

'Never? Isn't that a little strange?'

'There are a number of possible reasons, but it may simply have been that the authorities made it too hot for them. The U.S. Office of Strategic Services formed an Art Looting Investigation Unit. It was made up of experts in the field and their brief was to track down looted art treasures and return them to their rightful owners as quickly as possible. In a desire to establish good relations with freshly occupied countries it was given top priority.

'A lot of those who on the spur of the moment thought they were on to a good thing quickly discovered that stealing a lorryload of treasure is one thing, reaping the benefit is something else again. Actual cash can be laundered gradually over a period of time without arousing too much suspicion. Works of art have their own problems. How do you get it back home? What do you do with it once it is there? A lot of people must have written the whole thing off as a bad job; a kind of drunken spree which looked totally different in the cold light of day when they eventually sobered up.

'Even back home they weren't safe. The CIA and the FBI started watching bank accounts, looking for any sign of sudden wealth.

'Some people managed to solve the problem, but it didn't do them much good. Here, I will give you an example.' The *officier* leaned forward, reached across the desk and turned over the pages until he came across the one he wanted.

Monsieur Pamplemousse glanced at a press cutting taken from an American journal. It was dated 1 July 1990. On one side of the page there was a picture of a tumbledown group of buildings. It was captioned 'The Texas Connection'.

Alongside the opposite page someone had attached a translation of the accompanying text.

It had to do with the discovery in some small derelict farm town in Texas – a town of boarded up shops and deserted streets about an hour's drive from Dallas – of a cache of Nazi loot. Investigation showed it had been smuggled back to the States over a long period of time by a former GI whose unit had accidentally stumbled across the hoard in a cave outside Quedlinburg. It had been the subject of an investigation at the time, but that had ceased in 1949 when Quedlinburg became part of East Germany. The extraordinary part of the whole story was that over the years the man had had it sent home through the mail without a single item being queried. The total value was many millions of dollars. The man – respected owner of the local hardware store and an orchid-fancier in his spare time – had died of cancer ten years ago. Steps were being taken to return the property to its original owners.

'Truth,' said the *officier*, 'is often stranger than fiction. I could give you many more examples.'

'And you think something similar may have happened here in Arcachon?'

'Whoever stayed at the hotel didn't drive all that way for the oysters. It must have been because they wanted to bury something in the dunes.'

'But why Arcachon? It is a long way from Bavaria.'

'So much the better. Picture yourself in the same situation. There you are in a strange country: an alien land. You hardly speak the language. You certainly don't trust the natives. After all, for six years you have been at war with them. Suddenly you have the chance to get your hands on untold wealth.'

'The stuff that dreams are made of . . .'

'Dreams, yes – we all have them from time to time. Dreams of winning the *Loterie nationale* perhaps, or being left a fortune. But we are dealing with the harsh practicality of a lorryload of art treasures.

'What do you do with it?'

'Hide it?'

'Yes, but where? Bearing in mind you may not be able to touch it for a long time; certainly not for many months, possibly years, it needs to be somewhere safe.

'Then I know what I would do. I would get the hell out of it. I would drive as far away from the scene as I possibly could. Which is exactly what they must have done.

'Having made their getaway they probably talked it over between themselves. Someone suggests going to Paris. People are naturally more observant in the country; they know all that is going on. A big city would be safe. But no one knows Paris, so that is out. Lyon? Marseille? Nice? They are just names. Time is of the essence.

'They rack their brains. Then someone mentions Arcachon and its dunes. Perhaps they had passed through after the invasion and it stuck in their mind. In many ways it must have sounded ideal. The dunes are not getting any smaller. If anything, they are growing in size. No one is ever likely to build on them. Any tracks they left in the sand would have been obliterated almost immediately. It is safe from the elements . . . all, that is, except one.'

The *officier* reached across and turned to another page.

'They reckoned without the wind.'

Monsieur Pamplemousse recognised the press cutting. It was identical to the one Elsie had been carrying in her handbag. This time he took the trouble to read the caption beneath the picture: 'The hulk of an American-made Sherman tank found on a beach near Arcachon, south-western France. The tank, which had been buried in sand, was uncovered by heavy storms on Wednesday.'

Monsieur Pamplemousse looked up. 'The storms were that bad?'

'The worst ever recorded. Millions of pounds worth of damage was done.'

It was true. Paris had suffered that year. Trees in the Bois de Bologne and the Luxembourg Gardens had been uprooted.

'And you think Monsieur Bouet may have discovered something much more valuable than a tank?'

'I know he did. The first of the pictures began appearing on the walls of his hotel soon afterwards. It was spotted by one of our men when he was making a routine check about another matter. He happened to pass some lighthearted comment about business being good and Monsieur Bouet went into a great panic. Anyway, he carried on about it so much the officer's suspicions were aroused.'

'How about Madame Bouet?'

'She swears he never told her where he found them. He said it was better she didn't know. The fact is that by then, as he began to realise the true nature and value of his find, he was probably almost beginning to wish he hadn't come across it. Like the ones who originally buried them he suddenly didn't know what to do. Again, it was a matter of quantity and of ergonomics. His first instinct was probably "finders keepers", but where was he going to keep them?

'He was probably taking legal advice. Laws on these matters are not as clear cut as one might imagine.'

'They seldom are,' said Monsieur Pamplemousse drily.

'Establishing the rightful ownership could well involve a long and costly legal battle. The laws of each country are different. There are organisations whose sole purpose is to make sure the property is returned to its rightful owners. I think Bouet was biding his time until he got sound advice as to what to do next.'

'In the meantime the walls of the hotel were beginning to groan under the weight.'

'*Exactement.* We were about to pull him in for questioning when he disappeared. It is my belief that shortly after Bouet began hanging the pictures in his hotel someone must have stayed there – probably quite by chance – but someone who knew about these things. The art world is small. News travels fast.'

Monsieur Pamplemousse suddenly thought of his conversation with Elsie.

'It is a wonder that so far no one has attempted to steal the paintings,' he said innocently.

'They will. It is only a matter of time. Up to now they have held back for reasons of greed. They believe there must be more where the present ones came from and they don't want to draw attention to the fact. But when they do . . .' he reached under his desk and flicked a switch. An alarm bell rang. 'The pictures are wired.'

Monsieur Pamplemousse sat lost in thought for a moment. 'Why are you telling me all this?'

The question was met with another. 'In your experience, Monsieur Pamplemousse, what is the most important thing to do when you bury something for a long time?'

'First, make sure it is well protected – in a waterproof container of some kind.'

'And then . . .'

'Of equal importance, I would say, is to make absolutely certain you remember where you buried it: not the next day, or the next week, but possibly years later.'

'For that you would need either something very special and immovable to mark the exact spot or a very accurate bearing – preferably more than one – ideally a triangulation.'

'How about the blockhouse nearest to the hotel?'

'That would be useless. It started off at the top of the hill and now it is halfway down.'

'They wouldn't have known that was going to happen.'

The *officier* nodded. 'That is true. But instinct tells me no. You don't go to the trouble of transporting treasure all across France to the Dune du Pilat and end up burying it somewhere obvious like that. It has to be somewhere within the dune itself.'

'Have you tried looking?'

The *officier* gestured towards a cardboard box in the corner of his office. 'I have had men posing as tourists working on it with metal detectors for several weeks. So far we have unearthed two hundred and thirty francs in coins, three cigarette lighters, two powder compacts, two metal trouser buttons and a selection of items from a lady's handbag which even you might find hard to believe. If we keep going we could end up with the cleanest dune in western France and still be no further on. It is an impossible task.'

'Are there not more sophisticated devices these days? Can the army not help?'

'It would cause too much comment. Can you imagine what would happen once the word got out? It would trigger off another gold rush. The dunes would be swarming with people.'

He had an answer for everything.

'May I ask a question?'

'Of course.'

'You are not telling me all this for nothing.'

'It is my experience, *Monsieur*, that few people in this world ever do anything for nothing. You are in a position to help. You are sitting in the hot seat as it were. We would like more information on those who are staying at the hotel before we make our next move.'

'There are very few left now,' said Monsieur Pample-mousse. 'The English family have gone, so have the Germans. Now the restaurant is closed I suspect most of the others may have departed too. The only ones left apart from myself and my colleague, are Monsieur and Madame Blanche and the Americans.'

'Precisely! The Americans.'

'You think one of them may be the lieutenant who stayed at the Hôtel des Dunes all those years ago?'

'No. He is dead. That much we know. We checked back through the hotel records and got all their names. They were probably so sure of themselves they didn't bother with false ones. Besides, everyone was very identity conscious in those days.

'The FBI have been very helpful. The others have all either died of old age or disappeared without trace. However, it is my belief that before he died the lieutenant passed on at least part of his secret, perhaps quite inadvertently when he saw news of the storm. It would have brought back memories.'

Monsieur Pamplemousse looked at the newspaper cutting again. 'I see it has a Reuters' credit – it will have had worldwide circulation.'

The *officier* laid his hands flat on the table. 'Monsieur Pamplemousse, do not lose sight of the fact that this is no longer simply a case of looking for buried treasure. It is also a case of murder. Double murder.'

'Monsieur and Madame Blanche are neighbours of mine in Paris. Madame Blanche may be *une emmerdeuse* – a pain in the arse – but I doubt if she would ever be a party to such things.'

'*Exactement.*'

'If you suspect the Americans why do you not arrest them?'

'On what charge? If we arrest them on suspicion of murder where does it get us? Other than the fact that Monsieur Bouet disappeared soon after they arrived, we have no proof. At this moment in time we do not even have any bodies. All we have is a photograph showing a part of one.'

It suddenly occurred to Monsieur Pamplemousse that Pommes Frites could be charged with concealing vital evidence; worse still, destroying it! But he dismissed the thought. It would be impossible to prove.

The *officier* clearly felt the same way. After a slight pause he continued. 'We also have a big query against their names from the other side of the Atlantic. A query which says in effect – watch out!

'Other than that we have absolutely nothing against them. Their visas are in order. They pay their bills. They play the casinos – but they are not alone in that. It does not make them criminals.

'Once again, arresting them will only draw attention to the whole affair, and that I wish to avoid for as long as possible.'

'How can I help?'

'We would like more information about your . . . er . . . travelling companion. It seems to me that, yourself excepted of course, she does not always keep good company. I think she is in need of care and protection. It could be that through her association with the Americans she has learned something we do not know. In which case your co-operation would be appreciated . . .'

'That is not possible.' The words came out automatically, before Monsieur Pamplemousse recalled that Elsie had on occasions behaved very oddly.

The *officier* gave a sigh. 'I feared you might say that. It is a pity. It makes my job less pleasant than it might otherwise have been.' He reached across the desk again and turned the pages of the file until he reached the last one.

Monsieur Pamplemousse gave a start. It was a blow-up of a photo taken of him standing by the train earlier in the day; hat over face, watched in amazement by the occupants of the carriage; in colour. The *gendarme* must have been quick off the mark: not half as dozy as he had made himself out to be.

'That would not look good in *Ici Paris*. An unhappy follow-up to your unfortunate affair at the Folies, would you not say?'

'That is blackmail,' said Monsieur Pamplemousse indignantly.

'*Oui.*'

'Blackmail of the very worst kind.'

'*Oui.*'

'People are arrested every day for less.'

'*Oui.*'

'That is very unfair.'

The *officier* allowed himself a smile for the first time. 'Life is very unfair at times, Monsieur Pamplemousse.'

'And that is all you have to say?'

'For the moment, *oui*. I am sure we shall meet again.'

Monsieur Pamplemousse rose to his feet. 'One last question. The lieutenant . . . the one who stayed at the hotel all those years ago. When did he die?'

'Just over a month ago.'

'Of natural causes?'

'He was shot through the back of the head by a bullet from a .44 Magnum. A favourite weapon, I believe, of the American Mafia.'

'I think,' said Monsieur Pamplemousse, 'it is time I returned to the Hôtel des Dunes.'

9
A MATTER OF DEGREES

The Hôtel des Dunes was in semi-darkness when Monsieur Pamplemousse arrived back. The dining-room windows were shuttered and a piece of paper bearing the single word FERMÉ was pasted across the glass-fronted menu case. A quick glance around the parking area revealed only three other cars; the Blanches' Renault 25, the Peugeot belonging to the Americans, and a third – a Renault estate which had been there from the beginning and which he guessed must belong to the hotel.

A single light was burning in the entrance hall but there was no sign of Maurice. Monsieur Pamplemousse pressed the *minuterie* button for the landing light.

He paused halfway up the stairs and took a closer look at the painting. It was a Sisley. The signature in the bottom right hand comer was unmistakable. He couldn't think how he'd missed it. Somehow the very fact of knowing who it was by gave the work a whole new perspective, which he had to admit ruefully said something about his knowledge of art. It was certainly a picture he could 'live with': one of his main criteria when it came to passing any kind of judgement.

The light went out and he groped his way towards another illuminated switch. Then he made his way up the second flight of stairs and along the corridor to his room.

Elsie was sitting on the end of the bed eating a choco-late-finger sandwich. Pommes Frites lay on the floor at her feet. He jumped up licking his lips guiltily as his master entered the room. His tongue had a noticeably brown tinge to it.

''Ave one,' said Elsie. 'There's plenty more where this came from.'

Monsieur Pamplemousse didn't wait to be asked twice. It was the gastronomic equivalent of a smoker 'rolling his own'. The sandwich prepared, he took a bite from one end and then regarded the phenomenon of bread which never seemed to grow stale. Doubtless it was an acquired taste.

'Madame Blanche was looking for you earlier,' said Elsie. 'She looked quite put out when she found me in your room.'

'Did she see Pommes Frites?'

'I'm afraid so. If you ask me, I think your cover's blown.'

'Irretrievably,' agreed Monsieur Pamplemousse. At least it was Madame Blanche on the warpath and not her husband. 'Why do you think the Blanches were in Cap Ferret?'

'The same reason as everyone else, I suppose,' said Elsie. 'Taking a look at the lighthouse. Or rather, taking a look from it.'

'You did that too?' It confirmed his worst suspicions.

'Amongst other things.'

'Isn't it about time you came clean with me? You are not here because you have ambitions to be an Inspector with *Le Guide,* nor are you here for the simple pleasure of being by the sea.'

Elsie grinned. 'That goes for most of us,' she said. 'How about yourself? Don't tell me you're not intrigued too. A little hotel in the back of nowhere suddenly 'as its walls covered in valuable paintings. It's like a bleedin' art gallery.'

'I am here because you are here. I was sent; you came of your own accord, that is the difference.'

'Funny thing, differences,' said Elsie. 'I mean, take a simple thing like a shovel. There it is. It does the same thing the whole world over, dunnit. I mean, you'd think after all this time someone would 'ave come up with a Mark whatever world standard shovel. But, no. In England we have shovels that are flat and 'ave a proper 'andle you can grip. In France you 'ave shovels shaped like a heart on the end of a broomstick . . .'

'So what are you saying?'

'I'm saying that if you was to look in the boot of some of the cars parked outside I bet you'd find quite a selection. And what do their owners 'ave in common? Well, for a start they didn't none of them come 'ere to build sandcastles.'

'So why are they here?'

'You could say a love of art. Reginald thinks a tank wasn't the only thing what was uncovered by the storms that Wednesday. He reckons there were a few crates of goodies as well.'

Monsieur Pamplemousse remained silent. It was often the best way of finding out things.

'Reginald 'as been doing a spot of research while 'e's been inside. 'E thinks there must be a link between the storm and the paintings. How they got there in the first place is something else again, but apparently it all goes back to the last war. Some nut-case in the American army who found himself with a lorryload of loot and didn't know what to do with it. Anyway, Reginald discovered that he stayed in this very hotel.'

Monsieur Pamplemousse began to have a new respect for Elsie's boy friend. A force to be reckoned with. It was a pity he was on the wrong side of the fence.

'That is very enterprising of him.'

171

'Reginald has his methods,' said Elsie. 'And his contacts. Just 'cause 'e's inside doesn't mean to say he can't use them.'

'What put him on to it in the first place?'

'It's a small world,' said Elsie. 'Once the pictures had been spotted the buzz was on. It was a case of who got 'ere first. Reginald was otherwise engaged so I came instead. As it 'appens, so did one or two others.'

'Tell me,' said Monsieur Pamplemousse. 'Who would you put your money on? The Blanches or your American friends?'

'You must be joking,' said Elsie. 'The Blanches couldn't find a dog's doings in a snowdrift. My American friends mean business and they're not going back home until they've found what they came for, that's certain.'

Monsieur Pamplemousse made himself another sandwich. He wondered if they were addictive.

'I've been doing all the talking so far,' said Elsie. 'Now it's your turn. What's the most important thing to remember when you bury something?'

Monsieur Pamplemousse had a distinct feeling of *déjà vu*. 'It is as well to remember where you put it.'

'Right in one.'

'For that you would need some kind of landmark nearby. Or possibly one further away from which you could take a bearing. For safety's sake, preferably the latter.'

Elsie rose and walked to the window. 'Stand on this chair and tell me what you see.'

Monsieur Pamplemousse followed her across the room and did as he was bidden.

'Well?'

'To my right I see lights from houses dotted about here and there around the bay. If I stand on my toes I can just make out some fishing boats. Beyond them I can see the

172

outline of Cap Ferret silhouetted in the moonlight. I see the lighthouse flashing . . .'

'Exactly. It's just clear of the trees. That's why Reginald specially wanted me to 'ave this room. It's the same room what they 'ad at the time.'

Elsie offered Monsieur Pamplemousse a helping hand as he turned away from the window. 'Well, there you are then. It's simple innit. What more could you want?

'Reginald's been living with it for weeks now – eating, sleeping, drinking it. 'E's 'ad a map of the area pasted to 'is wall. The beauty of it is you don't even need a compass. You just go out the back door of the hotel, stand under the window of my room, then walk in an exact straight line towards the light. Somewhere along the route you'll find what you're looking for.'

'I see certain snags to that theory,' said Monsieur Pamplemousse. 'Your path would take you across some five hundred metres of soft sand. It wouldn't be easy to keep to a straight line. Also, you would need to know exactly where to stop. There must be some other measurement we don't know about. However, there is another even more fundamental problem.'

'What's that?' asked Elsie.

'The robbery took place in the spring of 1945. *D'accord?*'

'Yeah. Reginald reckons they got here in April. 20 April to be exact. He 'ad someone check the old register.'

'In that case they wouldn't have seen the lighthouse,' said Monsieur Pamplemousse.

'What do you mean – they wouldn't 'ave seen it? Don't tell me it was blacked out.'

'No. It simply wasn't there. The Germans destroyed it in 1944 – it wasn't rebuilt until 1946.'

Elsie looked at him disbelievingly. 'How do you know that?'

'Fate,' said Monsieur Pamplemousse. 'A combination of somewhat unusual happenings took me to the lighthouse this afternoon and by sheer chance I happened to overhear a conversation someone was having with the guide.'

He almost wished he hadn't told Elsie, she looked so crestfallen as she sat down on the side of the bed.

'I'll tell you something,' she said at last. 'If that's the case, Reginald's not the only one who's got it wrong. There's going to be hell to pay when the others find out, especially now someone's killed the goose that laid the golden egg. Old Monsieur Bouet was the only one who knew exactly where the loot was hidden and with him gone the secret's gone too. So everybody's back where they started. Only worse.'

'You think it was the Americans?' asked Monsieur Pamplemousse.

'Well, I don't know about that. Your guess is as good as mine. But from what I've seen and 'eard I wouldn't put it past any of them. It could be that they tried to force it out of 'im and 'e wouldn't play ball.'

'And his assistant?'

Elsie shrugged. 'Perhaps he came across something 'e shouldn't 'ave done. Or he just 'appened to be in the wrong place at the wrong time.'

'I do not wish to alarm you,' said Monsieur Pamplemousse, 'but if all you have told me is true, it seems to me that you could be in considerable danger yourself.'

'Why do you think I've told you all this?' said Elsie.

'I suggest you don't breathe a word to anyone and that you make sure you lock your door tonight.'

'I've got an even better idea,' said Elsie. 'Why don't I stay 'ere again? I feel sort of vulnerable in my room. Especially

174

'aving a double bed and all. It's ever so lonely all by yourself in a double bed.'

Monsieur Pamplemousse hesitated.

'Go on – be a sport.' Elsie adopted her little girl lost voice
as she pressed herself against him and ran her fingers up the
lapel of his jacket. 'I can't think of any good reason why
not, can you?'

All too aware of a tingle down the back of his neck,
Monsieur Pamplemousse tried hard to leave his mind a
blank. His conscience got the better of him.

'How about Reginald?'

'What the eye don't see the 'eart don't grieve for,' said
Elsie.

It was on the tip of Monsieur Pamplemousse's tongue to
ask if Reginald need ever know, but Elsie forestalled him.

'And don't say 'e need never know 'cause he would.
Reginald always does. Mind you, you're quite right. 'E'd
throw a fit. 'E 'ates dog hairs on the sheets.'

'Dog hairs?' Out of the comer of his eye Monsieur
Pamplemousse caught sight of Pommes Frites clambering
on to the bed. He was wearing his complacent 'you win
some, you lose some' look. He turned round twice before
settling down plumb in the middle.

'Reginald 'ad one go right up inside his big toe once.
Agony it was. It took them ages to get it out. 'E swore never
again.

'Night, night, then.' Dismissing Monsieur Pamplemousse, Elsie planted a kiss on his forehead, then reached
inside her dress and produced a key. 'See you in the
morning.'

The key still felt warm to the touch as Monsieur Pamplemousse let himself into room number eleven. He realised
suddenly that he had left everything in with Elsie, but he

was too tired to worry. Discarding his clothes on the nearest chair he slipped between the sheets and closed his eyes. Sleep came almost immediately.

How long it lasted he had no idea. All he knew when he woke was that he had been suffering a recurrent nightmare: one that he often experienced during times of extreme stress. It was the torture of *'les trois chocolate'*: worse than the fiendish Chinese water treatment, more deadly than the wheel.

It always began the same way. He would find himself dining alone at one of France's premier restaurants. Always he chose exactly the same menu – *Le menu gastronomique* – seven courses, a selection from the chef's repertoire, each one more exotic than its predecessor, each accompanied by a different wine. And always, no matter how the meal began, he would end up with the same dessert – *les trois chocolate*. A speciality of the house, it was a concoction of such extravagance and such unadulterated richness, it almost beggared description. Moist, yet firm, three different shades of brown . . . the thick cream . . . the raspberry *coulis* . . . the underlying flavour of *Grand Marnier* . . . eating it was an unforgettable experience. It was like hearing the Beethoven Ninth for the very first time.

L'addition taken care of, he would experience the usual difficulty in rising from the table. His 2CV would be waiting for him at the door. Willing hands would lever him into the driving seat and then, as he emerged from the entrance gates and set off down a long country road, a hand would reach round from behind and hold a pad against his face . . . there would be a whiff of chloroform . . . then darkness. When he came to he would find himself bound hand and foot to a chair, a spotlight directed on his face.

And then it would happen. Men in dark suits – usually masked – would emerge from the shadows and take it in turns to question him; one after the other, faster and faster, at the same time spooning more and more chocolate dessert into his mouth until he found himself crying out for mercy.

Monsieur Pamplemousse sat up in bed and wiped the sweat from his brow with the back of his hand. Somehow the dream had seemed even worse than usual, perhaps because on this occasion his torturers had manifested themselves as the Americans staying in the hotel. He felt for the pillow, but it must have fallen on the floor.

Gradually he became aware that the sound which had woken him came not from his own voice calling out in a dream, but from somewhere in the distance. It was a police siren and it was getting closer all the time.

Switching on the light, Monsieur Pamplemousse jumped out of bed and made a grab for a dressing gown hanging on the back of the door. He hurried along the corridor, pressing the *minuterie* button as he went. Reaching the stairs he peered over the banisters. As he feared, the painting was no longer there.

Hardly pausing in his stride, he made for his own room and knocked on the door. Elsie opened it almost immediately. Dressed in his pyjamas, she suddenly looked surprisingly small and defenceless. It was the first time he had seen her smoking.

'The picture on the stairs is missing.'

'The Sisley? Gone? Now who would have done a thing like that? You can't trust anyone these days.'

Something in her tone of voice stopped Monsieur Pamplemousse in his tracks.

'Look . . . if you know anything about it . . .'

'Me?' Elsie took a drag of her cigarette. Making an almost perfect O with her lips, she blew an equally perfect smoke-ring. They both watched it float away across the room. 'Why should I know anything about it? What a thing to say!'

Monsieur Pamplemousse tried hard to contain his impatience as he heard the sound of a car drawing up on the gravel outside the hotel. It was followed almost immediately by a second, then a third. Doors slammed. 'I'm telling you this for your own good. The pictures are alarmed. The police will be up here at any moment.'

'They'll 'ave to play hunt the thimble then, won't they?' said Elsie. 'I spy with my little eye something beginning with K.'

Monsieur Pamplemousse took a deep breath. Already he could hear footsteps coming up the stairs.

'Well, I suppose it wouldn't be a "K" in your language,' said Elsie, as she stood up to answer a knock on the door. 'I'm not sure what it is really.'

The *officier* took in the scene with the air of one who, though surprised by nothing in this world, left room in his mind for the occasional unexpected twist of its ingredients. He eyed the dressing gown Monsieur Pamplemousse was wearing. It was, to say the least, several sizes too small.

'I take it, *Monsieur, you* have been here all the time?'

Monsieur Pamplemousse hesitated, uncomfortably aware that, as ever, the Blanches were hovering in the background, hanging on his every word. They were both fully dressed. Monsieur Blanche was carrying a spade.

'You should ask Pommes Frites,' said Elsie. ''E could tell you a thing or three.'

'While you are about it, ask him what he is doing staying here under a false name?' Pushing her way to the front, Madame Blanche pointed to Monsieur Pamplemousse.

He glared back at her. '*Madame* . . . you have no proof.'

'Ask him to show us his knees then,' demanded Madame Blanche. 'If he has a mole on his left knee then he's not who he says he is.'

'I've never seen no mole, not on either of 'is knees,' said Elsie. 'Or anywhere else come to that.'

Monsieur Pamplemousse took hold of the two ends of a silken cord around Elsie's dressing gown and undid the knot. 'I will willingly prove you wrong, *Madame.*' It was a last ditch chance.

The *officier* stiffened. Clearly he had other priorities 'That will not be necessary.'

He turned to the Blanches. 'I must ask you to go to your room and remain there while we conduct a search of the building.'

Taking advantage of the commotion as the *officier* and his men clattered off down the corridor banging on doors as they went, Pommes Frites emerged from under a blanket and made his way downstairs. He was wearing his pained expression. Sleep was proving difficult. If it wasn't one thing it was another. Elsie had taken up a surprising amount of room. Not only that, but she had been very restless. In and out of bed like a yo-yo. The current goings-on were the last straw. In the circumstances, and in the absence of any orders to the contrary from his master, swopping Monsieur Pamplemousse's bed for the familiar surroundings of his inflatable kennel seemed a sensible move.

It didn't take Pommes Frites long to have second and even third thoughts on the matter. His pained expression gave way to one of puzzlement. No sooner had he settled himself down than he jumped to his feet again. For some reason the floor of his house felt strangely lumpy. He tried changing his position several times, but to no avail. In the end, unable to stand the discomfort a moment longer, he got up and went back outside in order to investigate the matter.

The cause was immediately apparent, although how it came to be under his kennel he had no idea. It certainly hadn't been there earlier in the evening.

Having removed the offending object, Pommes Frites stood for a moment holding it in his jaws, wondering what to do next. He was tempted to dispose of it behind the nearest bush, but being still in a decision-making mode he had another thought. He knew where there were some other objects just like the one that had been causing all the trouble. He might have temporarily mislaid the various bits and pieces belonging to the owner of the hotel and his assistant, but this was a chance to vindicate himself.

Following a built-in navigational system which owed as much to extra-sensory perception as it did to William Gilbert's discovery of magnetic north, Pommes Frites set forth without further delay.

His actions didn't go unnoticed by a *gendarme* who had been left sitting in one of the police cars. Reaching for his walkie-talkie, he opened the door and set off in pursuit. A moment later heads appeared at various windows of the hotel. Other walkie-talkies began to crackle; other figures appeared out of the darkness.

Pommes Frites' course took him towards the dune. Had he, in fact, continued in the same direction across sand and sea, it would have taken him to the very front door of the Semaphore Tower, a kilometre or so to the west of the light-house at Cap Ferret, but he didn't in fact go very far. Having reached a point which was exactly two hundred and ten metres from the hotel or, for those who were mathematically inclined but unwilling to trust their memory, ten times his master's room number, he stopped in his tracks and began to dig.

For a few moments sand flew in all directions; at such times Pommes Frites was no respecter of persons. The gendarmes who were standing a short distance away craning their necks in order to get a better view of what was happening stepped back a pace or two. Then, as heavy breathing gave way to the sound of claws against wood, they moved forward again in a body.

Pommes Frites paused in his labours and glanced round at them.

It really was a most satisfactory way to round off an evening. And if, in the heat of the moment the saliva from his mouth had caused some of the colours on the canvas to run, it was but a moment's work to drop the painting into the hole and cover it with sand before anyone noticed.

'*Merde!*' Hearing the sound of doors slamming, Monsieur Pamplemousse rushed to the bedroom window and was just in time to see the Americans' Peugeot leaving. Seconds later another car took off in pursuit.

'Don't worry.' Elsie joined him just as the tail-lights disappeared through the trees. 'They won't get far. Even if the police don't catch them, there'll be others on the look out Reginald may 'ave his faults, but 'e's never been into that kind of thing. There's a contract out on them. The underworld don't like innocent people being killed. They 'ave their code the same as anyone else.'

Monsieur Pamplemousse eyed her curiously as he absorbed the information, trying for a moment to reconcile the matter-of-fact way in which it had been conveyed with the Elsie he had come to know.

'All the same, forgive me, I must get dressed.'

'Before you look inside the wardrobe,' said Elsie, 'I think I should tell you – there's something in there . . .'

'Something?' He paused with his hand on the doorhandle.

Elsie took another drag on her cigarette. 'You'll see.'

'*Sacré bleu!*' Monsieur Pamplemousse stepped back a pace and gazed at a picture propped up against the back wall. It had an all too familiar look about it.

'Nice innit,' said Elsie. 'Told you it would be a surprise. I 'ope you don't mind me putting it there but it's the one place in the 'otel where no one's liable to look for it, you being who you are and all.

'Besides, there's no point in going home empty-'anded. Reginald wouldn't think much of that. He's very keen on Sisley, is Reginald.'

10
WASH DAY

'I must go to the launderette after dinner,' said Madame Pamplemousse.

'Oh, dear, must you, Couscous? Can't it wait until tomorrow?'

'You won't have a thing to wear if I don't. I can't think what you've been up to. Your clothes are in a terrible state.'

'It was the dunes,' said Monsieur Pamplemousse.

He buried himself in his newspaper. The news from Arcachon occupied several columns. Two people were helping the police with their inquiries. One had been charged with carrying an offensive weapon. There was no more to report on either Monsieur Bouet or his assistant. Nor, according to the special correspondent on the spot, was there likely to be for some time to come. The police had an impossible task. It was worse than looking for a needle in a haystack. There was nothing about Elsie. No mention of airports being watched. Most of the story was devoted to the police discovery of the loot and its legal ramifications.

'Anyway,' said Madame Pamplemousse, 'it's a chance to catch up on the gossip. Not that I ever listen to it.'

'No one ever does,' said Monsieur Pamplemousse vaguely. 'But everyone likes it all the same.'

'I want to hear the latest on the Blanches. It seems they're being held for questioning.'

Monsieur Pamplemousse pricked up his ears. 'The Blanches? Do I know them?' he asked innocently.

'You must do. He has a gallery and he writes about art for one of the *journaux*. I see his wife in the launderette sometimes. Apparently Monsieur Blanche was caught carrying an offensive weapon. Nobody knows what Madame Blanche is being held for.'

Monsieur Pamplemousse could guess. Trying the patience of an *officier* for a start. Something must have snapped.

'Funnily enough, Monsieur Blanche has a mole on his left knee just like yours.'

Monsieur Pamplemousse lowered the *journal* and stared at his wife. 'Do you mean to say you have been discussing my mole in a launderette? Is there nothing sacred?'

'People let their hair down in launderettes,' said Doucette. 'You find out all sorts of things. You would be surprised.'

After the latest revelation, Monsieur Pamplemousse had a feeling nothing would surprise him ever again. It gave truth to the old phrase about washing one's dirty linen in public. For all he knew the whole building was aware of his impediments. It was bad enough having the details entered on his P63, his personal detail file, back at *Le Guide's* headquarters.

Any further conversation was interrupted by the telephone ringing. Madame Pamplemousse picked up the receiver.

'It is from Arcachon.'

Monsieur Pamplemousse gave a grunt. He'd been expecting the call ever since his arrival back in Paris. Recognising the signs, Madame Pamplemousse disappeared into the kitchen.

The *officier* went straight into the attack.

'I take it I am talking to the real Monsieur Aristide Pamplemousse and not his twin brother?'

'You have a choice,' said Monsieur Pamplemousse, in an attempt to break the ice. He waited for an answering chuckle, but none was forthcoming.

'We have made an inventory of the pictures.'

It wasn't hard to guess what was coming next. 'There were a large number still in their original crates. A Cézanne, a minor Botticelli, a Seurat, a Fragonard or two. Together with those in the hotel they came to a total of seventy-five. Then there were a great many items in silver and bronze, statuettes and other bits and pieces. I won't bore you with all the details. A full list will be published in due course, along with the total value.

'However, there was one oddity – a painting – measuring some fifty centimetres by thirty. It was more recent than the others and it bore the name of a local artist.'

'It is a small world,' said Monsieur Pamplemousse.

'It was purchased at an art exhibition being held at the *Mairie* in Bélisaire. It depicts a scene not dissimilar to the one by Sisley which was stolen from the hotel. Would you know anything about that?'

'*Non,*' said Monsieur Pamplemousse. 'Definitely and most assuredly, *non*. I can say with my hand on my heart that I have never seen such a painting.'

'My understanding is that it was purchased by an English girl, answering to the description of your companion. She was most insistent that she be given a receipt describing the scene in detail; a canal in summer time. She said it was in case she was stopped at the airport.'

'It sounds like a sensible precaution,' said Monsieur Pamplemousse.

'The paint had run and there were teeth marks on the frame.'

'Perhaps,' said Monsieur Pamplemousse, 'she should ask for her money back.'

'That is all you have to say?'

'I am sorry, but it is a very bad line. Either that, or I have an attack of my old complaint – temporary loss of hearing.'

'Considering I stood up for you with Madame Blanche, I think that is very unfair. I have just let her go, but only under pain of being instantly rearrested should she so much as breathe a word.'

'Life *is* very unfair at times,' said Monsieur Pamplemousse. 'But at least Pommes Frites found the buried treasure for you. In return I would like to keep my self respect.'

There was a long silence.

'That is your final answer?'

'*Oui.*'

There was a click and the line went dead.

'*Dîner is* ready,' called Madame Pamplemousse from the kitchen. 'We have *filets de hareng marinés and poulet rôti.*'

The herrings came in a large tureen along with sliced carrots, thinly sliced onion and herbs. The accompanying potatoes, quartered, tossed with *vinaigrette,* olive oil and parsley and still slightly warm, were in a separate bowl.

Monsieur Pamplemousse poured two glasses of a lightly chilled Pouilly Fumé Les Charmes, and then took the precaution of removing his tie before he sat down.

'Who was that an the telephone?' asked Madame Pamplemousse.

'It was someone from the *gendarmerie* in Arcachon. One of the *officiers.*'

'You sounded very brusque, Aristide.'

186

'Not brusque,' said Monsieur Pamplemousse. 'I was merely being firm. He wanted some information which I was not prepared to give.'

They ate in silence for a while.

'Was it nice in Arcachon?' asked Madame Pamplemousse suddenly.

'Very,' said Monsieur Pamplemousse. 'You would like it. It is not too grand.'

'And the hotel? Was the hotel nice?'

'There was a lot to be desired.'

'I have never been to that part of France. Perhaps we could take a holiday there later in the year. When the crowds have gone.'

'I think we should leave it until next year,' said Monsieur Pamplemousse. 'People will be flocking to the Dune du Pilat all through the summer.' He also had no wish to meet up with the *officier* again until the dust had settled.

He wiped the plate clean with his bread. 'That was delicious, Couscous. The herrings were exactly as they should be – not too salty.'

'I took the precaution of soaking them in milk for several hours first,' said Doucette. 'They have been marinating in oil ever since you went away so the onions and carrots have had time to soften.'

While she was preparing the second course, Monsieur Pamplemousse picked up the telephone and dialled the Director's number in Deauville. It was answered on the first ring.

'*Monsieur . . .*'

'Pamplemousse! What news? I have been trying your hotel all day. The number seems ta be permanently engaged.'

It was hardly surprising. The Hôtel des Dunes was probably swarming with officials, not to mention the media, all of them wanting to use the telephone. He pitied the poor television cameramen lugging their equipment up and down the dune; worrying about getting sand in their lenses.

'I thought you would like to know, *Monsieur*, that you may put your ballpoint away.'

'My *ballpoint*, Pamplemousse? What on earth are you talking about?'

Monsieur Pamplemousse suppressed a sigh. Sometimes he wondered if his chief was being deliberately obtuse.

'The operation, *Monsieur*,' he hissed. 'My reason for being in Arcachon. It has reached a satisfactory conclusion.'

'You mean?'

'Elsie is returning to base. With luck she may already be there. She has given up all thoughts of becoming an Inspector. I doubt if she will need to work again for a while.'

'Aristide, what can I say? I cannot begin to tell you how much I have been through these last few days. I seem to have spent most of my time hiding beneath the duvet. Time has hung heavy.'

'I, too, have suffered, *Monsieur*. And I, too, have returned to base. I am speaking from Paris.'

'Paris? How extraordinary. Doubtless you have seen the news about Arcachon. It is on all the channels. There is no escape from it. How strange that it should all have blown up the moment you leave. You have missed all the excitement.'

'*C'est la vie, Monsieur*. That is life!'

The roast chicken came garnished with watercress. Monsieur Pamplemousse dissected it quickly and expertly.

Then Madame Pamplemousse put the legs back in the oven for himself and Pommes Frites later. It was what she called 'the men's portion'. While she was gone he took a quick nibble. It was what he called 'carver's privilege'. The flesh was done to a turn, the skin golden brown. The watercress leaves added a pungent taste.

He went to his wine cupboard in the hall and took out a bottle of '85 Faiveley Morey St.-Denis Clos des Ormes which he had been saving for a special occasion. Only ninety-five cases had been made.

'You are spoiling me, Couscous,' he said, as Doucette returned carrying a bowl of green salad and a plate piled high with frites. 'It is a meat fit for a king. I swear the *poulet* would not disgrace L'Ami Louis.'

Madame Pamplemousse looked pleased. 'The trick is in rubbing it first with goose fat, then seasoning it with salt. That is how they do it.'

Monsieur Pamplemousse poured the wine. 'You should have been an Inspector.'

'I haven't lived with one all these years without learning a few secrets,' said Doucette. 'I hope it makes up for all the bad food you had in the hotel.'

Monsieur Pamplemousse looked up in surprise. 'How did you know that?'

'The Director's wife was telling me.'

'Aah! Chantal. Did she tell you anything else?' In case the news was bad, Monsieur Pamplemousse took the precaution of filling his mouth with food so that if he were to be questioned he would have a little breathing space. He immediately regretted it.

'She told me about Elsie. It was such a pity the poor girl struck unlucky on her first time out. It must have put her off any thoughts of becoming an Inspector.'

'Elsie?' Monsieur Pamplemousse emitted a choking noise.

'Such a nice girl, and such a good cook. I think she is really very shy. I'm so glad it was she you had to take and not a lot of people I know. Although I must say I wouldn't have recognised her from the photograph you showed me the other night after the Director's party. Where you got it from I don't know.

'Chantal told me about all the telephone calls. It happened every time she went into the bathroom. She had to wait in there for ages some evenings. Why there had to be such secrecy I really can't imagine.'

'Perhaps,' said Monsieur Pamplemousse discreetly, *'Monsieur le Directeur* was worried on my behalf. He thought you might be jealous.'

'Men! You are such vain creatures. You think that every pretty girl is just waiting for the chance to jump into bed with you. I knew you would be safe with Elsie. It's the unlikely ones you have to watch. People like Madame Blanche.'

'Couscous! How can you say such things?'

'Because I know men. And I know Madame Blanche. I think she rather fancies you on the quiet.'

Not for the first time, Monsieur Pamplemousse reflected that there was no knowing women. But that, of course, was their attraction.

He lifted his glass. 'Here's to things past.'

The wine was smooth and full bodied; an explosive mixture of ripe fruit, with a promise of even greater things to come. Mentally he added a second toast; to Elsie – wherever she might be.

'The past is like a foreign country,' said Doucette, 'where they speak a different language.'

Monsieur Pamplemousse digested the observation for a moment or two. 'That is true,' he said at last. 'It was certainly very true of Elsie.'

Taking another sip of the wine he caught Pommes Frites' eye. Pommes Frites was wearing one of his enigmatic expressions. It was hard to say whether he was registering agreement about Elsie, or whether he was simply waiting for his chicken leg to arrive.

If it were the former, reflected Monsieur Pamplemousse, then Pommes Frites had the advantage over a great many people. At least he and Elsie had got to share the same bed. He hoped Reginald didn't ever get to know. He might be tempted to put out another contract.

Monsieur Pamplemousse on Location

Contents

1
OVERTURE AND BEGINNERS

For Monsieur Pamplemousse it began and ended in the Parc Monceau; that small but immaculately kept oasis of greenery situated in the 8th *arrondissement* of Paris, where uniformed nannies from well-to-do families forgather every afternoon in order to give the occupants of their *voitures d'enfant* an airing.

Fate had drawn him there in the first place. Fate and Pommes Frites, which more often than not amounted to much the same thing.

The day had started badly. *En route* to the office, he encountered a horrendous traffic jam in the Place de Clichy. An *embouteillage* of the very worst kind. A quick glance to his left as he joined the throng of impatient drivers revealed stationary traffic as far as the eye could see – all the way down the rue de Léningrad.

Without a moment's hesitation, Monsieur Pamplemousse abandoned his normal route and put Plan 'B' into action. After mounting the central reservation for a short distance, he wormed his way with great aplomb in and out of the waiting vehicles and headed westwards along the Boulevard des Batignolles as though that had been his intention all along.

A few minutes later, soon after they reached the Boulevard Courcelles to be exact, he felt a stirring in the back seat of his 2CV as Pommes Frites came to and registered this unexpected change to the natural order of things. Having treated the shampooed and pomaded occupants of a *Boutique de Chiens* to his right with the contempt he clearly thought they deserved, he turned his attention to the vista on his left. As he did so the Parc Monceau loomed into view.

Resting his chin on his master's shoulder, Pommes Frites gazed soulfully through the offside window. Anyone watching could have been forgiven for assuming the worst. A hard done-by hound if ever there was one, possibly on its way to the knacker's yard.

Monsieur Pamplemousse glanced at his watch. It showed a minute or so before nine o'clock. It was his first day back at work after a successful tour of duty in Arcachon. No one would expect him to arrive at the office dead on time, least of all the Director, who had good cause to be in his debt in more ways than one. Had not Monsieur Leclercq specifically said that the choice of a next assignment lay with Monsieur Pamplemousse himself? The world – at least that part of it which lay within the boundaries of metropolitan France – was virtually his oyster.

In the meantime the sighing in his ear was becoming almost intolerable. To stop or not to stop? The question resolved itself almost immediately when an empty parking space suddenly materialised ahead of them.

Entering the Parc Monceau through a pair of vast and gilded ornamental wrought-iron gates, Monsieur Pamplemousse returned the salute of an elderly gendarme who appeared from behind a large rotunda. It was nice to know there were still those in the force who recognised him from his days with the Sûreté. All the same, he was glad he had thought to put Pommes Frites on a leash; the man already had his whistle at the ready.

Monsieur Pamplemousse tightened his grip on the lead as he joined a stream of commuters heading across the park towards the Champs Elysées. There was a large sand pit in the middle of the path leading off to his right and he sensed that Pommes Frites might have designs on it; designs which would undoubtedly have been legislated against on one of the many notice boards. It looked like a 'no go' area in all senses of the word. That being so, he led the way along a path to their left. Out of the corner of his eye he could see the gendarme still keeping a watchful eye on them. It was a case of better safe than sorry.

In the days to come Monsieur Pamplemousse would more than once fall to wondering what might have happened had he risked the gendarme's opprobrium and gone to his right. Would everything have been different?

As it was, he strolled on his way past large areas of begonias and between beds filled with marigolds and busy lizzies, blissfully unaware that he was setting in motion his involvement in a train of events as bizarre as any he had yet experienced.

It was a tranquil scene. Roses were in full bloom everywhere. Pigeons waddled to and fro as they foraged for unconsidered trifles; sparrows followed in their wake. Only the soft swish of water from hosepipes playing over the freshly mown grass and the occasional heavy breathing of passing joggers disturbed the peace.

Their route took them towards the *naumachia basin,* an artificial lake modelled, so it was said, after pools the ancient Romans were wont to construct in order to simulate mock naval battles. Ducks swam lazily back and forth, pausing every now and then in order to dip their beaks into the water. In the coming months the colonnades beyond the lake would form the background to many a fashionable wedding photograph, but for the moment it wasn't hard to picture it peopled by toga-clad citizens of the Roman Empire, idly helping themselves from bunches of grapes as they spurred their model boats on to victory over a late breakfast.

Had Monsieur Pamplemousse taken the path to the right that morning his thoughts might well have been on madeleines rather than ancient Rome, for had he not once read that Marcel Proust used to play in the sand with his friend Antoinette Fauve? Marcel Proust, whose most memorable work was inspired by the simple act of dipping a spoonful of madeleine cake crumbs into a cup of lime tea.

And if his thoughts had been on madeleines, then it was more than likely he would have spurned the Director's offer of a trip to the Camargue, opting instead for a chance to sample the culinary delights in and around Illiers-Combray, home territory of the illustrious writer.

Pommes Frites had no such romantic notions. As far as he was concerned water was for swimming in, ducks were meant to be eaten, and birds and joggers were there to be chased. Unable to do any of these things, he strained at his leash, anxious to explore pastures new.

Monsieur Pamplemousse knew how he felt. It was ridiculous really. It was only a matter of days since their return from Arcachon and already he, too, was feeling restless. It was hard to put a finger on the cause. Perhaps it had to with the feeling of holidays in the air. All the way along from the Place de Clichy waiters had been busy putting out extra tables and chairs ready for *déjeuner*, anxious to make the most of things before the annual migration out of Paris began. Men in green overalls had been busy with their brooms. Pavements glistened from being freshly machine-washed. It was rather as though everything was being spruced up and made ready for putting into store. In a few weeks time Paris, at least as far as its residents were concerned, would be empty.

Studiously averting his gaze from the shadowy figures practising Tai Chi behind some bushes, he moved on round the gardens and stood for a while contemplating the spot where, on the 22 October 1797, a certain Monsieur Jacques Garnerin, the world's first parachutist, had caused consternation amongst the local populace by literally falling out of the sky. It didn't help.

Monsieur Pamplemousse's feeling of unrest lasted all the way to the office. Driving round the Arc de Triomphe he was struck by the thought that it needed but a turn of the wheel and he could head in any direction he chose; north, south, east or west. It was that sort of morning.

But duty called. As he went round for the second time, he abandoned the *carrousel* and headed towards the pont de l'Alma and the underground car park beneath the Esplanade des Invalides.

A few minutes later he turned off the rue Fabert and applied a magnetic card to a brass plate let into the wall. In response to the answering buzz he pushed open a small door marked *piétons* and let himself into a courtyard on the far side of which, beyond the fountain, lay *Le Guide's* headquarters.

Even old Rambaud, the gatekeeper, seemed to have caught the bug. The window of his little room just inside the entrance was wide open: an unprecedented event. No doubt if he caught a cold they would all suffer the consequences.

Crossing the courtyard, Monsieur Pamplemousse entered the main building through the large plate-glass revolving doors. He exchanged greetings with the receptionist and then, ignoring the lift, bounded up the main stairs two at a time.

The Inspectors' office on the third floor was empty. It was the time of year when most of his colleagues were scattered far and wide across the length and breadth of France, searching out new restaurants, checking on long-established ones, double-checking those earmarked for promotion, or in some cases demotion, following up unsolicited letters of praise or complaint.

Panting a little after his exertions, Monsieur Pamplemousse settled down at his desk and started to go through the contents of his In-Tray. There was the usual assortment of odds and ends. Some queries from Madame Grante about past expenses – he put those on one side to deal with later – she had yet to see the extras he had accumulated in Arcachon; they would need *Monsieur le Directeur's* approval before he even dared broach the subject. Explaining how and why Pommes Frites had come to bury one of *Le Guide's* issue camera lenses in the sand at Cap Ferret would not be easy: worse than filling in an accident report. Lips would be compressed. Unanswerable questions would be posed. Pleading that the lens had been in a pocket of his best suit which had also been engulfed by the incoming tide would be a waste of time.

There was a note from Trigaux in the Art Department saying a film he'd wanted processed was ready for collection. Bernard had left him a wine list containing several sale items marked with a cross. Bernard had connections in the wine trade and an eye for a bargain. Truffert had returned a tape he'd borrowed- *Gerry Mulligan Meets Ben Webster*.

Reaching across, Monsieur Pamplemousse felt in his tray in case he had missed anything. His fingers made contact with a small plastic envelope. A tag bearing his name was attached to the outside. Printed in red across the top were the words SECRET ET CONFIDENTIEL. Tearing open the top of the packet, he upended it over his blotting pad. Bottle was too grand a word for the object which fell out. True it was made of brown glass, but it was so small there was no room for a label, nor was there anything inside the envelope to say who had put it there in the first place or why.

He held the object up to the light, but it was impossible to see if there was any liquid inside. He decided it must contain something because it had a tiny glass stopper kept in place by a band of shrink plastic.

Taking a corkscrew from his pocket, Monsieur Pample-mousse released the knife blade and made a nick in the band. Still half-suspecting one of his colleagues might be playing a prank, he gingerly removed the stopper and applied it to the end of his nose. It was a perfume of some kind. Mildly assertive, yet with an underlying promise of other things to come; it was hard to put a word to it. Sensual? Decadent? That was it – decadent.

Analysing it as one might a glass of wine, isolating one part from another, he first of all registered musk. Beyond that he thought he could detect the smell of incense. There were spices too, spices . . . roses? . . . perhaps a damask rose? Certainly flowers of some kind. Jasmine? There was more than a hint of oakmoss. He added coriander to his list before he gave up. Doubtless there were many, many more, but it would need an expert and highly trained nose to isolate them. The overall effect wasn't unpleasant: very much the reverse. But why he should be the recipient of such a strange gift he hadn't the remotest idea. Perhaps someone was trying to tell him something?

He picked up the phial and dribbled the contents over the back of his other hand in the way that he'd seen women do when they were testing samples in a shop. Rather more came out than he had intended. It trickled off on to the desk and he was about to reach for his handkerchief when he thought better of it. Doucette might suspect the worst.

Catching sight of Pommes Frites stirring in his sleep, Monsieur Pamplemousse hastily crossed to the nearest window and flung it open. He had no wish for anyone to come in and catch him smelling to high heaven.

He was in the act of waving his arm to and fro when he happened to catch sight of a familiar car drawing into its official parking place to the right of the main entrance. The solitary occupant alighted and was about to slam the door shut when he glanced up as though to check the weather.

Monsieur Pamplemousse froze. It was too late to withdraw his arm, so he did the next best thing – he converted the waving motion into a form of salutation. The greeting was not returned. Instead, the driver stared up at him for several seconds, then reopened the door of his car and reached for a telephone on the centre console.

Closing the window, Monsieur Pamplemousse hurried back to his desk. He hardly had time to settle down again before the telephone rang. It was Véronique, the Director's secretary.

'Monsieur Pamplemousse. Monsieur Leclercq wishes to see you in his office.'

'Now?'

'*Oui. Tout de suite.*'

'Did he sound . . .?'

Véronique anticipated his question. '*Non. Au contraire.* He sounded very cheerful. He simply said as soon as possible. He is on his way up now. If you hurry you may beat him to it.'

Monsieur Pamplemousse hastily replaced the stopper in the phial and parcelled it up inside an envelope. Then he opened a drawer. The mystery would have to wait.

He glanced down. Pommes Frites' nose was twitching and there was the suspicion of a smile playing on his lips. It seemed a pity to disturb him.

Véronique made a thumbs-down gesture as Monsieur Pamplemousse entered the Director's outer office. Behind an open door he could see her boss already seated at his desk. Clearly the race had gone to the one with the private lift.

'*Entrez,* Aristide. *Entrez.*' Catching sight of his subordinate, Monsieur Leclercq rose to his feet and after a brief but undeniably warm handshake motioned towards an armchair.

Monsieur Pamplemousse did as he was bidden. Véronique was right. The signs were not bad. In fact, his chief looked in an unusually sunny mood.

'I trust you are fully recovered from your stay in Arcachon, Aristide?' he began.

'I think I have seen enough sand to last me for a while, *Monsieur.* The dunes are unbelievably large.'

The Director sniffed. 'I take it you have been at the bottle already.'

Monsieur Pamplemousse looked suitably injured. 'I assure you, *Monsieur,* that not a drop has passed my lips since yesterday evening.'

'No, no, Pamplemousse, you misunderstand me. I was referring to the sample fragrance I asked Véronique to place in your tray. Tell me what you think of it. I value your opinion.'

205

'It is . . . unusual . . .' Monsieur Pamplemousse hesitated. Something in the tone of the Director's voice prompted him to leave his options open for the time being.

'It is not one I have come across before,' he added cautiously.

The Director closed the door to his outer office and then glanced quickly round the room to make doubly certain the rest were properly shut. 'That, Aristide, is because it is not yet on the market. The launch date has yet to be fixed. Field trials are still in progress.

'A "come-hither" perfume would you say? Hard to resist?'

'I have not put it to the test, *Monsieur.*'

'Madame Grante has not been chasing you down the corridors overcome by barely concealed passion?'

'No, *Monsieur*. I am glad to say she has not. I came as soon as I received Véronique's call.'

The Director looked mildly disappointed. He gave another sniff and retreated towards the window.

While his chief's back was turned Monsieur Pamplemousse automatically glanced at the desk to see if it offered any clues as to why he had been summoned. Somewhat to his surprise he saw there was a translation of the works of the great Roman cookery writer, Apicius, lying open. Alongside it was a paperback book. As far as he could make out from the title on the spine it was a glossary of film terms.

Rather more ominously, he also caught sight of a P.27 – the standard form used by *Le Guide* in order to record personal details relating to members of staff. He was too far away to see whether or not his own name was at the top. The answer was not long in coming.

Having made himself comfortable, the Director picked up the form.

'I have been going through your records, Aristide. I see you spent some time attached to the fraud squad while you were with the *Sûreté.*'

Monsieur Pamplemousse gave a non-committal *'oui'*. He wondered what was coming next.

'No doubt you learned a great deal about perfume while you were there?'

'It was not really my area, *Monsieur*. I was mostly concerned with food. Food and drink. Unscrupulous fish-mongers who resort to varnishing the eyes of their wares when they grow stale. As for drink, believe me, *Monsieur*, you will find more ways of spelling Byrrh and Pernod in the Musée de Contrefaçon than you would have thought possible. People read what they expect to read. But I know there is a section devoted to perfume; there are numerous examples of passing off – names like Chanel become Cherel, or even Chinarl. Dior-Dior turned up once as Dora-Dora. Nina Ricci, Guy Laroche, Givenchy, even Guérlain have all suffered in their time.

'With a world-wide market for perfume worth tens of billions of francs, counterfeiting is big business these days. Perfume is the reflection of many people's dreams. It offers the promise of excitement in their lives: a touch of wicked-ness. And where there are desires to be satisfied corruption is never far away.'

The Director nodded.

'Tell me, Aristide, talking of wickedness, what do you know about sin?'

Monsieur Pamplemousse suddenly caught on. Although his annual increment wasn't due until October, the Director must be ahead of himself; clearing the decks before his summer holiday. At such times he had a penchant for plying members of staff with trick questions. Two could play at that game. He, Pamplemousse, was more than ready. It was simply a case of avoiding the obvious at all costs.

'Sin was a fortress in ancient Egypt, *Monsieur;* situated in the Nile Delta. It is famous because in the reign of Hezekiah, a certain general by the name of Sennacherib led an attack on it which had to be abandoned because a plague of field mice ate up his archers' bowstrings.'

Monsieur Pamplemousse felt pleased with himself. It was strange how these things stuck in one's mind. It was something he had learned at school in a year when the Auvergne had suffered a similar plague. His teacher had used it as an illustration of how even very tiny creatures can sometimes change the course of history.

He felt tempted to say 'ask me another', but something in the way the Director's lips were pursed caused him to think better of it. There were times when his chief's moods and intentions were hard to judge and he seemed less than happy with the reply.

'And Les Baux-de-Provence, Pamplemousse. What can you tell me about Les Baux?'

Monsieur Pamplemousse thought for a moment. He doubted if the Director expected him to eulogise on L'Oustau de Baumanière, Monsieur Raymond Thuilier's world-famous restaurant on the lower slopes; a restaurant where, in 1972, the Queen of England had dined on sea bass *en croûte,* followed by lamb, and strawberries and cream. The menu had stayed in his mind because shortly afterwards Doucette had cooked it for him as a surprise.

'Les Baux, *Monsieur?* Les Baux is a strange geological excrescence in the Apilles north of the Camargue; a natural fortress. The warlords of Les Baux are legendary. They claimed to be descended from Balthazar. It was there that another unfortunate incident took place, although

208

this time it hadn't to do with mice. The story goes that the Duke of Guise was staying for the night, and having indulged himself with too much wine at dinner he ordered a salute to be fired every time he proposed a toast. Unfortunately the very first time he raised his glass the canon nearest to him exploded. Although there is a tombstone bearing his name in a cemetery at Arles, it is merely a token gesture. In reality the Duke himself was scattered over a wide area.

'Another interesting fact is that the mineral bauxite was discovered nearby and was named after the village. As I am sure *Monsieur* knows, bauxite is a basic material of the aluminium industry . . .'

Suddenly aware of a drumming noise coming from the desk in front of him, Monsieur Pamplemousse broke off.

The Director heaved a deep sigh. 'Pamplemousse, I yield to no one in my admiration of the depth of your knowledge on a variety of subjects. However, I was not asking for a history lesson.'

But Monsieur Pamplemousse was not to be stopped that easily. 'I am sorry, *Monsieur*. I was lucky with my teacher. Although it was only a village school, she had a flair for bringing things to life.' Even as he spoke he wondered if deep down he wasn't trying to score over his chief, whose education had followed a very different path; a path available only to the rich and privileged.

He closed his eyes for a moment, the better to draw on his store of knowledge. 'Another of her favourite stories concerned Leonardo da Vinci. Possibly it was apocryphal – there are so many – but it tells of how he invented a giant watercress cutter which ran amuck outside the Sforza palace the very first time he tried it out and killed six members of the kitchen staff and three gardeners.'

Monsieur Pamplemousse paused. The Director looked as though he would have dearly liked to get his hands on such a machine himself.

'Tell me, Pamplemousse, to return to my first question, did she at the same time instil in you a knowledge of the seven deadly sins? Can you by any chance still enumerate them?'

But if the Director was hoping to win a round he was unlucky. This time Monsieur Pamplemousse didn't even bother closing his eyes.

'Pride, *Monsieur*. Wrath, envy, lust, gluttony, avarice and sloth.'

In spite of everything a look of grudging admiration crossed the Director's face. 'You were indeed lucky with your teacher, Aristide,' he said gruffly. 'Most people can hardly name more than two or three.'

'It was not my teacher who taught me about the seven deadly sins, *Monsieur*. It was the *curé*. He lectured the congregation on the subject most Sundays. He was of the opinion that all seven were rife in the village.'

'Aaah!' The Director sat in silence for a moment or two.

'I expect, Aristide,' he said at last, 'you are wondering where my enquiries are leading?'

Monsieur Pamplemousse thought the matter over carefully before replying. The Director's questions had been so diverse it was hard to find a common denominator. In desperation he glanced at the desk again and took in the open copy of Apicius's culinary work.

'Monsieur is gathering material for a spoof guide?'

The Director glared at Monsieur Pamplemousse for a moment, then he reached over and slammed the book shut.

'No, Pamplemousse,' he said crossly. 'I am not.' Rising to his feet with the air of a man badly in need of a drink he headed towards a cupboard on the far side of the room.

As he opened the door a light came on revealing a wine bucket, its sides glistening with beads of ice-cold sweat. The gold foil-covered neck of a bottle protruded from the top. Monsieur Pamplemousse recognised his favourite marque of champagne – Gosset. Clearly his being summoned to the top floor was not, as he had at first supposed, a spur of the moment decision.

'I have been trying to think of a way of expressing my thanks for all you did in Arcachon, Pamplemousse.'

Monsieur Pamplemousse made a suitably deprecating noise.

'It was far from being nothing,' insisted the Director. 'You averted a disaster of the first magnitude. Elsie is a lovely girl, but to have had her on our staff would have been disruptive to say the least, not to mention the problems I might have encountered *chez* Leclercq.'

Monsieur Pamplemousse was of the opinion that the Director's one-time *au pair* had never entertained the slightest intention of becoming an Inspector, but he remained silent.

'I have been considering your next assignment, Aristide. I had been toying with the idea of sending you to the Rhône Valley; Bocuse, Pic, and so on, but I have since been wondering how you would feel about going further south.' The Director handed him a glass. 'Loudier was really due to go, but in the circumstances I think you are the better man.'

'The circumstances, *Monsieur?*' Once again it all sounded a little too casual for comfort.

'Circumstances are like carpenters, Aristide. They alter cases. You may, of course, go anywhere you choose.'

'Anywhere, *Monsieur?*'

'A promise is a promise. It is the least I can do. However, before you decide, I have something else in mind, something a little out of the ordinary which I am sure will be right up your *rue.'*

While the Director was resuming to his seat, Monsieur Pamplemousse sipped the champagne thoughtfully. It was a Brut Réserve. A wine of quality, with over 400 years of family tradition behind it. He wondered what was coming next.

The Director fortified himself with a generous gulp from his own glass before he resumed.

'Earlier in the week I was dining with some friends and quite by chance found myself sitting next to the wife of one of our major *couturiers.* One thing led to another – I passed some comment on the perfume she was wearing – and she, for her part, was not unimpressed by my dissertation on the dish we had been served – saddle of lamb with truffles, chestnuts and a delicious *purée* of mushroom tart.

'For the time being the name of her husband's company must remain a closely guarded secret, but I can tell you they are about to launch a new perfume. It is to be called, quite simply, Excess – spelt XS.

'Soon, those two letters will be appearing on hoardings all over France. They will act as a teaser before the campaign proper.

'A major part of the launch involves the making of a series of commercials based on stories from the Bible. Work has already begun. Several episodes are already in the can. They will become classics of their kind. There is a star-studded cast and a budget of over 100 million francs. If I tell you they have engaged the services of no less a person than Von Strudel as the director you will appreciate the magnitude of the project.'

'Von Strudel, *Monsieur*? I must admit I didn't realise he was still alive.'

'There are unkind people in the business,' said the Director, 'who would say that even Von Strudel himself wasn't entirely convinced of the fact when they first approached him. He has been living the life of a recluse in his native Austria ever since biblical films priced themselves out of the market. He is, nevertheless, one of the greatest authorities on the *genre*.

'If he has a fault it is that he has become a little out of touch with present-day costs. He is not blessed, as we are, with a Madame Grante looking over his shoulder and he is already considerably over budget. Over budget and for one reason and another behind schedule.

'But to return to the dinner. The long and the short of it is that at the end of the evening my companion made me a proposal I could hardly refuse.'

'It happens, *Monsieur*.' Monsieur Pamplemousse assumed his man of the world tones as he drained his glass.

The Director clucked impatiently. 'It was not that sort of proposal, Pamplemousse,' he growled as he took the hint and reached for the bottle. 'Although I must say your reply does lead me to feel that in dispatching you to Les Baux I have made the right choice.'

'Les Baux, *Monsieur*?'

The Director sighed. 'Aristide, I do wish you would break yourself of the habit of repeating everything I say. It can be very irritating.

'The reason I am suggesting you go to Les Baux is because they are badly in need of an adviser. As I am sure you know, Pamplemousse, Von Strudel was renowned for his scenes of lust and gluttony. Naturally when I heard those two key words your name sprang immediately to mind. I can think of no one better qualified to advise on both those subjects.'

'*Merci, Monsieur,*' said Monsieur Pamplemousse drily. 'And what precisely am I expected to advise on?'

'Anything to do with food, Pamplemousse,' said the Director grandly. 'Anything and everything. Food as it was in Roman times. Food in the Bible. The essential culinary ingredients for an orgy if the need arises.

'I need hardly tell you that to be associated with such a project, even in a minor way, to have our name mentioned when awards are given out at the Cannes Festival, will be a considerable *plume* in our *chapeau.*'

Despite his misgivings, Monsieur Pamplemousse felt his mind getting into gear. It was an exciting prospect and no mistake.

'I believe the Romans were very keen on edible dormice, *Monsieur.* They first of all fattened them on nuts in special earthenware jars and then they stuffed them with minced pork and pine kernels.'

The Director looked dubious.

'Pamplemousse, I hardly think dormice, however edible they might be, would go down well with the cast. However, there are other things.' He picked up the copy of Apicius and turned to a marked page. '*Par exemple*, I see they ate bread and honey for *petit déjeuner.* Milk was strictly for invalids. Instead, they used to dip the bread in a glass of wine.'

He snapped the book shut. 'You may borrow this if it is of any help. Von Strudel has a reputation for being a stickler for detail. That is why I wish you to go, Pamplemousse. We must not let the side down.'

'With respect, *Monsieur,* if Von Strudel is such a stickler for detail and he is dealing with biblical times, why does he not shoot the film in the Middle East where most of the events took place?'

The Director dismissed the suggestion with a wave of his hand.

'The cost of the insurance would be too great. That part of the world is in a constant state of turmoil. Also, there is another reason. Von Strudel is not exactly welcome on the shores of Israel. His name has unhappy associations with certain events which took place in Europe during the last war. There are those who, some fifty years after the event, are still out to exact revenge. Even at the age of eighty-five life is sweet.

'Besides, we are not talking about real life. We are talking about make-believe. There are details and there are mere details. The simple fact, as I understand it, is that the Art Director happened to be staying with a friend at L'Oustau de Baumanière and he fell in love with the setting. In his mind's eye it has already been transformed into the Mount of Olives.'

The Director gazed dreamily into space. 'Mangetout is playing the part of the Virgin Mary. Before I met Chantal, Aristide, I was very much in love with her. She was France's answer to Rita Hayworth, with the added advantage of being half her age. I still have a signed photograph I sent away for. I remember the feeling of disappointment that came over me when I found the signature had been printed. It destroyed something very special and private.'

'There was always hope, *Monsieur.*'

'The magic of the silver screen, Aristide. We all thought we were the only one.'

The Director hesitated. 'That still doesn't answer my question.'

Monsieur Pamplemousse felt himself weakening. As an avid cinemagoer, the chance of being involved in the making of a film – even a commercial – was too good to turn down. If he didn't want to talk himself out of a job any protests he made from now on would need to be of a token variety.

'Madame Pamplemousse will not be pleased. As you know, *Monsieur*, I have only just returned from Arcachon.'

'Madame Pamplemousse is welcome to accompany you,' said the Director generously. 'I am sure she can be budgeted for. We will think up a title. She can be your AAO. Assistant to the Adviser on Orgies.'

'That is kind of you, *Monsieur*,' said Monsieur Pamplemousse hastily, 'but that won't be necessary. In any case Doucette would not be happy staying at L'Oustau. It is a little too *chic* for her tastes. She would be worrying all the time about what to wear in the evenings.'

The Director dismissed his protest. 'The problem will not arise, Pamplemousse. The hotel has been taken over lock, stock and barrel by the film company. They are using it as their production headquarters.'

'How about its off-shoot further down the hill, *Monsieur* – La Cabro d'Or?'

'That is being occupied by lesser mortals: those who I believe are known somewhat prosaically in the film business as gaffers and grips.'

Monsieur Pamplemousse puckered his brow in thought. 'There are not many other hotels in the area.'

'*Pas de problème,* Pamplemousse. You have been allotted a caravan.'

'A caravan?' Monsieur Pamplemousse tried hard to keep the note of disappointment from his voice. 'In that case Madame Pamplemousse will certainly not be accompanying me. We have an agreement.'

Memories of a caravan holiday they had spent in the Dordogne soon after they were married came flooding back. It had been impossible to boil a kettle without first taking something else apart. Going to bed at night and getting up again in the morning had been a nightmare. They had both sworn never again. And that was long before Pommes Frites appeared on the scene.

'There are caravans, Pamplemousse,' said the Director, 'and there are caravans. Wait until you see what yours will be like.' Opening a desk drawer, he removed a large, glossy brochure.

'A whole fleet of these was ordered from America. They have been strategically placed so as to form the nerve centre of the whole operation. Make-up, wardrobe, rest rooms . . . you will be surrounded by other experts in their various fields. There is even a resident chef.'

Monsieur Pamplemousse suppressed a whistle as he gazed at the picture on the cover. It was an artist's impression and therefore one had to accept that certain aspects of the scene were probably grossly over-exaggerated; the man standing on the steps of the caravan clasping a glass in his hand must have been at least seven feet tall – he would have needed to duck in order to get through the doorway – if, indeed, he was capable of bending at all; the surrounding foliage was a shade too luxuriant even by Californian standards.

However, it was the final artistic embellishment which caused Monsieur Pamplemousse to make up his mind without any further hesitation. There was a bloodhound sitting on the grass outside the caravan and it bore an uncanny resemblance to Pommes Frites. The likeness was so great, for a moment he almost suspected the Director of having engineered the whole thing. He dismissed the thought from his mind. There would not have been time. Clearly, the whole thing was meant.

217

'So what is it to be, Aristide? *Oui ou non?*'

'I think you may safely assume, *Monsieur,* that the answer is *oui.*'

'Good man! I knew I could rely on you.' The Director poured out the remains of the champagne and having gulped down the contents of his own glass with a haste bordering on the indecent, he reached inside the drawer again and withdrew a long white envelope. 'In fact, I was so convinced you wouldn't let me down I had Véronique prepare an introductory letter to Von Strudel himself.'

'*Merci, Monsieur.*' Taking the hint, Monsieur Pamplemousse pocketed the letter, downed his own champagne, and made for the door. As he turned the knob he felt the Director's hand on his shoulder.

'Take care, Aristide. In the meantime I would strongly advise you to stay away from the typing pool. One of the major selling points of the new perfume is that a little XS goes a long way and I suspect you may have been over-generous. Portion control on your part is sadly lacking.

'And if I may offer one final word of advice. When you get to Les Baux watch out for the "best boys". I have no idea what their precise function is, or why they should receive a credit for doing it, but whenever their names appear on the screen I always fear the worst.'

Monsieur Pamplemousse was aware of a certain excitement in his step as he left the Director's office. He couldn't wait to show the brochure to Pommes Frites.

Waving goodbye to Véronique, he caught a whiff of XS and wondered for a moment whether he should put the Director's theory to the test and try it out on Madame Grante, perhaps even take a short cut to her office via the typing pool, waving to the girls as he went?

Reason prevailed. He slowed down as he made his way along the corridor. His inner warning system was already hard at work. Thinking back on the meeting it seemed too good to be true. In retrospect, the conversation – the champagne on ice – the little tidbits of information dropped in here and there – had all felt too pat, too carefully rehearsed.

By the time Monsieur Pamplemousse reached the lift he had a growing presentiment that watching out for 'best boys' might well turn out to be the least of his problems in the days to come.

2
DINNER WITH A BANG

Monsieur Pamplemousse's caravan manifested itself in the shape of an American custom-built Star Wagon trailer of vast proportions, some twelve metres in length by perhaps two and a half metres wide. It was one of a number parked beneath a row of plane trees on the lower slopes of Les Baux-de-Provence. They were all of a luxury beyond anything he could have imagined.

Having turned off the A7 Autoroute du Soleil at Cavaillon, hot and tired after the long drive from Paris, he had approached his destination via St Rémy and the D5. His first sighting of the film company's location came as he rounded a bend in the twisting road which skirted the old town of Les Baux. The detritus of previous days' filming awaited collection – a discarded city of partly dismantled sets, façades of buildings, transport of all kinds – bullock carts, carriages of various shapes and sizes, a chariot or two, plus a motley collection of vans, lorries and cars. Beyond that lay sundry pieces of film equipment – camera cranes, lighting gantries, switch-boards, generators spewing out thick cables in all directions. In the distance, although there was no water to be seen, was what looked like the carcass of a large boat left high and dry by a tide which had long since receded never to return.

Monsieur Pamplemousse braked sharply and a crowd of

spectators sprawled across barriers set up at the side of the road turned their heads as his car ground to a halt.

A buzz of excitement went up as someone registered an official sticker on his windscreen. Faces peered in through the open windows as others parted to let him through. Autograph books appeared as if by magic. Fingers pointed towards the passenger seat. Never one to miss a trick, Pommes Frites assumed a faintly regal air while his master conferred with a uniformed man at the entrance to the site. Cameras clicked as a barrier was raised and they were waved on their way.

Monsieur Pamplemousse drove a short distance along a track indicated by the guard. He parked his 2CV in the shade of an olive tree and then set about unloading their belongings from the back seat. Cameras went into action again as Pommes Frites climbed out after him, stretched, and then obeyed an urgent call of nature. Photographically speaking, it was clearly a case of grasping at straws. In the fullness of time albums the world over would testify to the fact that until their arrival action had been thin on the ground. Entering into the spirit of things, Pommes Frites turned his best side towards the cameras.

Entering the trailer by what turned out to be the back door, Monsieur Pamplemousse found himself in a make-up area. Behind the make-up table itself there was a large mirror lit by rows of small, unshaded light bulbs along the sides and top. The reflection showed he had already caught the sun.

Laid out on a towel in front of the mirror were the tools of the trade; a selection of brushes in sanitised wrappings, tissues, sponges, eyebrow pencils, mascara, a jar of cleansing cream. On the other side of the room there was a telephone, and a colour television.

A curtained-off area to one side of a large wardrobe revealed a marine-style toilet and a full-size bath. The temptation to take a cold shower was hard to resist; the last 100 kilometres or so of the journey down had been like driving through a furnace. Air-conditioning was not one of the *Deux Chevaux's* optional extras – unless you counted having the roof rolled back.

Curiosity got the better of Monsieur Pamplemousse. Opening a full-length mirrored door beyond the bath, he found himself in a kitchen area complete with a Westinghouse refrigerator, a Sharp Carousel II convection microwave oven and a gas cooking hob. Alongside the hob was a stainless steel double sink unit. On a tiny shelf to the left of the oven stood a copy of Barbara Kafka's *Microwave Gourmet Healthstyle Cookbook* – an all-embracing title if ever he'd seen one, but a welcome sight nevertheless. The word microwave was banned *chez* Pamplemousse and the whole process remained a mystery to him.

There was a cupboard with a range of pots and pans and a shelf of dry foodstuffs. To his left was an alcove with a small face-to-face dinette. In the centre of the built-in table stood a glazed pottery bowl containing sprigs of broom; a gathering of golden butterflies.

Monsieur Pamplemousse opened the refrigerator door. Someone had done their job well. It was replete with fruit and vegetables; soft drinks – fruit juices and mineral water – tins of beer and a supply of local wine – Terres Blanches and some Listel *gris-de-gris*.

There was red wine in a rack above the working surface – some Châteauneuf-du-Pape and a bottle or two of Cabernet-Sauvignon: Mont Caume from the Bandol. Alongside it was a rack of culinary implements. They looked unused.

On an upper shelf stood an unopened tin of black olives from a Monsieur André Arnaud of nearby Fontvieille.

Having filled a bowl with some ice-cold water from a tap attached to the refrigerator, Monsieur Pamplemousse helped himself to an equally cold Budweiser while Pommes Frites noisily slaked his thirst.

Another door led to the main living-room. The beige carpet, striped with bars of sunlight filtering through a venetian blind covering a picture window at the far end, felt thick underfoot. An elevated area beneath the window supported a double bed.

Closer inspection revealed a second colour television receiver, a larger one this time – a Mitsubishi with a matching B82 video recorder – a Sony stereo cassette player, yet another telephone and a FAX machine. He could hardly complain of being cut off from the world.

After the canvas front seat of his *Deux Chevaux* the bed felt deeply luxurious. From somewhere overhead came a welcome draught of cool air. It accounted for the faint hum of a generator which he'd heard on entering the trailer. Come night-time it would probably be the usual toss-up between being kept awake by the noise, or opening windows and risking being bitten. Nearby Arles was reckoned to being the mosquito capital of France. No doubt they had plenty of relatives in the surrounding countryside. The news of fresh arrivals from the north would travel fast.

Monsieur Pamplemousse lay where he was for a moment or two, then he reached across and parted the blind. Dotted here and there were signs of civilisation – the odd patch of terracotta roof tiles or an occasional scattering of sheep or goats left behind for whatever reason while the rest of the flock enjoyed a summer diet of wild herbs in the surrounding uplands – but mostly the limestone terrain was bare and forbidding. Val d'Enfer – Hell Valley – wild and unruly; in the old days it must have earned its name. The light was dazzlingly clear. No wonder Van Gogh had been drawn to the area. A thermometer leading from an outside sensor was nudging 32°C. The thermometer inside the trailer showed a pleasant 19°C.

Pommes Frites came into the room, padded silently round on a tour of inspection, sniffed and went out again.

Monsieur Pamplemousse took the hint. He got up and began unpacking his bags, most of which were filled with reference books he had literally thrown in at the last moment; the Director's copy of Apicius, and as many other books relating to the subject as he had been able to lay his hands on at short notice. They took their place among a scattering of others on a mahogany shelf at the end of the bed.

Leaving the rest of the unpacking for the time being, he fed the cassette player with the tape Truffert had returned to him. As the sound of Billy Strayhorn's 'Chelsea Bridge' filled the air he squeezed a tube of *Eau Sauvage* gel into the bath and turned on the taps.

Anxious to share the news of his good fortune, he lay back in the foam for a while, composing a fax to the Director, then rapidly amended it. There was no point in making life sound too attractive. If Madame Grante got wind of it she would go through his expenses with a fine tooth comb. Something along the lines of 'TEDIOUS JOURNEY DOWN, BUT ARRIVED SAFELY, DESPITE INTENSE HEAT, WORK GOING ACCORDING TO PLAN' would suffice. If he dispatched it as late as possible before going to bed that night the automatic recording of time of origin might earn him Brownie points.

That problem out of the way, he had to admit to a feeling of unease. Even the music, far from giving him the lift it normally did, had a reverse effect. The sheer professionalism of the way Mulligan and Webster played together sowed seeds of doubt in his mind about his own capabilities for the task ahead. Despite his performance in the Director's office, all he really knew about the period he was supposed to advise on could have been written on the back of a spoon. He had to admit with a sense of shame that he didn't even know the date of the Crucifixion. As for what had been eaten at the Last Supper . . . the few books he had glanced through conveniently glossed over the subject.

It was another hour and a quarter before Monsieur Pamplemousse finished his ablutions. Allowing the last soulful strains of Ben Webster's rendering of 'Blues in B Flat' to die away, he looked at his watch. It showed nearly seven o'clock. There was a click as the machine switched itself off.

Emerging from the trailer he had an immediate reminder of just how hot the Camargue could be in July, even at that time of the day. It was as though he had opened an oven door. At least the Mistral wasn't blowing.

An immediate reminder of Pommes Frites' whereabouts came via a loud bang from inside the trailer.

Monsieur Pamplemousse turned to go back up the steps, and as he did so he had a pleasant surprise. If only Doucette could have been there to see it too – she would have been very proud. He reached up to touch the name board screwed to the top of the door. The 'M' on M. PAMPLEMOUSSE still felt slightly tacky. Flecks of dust had stuck to the white paint. A salutary warning, Hollywood style, that nothing is for ever, least of all in the world of make-believe. A few strokes of a brush and he would cease to exist. He wondered how many other names had graced that very same board, and whose for that matter?

'Hullo there! *Comment ça va?*'

Looking round, Monsieur Pamplemousse spotted a lone figure sitting at a table beneath a large sunshade advertising Ricard. There was a matching bottle on the table, together with a jug of water and some glasses.

'*Bien, merci.*' Returning the wave, he followed Pommes Frites along a path worn by the occupants of the neighbouring trailers. On his way he stole a glance at the names on some of the doors. Mostly they meant nothing to him. Brother Angelo – he guessed he must be an adviser of some kind; Gilbert Beaseley – the name rang the faintest of bells; he spotted Mangetout's quarters a little way back from the others. Alongside it were two other unmarked trailers. All three had their blinds drawn.

The person who had called out the greeting rose to his feet as Monsieur Pamplemousse drew near. He was wearing a white shirt, the long sleeves of which were folded back rather than rolled, a cravat, immaculately pressed beige trousers and suede boots. If Monsieur Pamplemousse hadn't already guessed from the accent, his nationality radiated from every pore. He was clutching a half empty glass in long, thin fingers. From his demeanour it looked as though it wasn't the first that evening.

Monsieur Pamplemousse accepted the proffered hand. That, too, was droopy. 'Gilbert Beaseley . . .' The greying quiff of hair casually tossed to one side matched his eyes. 'You may have heard of me. Writer. Go anywhere. Do anything. Distance no object. Masonics and biblical films a speciality.'

I have seen your name.'

'I saw yours being put up, too. Welcome to Babylon.' Monsieur Pamplemousse's suit was noted with approval. 'I see you haven't gone native yet. Good chap. Must keep up the standards.'

'I came away in a hurry,' said Monsieur Pamplemousse simply. It was all too true. Thoughtlessly, he hadn't even bothered to pack any short-sleeved shirts. Doucette would raise her eyes to Heaven when she found out.

'Would you care to join me in an *aperitif,!*'

Monsieur Pamplemousse hesitated. 'You look as though you are expecting company . . .'

'Not expecting . . . hoping. There is a crisis Ark-wise and I have been deserted.'

Refusal being clearly impossible, Monsieur Pamplemousse lowered himself into the remaining chair. As he did so he gave a start. Surprise gave way to embarrassment. The noise was loud, clear and unmistakable.

Gilbert Beaseley looked away, made a languid effort at swotting a passing fly and edged his own chair slightly away from the table.

Monsieur Pamplemousse shifted uneasily. The noise was repeated.

'*Pardon.*' The word came out automatically: an admission of guilt where none existed.

'Not at all.' Beaseley beamed at him. 'Are you taking anything for it?'

'It is nothing . . .' Monsieur Pamplemousse broke off. It was too late to deny responsibility even though his conscience was clear. The damage was done. He sat very still.

Pommes Frites eyed his master with interest for a moment or two. Then, before any attempt was made to shift the blame in his direction – as had been known on past occasions – he set off on a voyage of exploration. There were signs of activity down by the boat. Lights were coming on. A solitary dove winged its way low overhead, then turned and flew back again. It all looked worthy of investigation.

Gilbert Beaseley glanced after him. 'I see you've brought your own bodyguard. Very wise. I wish I had. Is he an only one? He hasn't a friend I could borrow?'

'It is not as simple as that,' said Monsieur Pamplemousse. 'He is unique. I do not know where I would be without him.'

'Pity. Everybody in this business ought to have a stand-in. You never know.'

Monsieur Pamplemousse forbore to ask why and the subject was abruptly changed as his host reached for the bottle.

'Forgive me. I'm being neglectful. I'm afraid you find Gilbert Beaseley not at his best. I should make the most of me. I may not last until morning.' He pushed a stiff measure of pastis across the table. 'I will leave you to do the necessary.'

'*Merci.*' Monsieur Pamplemousse removed a perforated spoon from one of the glasses, added a knob of white sugar, and began adding water from the jug slowly and carefully, drop by drop, partly for the sake of the ritual and partly because he feared a repeat performance of the dreaded noise. The water was satisfactorily cold and they both watched while the colourless liquid turned a tawny-yellow. Hoping to achieve a classic 5:1 ratio, *à la Marseillaise*, he was disappointed. It was as he feared; the helping of *pastis* had been more than generous.

'So you are a writer? I am sorry, I am afraid I have not read any of your works.'

Gilbert Beaseley sighed. 'My penetration of the French market is, I fear, fairly minimal. The sad fact is, many of my titles lose in the translation. They had great difficulty with my very first work – *Whatever Happened to the Sandcastles I Built when I was Young*? It ended up as *Chateaux* and everyone thought it was a book on doll's houses. It put them off buying any more. It was a slight work – a mere fifty pages in free verse – but I like to think it caught the mood of the Swinging Sixties in England – the end of it anyway, when people were eager to wallow in nostalgia.'

'In France,' said Monsieur Pamplemousse, 'we still do. Wallow, I mean.'

'Would you believe me if I told you I was also Rita Harridge?'

Monsieur Pamplemousse shook his head. He was unprepared for the question. 'She is a writer too?'

'Was,' said Gilbert Beaseley. 'Was. For a while I worked in a joke factory making stick-on phallic symbols for people who can't draw. Then I found employment in a firm of printers. One day I was typesetting a book and I thought to myself "I could do that". That's when Rita first saw the light of day. She had a short life, but a happy one. I think I may say with all due modesty that while she was around Rita caused many a housewife to lay down her feather duster of an afternoon and take to her bed.'

'What happened to her?'

'She had to be put down, poor dear. She was long past her "sell-by" date anyway. Husbands in Ruislip began to complain about the state of their semis. Pity. I think you would have liked her.'

'And your castles which were made of sand?'

'They got washed out to sea, like so much of my life.'

'So what brought you here?' Monsieur Pamplemousse gave an all-embracing wave.

'Ah, well may you ask. I was indulging in my current obsession- a history of Les Baux in the Middle Ages. I thought it would be nice to write a book which didn't dwell on all the carnage over the years: episodes like the well-known after-dinner sport called "Making Prisoners Jump off the Castle Walls and Listening to Their Screams as They Fall to their Death"; that kind of thing. I want to concentrate on the romantic side. The days when the City of Baux was a place of love and played host to troubadours and minstrels; when to be accepted, the ladies of the court had to be pretty and high-born. As you may have noticed, I specialise in slim volumes. Alas, if you leave out all the gory bits about Les Baux's past, there isn't a lot left. I've begun to think that Raymond de Turenne, inventor of the jumping game, was on to something. Every time I go up there and see the coach-loads of tourists arriving I think how nice it would be to resurrect it. "Now here we have the very spot where it used to take place. Come a little closer . . . closer still . . ." SHOVE. Posing as a guide you could build up a tidy score in no time at all and no one would be any the wiser.'

'The world,' said Monsieur Pamplemousse, 'is getting vastly overcrowded. The very things people travel miles to see are spoilt before they even get there.'

'How true. Anyway, one day I was doing some research up in the old town when I happened to get into conversation with the producer of this epic at a moment when writers were suddenly thin on the ground. One had gone into a home. Another is reputed to have joined the Foreign Legion. The other three simply walked out and haven't been seen since. On the strength of an old copy of *Sandcastles* I just happened to have with me and a CV I concocted on the spur the moment, he made me an offer I couldn't refuse. *Voilà* . . . here I am.

'I said to him – you'll have to take me as I am. If you don't like what you find, just tell me. I know when I'm not wanted.'

Replenishing his glass, Gilbert Beaseley pushed the bottle across the table. 'I'm talking too much. Tell me about yourself.'

Monsieur Pamplemousse was about to lean forward when he thought better of it. He was also momentarily distracted by the sight of Pommes Frites hurrying back up the slope away from the boat. From the way he kept peering over his shoulder it looked as though he could be in disgrace about something. Guilt was writ large all over his face.

'I am here as a food adviser.'

'A bit late in the day isn't it? I mean, there's only the Last Supper and the Crucifixion to go. No one will get very fat on that, least of all you. There won't even be any leftovers worth speaking of.'

'That is not what I was given to understand.'

Gilbert Beaseley shrugged. 'You may well be right. Things change from minute to minute. The Red Sea was all set to part three days ago – or the Red Sea as represented by a local stretch of water – but it never did. The *Etang de Vaccarès* turned out to be part of the *Réserve Naturelle*. All hell broke loose. They're very hot on conservation down here and no one had got permission to part it.'

Pommes Frites arrived back panting and settled himself under the table. For some reason he was soaked to the skin. Monsieur Pamplemousse also couldn't help noticing there were several small white feathers stuck to his chin.

Gilbert Beaseley glanced down. 'Did you distract the nasty lady, then? Mr Strudel *will* be pleased; so will the crew – they're all on double-time. I only hope you didn't bite her. You could wake up with lock-jaw.'

He turned back to Monsieur Pamplemousse. 'Mrs Noah's being difficult. She has but three lines to say –

"Hurry along there", "Two at a time" and "Don't push there's room for everyone" – not the kind of deathless prose I wish to be remembered by, but at a thousand dollars a word, who's complaining? Besides, in a forty-five-second commercial simplicity is all. Now she's demanding a dialogue coach.'

Monsieur Pamplemousse stared towards the boat. 'Von Strudel is down there?'

'I doubt it. It's the second unit working on some fill-in shots for the Ark sequence.' Beaseley read his thoughts. 'Anyway, I should stay where you are. You'll have plenty of time to see him in action. If you're working on the project there are two things you should know. One: speed is not Von Strudel's middle name. Two: he may be the greatest living authority on biblical films, but to say he is a little out of touch with the stark realities of making television commercials is the understatement of the year. His first shooting script lasted over an hour. That's when they began bringing other writers in, and one by one they have gone – all except for me. He still insists on using his original mega-phone.' Beaseley cupped his hands in the shape of a horn. 'Do you vrealise it vas through zis very megundphone zat I called Dietrich *eine Dummkopfe!* If you ask me he's a little bit bonkers.'

'*Comment?*'

'Bonkers. Round the bend. He's been living by himself for too long.'

'Can they not get rid of him?'

'I wouldn't like to be the person who tried. Besides, it would cost too much and the films are vastly over budget as it is. He's getting paid more than the rest of us put together. At his age he doesn't need the money, but he's no fool. Salaries establish the pecking order in this ego-intensive industry. Besides, you know what they say. If you owe someone a thousand dollars you don't sleep at night; make it a million and *they* don't sleep at night. I'll wager Von Strudel sleeps like a log. Apart from that, to fire him would be counter-productive. Time is running out. It could raise all kinds of problems and leave them even worse off.'

'In what way?' Monsieur Pamplemousse was finding it hard to follow the logic.

'The whole thing has to be seen in perspective. This series of commercials may have a bigger budget than *Ben Hur*, but in relation to the potential gross income from the product it is but a drop in the ocean. World-wide we are talking in space-programme terms.'

It occurred to Monsieur Pamplemousse that either he was very low in the pecking order or *Le Guide* must be doing exceptionally well out of him on the quiet. Draining his glass, he made a mental note to tackle the Director on the subject when he had a chance.

'Help yourself,' said Beaseley. 'It's on the house. Von Strudel may be a shit, but at least he's generous with other people's money.'

Monsieur Pamplemousse declined. He was already beginning to feel the effect.

'If it is all so bad, why did you take the job on?'

'A question I ask myself every time I open my eyes in the morning. The sordid truth can be summed up in three words – money, money, money. Also the experience. When it's all over I shall write a book about it. The fact is, ducky, there's more material here than I shall use in a lifetime.'

Gilbert Beaseley looked as though he was about to develop his theme still further but at that moment a loud bang like a pistol shot rang out from somewhere behind them. It was followed by a series of high-pitched bleeps.

Monsieur Pamplemousse turned and was just in time to see the gowned figure of a man carrying a large bundle wrapped in a white sheet disappear into one of the trailers. A second loud bang echoed round the clearing as the door slammed shut, but not before he managed to catch a momentary glimpse of a round, whiter than white face surmounted by a mop of curly black hair and behind that, just inside the trailer, a girl whose hair, in striking contrast, was long and ash blonde. She looked as though she was wearing a nurse's uniform.

'*Sapristi!*' He was glad he had resisted the offer of another Ricard. 'Who or what was that?'

'That,' said Gilbert Beaseley, 'was Brother Angelo. The girl is what is euphemistically known as an *au pair* – Swedish version.

'We do sound in a tizz today. It's a good thing he's wearing his bleeper.'

'Brother Angelo?' Monsieur Pamplemousse looked puzzled. 'He is also an adviser?'

Beaseley gazed at him in amazement. 'You must be joking. Don't tell me you've never heard of Brother Angelo? Late of "The Friars" – before he went solo.' He gave a hollow laugh. 'The only thing Brother Angelo could advise anyone on is where to get their next shot of coke. Brother Angelo – whose real name, by the way, is Ron Pickles – is the Pavarotti of the pop world. The one big difference being that Pavarotti doesn't end his act by urinating on an electric guitar. Come to that, neither does Brother Angelo any more. He did it once too often at a concert in Manchester. There was something wrong with the wiring and he received what he fondly calls "a packet up his privates". He could neither let go, nor could he stop peeing. In the end his trousers parted under the strain and a certain HRH who happened to be present complained. Not even his laser-controlled halo could save him from being arrested for indecent exposure. He was lucky not to end up being sent to the Tower.'

'I am afraid I am a little out of touch with the pop world,' said Monsieur Pamplemousse. 'The last concert I went to was with my wife. Jean Sablon was top of the bill. "Sur le pont d'Avignon" was all the rage that year.'

'But was it *numéro un?*' said Beaseley.

'I don't think they had numbers in those days,' said Monsieur Pamplemousse. 'It was done alphabetically. But it was a very good song. It was on everyone's lips.' He stared at the closed door of the trailer. 'So what is the secret of his success?'

'Perfectly simple. Despite everything, our Ron looks the picture of innocence. Innocence radiates from every pore. It's that black, curly hair. Women the world over-that is to say, girls of thirteen plus – all want to mother him. Mind you, I wouldn't care to be the one who got to do it. She would be torn limb from limb by the rest of the mob. In some ways, casting him as Our Saviour was a stroke of genius, but it is not without its problems.'

'You mean . . . Brother Angelo – Monsieur Pickles – is playing Christ?' Monsieur Pamplemousse looked aghast at the thought. 'It is not possible.'

'You could do a lot worse. Can't you just see him in the part?'

'If you want my opinion,' said Monsieur Pamplemousse, 'the very idea is so grotesque it will offend many people.'

'Undoubtedly. That's one of the reasons why Von Strudel was engaged in the first place. There's no such thing as bad publicity. At least it will get the product talked about. Strudel has spent his whole life offending people. His films are monuments to bad taste, but they are beautifully made. The grammar is immaculate. Nothing tricksy. Long shot, medium shot, close-up. No playing around with the sound perspective. You always know exactly where you are.

'Anyway, let's not be stuffy about it. By all accounts Christ was one of the people, with the power to draw the multitudes. That describes Ron Pickles down to a tee. It's the "in" thing – identifying a well-known person with a perfume. It began in England. The pulling power of Henry Cooper persuaded British men that wearing Brut could be macho; Chanel called on Jack Nicholson when they launched L'Egoïste. They didn't get him, but they called. Besides, who is it going to offend? Not the people who buy XS. They are hardly likely to be offended by anything – and certainly wouldn't admit to it even if they were. Those who might be offended are unlikely to buy it.

'The main trouble lies with Brother Angelo. They have come up against one tiny snag. He suffers from acute coprophalia . . .'

'*Qu'est que c'est?*' Monsieur Pamplemousse's command of English was beginning to desert him. He felt his concentration going.

'Coprophalia? It is an uncontrollable desire to be foul-mouthed. For years he has been totally unable to construct the simplest sentence without using the word "fuck". That may have been all right in the Sheffield steelworks where he first started out, but it doesn't go down too well in the world at large. He's been fitted with a bleeper attached to his voice-box. A kind of early warning system. It is programmed to obliterate certain key words. Luckily the Anglo-Saxons are sadly deficient in the oaths division, so the electronics are comparatively simple. Had our Ron been born in Italy the technical problems would have been immense. It would have needed an entirely new chip. As it is he sometimes sounds like a walking cash register. Fortunately Our Lord was a man of few words and it makes writing the script that much easier.'

'*Excusez-moi.*' Monsieur Pamplemousse reached for the bottle. He suddenly felt in need of a drink.

'Whoever said "you don't have to be crazy in this business, but it helps" knew what he was talking about.' Gilbert Beaseley glanced in the direction of the boat. While they had been talking the lights had been struck and everyone had disappeared. Filming was over for the

day. He lifted a wrist and focused on his watch.

'Delightful though it is, I'm afraid we shall have to continue this *conversazióne* some other time. There is an emergency script conference at the Oustau de Baumanière in less than an hour's time.'

'You will not be eating first?' Monsieur Pamplemousse's taste buds were beginning to register the smell of food from somewhere nearby. Pommes Frites was getting the message too. Every now and then he sat up, nose twitching.

'Sadly, no. I may cook myself some sardines on toast later. The muse is calling. Or, to put it another way, I feel it may be expeditious to work on a stand-by script for the Last Supper. Something tells me it should be possible to do better than "someone isn't wearing you-know-what, pause, all but one turn. Cut to BCU of Judas Iscariot. Dissolve." I feel like a schoolmaster, trying to keep one step ahead of his class. I can't stand it when everyone looks at me for an answer and I haven't got one. It makes me feel terribly lonely.

'But as for dinner, far be it from me to tell a food adviser where to eat, but if you take my advice you'll skip the unit caterers, Ratatouilles et Cie. Take advantage of Mr Strudel's absence and dine Chez Montgomery.'

He directed his thumb towards an olive tree some fifty or so metres away, beneath the branches of which a figure in white shorts and a white chef's jacket and *toque* was busying himself over a field kitchen.

'Montgomery is Von Strudel's personal chef. An unlikely name for an Egyptian, but he was born at the time of El Alamein, so he was named after one of our generals.' Beaseley shrugged. 'If things had gone the other way I suppose he would have ended up as Rommel. Only one word of warning. Montgomery is a splendid fellow and he cooks like a dream, but he is given to occasional excesses. Given your problem, I should steer clear of his version of Strawberry Romanov. It goes under the name of *Erdbeeres Von Strudel.* I've heard tell it is positively lethal.'

Gilbert Beaseley paused as he turned to leave. 'Technical question: if comedy is unreal people in real situations, and farce is real people in unreal situations, what do you call unreal people in unreal situations?'

'*Dummkopfs?*'

Beaseley laughed. 'You're learning.'

Monsieur Pamplemousse watched Gilbert Beaseley as he made his way slowly and unsteadily in the direction of his trailer. He had a feeling he had passed some sort of test, but he wasn't sure what.

As the other disappeared from view he rose. Instinct told him to follow Beaseley's advice. No chef likes to be idle. In a profession dedicated to giving pleasure, idleness was like the sounding of a death knell. Never one to miss an opportunity, Pommes Frites followed suit. Although for reasons best known to himself, dinner didn't appear to be high on his list of priorities, it was clear that he, too, recognised the signs.

They were neither of them mistaken.

As the pair of them drew near, Montgomery's face lit up. There followed a burst of frenzied activity. Monsieur Pamplemousse's request for a *pastis* was brushed aside in favour of a Kir.

'I make it for you specially. For you I add just a touch of honey. Try it. If you no like, then I will bring you a Ricard.'

The kir arrived at record speed along with a bone for Pommes Frites. Monsieur Pamplemousse tasted the former and murmured his approval, adding that it would perhaps need another to offset the taste of his pastis; in a moment or two – there was no hurry. Seeking Pommes Frites' opinion as to the quality of the bone would have been superfluous. He was managing to force it down.

Moments later a plate of *amuse-gueules* appeared with a flourish: *Caillettes* – tiny meatballs made of pork liver and spinach, flavoured with herbs; and some wafer-thin square slices of toast covered with *Anchoïade* – a combination of anchovies, olive oil, lemon juice and garlic – topped by a slice of fig. The anchovies had been mashed by hand before being blended with the other ingredients and the mixture pressed hard into the toast so that it would absorb the flavour.

After a suitable interval and a second kir, a salad arrived: on a bed of crisp lettuce leaves lay prawns, sliced tomatoes, black olives, *crème fraîche* to which a squeeze of lemon juice and a little basil had been added, mushrooms and asparagus tips. The *vinaigrette* dressing was immaculate. Monsieur Pamplemousse helped himself sparingly to some *aioli* which came in a separate bowl. He doubted if he would be going short of garlic and what was left would keep the flies at bay.

It was a wise move. The monk fish in the *Lotte en Broche* which followed had been marinated with lemon juice and garlic before being interspersed between slices of pepper and onion on skewers fashioned out of rosemary branches. Out of the corner of his eye he'd seen Montgomery basting it every few minutes with a sprig of rosemary dipped in olive oil as it grilled over a charcoal fire. It tasted divine, the rosemary implanting a wonderfully delicate flavour.

The wine was a Côtes de Provence L'Estandon; young and fresh, suitably chilled and in a 'serious' bottle – not one of the traditional fanciful shapes. It was an ideal accompaniment for the spicy food. Fruity, yet with a faint hint of acidity about it.

Rather like Gilbert Beaseley. Beaseley had a touch of acidity. Monsieur Pamplemousse wasn't sure whether he liked him or not. That was probably the way most people felt. He must go through life treating it as an arm's length transaction. Perhaps he'd suffered some great tragedy or disappointment which made him shy of getting too close to people.

The cheese was a *banon*, a small disc-shaped piece covered in chestnut leaves bound with rafia. With it came a glass of red Côtes du Ventoux. The bottle was left on the table. He examined the label. It was from Jean-Pierre Perrin. Once again, a perfect choice. It would accord well with the mildly nutty flavour of the cheese.

Monsieur Pamplemousse sank back into his canvas chair feeling at peace with the world. He didn't envy a soul, not even those who by now would be dining in state at the Oustau de Baumanière. It was a pleasant change to have someone else choose his meal, nicer still not to feel obliged to sit down and write copious notes about it before he retired to bed.

The smell of lavender mingling with that of burning charcoal and rosemary reminded him of the reason for his being there. What a strange world it was, the world of perfume and *haute couture*. XS was a very apt name for one of its products. It summed it all up.

While he had been eating, it had grown dark and lights were twinkling like fireflies around Les Baux. He wondered how Beaseley was getting on. Probably rewriting an abridged version of the Bible. To all intents and purposes it had been written by committee anyway, and then amended down the centuries.

Brother Angelo, too. He hadn't heard or seen a sign of him since his brief appearance. The trailer he'd entered was dark and silent, the curtains tightly drawn.

He wished now that he had asked about Mangetout. From all he had heard she led the life of a recluse these days. Garbo had nothing on her. No doubt Beaseley would fill him in if he asked. It would be something to tell the Director.

'For you, I add a little curaçao.'

A dish of sliced strawberries macerating in orange juice floated before his eyes and he suddenly realised the chef was talking to him.

It was *'Erdbeeres Von Strudel'* time. The combination of fruit and liqueur seemed overpoweringly heady in the night air. The smell reached out to him and then faded as the dish was whisked away to a nearby table.

'Then . . . a touch of *crème Chantilly.'* The strawberries vanished under a mound of cream.

'Then I add some pepper. Not too little . . . not too much. It is how Herr Strudel likes it.'

Watching Montgomery wielding the giant mill, Monsieur Pamplemousse wondered what would constitute too much. It looked a lethal amount. No wonder Beaseley had warned him against it.

'And then . . . just for you' – Montgomery made his way quickly to the stove, glowing red in the twilight – 'I pass it under the grill . . . like so . . .'

The words had hardly left his mouth when there was a flash like a sheet of lightning. It was followed a split second later by a loud explosion. A cloud of black smoke rapidly enveloped the stove, momentarily obliterating it from view.

Monsieur Pamplemousse picked himself up, but in his haste to see what had happened to Montgomery, who had borne the full brunt of the blast, he tripped over Pommes Frites, lost his balance and landed on the ground again. It was only then, as he gazed up at the back of the chair he had been sitting in a few moments earlier, that he realised whose seat he had appropriated.

Stencilled across the canvas back were the words VON STRUDEL – DIRECTOR (KEEP FOR SERIES).

As he registered the words it occurred to Monsieur Pamplemousse that given Von Strudel's advanced years, had he been performing his party piece that evening, they might well have had cause to replace KEEP FOR SERIES with the letters RIP and yet another chapter in the history of the cinema would have been closed for ever.

3
A STAR IS BORN

'It is good, Herr Strudel, that you have managed to assemble such an agreeable cast.'

Monsieur Pamplemousse hadn't intended using the word *agréable*. It slipped out. He had meant to say *distingué*, but at the last moment he'd wondered whether Von Strudel's French was up to it. So far there had been no indication that it might be. Conversation had been minimal: a one-sided series of guttural grunts.

He could hardly complain, however, at not receiving an immediate reaction to his attempt at breaking the ice.

Reaching for his monocle, Von Strudel screwed it firmly in place over his right eye and glared at Monsieur Pamplemousse as if he had suddenly taken leave of his senses. What was clearly a long-perfected trick of closing his other eye at the same time only served to intensify the effect.

'Zer is no such thing as *ein* actor who is *agréable*,' he barked.

'No actor is *agréable*. Zey are all *Dummkopfs*. Eisenstein vas right. You can do zee same thing *mit eine* dummy. Better! Every one of zem is *ein Dummkopf*.'

Having delivered himself of what he clearly considered to be the final word on the subject, Von Strudel placed the thumb and forefinger of both hands together to form an oblong frame. Peering through the opening, he turned his back on Monsieur Pamplemousse. A squeak which sounded uncannily like two pieces of unlubricated wood rubbing against one another arose as he pivoted on his right leg whilst endeavouring to pan across the pine-clad hills in the far distance.

It was a long pan, for the view from the top of Les Baux afforded an unbroken view of an horizon which seemed to stretch on and on to infinity. Fearful that he might unwittingly be the cause of Von Strudel losing his balance, Monsieur Pamplemousse followed him round.

'Vy do you say zey are *agréable?*'

Monsieur Pamplemousse was rapidly reaching the stage of fervently wishing he'd never mentioned the word. In fact, more than ever he regretted not having postponed delivery of the Director's letter until later in the day. He looked around for a friendly face, but there was no one else in sight. Even Pommes Frites had taken himself off somewhere immediately after breakfast.

Petit déjeuner, taken at a white wooden table beneath a parasol which Montgomery had set up outside his trailer while he was still asleep. It had been a delicious meal. A *petit déjeuner* to be enjoyed at one's leisure and remembered in tranquillity. Closing his eyes while he silently counted up to *dix,* he could still taste it.

Fresh *jus de orange.*

Fromage blanc with cream.

Wild strawberries.

A jug of hot *café.*

Honey and two kinds of *confiture.*

A bowl of cherries.

A wicker basket containing *croissants,* two kinds of toast and a selection of home-made *brioches.*

Beurre.

A white honey-scented buddleia nearby had been alive with bees. Taken in the morning sunshine, they were the ingredients which made it good to be alive. Had such a meal been presented to him at an hotel during the course of duty, there was no question but that he would have marked the establishment down as being worthy of three Stock Pots in *Le Guide*.

And all because he'd been anxious to locate Von Strudel before work started for the day, he had hurried over it!

Life was full of regrets. He should have made the most of his good fortune while it lasted; savoured every mouthful. Given his reception, he was sorely tempted to retrace his steps down through the old town of Les Baux, where he had eventually tracked down his quarry, climb into his car and drive back to base in the hope that he could go through it all again at a more leisurely pace.

He decided to try another tack. 'I have been doing some research on the Last Supper, *Monsieur*. Clearly, it was not an occasion for a banquet. It would have been a simple meal: some lamb, perhaps, with bitter herbs and other condiments, a little bread, some wine. There would have been a bowl of sauce at Our Saviour's side for the moment when he dipped his bread and handed it to Judas. It is hard to say what the wine would have been like; most probably white, possibly sweetish. It would have been kept in a two-handled clay jar holding nine litres, which was the official measure at that time, and would then have been served from a pitcher, which may well have been decorated. The Romans were fond of such embellishments. Some of them were very elaborate. If you like, I can show you an illustration of one – it would look very well on film. Four cups of wine would have been drunk during the meal to accompany various blessings. To symbolise the haste with which the Passover meal would have been eaten at the time of the great escape from Egypt, the bread would have been unleavened, that is to say nothing would have been added to produce fermentation. The lamb would have been roasted . . .'

Monsieur Pamplemousse felt pleased with his discourse. He had no idea what message the Director had conveyed in his letter, but given the limited time available, he felt he hadn't done at all badly in establishing his credentials. Beaseley was right; it was necessary to keep one step ahead of the field.

Von Strudel abandoned his pan in mid flight; Arles and the Grand Rhône were left unexplored. Replacing his monocle, he fixed Monsieur Pamplemousse with a basilisk-like glare. 'Who cares vot zey ate? Actors are not paid to eat. Miming, zey are paid to do. Eatink *nein.*'

Monsieur Pamplemousse tried hard to conceal his disappointment.

'I am afraid I do not understand you, *Monsieur.* The purpose of an adviser, surely, is to advise. If you do not choose to follow the advice, that is your decision. But if such is the case, then I fail to see the purpose of my being here. You do not call in a doctor and then disregard his advice.'

'Advice? Advice? I am surrounded by advice. I cannot even go to the *Badezimmer* without being given advice. I hov advice coming out of *mein Trommelfells.*'

'In that case,' said Monsieur Pamplemousse, 'I will not bother you any further. I am afraid I must ask you to accept my resignation.'

'And I am afraid zat I do not accept it. No vun resigns on zis picture! OK?' Von Strudel glared at him. 'All I vish to know is hov you discovered who is buggink me?'

'*Comment?*'

'Every day since we arrive here somezing goes wrong. Disappearing ink on *mein* script. Toads in *mein* bed. Sand in ze camera vorks. Tyres on *mein* automobile *kaputt*. Now, exploding *Erdbeeres!*' Von Strudel tapped the Director's letter. 'You are here to find ze bugger who is buggink me, is zat not zo, huh?'

'No, zat is not zo,' was the reply which immediately sprang to Monsieur Pamplemousse's mind, but as light slowly began to dawn he paused. He must be getting old. He should have known better. The Director was up to his old tricks again. No wonder the chief had been so anxious to get the meeting in his office over and done with. Just wait!

His silence was misconstrued.

'Zat is good. Now ve know ver ve stand, huh?' Von Strudel beamed *bonhomie*. Exuding brotherly love, he placed an arm round Monsieur Pamplemousse's shoulder.

Monsieur Pamplemousse managed a nod.

'No more of zis talk of resignink?'

With an effort Monsieur Pamplemousse converted the nod into a half-hearted shake. He felt like the victim of some cheap con trick and he didn't as yet trust himself to speak.

'Zat is good,' said Von Strudel. 'Now zat ve understand each other I vill tell you somezing. You are fired!'

The last Monsieur Pamplemousse saw of his erstwhile employer, he was striding purposefully up the hill, peering once again through his makeshift viewer. There was a bang and a whoosh as low-flying air-force jet suddenly shot past without warning, skimming the rooftops. As the noise died away a cry of '*Dummkopf*' echoed round the narrow streets and alleyways of Les Baux.

'Don't take it to heart,' said Gilbert Beaseley. 'Strudel fires people in much the same way as other people offer you a cigarette. He'll have forgotten all about it by the time you next see him. He really should be fitted with a bleeper like Brother Angelo. As for your advice on the catering arrangements at the Last Supper, I shall accept it with gratitude and all due humility.'

He glanced idly at Monsieur Pamplemousse. 'If it's not a rude question, why *did* he fire you? It must be something of a record. Most people manage at least one full day.'

'We had a little misunderstanding.' Monsieur Pamplemousse was reluctant to divulge what had taken place between himself and Von Strudel, least of all to Gilbert Beaseley, who seemed to thrive on other people's business. He had already said more than he'd intended. Despite everything, and much against his will, he felt himself being drawn into the affair, his appetite well and truly whetted. If he intended taking his mission seriously the least said about it the better. Now that the initial shock of his first encounter with Von Strudel had worn off he had already made up his mind to stay, come what may. 'A confusion of identities, that is all.'

'Conversation with Von Strudel is never easy.' Beaseley took the hint and abruptly changed the subject. 'I heard about last night's kerfuffle. No ill effects, I trust?'

'Some stiffness, that is all. I was sitting far enough away to avoid the blast, and Montgomery managed to roll with the explosion. I saw him at breakfast this morning. Apart from a few strawberry pips embedded in his face, he seemed little the worse for his experience. At some point they will need to be removed.'

'Rumours of sabotage are rife,' said Beaseley. 'It isn't the first thing that's happened. If you ask me, I think someone,

248

for reasons best known to himself, is trying to delay the production.'

'It was more spectacular than lethal. If the speed of the flame which preceded the explosion was anything to go by I suspect some form of *poudre brugère* – the "black powder" which is commonly used in the fireworks industry. Contained, if I am not mistaken, in the pepper pot.'

Beaseley gazed into the middle distance. 'In short, a rather upmarket version of the exploding cigar trick. An interesting theory. Now who on earth would want to do a thing like that? Montgomery wouldn't harm a fly.'

Monsieur Pamplemousse gazed at Gilbert Beaseley speculatively. He sounded genuinely sorry, and yet . . .

On his way back from the abortive meeting with Von Strudel, he had idly straightened the chair he had been sitting in the night before. It was the Capricorn in him. Something made him look under the seat cover and there he'd come across a small rubber cushion. The name of the maker was emblazoned across it: The Whoopie Joke Company, Chicago, Illinois. Relief had been tinged with mortification at being taken in by such a crude joke. He decided to store the information for the time being.

'I doubt if it was meant for Montgomery,' said Monsieur Pamplemousse. 'Apparently it was the first time he had ever made the dish. Normally Von Strudel insists on finishing it off himself. It is his party piece and he is rather proud of it. I suspect Montgomery was a little heavy-handed with the *mouli.*'

Pointedly picking up a copy of a child's version of the Bible he had been reading, he removed a bookmark and opened it at a point where the Easter Story was about to begin. Despite the news that his services as Food Adviser were to all intents and purposes redundant, professional pride made him want to go over the details of the Last Supper one more time.

'Would you care for an up-to-date run-down on today's latest piece of gossip – as at 09.55 this morning?' It was a rhetorical question. Without leaving time for a reply, Gilbert Beaseley pulled up a chair. Monsieur Pamplemousse heaved an inward sigh as he lowered his book again. He gave a non-committal shrug. He had enough on his mind as it was without worrying about the problems of others.

'If you think I am up to it.' He caught sight of some ants on the ground near his feet. One of them was carrying off a breakfast crumb. Relatively speaking it must have weighed a ton; the size of a caber.

'The "Golden Proboscis" has received a nasty letter. It came with this morning's mail.'

'*Le Nez d'Or*?

'Monsieur Parmentier, *parfumier extraordinaire;* inventor of XS. A rare bird indeed. A man of exquisite taste and possessor of a very unique talent. A man blessed with the ability to remember and identify something in the region of 3,000 different odours. There are only about a dozen others like him in the whole world. Their names never appear on the label, but without them the perfume industry, the top end of it anyway – the part that doesn't rely on chemical substitutes – would collapse overnight.

'I consider myself lucky if I manage to identify one smell at a time. Add brandy and cointreau to my pastis, as is the current ghastly trend, and the old computer in my brainbox goes up in smoke. Utter confusion sets in.'

'What did the note say?'

'The very worst. Some person – or persons – unknown is or are threatening to cut it off.'

'It?'

'His olfactory organ. That organ without which he would be unable to function. Monsieur Parmentier is very unhappy, as well he might be. If I'd spent all those years nurturing my nose, treating it like some rare hothouse plant, keeping it clear of draughts, never going out of my depth in a swimming pool in case the change in pressure affected my sinuses, spraying it morning and night with lightly salted water instead of having a good old-fashioned wash, and then some idiot appeared on the scene threatening to remove it, I'd feel pretty pissed off. It's like having an oil well in your back garden and waking up one morning only to find it's about to run dry.'

'But is he not insured?'

'A very down-to-earth, practical French attitude, if I may say so. Naturally he is insured. But what good does that do anyone? The formula for a perfume is not something you can commit to paper.'

'You mean without Monsieur Parmentier the whole thing would fall apart?'

'His loss would be a disaster. Worse than an opera singer losing his voice. The original formula for XS is a closely guarded secret. Chemical analysis may reveal the basic ingredients, but it won't show how they are put together. Once the current stocks are gone, repeating them will be a major problem. You can't say "take a ton of rose petals or half a ton of this or that, plus a pound of the other". Crops vary for all sorts of reasons; the weather, the time of day when they are picked; Jasmine, for example, needs to be gathered early in the day, ideally before dawn. Ensuring continuity is an art in itself.'

Beaseley broke off as a messenger came roaring up on a scooter and handed him a note. He scanned it briefly, then gave a nod. 'We'll be there.'

'Isn't it delightful,' he remarked to Monsieur Pample-mousse. 'Only in the film business would they call a messenger a gofer – "go for this – go for that . . ." We have received a summons. The "dailies" – yesterday's rushes – are about to be shown.'

'I am included?'

'That's what it says. I told you not to take any notice about getting the sack. Reinstatement is usually swift and painless.'

Monsieur Pamplemousse gave another sigh – audible this time. He marked the place in his book and excused himself while he put it in the trailer for safe keeping.

'It'll be worth going if only to see a minor miracle take place,' called Beaseley. 'I'll wager there won't be a car or a telephone pole or an electric cable or a television aerial in sight. Believe me, that isn't easy. You may think you're out in the wilds, but take a closer look – civilisation is never very far away.'

As they passed Mangetout's trailer they heard the sound of raised voices, interspersed with bleeps.

Beaseley made a face. 'The path of true love never did run smooth. Mangetout doesn't take kindly to the sight of a three-year-old infant mewling and puking in its nurse's arms. The dreaded child has been banished along with Miss Sweden to another caravan. Brother Angelo has taken umbrage. That was the cause of all the fuss yesterday evening.'

'Mangetout and Brother Angelo? But she must be old enough to be his mother.'

'Even worse,' said Beaseley. 'She's the mother of the child.'

Monsieur Pamplemousse stopped in his stride. 'That is not possible.'

'That's probably what they thought at the time. Medically speaking, the odds must have been very much against it. A minor miracle in itself – one for *The Guinness Book of Records*. I looked it up and the last incumbent for the Oldest Mother entry was a Mrs Kistler of Oregon, who was a mere 57+. Brother Angelo and Mangetout aren't exactly in an Abelard and Heloïse situation, but it does make for an interesting subplot in the circumstances. It adds a certain air of incest to the casting. Ron's sponsors would skin him alive if they knew, not to mention the fans. Talking of which, we shall be blessed with several thousand of them over the next few days.'

'They are being allowed in?'

'It's one of Von Strudel's happier thoughts. In some ways it is a stroke of genius. Having Brother Angelo play the lead means Von Strudel has immediate access to his fan clubs and as many extras as he needs. Tomorrow they descend on us ready to line the streets of Les Baux for the filming of the Crucifixion. They would probably carry out the deed for free as well if they knew the truth.'

'All for the sake of a bottle of XS!'

'All for the sake of a bottle of XS. I'll tell you something else about the perfume business. On the one hand it is a very precise science and on the other hand it is an extraordinary hit and miss affair. Enormous risks are taken. Rumour has it that when XS was first presented it was one of some thirty samples. The owner of the company – he whose name on a product causes women's hearts to beat faster and men to reach for their wallets – blanched at the sight of so many bottles laid out before him. He could have cried out *Sacré bleu!* or even *Nom d'un nom*, but instead he threw up his hands, pointed vaguely in the direction of the twenty-third bottle, and uttered the immortal words *c'est excessive!* Which is how it got its name.'

'Do you believe that?'

'It's a nice story – the kind of story you *want* to believe. Repeated often enough – and it will be if the Press Office are doing their stuff – it will become true.

'Anyway, it's in the best Coco Chanel tradition. She is reputed to have chosen No. 5 out of ten sample perfumes because it happened to be her lucky number. She lived on the royalties until the day she died.'

As they reached the viewing theatre, Gilbert Beaseley ushered Monsieur Pamplemousse up some steps and into a large air-conditioned room. Some ten or a dozen velvet-covered armchair seats faced an uncurtained screen on either side of which were two enormous loudspeakers. At the back of the room there was a small sound console and behind that a projection booth. There was a cabinet in one corner on top of which stood an espresso coffee machine and a jug of iced water. The walls were lined with velvet drapes. The ceiling was faced with non-reflecting material and there was thick carpet underfoot. Not surprisingly, voices sounded muted. More than half of the seats were already occupied and Beaseley performed the introductions.

There was hollow laughter when Monsieur Pamplemousse gave the official reason for his presence. An American sound engineer suggested he might start by advising the unit caterers. The second unit director echoed his agreement.

'When I leave here I'm gonna have *ratatouille* withdrawal symptoms.'

The subject of Monsieur Parmentier's letter came up. Various theories were propounded. Anne-Marie, the key make-up artist – dark, green-eyed and unmistakably French –

254

suggested it might be the work of a rival perfume company. Láslo, the Hungarian art director, threw up the thought that it might be one of the local growers who'd been done out of a contract. More and more distilleries were turning to the Middle East for their flower crops. The French director of photography, Jean-Paul, was convinced it was the work of a religious group – possibly Christian fundamentalists. The continuity girl – who could have been German – disagreed. It was the Jews. In a matter of moments a multilingual argument was in full spate.

Beaseley led the way to two vacant seats at the back of the room.

'All this is a bit of a waste of time,' he murmured. 'They're giving up on the Ark. I managed to talk them out of it last night.'

Monsieur Pamplemousse glanced at his companion with renewed respect. There must be more to him than he'd imagined.

'Have you ever thought about it?' Beaseley went on. 'I mean – *really* thought about it? What the Ark must have been like. All those animals packed in one small boat, crapping and fornicating all over the place. It's the last setting I'd choose for a perfume advert. You can hardly repeat the "Someone isn't using XS" gag.'

The buzz of conversation died down as Von Strudel entered with his 'fixer' and took his seat in the front row.

'I am ready for ze *Bildmusters,*' he announced.

The fixer clicked his fingers and an unseen hand dimmed the lights.

A leader appeared on the screen followed by a shot of the clapper board. The name of the production, the director and the cameraman filled the top half. The scene and take number were chalked on the bottom section.

'Has anyone thought,' whispered Monsieur Pample-mousse, 'that XS wouldn't even have existed in those days. Distillation wasn't invented until the tenth century.'

'Ssh!' Beaseley put a finger to his lips as the hinged clapper stick came down with a sharp crack, providing a start mark for sound synchronisation. 'You'll do us all out of a job. Ours is not to reason why. Ours but to carry out such crumbs of ideas as the agency people throw at us.'

'So why are we bothering to watch?'

'Questions. Questions. Quite honestly, I don't know. There are moments in life when it's easier to toe the party line.'

Monsieur Pamplemousse sank back into his seat and watched while a succession of shots, each with its separate number, came and went. Water from a rain machine started up. There were shots of the Ark's prow. Shots of the stern. Shots of the gangway. Close-ups of Noah and his wife. Their three sons and their wives were nowhere to be seen. Retake followed retake. The reasons multiplied. Fluffed lines. Passing aircraft. A flock of birds when there should only have been two. There was enough film to make fifty commercials. The sky grew darker and all the time the rain came down, unremitting in its intensity. Whatever else one might say about Mrs Noah, she was certainly earning her money in one respect. She looked soaked to the skin.

'What about the animals?' whispered Monsieur Pample-mousse.

He felt Beaseley's pitying glance. 'This is the cinema. The quickness of the cut deceives the eye. The animals are all over the world. Cairo, Washington, Tokyo – you name it. They get edited in later. Only the Ark is here and that, as we all know, has its problems. Imagine what it would be like if you had animals too.'

'And the doves?'

'They belong to one of Jean-Paul's many cousins.'

'Of course,' said Monsieur Pamplemousse, drily.

'Halt!

'Hold it!' The fixer, whose sole function appeared to be that of acting as Von Strudel's shadow, repeating his words and translating them when necessary into an understandable language, echoed the command.

'Merde!' Jean-Paul's voice came out of the darkness. 'I said to lose that shot.'

The editor apologised.

'We're coming to the end anyway,' said the second unit director. 'That's when we ran out of doves. Remember? Fifteen Goddamn doves and they all disappeared!'

Monsieur Pamplemousse, who had been contemplating trying to catch up on some lost sleep, sat up, the memory of the look on Pommes Frites' face the night before still fresh in his mind: the look, the feathers. It was no wonder he hadn't seemed particularly hungry.

'Umrollen.'

'Roll back.'

He sank back into his seat as a familiar image filled the screen. Caught during a break in the filming, Pommes Frites was standing on three legs gazing in astonishment at something just out of frame to his right. As the camera zoomed back to a wider angle, a palm tree which had been lying on the ground a short distance away, pivoted on its base until it was in vertical juxtaposition with the principal subject. Through the magic of reverse projection the reason for Pommes Frites' stance became clear, as a stream of water emerged from the tree and made its way rapidly back to source. The action completed, Pommes Frites replaced his nearside rear leg on the ground and backed out of shot.

'Halt!'
'Hold it!'
'Vroll!'
'Roll!'

Pommes Frites re-entered the picture, eyed the palm tree for a brief moment, then lifted his leg and stood contemplating his immediate surroundings while he obeyed the call of nature. As the tree began to topple over he did a double-take. The camera zoomed in again to show him registering a mixture of alarm and disbelief.

'So much for *papier-mâché* trees,' said someone. 'They'll never replace the real thing.'

Láslo, the designer, gave a groan.

'Not a very good advert for the local water,' murmured Beaseley. 'It confirms my faith in Ricard.'

They watched as Pommes Frites continued on his way. Recovering from the shock, he gave the fallen tree a tentative sniff. Then, having ignored what was obviously a genuine almond tree in favour of conserving his supplies for another occasion, he headed towards the Ark. Whether by accident or design, he was halfway up the gangway when the rain machine started up again.

'Halt!'
'Hold it!'
'Beleuchten!'
'Lights!'

A large digital clock above the screen showed that from beginning to end the whole sequence had lasted no more than a minute and a half, but during that time Pommes Frites had run the gamut of his emotions. Dignity in repose had given way to alarm and bewilderment. Guilt became friendly interest, then on an instant changed to shock as the rain came down. Disappointment and disgust with mankind in general

258

had permeated his visage as he made his final exit down the gangplank. It was Lewis Milestone's Judge Hardy combined with the natural elegance of Ronald Colman. It was Olivier at Agincourt. At moments it recalled both Edward G. Robinson and W. C. Fields. Edward Everitt Horton sprang to mind; there were shades of Walter Matthau.

Only reproach and a desire for revenge were absent from his face, neither qualities being part of Pommes Frites' make-up, but by the time he had disappeared from view the house lights were on and Von Strudel was addressing the others.

'I vant zat *hund*.

'But . . .'

'No buts . . . Zat *hund* has star quality. I vent him in ze picture. Zat *hund* is *ein* genius.

'So ve write him in, huh?' He glared across the room at someone who'd had the temerity to point out a basic problem with his thinking.

'Here we go again.' Beaseley looked gloomy. 'I knew it was all too easy. Never write for films. It's like throwing your nearest and dearest to the wolves. If you don't like watching your brain child being butchered first thing every day, forget it.'

An argument broke out near the front over the ethics of using a dog in a biblical scene.

'Wait till the network committees back in the States get to see it!'

'It'll be hacked to pieces.'

'You won't even have to go that far. How about the agency?'

Von Strudel's voice overrode them all.

'Who says Christ did not have *ein* dog? Ver is it written in the Bible that Christ did not have *ein* dog? Show me ver it is vritten. Zat *hund* vill provide the missing link. He vill bind ze whole thing together. Ve vill have him appear in every episode. Zer vill be continuity.'

'Bloodhounds weren't around then.' It was clutching at straws time on someone's part.

'Send him to make-up. Tell them ze problem. By the time zey have finished with him no one vill know him from *ein Wiener Schnitzel.*

'Vat is his name? Ver can we contact him?'

'His name is Pommes Frites!' Monsieur Pamplemousse felt it was high time he made a contribution, however slight.

'That'll have to be charged.' The fixer added his mite to the argument. 'You know what that means in America? French fries. That's something you get on the side.'

'Who cares what he's called?' said a voice. 'It's a commercial. There won't be any credits.'

'What about when he goes up for his awards?' It was hard to tell whether or not Láslo was being serious. Monsieur Pamplemousse suspected not.

'What awards?'

'Who knows? He could get his paw-mark in the cement outside Grauman's. You can't say it was made by a Pommes Frites.'

'Think of Lassie.' It was the second unit director. 'Lassie started off as a Laddie and before that he was called Pal.'

'How about Pommes Nouvelles?'

'Or Duchesse? It doesn't have to be a he.'

'In that case, how about Dauphine? Dauphine would be great.'

'Does he have a ten percenter?'

'Ja! Ver is his agent?' Von Strudel gazed around the room.

'I think he means you,' murmured Beaseley. 'Now's your big moment.'

Monsieur Pamplemousse rose to his feet. 'I think there is something you should all know,' he said. 'I am not, as it happens, Pommes Frites' agent. He is perfectly capable of looking after himself. But I think I know him sufficiently well to speak on his behalf and to say that under no circumstances would he agree to changing his name – let alone his sex. As for his appearing in a film advertising perfume, that is up to him. He may or may not agree to it. If he does not want to take part, then nothing on earth will persuade him otherwise. If you wish to contact me in order to discuss the matter further, you will find me in my quarters. I am at your disposal.'

Utter silence prevailed as Monsieur Pamplemousse made his way towards the exit. As he closed the door behind him he heard Von Strudel's voice.

'Who vas that person? Ver have I seen zat man before? Vy does he keep buggingk me?'

Back in his trailer, Monsieur Pamplemousse picked up the telephone and dialled his office number. He was put through to the Director's office straight away.

'Monsieur Pamplemousse? It is Véronique. *Comment ça va?*

'*Non, Monsieur* . . . the Director is not here. He left a little while ago for an unknown destination . . . *Oui, une destination inconnue* . . .

'*Non, Monsieur* . . . he did not even tell me . . .'

There was a pause. 'Monsieur Pamplemousse . . .'

'*Oui*, Véronique?'

'Perhaps I should not say this, but before he left he sent out for a bottle of *huile de soleil* – a large one – and he took with him a case containing his summer clothes. I think it is possible he may be heading south.'

'Aah! Ah, I see.' Monsieur Pamplemousse thanked the Director's secretary and then replaced the receiver.

He picked up his book and removed the marker. It was the beginning of Jesus' last week on earth. He was about to set out with his disciples on their pre-ordained journey to Jerusalem.

Without being in the slightest bit blasphemous and on a totally different level, Monsieur Pamplemousse couldn't help but sense a parallel in his own life. The news that *Monsieur le Directeur* had set out from Paris for an unknown destination had more than a touch of inevitability about it too.

lt was after midday – Jesus had just acquired a donkey and her foal in Bethfage – when Monsieur Pamplemousse happened to glance up from his book, distracted by movement outside his window. Halfway between his own quarters and those of Mangetout a man in blue overalls was screwing a name board on to the door of one the spare trailers he'd noticed the previous evening.

Opening *Le Guide's* issue case, he removed the Leitz Trinovid binoculars and directed them towards the board. As the man stood back to admire his handiwork, the words POMMES FRITZ swam into sharp focus. So Von Strudel had got his way after all: willingly or unwillingly, Pommes Frites was setting out on the road to stardom, nobbled while his master's back was turned, and was exchanging his usual sleeping accommodation on the floor for a bed of his own. And he had succeeded in keeping his own name – more or less.

Monsieur Pamplemousse lowered his glasses. He was about to reach for the telephone handset when he hesitated. The whole thing was utterly ridiculous. Talented though he undoubtedly was, there were some things beyond even Pommes Frites' capabilities. Answering the telephone was one of them.

What was it Beaseley had said? 'You don't have to be crazy to work in films, but it helps'? Clearly, as a disease, it was catching.

On the other hand – he checked Pommes Frites' number against a plan on the wall, then reached for the telephone again – on the other hand, it was tough at the top and already Pommes Frites could be feeling a trifle lonely, wondering perhaps if he had made the right decision. A single ring might well provide a much- needed crumb of comfort; a sign that someone, somewhere, was thinking of him.

4
THE LAST SUPPER

They began to arrive in the late afternoon of the day before the shooting of the Crucifixion; by van, by car and on foot. Some were dressed in shorts and sleeveless tops, others in factory-frayed, cut-off jeans and T-shirts bearing the motto 'Brotherly Love' stencilled below a picture of their hero.

The more enterprising, aware of the fact that they would be paid extra if they came in costume, wore the dress of the period. The women were mostly clad in long, plain black or dark-blue gowns, with a wide leather girdle round the waist. They wore a square piece of folded cloth of the same colour on their head, either hanging down behind or used as a turban. Others wore plain, homespun woollen dresses, relieved by coloured handwork at the neck.

Some of the men – who were mostly older and in the minority – wore loincloths, often supporting a *bedon* which was far from *petit;* many were bearded, and almost all wore thonged leather sandals. The more adventurous sported priestly robes of blue-edged purple over linen breeches and undershirt. The tinkling of bells as they walked could be clearly heard across the valley.

They converged as if by common consent on an area just outside the perimeter of the location site. Tents were erected. Smoke began to rise from camp fires. It was like a remake of the trek to the Promised Land.

Using a borrowed lighting stand as a support, Monsieur Pamplemousse set up his Leica and began shooting off a reel of FP4. With the mountains in the background and the smoke and the Brueghel-like wandering figures it cried out for black and white. It would make a good illustration for an article in *Le Guide's* staff magazine. Calvet, the editor of *L'Escargot,* might welcome it as a change from Guilot's endless articles on hiking or one of Bernard's treatises on the cultivation of the rose.

'Setting up in opposition?' Beaseley materialised beside him, smelling of pastis and after-shave.

'Hardly.'

'It's quite a sight. Rather awe-inspiring in a way.'

'It would be interesting to know what motivates them.' Monsieur Pamplemousse moved his makeshift tripod a little to the left and changed the lens to a narrow angle.

'Word gets around,' said Beaseley. 'It's something to focus their energies on. All the same, some of them must have travelled thousands of miles to be here. I can't see myself doing it. It makes me feel old.'

'Don't tell me,' said Monsieur Pamplemousse wrily. 'Policemen are starting to look younger.'

'Chief constables are starting to look younger,' said Beaseley gloomily.

Monsieur Pamplemousse glanced at him. 'With respect, you are no longer seventeen.'

'Neither are a good many of that lot,' said Beaseley. 'Take away the teeny-boppers and the average age is higher than you'd think.'

'Perhaps,' said Monsieur Pamplemousse simply, 'Brother Angelo is blessed with that mysterious ingredient known as "star" quality. It is a God-given attribute. You either have it or you don't.'

'I suppose that's why he got the part.' After his exposition of the night before Beaseley sounded less sure of himself, as though he were having second thoughts. 'You're right, though. Whatever it is, our Ron's got more than his fair share. I happen to know from the person who looks after his fan mail that all over the world – from Winnipeg to Wellington, from Florence to Folkestone – there are women awaiting his call. They have a bag packed and stashed away under the bed ready to leave home at a moment's notice.'

'That is true?'

'It's not only true, but I have a feeling my informant wouldn't mind dropping everything herself if the chance arose.'

'Some people need to live out their fantasies with a person who, deep down, they know will never be theirs,' said Monsieur Pamplemousse. 'It avoids the moment of truth.'

'I wouldn't go so far as to say that,' said Beaseley. 'By all accounts Ron has done his bit towards making other people's fantasies come true. Whenever he gives a concert he hands his manager a list of the ones in the front row he'd like to stay behind. Most of them are only too happy to oblige. Who knows what exposure to hot Provençal nights will do to some of those out there. There have already been several attempts at breaking into the site just to be near him and it isn't even dark yet. I fear the worst.'

Monsieur Pamplemousse listened with only half an ear. He was concentrating instead on trying to take a picture with the minimum number of vehicles in shot. It wasn't easy. More were arriving every minute. Even as he checked the focus on what he thought would be his final shot, a car rather larger and more opulent-looking than the rest entered the frame. It disappeared momentarily behind an outcrop of rocks, then came to an abrupt halt as it emerged on the other side and came up against a veritable wall of human bodies, completely ruining his composition.

It was a Citroën DX25. A black Citroën DX25.

Monsieur Pamplemousse's heart sank as he watched the driver climb out of the car and, after engaging some of the crowd in conversation, turn and begin heading in the direction of the location, signing autographs as he went. The mannerisms, the walk, the air of authority were all too familiar.

'Is anything wrong?' asked Beaseley.

Monsieur Pamplemousse pressed the shutter for luck. 'Not really. It is just someone I would rather not see.'

'Ah, the world is full of those,' said Beaseley sympathetically. 'Talking of which reminds me of Von Strudel. We have just been locked in mortal combat. The good news is I may never be asked to work on a film script again.'

'It is that serious?' Monsieur Pamplemousse reloaded his camera and then started packing up the equipment, slotting the various items into their allotted places in the tray which was part of *Le Guide's* issue case. He couldn't help but feel rather more concerned about his own affairs than Beaseley's. It was bad news if the Director had taken it into his head to pay him a visit. Any hopes of a quiet few days would be gone. He should have realised what was afoot from his telephone conversation with Véronique.

He forced himself to return to his companion. 'Did you get the menu for the Last Supper? I asked the gofer to make sure it reached you before work started.'

'I did, thank you very much,' said Beaseley. 'Apart from the lamb – I feel it is a moot point as to whether it would have been roasted or boiled – I couldn't fault it. However,

I'm afraid that's where the trouble started. It seems that Mangetout is a Vegan.'

'Mangetout?' Monsieur Pamplemousse came down to earth with a bump. 'But surely the Virgin Mary wasn't present at the Last Supper?'

'My words exactly,' said Beaseley. 'That was when I ran foul of her agent – an American gentleman from one of the less salubrious areas of New York. He has never learned the meaning of the word "No"; although, in fairness, I suppose that's what makes him a good agent.

'You know what he said? "That's her boy up there. You think she's going to let him be all alone on his last night?"'

'Picture the scene,' continued Beaseley. 'A patch of hilly ground in the Camargue. A crowd of people are gathered round a room which, for practical reasons, has only three sides made out of canvas and plywood to resemble a house in Jerusalem circa AD30. The fourth side is peopled by some of the highest paid technicians in the world, all set to go. They have the benefit of the greatest lighting engineer in the business overhead, but filming being a belt and braces operation, arc lights are standing by at the ready lest He should take umbrage, as well He might when He hears what's going on down below. The Heavens could grow dark.

'Seeing that something was expected of me, I made what I still think is a valid point.

'"How," I asked, "does she know it's his last night?" Do you know what the answer was?'

Monsieur Pamplemousse shook his head.

'"It ain't negotiable. It's in her contract. Where he goes – she goes." It seems Mangetout is insisting on having her part built up. Short of having her say things like "Watch out – the plates are hot," or "Anyone for mint sauce?" I'm afraid my mind went a total blank on the subject. "If that's the way it is," I said to her agent, "why don't you play the one who isn't wearing XS? You can be Judas and all the other agents can be the rest of the disciples – then everyone will be happy." As a suggestion it went down like a lead balloon.'

'But the whole thing is monstrous. *Incroyable*. It is little short of *sacrilège*.'

'I take heart,' said Beaseley, 'with something the editor whispered to me as I made my exit. "There's always the cutting-room floor." The whole episode, from the opening establishing shot until the villain of the piece, Judas Iscariot, is revealed, lasts less than a minute. The cameraman's no happier than I am – he's having to shoot Mangetout through gauze.'

'What did Brother Angelo have to say about it all?'

' "****ing ****!" I quote. Then he buried his head in his hands. Which sums up my feelings too. I have an idea that particular clause in Mangetout's contract wasn't of his making, nor that of his own agent.

'Come,' Beaseley beckoned to Monsieur Pamplemousse. 'I suggest we take a little stroll in the general direction of Jerusalem and you can see for yourself. Unless, of course, you want to stay and see your friend.'

Monsieur Pamplemousse's moment of hesitation was but a token gesture. 'I shall be happy to join you. If I stay I may end up saying something I regret.'

'Heaven forbid!' said Beaseley. 'Follow me. But don't say I didn't warn you.'

Monsieur Pamplemousse and Beaseley arrived on the set during a break in filming. Jesus and his disciples were seated round a long table in what purported to be the upper room of a house. The beginnings of a mock staircase to what

269

would normally have been the stables in the room below led nowhere. At the head of the table, Brother Angelo was hardly recognisable with his moustache and beard. Mangetout stood a little behind him, but just out of shot, holding a dish of lamb. She looked decidedly unhappy.

It was all much as Beaseley had described it: Rome might not have been built in a day, but a very passable replica of a street in old Jerusalem had been constructed overnight. Façades of houses were supported from behind by scenery props kept in place by weights and sandbags. Scaffolding held up the Palace of the High Priest, Caiaphas, which towered above everything else. Giant white screens reflected the sunlight on to the set, filling in the shadows. Cables snaked in every direction.

As with all film sets, technicians and hangers-on seemed to outnumber the actors by something like ten to one. Each had their part to play; all were ready to do their bit at a moment's notice.

The make-up girl Monsieur Pamplemousse had seen during the screening of the rushes – Anne-Marie – darted in with a palette-shaped board and some brushes. She dabbed Brother Angelo's brow dry of sweat, repaired the damage with a dusting of powder, automatically removed a strand of hair from his shoulder, then darted off again. A male dresser wielding a clothes brush looked put out. A demarcation line had been crossed.

Monsieur Pamplemousse couldn't help but notice that Mangetout looked more than put out. Perhaps other demarcation lines had been crossed as well?

Beaseley noticed it too. 'I wouldn't like to be in Ron's shoes,' he murmured. 'I bet he doesn't get "Happiness Is . . ." sung to him over breakfast. She's jealous as hell of anything in skirts that moves.'

Someone called for quiet.

Monsieur Pamplemousse glanced around for Pommes Frites and spotted him with his wrangler in a mock-up stable area near to where Mangetout was standing. Half hidden by a lamp, he was probably waiting for a cue. One thing was certain – if he hadn't yet had lunch he must be feeling hungry.

The cameraman climbed aboard his dolly and the sound engineer racked out the microphone, swinging it up and down, testing for shadows.

'I thought the Last Supper took place after dark,' whispered Monsieur Pamplemousse.

'It will by the time they've finished with it,' said Beaseley. 'Day for night filming. Filters.' He put a finger to his lips.

Von Strudel was sitting nearby, a green eye-shield pulled down over his brow, his wooden leg resting on another chair. It was hard to tell if he was awake or not. He raised his right hand.

'Roll camera.' His fixer translated the signal into words.

After a few seconds the camera operator called 'Speed.'

'Mark it.'

The clapper boy ran in front of the lens and held up his board.

'Scene twenty-three. Take seven.'

'Action.'

As the camera started to dolly in there was the distant drone of an approaching aeroplane.

'*Scnitt!*' Von Strudel raised his left hand.

'Cut!' The fixer echoed his command.

Von Strudel glared up at the sky. He placed the megaphone to his lips. '*Dummkopf*'

Everyone waited patiently for the plane to pass. When all was quiet the whole procedure began again.

'Roll camera.'

'Speed.'

'Mark it.'

The clapper boy ran on. 'Scene twenty-three. Take eight.'

'Action.'

The camera began to dolly in once again for the opening establishing shot and then stopped. The sun had moved and there was a shadow which hadn't been there before. In trying to avoid it the camera operator was shooting off. There was also a troublesome reflection.

After a brief discussion with the director of photography, the set designer had a word with the unit manager. A carpenter appeared and added a strip of plywood to one side of the third wall. A scenic artist carrying a giant pot and a huge brush followed in his wake, splashing paint around with an air of abandon. In a moment the wood was transformed into stone. It looked as though the rocks had been there for ever.

Jean-Paul called for someone to 'Chinese' a barn door. The lighting gaffer called across to the best boy, who reached up with a pole and knocked the metal covering of a lamp through ninety degrees so that a vertical strip of light became horizontal. It was another world, and like all other worlds it had its own language. It would have been hard to justify the arrangement to a time and motion study person, but then time and motion people didn't make films.

Someone else ambled on to the set and sprayed a dish with dulling liquid.

The camera operator announced there was a hair in the gate. He climbed off the dolly and began removing a large soundproofing blimp covering the camera. The focus puller seized the opportunity to reload the film.

'All right, everyone. Take five.'

A buzz of conversation went up all around as those who weren't involved relaxed. Mangetout put her plate down on a stool near Brother Angelo and passed a comment. He gave a shrug and she retired into the shadows. It was easy to see why. Daylight didn't lend enchantment.

The wrangler said something to Pommes Frites, then left him to his own devices. Pommes Frites hesitated for a moment before settling down to await his next instructions. He was wearing his enigmatic expression and it was impossible to tell what, if anything, he was thinking. Monsieur Pamplemousse would have given a lot to know, but Pommes Frites seemed to be studiously avoiding his gaze – whether out of pique or guilt it was impossible to say, and before he had a chance to make the first move Beaseley took hold of his arm.

'Feel like a stroll?'

'*Une bonne idée.*'

They walked in silence for a while, picking their way in and out of the cables and equipment and groups of extras taking time off for a quick smoke.

'What gave them the idea?' asked Monsieur Pamplemousse idly as they finally reached open ground.

'You mean the Last Supper?'

'Not only that – the whole thing – using scenes from the Bible to sell perfume.'

'Don't ask me. I came in halfway through. I suppose it hasn't been done before. It's the ultimate. It has everything. Someone once said there are only six plots in the world and they are all in the Old Testament. Follow that, as they say.'

'But someone must have suggested it in the first place,' persisted Monsieur Pamplemousse.

'Who knows where ideas spring from?' said Beaseley. 'Normally it would start with the agency. A company entrusts itself to one of the big boys and relies on them to come up with ideas. Why do you ask?'

Monsieur Pamplemousse didn't really know. It was simply a little nagging question in the back of his mind. A tiny voice.

'It seems to have upset a lot of people.'

'You mean all the sniping that's been going on?'

Sniping was one way of putting it. Monsieur Pamplemousse felt he would have used a stronger word. Someone was trying to make a point and the method of doing it ranged from schoolboy practical jokes to verging on the deadly serious. So far no one had been injured, but there was always a first time. As far as he could make out there was a list as long as his arm of people who had it in for Von Strudel. Or, if not for Von Strudel himself, for those he represented. It was strange that so far no one had claimed responsibility.

'There must be simpler ways of making a commercial. Less likely to offend. Less costly.'

'We are talking films,' said Beaseley. 'Films, perfume and advertising – a lethal combination. Cost doesn't enter into it. I'll give you an example. Chanel never give out figures, but when they launched Egoïste Jean- Paul Goude was commissioned to make a thirty-second commercial featuring the Carlton Hotel in Cannes. He had a mock-up of it built in Brazil, flew everyone out there and took ten days over the shooting. The cost must have been horrendous. You might ask, why Brazil? Answer: because the Director decided the light was better.'

'And was it?'

'Possibly.'

'Would anyone have noticed the difference?'

'I doubt it. But the publicity which followed was worth its weight in gold. And that was nothing compared to this.

The column inches already written about XS would stretch from here to Grasse and back. Come up and see me some time and I'll show you my press cuttings.'

Beaseley caught the sidelong glance Monsieur Pamplemousse gave him.

'I was only joking,' he said hastily. 'The point I'm trying to make is that advertising is the stuff that dreams are made of – to misquote William Shakespeare. The life it pretends to portray doesn't, couldn't and probably should never exist. In my view it is responsible for a great many of the ills of this world, for it makes people restless for the so-called "better life". In that respect it offers up much the same thing as Brother Angelo, and there is about the same chance of achieving it.'

'It seems to me,' said Monsieur Pamplemousse, 'that a great many people would envy Brother Angelo.'

'Brother Angelo, perhaps,' said Beaseley. 'But is Ron Pickles happy? Not from all I've seen.

'As for choosing something simple, simple ideas are the hardest of all to come by. Anyway, it isn't such a bad notion. It's going back to basics. The Romans were into perfume in a big way. What did the Three Wise Men take with them as gifts when they visited Bethlehem after Jesus was born? Gold, frankincense and myrrh. Two out of three can't be bad. If Von Strudel had his way he would skip the gold and show them taking a bottle of XS as well. It's lucky no one's thought of it.'

'Mangetout is hardly my idea of the Virgin Mary,' said Monsieur Pamplemousse. 'Seen close to she is something of a disappointment.'

'Ravaged is the word,' said Beaseley. 'I agree it isn't exactly type-casting, but we all see things in our own way. With great respect to your lovely country and your good self, I suppose I've always seen Virgin Mary as being rather English – probably born somewhere near Guildford. In much the same way as I've always pictured Christ being British. A bit chauvinistic really. I daresay you people think he was French.'

'*Naturellement*,' said Monsieur Pamplemousse drily.

'Exactly. You could say that in choosing someone as unlikely as Mangetout nobody gets really upset because they know it isn't definitive and it still leaves them with their options open. Our heroine is mean, moody, magnificent and available – always has been. Did you know her real name is Haricot? Mangetout is much more apt. She devours anyone who comes near. I'm told that at one period in her career – when she was "resting" – she was known as Madame Flageolet.'

'And yet she decided to have Brother Angelo's baby.'

'Ron power,' said Beaseley. 'She knows he'd be off like a shot otherwise and she probably needs his money to keep her in the style to which she has become more than accustomed.'

As they arrived back on the set they heard Von Strudel's voice raised in anger. An argument appeared to be in progress between him and Brother Angelo.

'This bread,' said Brother Angelo, 'is ****ing awful. It tastes like ****. There's something ****ing wrong with it.'

Von Strudel raised the megaphone to his lips. 'You vill eat it und like it,' he bellowed. 'Zis is your chosen profession.'

'No it ****ing isn't!' Brother Angelo sounded equally incensed. 'And don't ****ing shout at me. I'm not * * * *ing deaf.'

Clearly an impasse had been reached. How long it would have gone on for or what possible solution might have been

276

arrived at, was hard to say, but attention was suddenly diverted by a cry from Mangetout.

'*Merde!*'

She held aloft an empty serving dish.

'*Le chien!*'

The delivery of the words *le chien* was on a par with the celebrated mouthing by Dame Edith Evans of the phrase 'a handbag' in *The Importance of Being Ernest*, but there the similarity ended. It was followed by a stream of invective which would have blown the fuses on Brother Angelo's bleeper had he been given the lines to say.

Gradually, as Mangetout's anger subsided, those around became aware of some singularly unpleasant noises coming from somewhere outside their line of vision. The cause became clear almost immediately as Pommes Frites tottered into view, his head held low, his legs looking as though they might give way at any moment. The sight of the empty plate in Mangetout's hand gave rise to fresh paroxysms. Unhappiness rubbed shoulders with both guilt and regret as he averted his gaze.

'The *lamm,*' shouted Von Strudel. 'Somevun has poisoned ze *lamm!*'

Brother Angelo gazed triumphantly round the assembly.

'What did I ****ing tell you?' he cried. 'It takes a ****ing dog to show you who's ****ing right. Now, do you ****ing believe me.'

Despite the glowing testimonial from such an unexpected source, Pommes Frites had the grace to look ashamed of himself as he made a beeline for the nearest bush and began another bout of retching.

It was difficult in the circumstances not to feel slightly holier than thou.

'The Lord giveth,' said Beaseley, 'and He taketh away. I'm glad I'm not a wrangler. I think there's some clearing up to be done.'

Having seen Pommes Frites safely to the unit vet's quarters at the other end of the location, Monsieur Pamplemousse made his way slowly back to his quarters.

Animal-like, Pommes Frites was already looking little the worse for his experience, but there was no sense in taking chances. The vet was English and a man of few words. He promised to keep Monsieur Pamplemousse informed if there was any change for the worse. Otherwise . . . a shrug indicated that he shared Pommes Frites' views on such matters. A few blades of grass would probably work wonders – were there any grass to be found. The patient would soon be back on solids. In the meantime he would keep him under observation.

Back in his trailer, Monsieur Pamplemousse decided it was time for *déjeuner*. He examined the contents of his refrigerator, and after a moment's thought removed four eggs and broke them into a bowl. It was hard to say how fresh they were, but they looked a good colour. He beat them lightly with a fork, then added some pepper and salt and put them to one side.

Rummaging around in the cupboard he found a lipped saucepan and a small basin. Pouring a little water into the saucepan, he put it on the hob to boil. The basin fitted snugly enough, the lip leaving enough of a gap for the steam to escape. It could have been made to measure. He dropped in a large knob of butter and while he waited for it to melt, added a few smaller shavings to the egg mixture.

It was at such moments that he missed Pommes Frites. He must have been very hungry to have taken the meat. It was quite out of character. Perhaps stardom was having an adverse effect on his behaviour. Either that, or some temporary aberration had caused him to think he was back working for *Le Guide*.

Opening a bottle of the Mont Caume, Monsieur Pamplemousse poured himself a glass. It looked as dark as night. Only in the south did you get quite such dark wine: a product of the late-ripening Mourvèdre vines. As the butter in the basin began to spread he tipped the egg mixture into the bowl and began stirring it with a plastic spatula.

Considering all the hazards and the things that could go wrong, it was a wonder films got made at all. Shadows, hairs in gates, passing aircraft – it wasn't until someone called for quiet that you realised just how noisy a place the world could be – doctored food; it wasn't surprising Von Strudel had gone over budget. Although you could hardly count the last episode as in any way normal.

Opening the tin of olives, he sliced several of them into small pieces. They were fat and succulent. He added them to the mixture. It was starting to thicken.

The vet had promised to examine the meat – if necessary he would get it analysed – but if Pommes Frites' rapid recovery was anything to go by, it didn't look like a serious attempt at poisoning. Another minor act of sabotage?

Monsieur Pamplemousse sat down to eat. The scrambled egg would have benefited from the addition of a little cream during its final stages and he would have given a lot for a slice or two of *baguette*, but . . . as he scraped up the remains with his fork he found himself wondering what had happened to the Director. Any guilt he might have felt about not searching him out and issuing an invitation to share the improvised lunch was quickly dispelled. The Director was more than able to look after number one. He was probably even now indulging himself in something much more exotic.

The telephone rang. It was Beaseley.

'I've found out the answer to your question.'

Monsieur Pamplemousse felt confused. He had no idea what Beaseley was on about.

'You know . . . where the idea for casting Brother Angelo came from. Apparently there was a period when he "trod the boards" for a while. Someone on the unit saw him back in the UK. He was appearing in a touring production of a musical called *Godspell*. He played Christ and by all accounts was a bit of a "wow". Slayed them in the aisles as they say, until disaster struck.'

'*Désastre?*'

'Unfortunately it happened during a matinée, so there were a lot of school parties. He was in the middle of doing some conjuring tricks when a piece of the scenery fell on his head. The air was so blue most of the children in the audience burst into tears and were whisked out by their teachers, the other half asked for their money back under the Trade Description Act. Question period the next day must have been rather fraught. It was shortly after that he was fitted with his bleeper.

'Anyway, whoever caught him in *Godspell* suggested him for the part and as soon as Von Strudel saw his photograph that was it.'

'As simple as that?'

'It's how lots of casting gets done. People play hunches. How's the invalid?'

'I think he will live.'

'Good. Tell him to keep taking the tablets.'

Monsieur Pamplemousse thanked Beaseley. He poured himself another glass of wine, then, after a moment's thought, checked in his diary and picked up the receiver again.

He dialled for an outside line, then 19 – a pause while he got International – then 44 for England. It was time he spoke to his old friend, Mr Pickering.

One of the very special things about Mr Pickering was that he was always the same. He was never taken aback. There were no questions asked. Niceties were kept to a minimum, but were no less sincere for all that. He was also extremely knowledgeable on a surprising number of subjects.

'*Oui. Ça va, ça va.*'

'Brother Angelo? The pop star? His real name is Ron Pickles.'

Monsieur Pamplemousse couldn't help smiling. As usual Mr Pickering was turning up trumps. 'You are one of his fans?'

'Not really. It stuck in my mind because of the similarity . . . Pickering . . . Pickles.'

'*Godspell?* Good Lord! I saw that in . . . let's see . . . must have been in the fifties.'

'Really? I hadn't realised it was still running anywhere. There are so many of them now. *Joseph and the Amazing Technicolor Dreamcoat. Jesus Christ – SuperStar.* I lose track. I shall have to ask my daughter.'

'Delightful. We enjoyed it enormously. David Essex. I've got the record somewhere.'

'Yes, of course. I'll ring you back.'

Monsieur Pamplemousse washed up the debris from his cooking- there was a notice pinned to the side of the cupboard concerning maid service when required – but he had no great desire to have someone else bustling about the trailer. No doubt the same person who had tidied up and made the bed that morning came every day, bringing fresh linen and replenishing the stores. Anything else could wait.

Searching out his binoculars, Monsieur Pamplemousse wandered outside for a breath of unconditioned air. If he stayed indoors for very much longer he would find himself lying back on the bed and that would be fatal. He felt at a loose end. Normally he could have walked it off with Pommes Frites, but that, for the moment at least, was a pleasure he would have to forgo. They would have a lot of catching up to do when things returned to normal. The thought gave rise to others – a bitter-sweet mixture; a certain nobility that he had not stood in Pommes Frites' way coupled with a feeling of being slightly let down.

He scanned the surrounding countryside. The area where all the extras had gathered was almost full. It looked as though most had now arrived and taken up temporary residence. Someone – it could have been the unit manager – was addressing a group of them through a loud hailer, but he was facing the other way and it was impossible to catch the words.

Monsieur Pamplemousse trained his binoculars on the Director's car. It was now almost hidden from view behind a sea of new arrivals.

He heard a voice behind him.

'Surveying the field, Pamplemousse?'

Monsieur Pamplemousse turned. Talk of the devil! As always the Director was dressed for the occasion. White Panama hat, dark glasses, a Pierre Cardin flowered shirt worn outside immaculately pressed designer jeans . . . his gaze travelled down . . . thonged leather sandals! Light began to dawn.

The Director pretended not to have noticed the reaction.

'All is well I trust?'

'I did not expect to see you here, *Monsieur*,' said Monsieur Pamplemousse coldly.

'I happened to have some business to attend to in this part of the world, so I thought I would drop by and see how things are going.'

And land a part in the film, thought Monsieur Pamplemousse.

'They are going much as I am sure you planned them to go, *Monsieur*,' he replied.

'Good. Good. I knew I could rely on you.' The Director rubbed his hands together. 'I am reliably informed that they could have need of an extra or two to mingle with the crowd, so I may stay on for a few days.'

Monsieur Pamplemousse contemplated his chief. It occurred to him that if the Director had been born an orange he would have been a remarkably thick-skinned one. A Navel rather than a Seville.

'You plan to stay, *Monsieur*? Accommodation is impossible to get. You told me so yourself.'

The Director brushed aside the problem. 'I have had a word with the unit manager. He has allocated me a trailer. My name has already been attached to the outside door.' He looked at his watch. 'Which reminds me, I must ring Véronique.'

Monsieur Pamplemousse waved towards the camp site.

'Then it is a good thing you have a trailer, *Monsieur*. I doubt if you will be able to use your car telephone. There is already a long queue.'

'What's that?' The Director gave a start. 'What did you say?'

'You can hardly blame them. Most have probably been away from home for a long time . . . America . . . Japan . . .

Pakistan. They will want to ring home. Doubtless, they will have a lot to relate.'

'*Sacré bleu!*'

'I am sure Madame Grante will understand when you explain, *Monsieur*. . . she is not as black as she is painted.'

Monsieur Pamplemousse's words fell on stony ground, as he thought they might. He wasn't normally given to playing practical jokes, but it must be catching. He had to admit to deriving a certain wry satisfaction over the speed at which the Director took off. Beaseley would appreciate it when he told him.

His own telephone was ringing when he opened the door to his trailer.

As suspected, Pommes Frites' indisposition boiled down to a matter of something he'd eaten. He could have told the vet that. What he wished to know was the precise cause of the trouble.

'Soup?' At first Monsieur Pamplemousse thought he had misheard.

'*Savon!*'

Soap! Everything had been laced with it. The lamb must have had a whole bar inside it. Slithers of soap had been inserted into the bread too. Brother Angelo was confined to his quarters. It was no wonder he had complained. There was a real Judas in the camp and no mistake. It was a sobering thought that if such a thing had happened in reality the whole course of history might have been changed.

Monsieur Pamplemousse had hardly replaced the receiver when the telephone rang again. This time it was Von Strudel.

'Zat *hund* of yours . . . Pommes Fritz . . .'

'*Oui*?' Monsieur Pamplemousse wondered what was coming.

'He is vorth his veight in gold. He is *ein* hero. Ze whole cast could have been poisoned. I am raising his salary.'

It was the first Monsieur Pamplemousse had heard talk of any kind of payment. Perhaps it really was time Pommes Frites got himself an agent. He made a mental note to get the matter in writing before Von Strudel heard the true reason for his indisposition.

'I hov decided to promote him. I am making him my personal food taster. From now on he vil taste everyzing before me.'

'Pommes Frites is a dog of many talents,' said Monsieur Pamplemousse, 'but I think you will find tasting food is his particular forte.' He nearly added the rider that if it meant tasting the output of Montgomery's kitchen, there wouldn't be much left for Von Strudel. On the other hand, if Von Strudel was dining *chez* La Baumanière that evening, the chances were they wouldn't take kindly to Pommes Frites being given first go at everything. He could foresee problems.

'Good. Zat is settled zen?'

'I am happy if Pommes Frites is happy,' said Monsieur Pamplemousse, staunchly. 'He is receiving medical attention after his last meal, so he may not be able to start work immediately, but recovery is often swift.' He hesitated. 'There is one other thing . . .'

'Ja.'

'I have been thinking . . . as my services as a food adviser are not keeping me fully occupied, and as the purpose of my being here is really to keep an eye on things, I wonder if it would be possible to combine the two during the shooting of the Crucifixion. It is the last time anyone will have an opportunity . . .'

Even as he spoke, Monsieur Pamplemousse realised he was laying himself open to a charge of failing miserably in his duty over the latest incident, and he was fully prepared for an explosion at the other end of the line, but to his relief he could almost feel Von Strudel beaming at the thought.

'You know somezing. You are *ein* good man. I liked you the first time I saw you. Vy? Because you stood up to me. You tell ze truth. You don't know vat it is like to be surrounded all your life by "Ja *Herrs*".'

Monsieur Pamplemousse didn't offer an answer and clearly none was expected.

'If you like I will give you *ein* part in ze film. You can vear *eine* galabiah and you can mingle mit ze crowd. Better still,' inspiration struck, 'you can be on zee route. You can be *ein* peanut seller. Zat vay no one vill suspect you. No one suspects peanut sellers.'

Ignoring the temptation to ask why, Monsieur Pamplemousse ventured to push his luck once again. 'May I have an assistant?'

'Of course. Have *zvei, drei, vier.* Take as many as you vould like. Phone ze casting director. Nothing must go vrong. I am relying on you.'

'One will be quite sufficient,' said Monsieur Pamplemousse. 'And I know just the man.'

His conscience was beginning to prick him. At the time he had made up the story about the car telephone almost without thinking. It had seemed like rough justice for the cavalier way in which the Director had plotted his being in Les Baux. Now that honour had been settled, the least he could do was make sure his chief got a part.

The last call of the day was again incoming. It was Mr Pickering.

'Sorry it's taken me so long . . . Not very good news, I'm afraid. *Godspell* hasn't been done professionally in years. It isn't even published in script form. Due for a revival.

'I can get hold of what they call a "perusal" copy if you like. You can have it on loan for a month if that's any help.'

'I don't think I shall be mounting a production,' said Monsieur Pamplemousse.

'No? Well, if you change your mind, you have only to ask. Rum business. You may be interested to know that in England the current odds against a Second Coming are a thousand to one.'

'How about the reappearance of Elvis Presley?' asked Monsieur Pamplemousse.

'The same.'

'And Ron Pickles?'

'I think the bookmakers are hedging their bets. Hope it doesn't upset your calculations . . .'

'*Oui.* Same to you.'

'Give my regards to Doucette. *Bonne chance.*'

Monsieur Pamplemousse replaced the receiver and gazed at it thoughtfully for a moment or two.

He wasn't sure if it upset any of his calculations or not. He didn't have many to upset. But if what Pickering said were true, then either Brother Angelo was a congenital liar, or he must have wanted to be in the commercial very badly indeed; badly enough to have enlisted the aid of an accomplice. It would be interesting to know exactly who in the company had suggested him for the part in the first place.

5
THE CRUCIFIXION

It was the last Friday before the start of the August holiday and there were ROUTE BARRÉE signs everywhere. Traffic in both directions on the winding D27A leading to Les Baux was at a standstill. Tempers outside the car park were frayed to breaking point. Coach drivers, their passengers pressing downcast faces against the inside of the windows, shouted at all and sundry as they tried in vain to back their vehicles. Lorry drivers, who had merely been taking a short cut, sat with folded arms. Car horns sounded. Gendarmes barked instructions. Whistles blew. Bedlam reigned supreme.

Monsieur Pamplemousse could almost feel the waves of dislike bordering on hatred as he wormed his way up the centre of the only wide section of road and, having shown his pass, was waved on his way by a poker-faced gendarme, oblivious to all but the appropriate signature on a piece of paper. He could hardly blame the other drivers. Most of them had probably come a long way hoping to arrive early and beat the crowds.

Les Baux was closed to anyone not involved in the filming. Presumably someone in authority had failed to pass on the news far enough afield. To be practical, it was hard to see how they could have done so, given the probable vagueness as to when it would actually take place, but explaining that to those who were being refused entry wasn't easy.

He drove straight through the main Porte Mage gate and on up the steep cobbled streets of the restored part of the town until eventually he managed to squeeze into an empty space in the Place St Vincent.

Normally at that time of day it would have been full of visitors, training their cameras on the sixteenth-century church with its 'lantern of the dead' bell tower and its Max Ingrand windows. Today, it was jam-packed with vehicles belonging to the unit.

Monsieur Pamplemousse continued his journey on foot up the rue du Trencat towards the *Ville Morte* – the Deserted City – where most of the activity seemed to be. He stepped round a ladder being used by a workman who was spraying grey latex over the side of a building in order to cover up an advertisement. What the shopkeepers were losing on the tourist trade they would be making up for three-fold in disturbance money. Despite that, some of them looked as though they were already beginning to regret the whole idea.

'Oui, Madame,' shouted the workman wearily. 'It will peel off again. You will never know it has been there.' It sounded as though he'd answered the same question many times before that morning.

Temporary dressing-rooms for the main cast had been set up in the the elegant *Mairie.* Cables disappeared through open windows. There were lights everywhere.

Further up the hill, past the ancient bread ovens, the crew were already hard at work setting up their equipment. All the stops were being pulled out to get the filming completed. The shooting of the Last Supper had gone on until late the previous evening. The sets had been struck overnight and now everything was being made ready for the Crucifixion.

Jean-Paul was supervising the setting up and positioning of the cameras. The platform of a large Louma crane with a remotely controlled camera pan and tilt mechanism rose high into the air, then swung down again as the operators watching a television monitor on the ground below made sure they didn't show anything untoward, or were themselves in danger of being revealed. Another camera, mounted on a dolly and pushed by two stalwart grips, went past on a set of rails, rehearsing a long tracking shot up the street. The focus puller sat astride the arm, checking his equipment.

Near the top they branched off to their left and continued the shot on to open ground towards the highest point where the Crucifixion itself was to take place.

Electricians were busy concealing their cables or laying ramps across them wherever there might be passing traffic.

Further on up the hill a third camera mounted on a 'cherry picker' stood by, ready to get an overall view of the scene – the streets of Jerusalem; a Jerusalem which was half the real village of Les Baux and half the product of the scenery department. It was hard to tell where one ended and the other began.

An operator with a hand-held Steadicam concealed beneath a voluminous white robe was practising taking close-up shots where those lining the streets would be standing. It struck Monsieur Pamplemousse that he wouldn't be the only one 'mingling' with the crowd that day.

Ahead of him the large perpendicular sided, unfenced plateau was packed with extras. The inevitable loud hailer boomed out barely comprehensible instructions, coupled with warnings about not straying too near the edge. The costume department, having set up headquarters beside the ruins of an old windmill, were having their work cut out exchanging T-shirts for more seemly wear. Near the monument to the Provençal poet, Charloun Rieu, make-up were equally busy, adding a beard here, a moustache there. A team of girls was working overtime with jars of skin toning; others were hard at work dressing hair. They all looked tired. There was no sign of Anne-Marie. She must be busy with the principals down at the Town Hall.

In a far corner of the plateau an assistant director was rehearsing a group in the art of murmuring. It grew more bloodthirsty by the minute. From a distance it sounded like a football crowd baying for blood.

The dolly came back down the hill, then a moment later reappeared again on its way up for yet another dry run. This time the arm was facing the other way so that the camera could shoot back on itself, following the progress of Jesus carrying the cross.

'*Lentement . . . Lentement. . .*' The cameraman waved his hand, palm downwards. The men pushing him were only too pleased to obey. They looked worn-out already.

Jean-Paul surveyed the scene pensively through a viewfinder, checking his findings from time to time with a light meter. The ambient colour in Les Baux changed by the hour according to the position of the sun. Sometimes yellow, often blindingly white; in the evening the stone could take on an almost fiery-red hue. It would need careful exposure. There was a limit to what the laboratories could do when it came to matching shots taken at different times of the day.

Monsieur Pamplemousse spotted the Director in an area to his left, between the end of the restored section of the town and the ruins of the old. Dressed as a Roman senator, he was standing gloomily beside a canopied barrow laden with nuts.

His costume, an embroidered silk tunic beneath a volu-minous rectangular cloak, looked as though it had been hired from a Paris theatrical agency. So much for his story of 'happening' to find himself in the area. It was hardly the garb of an itinerant peanut seller. Clearly he'd had his sights set on higher things.

Hoping he hadn't been seen, Monsieur Pamplemousse took advantage of a passing donkey laden with bread-filled panniers. As it ambled slowly by, momentarily acting as a screen, he made for the plateau.

It was worse than sale time at Galeries Lafayette. There were queues everywhere.

He recognised the continuity girl. She had been at the screening of the rushes. She was joined by the script girl and the call boy, both carrying a clipboard. They waved as they caught sight of him. All three looked harassed.

The call boy reappeared a moment later and took Monsieur Pamplemousse to the front of the costume queue. It was nice having friends in high places. He chose a simple white, high-necked robe and some sandals. There was no sense in trying to compete with the Director. Placing his surplus belongings into a sealed bag, he joined another queue to check them in with Security.

On his way back he bumped into Beaseley. He, too, looked harassed. His cravat had a distinctly ruffled look to it.

'*Comment ça va?*'

'Script changes,' said Beaseley. 'They're leaving the actual Crucifixion until tomorrow. The way things are going they'll be lucky to get the journey to Golgotha and the burial in the can.

'Rumours abound. The good news is that Mangetout has locked herself in her trailer and won't come out. On the other side of the coin, Brother Angelo is complaining of a bad back and says he can't carry the cross all that way. Von Strudel is with him now. Voices were being raised even as I came past the *Mairie*. My money, as always, is on Von Strudel. He has the megaphone.'

'As I recall,' said Monsieur Pamplemousse, 'Jesus had a similar problem. They called on Simon, from Cyrene, to carry it for him.'

'Good point,' said Beaseley. 'Yet another paradox. Do you realise today is a Friday. It was on a Friday – 3 April AD 33 according to the latest scientific evidence – that Christ is supposed to have died. That was why there was such a rush to bury him. The Sabbath started at nightfall . . .' He broke off and took a closer look at Monsieur Pamplemousse. 'So this what the average food adviser wore in Roman times? I've often wondered.'

It occurred to Monsieur Pamplemousse that he had never let on to Beaseley the true purpose of his being there. It didn't seem an ideal moment to come clean, even if he'd wished to. He still wasn't sure how far to trust his companion. 'It was a lowly position,' he said. 'The Romans were seldom in need of advice, least of all on food.'

'True,' said Beaseley. 'True. Fortunately for you, they bequeathed France their recipes. They only left us their roads. Which is why if it moves you French eat it, whereas we British lay bets on it. Care for a drink?'

He gestured towards yet another queue, longer than the rest, lining up outside one of the catering wagons.

Monsieur Pamplemousse made his excuses. 'There is someone I have to see.'

He found the Director lolling disconsolately on a shooting stick partially concealed beneath his robes. There was a small pile of peanut shells at his feet.

'Trade is far from brisk, Aristide,' he said gloomily. 'A difficult role to sustain when custom is thin on the ground. I hope things will pick up when shooting begins.'

Monsieur Pamplemousse couldn't resist a sly dig. 'It could be that you are looking too prosperous, *Monsieur*. Customers may find you intimidating.'

It was like water off a duck's back. The Director gazed at him. 'At least I have made the effort, Pamplemousse,' he said severely. 'I hardly think your present attire would have labelled you a trendsetter in AD 30. Heads would not have turned when you passed by.'

'It is a good "mingling" colour, *Monsieur*,' said Monsieur Pamplemousse stiffly.

The Director had the grace to acknowledge the point. Having taken a quick look over his shoulder, he lowered his voice. 'I cannot begin to tell you what a comfort it is to know you are keeping an eye on things, Aristide. It will not go unremarked in certain circles I can assure you.'

'That is nice to know, *Monsieur*,' said Monsieur Pamplemousse drily.

'Do you have any news?' asked the Director.

Monsieur Pamplemousse shook his head.

'No thoughts as to where the miscreant may strike next?'

'It depends,' said Monsieur Pamplemousse, thoughtfully, 'as to which miscreant you are referring. I suspect there may be more than one.'

It was the first time the Director had made positive mention of the true reason behind his assignment, and he was wondering whether or not to tackle him on the subject, when there was a shifting of attention as those gathered on the plateau began a concerted movement in their direction.

'Well, let us hope the wrong one doesn't get the upper hand,' said the Director, helping himself to another peanut.

Von Strudel strode into view, fixing the approaching masses with a gimlet eye. Clearly he must have won his battle with Brother Angelo. Raising the megaphone to his lips he began bellowing orders. Cries of *'Dummkopf!'* filled the air. People began to put on speed.

'It is an interesting fact,' said the Director, 'that even in this age of protest and rebellion, one man can inspire absolute terror and obedience amongst so many. Film making is one of the last havens of the true despot. Hitler would have been good at it.'

If Monsieur Pamplemousse detected a note of envy, he didn't dwell on the fact. His heart sank as he took stock of the crowd. The Director was right to be worried. If anyone did intend causing a disruption, now was their big chance, and there would be no possibility whatsoever of stopping them. He only hoped nothing happened to cause a panic. The prospect of people falling and being trampled on by a crowd rushing headlong down the narrow streets towards the only means of exit from Les Beaux or, worse still, disappearing lemming-like over the edge of the surrounding cliffs, didn't bear thinking about.

It was late morning by the time the extras had been herded into place and received their final instructions . . . 'You are not here to enjoy yourselves. You are here to vork. I do not vish to see anyvun *mit* ze smile on zer face. Anyone found smilingk will be given ze order *mit* ze bootz.'

The possibility of anyone enjoying themselves seemed remote, but Von Strudel was taking no chances.

A hush fell over the assembly as shooting began; a hush which communicated itself to all those lining the route.

As the cameras drew near, the Director edged away from the barrow and assumed a more imposing stance.

Clearly, he didn't wish to be identified in such a lowly role.

Monsieur Pamplemousse watched carefully as the mob moved slowly past. It was hard to tell how much of Brother Angelo's performance was acting and how much was in earnest. His face was certainly white from the strain. The stage blood on his back had started to congeal from the heat of the sun, which was now directly overhead. The crown of thorns looked all too real. The sweat running down his face undoubtedly was. The two thieves following on behind looked equally haggard.

Despite everything, it was surprisingly moving. The noise of the crowd, the heat, the flies, the sheer intensity of it all, combined with the concentration of the crew made the scene seem strangely real. It was like witnessing a live event, having grown blasé over the years through seeing the same thing on television too many times in the comfort of one's own home. The extras left behind as the pageant moved on up the hill looked equally affected as they drifted slowly away. Many remained where they were to watch, unable to tear themselves away.

Stopping for one reason or another, starting, repositioning, a much needed tea break . . . the day melted away, and it was evening before a temporary halt in the shooting was called. Apart from taking a few 'wild shots' of Brother Angelo for editing purposes, it was time to move on.

That there had been no accidents was a minor miracle in itself. As an exercise in crowd control it had been beyond reproach.

Leaving the Director to carry on by himself, Monsieur Pamplemousse made his way towards the ruins of the old city, where preparations had been made to shoot the burial sequence.

Beaseley was already there, along with Von Strudel and Jean-Paul. The crowd, having been put on stand- by until the next day, had largely dispersed.

There was a sense of urgency among those gathered round the cave. The sun would shortly disappear over the horizon. Timing was as critical for the unit as it must have been for the friends of Jesus who needed to carry out the ceremony before the Sabbath began.

There was still enough natural light to see shadowy details, but Jean-Paul added a little more. The level was changing with every passing moment. Standing alongside Monsieur Pamplemousse, he called for the camera to be lowered still more until it was shooting up.

'Do you know the painting by Caravaggio? That is the effect I am trying to achieve,' Jean-Paul whispered.

Watched by Mary, Mother of Joseph, and Mary of Magdala, Joseph and Nicodemus were rehearsing the rolling of a vast rock across the mouth of a tomb supposedly carved in the side of a hill outside Jerusalem where the body of Jesus was to be laid to rest. It was easy to see now why Les Baux had been chosen. It was a natural setting. The rock was circular, it could have been the grindstone from an old flour mill. Getting it moving at all was one thing. Stopping it in exactly the right spot so that it blocked the opening to the cave was something else again.

'Faster,' bellowed Von Strudel. 'Faster. *Mein Gott!* You are like ze snails. It is Friday eveningk. *Samstag* vil have come und gone by ze time you hov finished. You need to be faster. Faster, but *mit* ze reverence.'

'The sound of popping blood vessels,' murmured Beaseley, 'is really quite unique.'

'Places everyone.'

Jean-Paul made a quick check of the exposure, called for the gaffer to remove a layer of scrim from a lamp to bring up the light a bit more and restore the balance, then gave the thumbs-up sign.

'This is a take. Let's make it a good one.'

The clapper boy rushed on.

'Cue action.'

Joseph and Nicodemus entered shot carrying the body of Jesus, wrapped now in linen cloths to cover the wounds left by the soldiers. A strong smell of burial spices – a mixture of myrrh and aloes – mingled with that of human sweat. Placing the body reverently on a slab just inside the cave, they quickly withdrew and took hold of the rock. Their bodies glistened as it threatened to roll past its mark and they took up the strain.

'Cut!'

Everyone waited patiently while Von Strudel, Jean-Paul, the second director and others went into a huddle. Monsieur Pamplemousse looked around. It was as though time had stopped. Everyone had frozen in their position. In the short length of time it had taken to run the scene the sun had already set. The surrounding ruins, pockmarked and shadowy, had taken on the appearance of a gaunt and eyeless audience.

'OK. Print it.'

'Thank you, everyone.'

'*Ja*. Zat vas good.'

An almost audible sigh of relief went up all round the set as everyone relaxed and began talking at once.

Jean-Paul turned to his crew. '*Merci. Terminez* . . . *Emballer* . . . Wrap it up.'

The words were hardly out of his mouth when the lights all round the entrance to the cave suddenly went out. For a moment or two there was chaos. Voices came out of the darkness. *'Merde! Sacré bleu! Scheibe!* What the . . .'

Just as suddenly they came on again. Jean-Paul hurried back on to the set. 'Some *imbecile* must have tripped over a breaker switch. The plug had been pulled out.'

'Thank Christ it wasn't during the take.' The Assistant Director's shake of the wrist echoed everyone's feelings. 'OK. Strike the rock.'

A prop man ambled on and trundled the stone away with one hand. It bounced on some pebbles, then rolled over on to its side, jogging up and down as it settled. He raised a laugh by adopting a 'muscle-man' stance.

'What would we do without polystyrene?' said Beaseley.

'You don't think . . .'

'What?'

'Je n'en sais pas.' Monsieur Pamplemousse suddenly felt uneasy, that was all. He had no idea why.

'All films are an illusion,' said Beaseley. 'The quickness of the shot deceives the eye. Half the time the screen is blank anyway. If man hadn't been born with persistency of vision someone would have had to invent it . . .'

Beaseley's theme remained undeveloped as their attention was suddenly distracted by an outbreak of chatter from the mouth of the cave.

'C'est impossible!'

'Hey, everyone, come and look at this!'

'Jesus!'

'Mein Gott!' Von Strudel pushed his way to the front of the group and stared into the darkness. For once he seemed at a loss for words.

'I think,' said Beaseley, as he and Monsieur Pamplemousse joined the others and craned their necks to see what was going on, 'that what we have is a classic case of the "Old Mother Hubbards".'

'*Comment?*'

'Old Mother Hubbard,' said Beaseley, 'went to the cupboard, to fetch her poor dog a bone. But when she got there, the cupboard was bare, and so the poor dog had none. For bone, read Brother Angelo. In short, we are witnessing yet another attack of the dreaded *bugginks!*'

6
THE SACRIFICE

It hadn't taken Monsieur Pamplemousse long to find what he was looking for: a gelatin filter lying on the ground near the Ark. It was slightly blackened in the middle from the heat of a lamp – which was probably why it had been discarded – the dark patch would change the colour temperature of the light – but it was ideally suited to his purpose: tough yet pliable.

It took him even less time to put it to good use. Crouching down, he bent one edge of the plastic slightly, then slipped it behind the stop batten of the door frame and round between the casing and the leading edge of the door itself, applying pressure at the same time so that it slid even further between the two. Luckily, as with most modern exterior doors, slight warping had taken place, leaving a larger gap near the bottom than there was halfway up. The lock was a standard cylinder rim type, identical to the one on his own trailer. Nothing special. There was no deadlock bolt – neither the automatic variety nor the kind which was operated by a second turn of the key. It was an open invitation to anyone with an old credit card – or a discarded gelatin filter found on a film location.

He slid the plastic up the gap, once again applying pressure. The higher he went the more resistance he encountered. The first time it jammed just below the lock. He changed the angle slightly and tried again with one swift,

301

sweeping motion. This time it slid between the rounded bolt and the staple. There was a satisfactory click as the mechanism responded. The bolt slid back into the body of the lock and the door swung open.

Probably at that very moment there were other equally satisfactory clicks taking place all over the world. He knew from his time in the *Sûreté* that Friday night in Paris was always a particularly busy night for the police, with people going off for the week-end and leaving their apartments unattended. Except it wasn't Paris, and he would have been as hard put to justify what he was doing as any common or garden *cambrioleur*.

Monsieur Pamplemousse took a quick look over his shoulder to make sure no one else was around. The next moment he was inside Brother Angelo's trailer, closing the door gently behind him.

Only after he had made absolutely certain that the curtains were tightly drawn did he turn on his torch. His Cupillard Rième watch showed 1.18.

The trailer was basically identical to his own, if considerably less tidy. There were discarded magazines strewn everywhere. Unwashed glasses stood where they had been left. The remains of long since melted ice-cubes gave off an odour of whisky. There was also a smell of stale cigar smoke, Cigar smoke and . . . Monsieur Pamplemousse sniffed . . . powder rather than perfume.

He made his way through the kitchen to the back end of the trailer. The make-up area had certainly been put to good use. The table was littered with discarded tissues. The waste bucket was chock-a-block. Whoever had the task of clearing up in the morning was in for a busy time. He checked the bath and the washbasin. Neither appeared to have used recently. The towels felt dry.

He slid open the cupboard doors. It was hard to say if any clothes were missing. The hanging wardrobe was reasonably full, as were the drawers below it; socks, under-clothes, monogrammed handkerchiefs . . . all the things one might expect. Perhaps they weren't as full as they might have been, but they were nowhere near empty either. There were certainly no telltale signs of a hasty packing. There was nothing hidden behind the hanging clothes, nothing in any of the pockets, nothing untoward tucked away in any of the drawers.

He drew a blank in the kitchen area. Apart from a few vegetables in the bottom drawer, the refrigerator was empty. The end of a *baguette* lay dry and abandoned on the working area. Alongside it was an open tin containing a few black olives. They were from the ubiquitous Monsieur Arnaud.

There was some unwashed crockery in the sink. Two of everything.

Hoping it might prove more productive than the rest of the trailer, Monsieur Pamplemousse went back into the main area and began an inch by inch search of the room.

In a sense he was hampered by not having the remotest idea what he hoped to find. It was easier to say what he wasn't looking for.

If Ron Pickles's disappearance had been planned, it was doubtful if he would have left any evidence of that fact behind. Everything he had seen so far bore all the hall-marks of someone who had nothing to conceal. That being so, there was no point in looking for conventional hiding-places – inside hollow brass curtain rods, objects taped to the underside of drawers or wrapped in aluminium foil and put inside the freezer compartment of the refrigerator.

Also, space being at a premium, a trailer lacked many of the possibilities of an ordinary house – the glass fibre insulation between the roof rafters, for example, made a good hiding place; or fake plumbing – a false plastic waste pipe could hold a surprising amount. Luxurious the trailer might be, but everything about it was starkly functional. It had to perform a useful task, or else . . .

Hollowed-out books? The only book he could see was, rather surprisingly, an English edition of Daudet's *Letters from a Windmill*, a slim volume, one page of which was marked by a ticket stub from a show called the *Cathédrale d'Images* which was taking place in one of the local disused bauxite mines. *Prix d'Entrée 33F* Adulte. Neither the book nor the *Cathédrale d'Images* sounded exactly Ron Piddes's cup of tea. There was really no predicting other people's tastes.

He came across a second book on the floor beside the bed, a guide to the area, again in English. A sectiondevoted to the Massif de la Sainte-Baume, west of Marseille, was marked by a tourist's brochure describing the delights of Fontvieille. There was a picture of Daudet's windmill on the front. It must have ben picked up in Fontvieille itself because it bore the stamp of the Office de Tourisme. Perhaps Daudet's letters hd made an effect on Brother Angelo?

A waste-bucket in a corner of the room yielded up a half-used packet of book matches bearing the name of a restaurant called Le Croissant d'Or in the coastal town of Les Saintes-Maries-de-la-Mer, some screwed-up pages of script on yellow paper, and three more ticket stubs for the *Cathédrale d'Images*. Monsieur Pamplemousse wondered who Brother Angelo's companions had been. Mangetout, along with the Swedish *au pair* and the child? Except all the tickets were marked *Adulte*.

Monsieur Pamplemousse shone the torch on to his watch again. The search had taken over half an hour. There wasn't a lot to show for it.

He lay back on the bed turning the problem over in hismind, trying to picture what, if anything, his search had yielded. He looked in vain for a common link between a windmill, a meal by the sea, a walk in the mountains and a visit to a show. They were all ordinary enough: the kind of outings anyone might make if they were staying in the area and had time to spare.

And yet . . . and yet somehow that didn't ring true. None of the parties involved was exactly ordinary. None could have had that much time to spare. Mangetout kept herself so much to herself she made the late Marlene Dietrich look like Zsa Zsa Gabor, and from all he'd seen of Brother Angelo, he didn't exactly court being seen in public. He must dread going out at times. Worse than being royalty. At least they weren't besieged by autograph hunters.

Monsieur Pamplemousse switched off the torch and closed his eyes. The window must be open a fraction, for above the hum of the air-conditioning and the faint sound of the generator he could hear music in the distance – a guitar and a girl singing – coming from the camp site where all the fans were living.

He wasn't sure how long he had been lying there . . . fifteen minutes? . . . twenty? . . . when he heard a noise. It was the faint, but unmistakable rasping sound made by a key being pushed very gently through the pin tumblers of a door lock.

Mentally cursing himself for not throwing the bolt after he had entered, Monsieur Pamplemousse lay where he was, his right hand grasping the edge of the bed, ready to spring up at a second's notice. With his other hand he searched for the torch.

There was a shaft of moonlight, momentarily obscured by a shadowy figure, then the key was quickly withdrawn and the door closed again. Fully expecting the room to be flooded with light, Monsieur Pamplemousse braced himself. But instead, the newcomer moved swiftly across the room and leant across the bed as though searching for something. He felt the other person's warmth and there was a smell similar to the one he had noticed earlier, only much stronger this time. Resisting the temptation to reach up, he held his breath. There was a sudden gasp as whoever it was realised they were not alone.

'Tu!' The cry was one of pleasurable surprise rather than fear.

The figure straightened.

'*Mon chou! Mon chou!*'

Something heavy was discarded.

'*Mon chou!*' There was a wriggle as something lighter went the same way. A moment later he felt a body pressing itself against him: warm, sensuous, alive. Inviting lips sought his. Hands reached out and down . . .

The moment ended even faster than it had begun. The gasp this time was of total horror. The figure leapt from the bed and made a wild dash for safety. The door shot open and slammed shut again.

Monsieur Pamplemousse struggled to his feet. There was a thump as something heavy landed on the floor. Groping around, he made contact with his torch and switched it on.

A crumpled silk *négligé* lay in a heap where it had been abandoned. Beneath it was a top coat of some kind. He bent down. The *négligé* bore a La Perla label. Hardly what one might have expected anyone from the camp site to be wearing. On the other hand, he would have been willing to swear on oath that his visitor hadn't been Mangetout. It had been someone a good deal younger. He picked up the coat and was about to discard it when something prompted him to feel in the side pockets.

The first one contained a key, the second a ticket stub. It was yet another for the *Cathédrale d'Images*. There was a number across the top – 067174. He compared it with the numbers on those he had already found. One of them was 067175. It was only then that he realised that none of the other three numbers were consecutive. Brother Angelo must have been by himself when he went there on the other occasions.

Taking one last look round the room, Monsieur Pamplemousse let himself out. There was no point in lingering.

Closing the door gently behind him, he stood for a moment or two pressed hard against the side of the trailer, merging with the shadows, but nothing moved.

The night air was heavy with the smell of lavender and herbs. Cicadas were in full throat. Les Baux, starkly white and pockmarked by day, looked impossibly romantic in the moonlight; the twinkling lights gave it the appearance of some huge ocean liner sailing into the night. Romantic and at the same time still charged with horrors of the past. Its jagged outline against the night sky was like an illustration from a fairy tale by the brothers Grimm; a reminder that it was from the top of those very same rocks that Raymond de Turenne had rounded off his evenings by forcing prisoners to leap to their death. Their screams must have echoed round the Val d'Enfer, drowning the drunken laughter.

The heat was oppressive. In the distance, beyond the perimeter of the lot, he could see lights coming from the area where the extras were camping out, and there was the occasional flicker of a camp fire. Many of the fans had already left, but there was still a large body of those eager to see things out to the bitter end. The music sounded louder now and the mood had changed; it was somehow more restless, like the voice of a tormented being.

Detecting a glimmer of light in Mangetout's trailer, Monsieur Pamplemousse moved away in the opposite direction, making a detour round the back of the other vehicles. He thought he heard a baby crying somewhere. It stopped as quickly as it had begun. It could have been the plaintive cry of a sheep.

As he rounded the far corner of Gilbert Beaseley's quarters he almost collided with someone coming the other way.

It was the Director. A Director, moreover, who was clutching his right eye as though in pain.

'Ah, there you are, Pamplemousse. I have been looking for you everywhere.'

'Is there something wrong, *Monsieur?*'

'Wrong?' repeated the Director. 'Wrong? I have been attacked!'

'Attacked?' As was so often the case with his chief, Monsieur Pamplemousse found himself reduced to echoing the other's words.

'Attacked,' repeated the Director. 'I must admit, when I found a certain person occupying your quarters I thought the worst, but in no way did it prepare me for what transpired.'

Monsieur Pamplemousse stared at him. 'There is someone in my trailer, *Monsieur?*'

It was the Director's turn to gaze in disbelief. 'You are not trying to plead innocent, Pamplemousse?'

'I give you my word, *Monsieur.*'

'Come, come, Aristide, you know me better than that. In

matters of love and war, everything is fair. The best man has won. Let us say no more about it.'

'I repeat, *Monsieur*, I have no idea what you are talking about.'

Monsieur Pamplemousse might just as well have saved his breath. The Director had clearly got the bit between his teeth and did not intend letting go until he'd had his say.

'Unable to sleep for whatever reason – I think possibly it was the noise of the music – if that is the word to describe what sounds more like the cacophonous ramblings of those on whom the full moon has had an adverse effect – I got dressed and went for a walk. I found myself irresistibly drawn towards Les Alpilles and I went further than I had originally intended.

'When I returned, I have to admit that in approaching the site from a different direction I found myself totally disoriented. Seeing a chink of light coming from your quarters, I thought I would call in for a chat. I knocked on your door several times, but to no avail, and I was about to go on my way when to my surprise it was opened by none other than Mangetout. I was so taken aback it took me a moment or two to recognise her.

'The light, Pamplemousse, was the only thing she had on.

'It was a case of having to think on my feet. I pretended I had come to ask for her autograph. It was the best I could do on the spur of the moment. Clearly she did not have a *plume* about her person, and I was in the act of looking for mine when she attacked me. I cannot begin to tell you the language she used. I was lucky to make good my escape.'

Monsieur Pamplemousse stared at the Director. 'Mangetout was in my trailer?' he repeated. 'But that is not possible.'

'Pamplemousse,' the Director put a hand to his face again, 'there is no need to pretend. I know she is there. I saw her with my own eyes – as large as life and twice as powerful. I fully understand why you feel the need to be on your own for a while. Doubtless your batteries need recharging. Have no fear, the matter shall remain a secret between us. *C'est la vie.* I hope I am man enough to accept defeat gracefully.'

'But, *Monsieur,* there must be some mistake . . .' Monsieur Pamplemousse suddenly felt at a loss for words. 'If you come with me I will prove to you . . .'

'Not for all the *café* in Maroc, Pamplemousse. It was an illusion destroyed. One should not get too close to one's dreams. The reality seldom lives up to them. I will leave you to your own devices, such as they are. I see now why you and Pommes Frites are occupying separate trailers.' He reached out a hand. 'If I may, I will borrow your *torche de poche* and find my own way back.'

The Director broke off and stared at the object in Monsieur Pamplemousse's other hand. 'What is that you are holding, Pamplemousse?'

'It is nothing . . .' Monsieur Pamplemousse hastily stuffed the *négligé* under his jacket.

'Nothing?' exclaimed the Director. 'It is no wonder Mangetout was in a state of *déshabillée.*'

'*Monsieur!* . . . This does *not* belong to Mangetout. It is . . .'

'Well, Pamplemousse?' The Director assumed his magisterial tones.

'It belongs to someone else,' said Monsieur Pamplemousse lamely.

The Director gazed at him as if he could hardly believe his eyes.

310

'Is there no end to your depravity, Pamplemousse?' he boomed. 'Are you totally insatiable? Can you not be alone for five minutes? That poor woman. Small wonder she was distraught and smelling of gin.'

'It is a long story, *Monsieur . . .*'

'And I do not wish to hear it,' said the Director.

'*Monsieur . . .*'

'The *lumière*, Pamplemousse.'

Monsieur Pamplemousse took a firm grip of his torch. 'I hardly think that will be necessary, *Monsieur.*' He turned and pointed towards the nearest trailer. 'Your quarters are there in front of you.'

Relenting long enough to shine the light as far as the steps, Monsieur Pamplemousse waited until the Director was safely inside, then he turned and made straight for his own trailer, feeling for his key as he went.

Fully prepared for the worst, he flung open the door. The living-room was empty, the bed untouched. He went through into the kitchen. That, too, was exactly as he had left it. He drew a blank in the make-up area.

Returning to the main room, Monsieur Pamplemousse sat on the edge of his bed for a moment or two. It was a puzzle and no mistake. The Director could hardly have imagined all that he had described. Nor would he have made it up. His black eye was real enough. And if Mangetout had been in the trailer she would hardly have had time to vacate it. Unless, of course, the Director had been wandering around in a daze for longer than he realised. It was possible.

As he began to undress, Monsieur Pamplemousse looked at his watch again. Less than half an hour had passed since he had last checked the time; it felt much longer.

He lay back on the bed and closed his eyes. The mysterious visitor to Brother Angelo's trailer had been another

311

strange business. At the time it had seemed all too real . . . his mind drifted back to Mangetout. He wondered where she was now? Back in her own trailer? And what was she feeling about Ron's disappearance? Did she even know about it? It was quite within the bounds of possibility that she didn't. If they were in the middle of one of their periodic rows she could well have gone into a sulk. Not many people would be brave enough to knock on her door to break the news.

His head was throbbing from the incessant drumming coming from the camp site. It was getting louder; ever more urgent, but he was too tired to let it worry him. Pulling the duvet over his head, Monsieur Pamplemousse fell fast asleep in a matter of moments.

He had no idea how long it lasted; it could have been minutes, it could have been hours. All he was conscious of was being woken abruptly some time later by the sound of the telephone ringing. He struggled into a sitting position and reached for the receiver.

'Pamplemousse, are you all right?' It was the Director. He sounded agitated.

'Oui, Monsieur.' Monsieur Pamplemousse manfully resisted the temptation to say he would have felt better still had he not been woken.

'You have not been experiencing tremors?'

'Tremors, *Monsieur?*'

'The ground keeps shaking. This is not an area subject to earthquakes is it?'

'Not so far as I am aware, *Monsieur.*'

'There seems to be a wind getting up. Listen . . . can you hear it? Could it be the Mistral? I . . . Pamplemousse . . .' The Director's voice rose an octave or two. 'The whole room is moving. I . . . *Sacré bleu!* Come quickly! *Mon Dieu! . . .*'

There was a click and the line went dead.

As it did so, Monsieur Pamplemousse became aware that the noise which he had at first taken to be some kind of interference on the line, a fault in the air-conditioning perhaps, or, indeed, as the Director had suggested, the Mistral making an unseasonable sortie down the Rhône Valley, was actually much closer to hand.

Making a dive for the window, he operated the blind and was just in time to see the upper half of a trailer go past. Swaying as it went, like a ship at sea or some giant artificial monster in a Chinese New Year festivity, it was borne on a vast, undulating, heaving, tidal wave of bodies; some clad in galabiahs left over from the previous day's shoot, others wearing T-shirts bearing motifs and illustrations which even from a distance were clearly of a sexual nature. Others again had discarded everything completely. Brother Angelo's fan club were on the rampage and it was an awesome sight.

As the trailer disappeared behind some rocks Monsieur Pamplemousse caught his breath. The blind on one of the windows was raised and he had a momentary glimpse of a white face pressed against the inside of the glass. There was no need to look for his Leitz Trinovids in order to identify the owner of the countenance. It belonged to the Director, and terror was writ large all over it.

Monsieur Pamplemousse made a dive for the telephone again and dialled the duty security officer. A girl answered.

'Which service do you require, *Monsieur?*'

'I think,' said Monsieur Pamplemousse urgently, 'you had better send one of everything . . . *tout de suite!'*

7
IMAGES GALORE

Following a sign marked *Cathédrale d'Images,* Monsieur Pamplemousse took the back road out of Les Baux towards Arles. He had been driving for less than a minute when he rounded a bend and there on his right he saw a great rectangular hole carved out of the hillside. It was much grander than he had expected – cathedral was an apt description. Great slabs of white limestone left over from the days when it was a working quarry were stacked on either side of the opening. He drove into an empty car park and crunched his way across the gravel towards a small ticket office to the left of what must once have been the loading area.

He still wasn't quite sure why he was there, other than playing a hunch. A process of elimination really. It was also a means of passing the time. The Director had been admitted to a *hospice* in Arles and was under heavy sedation, so there was no point in trying to visit him. Work on the film had ground to a halt.

He scanned a notice board displaying various facts and figures about the mine. Forty slide projectors programmed to display some 2,500 slides, each one enlarged up to 10,000 times on to 4,000 square metres of surface area spread over 300 metres of walkway. A magical and unforgettable world, according to the blurb, born from the talent and imagination of its creator, the late Albert Plecy. The *Image totale* process made it possible for the spectator to wander at will through a gigantic audio-visual show. The whole sight and sound spectacular lasted thirty minutes.

The girl in the cash desk seemed surprised to see him. It was hard to say whether she was pleased or not. Probably not from the way she put down her magazine. He decided to ply her with a few tentative questions.

'*Oui*, business had suffered since the film company had taken over Les Baux. Not many people knew the *Cathédrale* existed and there was not much through traffic on the D27. They relied on tapping the overspill of visitors to the old town who came across their advertisements. Normally on a Saturday at this time of the year there would be crowds, but now . . . poof! See for yourself! was the general tenor of her responses. Her final question, 'You are from the company?' was slightly more animated.

'I am . . . attached . . .' Monsieur Pamplemousse tried to make his connection sound as tenuous as possible.

'I would be better off as an extra.' He wasn't sure if it was a statement, a moment of dreaming, or a hint. Perhaps she was hoping he was a casting director.

Hearing some pop music coming from a portable radio in the background, he tried another tack. 'You are a fan of Brother Angelo?'

The girl brightened. '*Oui*. And he is a fan of the *Cathédrale*. He has been here several times.'

'It is possible to see the same show more than once?'

'Of course! People come back all the time.'

Realising he had made a tactical error, Monsieur Pamplemousse tried to bring the conversation back again.

'When was the last time he was here?'

'The day before he disappeared. He didn't stay for long, but then he never did.' She brushed the hair away from her eyes. 'It is a strange business. Disappearing like that.'

'You know about it?' He felt in his trouser pocket for some change.

'Who doesn't? Nobody talks about anything else around here.'

'And you have not seen him since?'

'I wouldn't be sitting here if I had, would I?'

There was no one like the young, thought Monsieur Pamplemousse, for expressing with a single glance total and utter contempt for asking ridiculous questions.

He suddenly felt his age.

'At least you will have the cave more or less to yourself,' said the girl. 'There is only one other customer this morning.

'It doesn't matter if the show has already started. You can stay in there as long as you like. One show ends - another begins.'

Monsieur Pamplemousse thanked her and then pushed his way through the turnstile. He stood for a moment or two in the open area between the box office and the entrance to the cave, taking in the unexpected grandeur of the scene. It all seemed so much larger than life; it was like coming across a film set for some Cecil B. de Mille biblical extravaganza, or a theatre modelled after an Egyptian temple which had somehow been left over from the great days of Hollywood. It would certainly make a wonderful hide-out.

Could anyone get in and out without paying? There was a long metal barrier between the ticket office and the oppo-site side of the area where the entrance to the old mine lay. But if the girl were distracted, or if she left her post for a moment? She would hardly leave it unattended if there were any potential customers around. It certainly wasn't something to bank on. Even if he had changed his appearance, Brother Angelo had clearly already made his mark and he wouldn't risk being recognised.

Wandering towards the back and into a cavernous hollowed-out part of the hill, he passed the window of a little room where a plain deal table was laid with two plates. There was a *baguette,* some cheese and a bottle of red wine. A man was busying himself at a stove. Early *déjeuner* for himself and the girl at the cash desk? It looked like some kind of off-duty rest room. The window commanded a view of the car park and the approach road. He couldn't see anyone else around, although there were some official-looking offices to his left. They looked as though they were closed for the day.

He walked on a little, then came to an abrupt halt. Various *Danger* and *Passage Interdit* notices barred further progress. Presumably they were meant to be off-putting, because beyond them he could see patches of blue sky, so presumably anyone approaching from the other side – over the top of the hill – could gain access that way. If no one was watching.

A moment later the question was partly answered for him. A car drew up outside the car park and the driver – presumably a tourist or someone from a nearby camp site – tried to deposit a cardboard box full of rubbish alongside a litter bin. The man he'd seen a moment before rushed out of the rest room waving his arms and shouting.

It was a private litter bin. It belonged to the Company. How dare he!

The driver disappeared into his car like a scalded cat and drove off hell for leather down the hill. It looked as though it wasn't the first time such a thing had happened.

All the same, if the man was able to spot it from a distance of some fifty or sixty metres, he would surely have seen someone trying to get in without paying. There was no means of telling without testing the system.

On the other hand, if there were two people. One to divert attention . . .

It was time he went in. If he lingered much longer he would become an object of suspicion himself.

The door into the *Cathédrale* proper was reached via a long hallway hollowed out of the cliff. It was lined with display cabinets and posters giving more facts and figures, mostly about Albert Plecy and how he had established a research centre in the quarries. There were lists of past shows – amongst them one devoted to the paintings of Vincent Van Gogh. This year it was 'The Magic of Stained Glass'. The best things in life had always just been or were 'coming shortly'.

Entering through a door at the far end Monsieur Pamplemousse suddenly found himself in almost total darkness. Darkness with a chilly edge to it. He wished he had brought something warmer to wear. Ahead of him he could hear music and there was a faint glow of light. As his eyes grew accustomed to the lack of light he began to edge his way forward. Suddenly there was a burst of music directly overhead and on a wall to his left a picture of an illuminated church window appeared. It was followed by others to his right. The music grew louder, then faded as a commentator's voice took over. The whole cave seemed alive with shapes and sound. Nothing he had read outside had quite prepared him for the experience. The smooth white walls made perfect screens, and the texture and shape provided exactly the right amount of reverberation. He was surrounded by sound and by constantly changing pictures. It was quadrophonic, three-dimensional theatre in the round, and a totally unique experience.

Monsieur Pamplemousse began to work his way deeper into the mine, past supporting pillars and on into other vast chambers. There was constant clicking from all directions as the computerised projectors changed slides, mixing automatically from one to another. He was so absorbed by the sheer complexity of it all that for a while it commanded his whole attention. It wasn't until he found an optimum point which offered an almost 360 degree view of the cave that he paused for a moment, and leaning against a pillar, away from the criss-crossing beams of light, posed the simple question to himself. Why was he there?

The answer was nowhere near as clear cut as he would have liked. A faint hope that Brother Angelo might be in the *Cathédrale* too? Perhaps even now hiding in one of the many dark areas out of range of the projectors? It was possible – all things were possible. But was it likely? It was an eerie thought; the more so because as far as he could tell there was no one else about. Certainly nobody he could see or hear. There was no sign of the other visitor the girl at the cash desk had mentioned. He hadn't been aware of passing anyone. Whoever it was might well have left by now. A dozen people could have crossed his path and he would never have known. Looking around, shadows manifest themselves in unlikely places.

Deep down, Monsieur Pamplemousse began to wish he had been firmer with the *vétérinaire* and insisted on Pommes Frites' immediate discharge. Now filming had stopped, surely he would have welcomed a return to his old duties? Although, having said that, quite what he would have made of the present surroundings was hard to say.

The music swelled. It was modern, specially composed, loud, strident, synthetic; not to his liking, yet he had to admit it was somehow right for the setting. The rate at

319

which the images changed increased with the volume; a never-ending montage of stained glass windows, of saints and ecclesiastical figures one after another, a riot of reds and blues and all colours of the rainbow. The overall effect as both sound and vision reached a crescendo was so intensely theatrical, he found himself unable to resist an overwhelming urge to take advantage of being on his own and join in; to hold his ears and shout out.

'Brother Angelo! Ron Pickles! *Avancez!* Come out! *Ici!* I know you are here!' His voice rose above the sound of the music.

Monsieur Pamplemousse never knew what hit him. There was a crash and a glancing blow across the back of the head sent him sprawling.

He lay where he had fallen for a moment or two, vaguely aware of a strange sound like the ticking of a myriad clocks echoing round the vaulted chambers. It was a moment or two before he came to his senses and realised that the house lights were on and that the noise was coming from the projectors as they recycled themselves for the next performance.

Climbing unsteadily to his feet, he looked up. Immediately above his head there was a steel bracket attached to the pillar. It supported a small platform for one of the projectors. There was a mark along the edge as though it had been struck by some heavy object. The metal was shiny where the paint had been removed. Glancing down he saw some splinters of wood on the ground. He rubbed his head ruefully. His senses were still spinning, but at least the bracket and the fact that he was wearing his hat had saved him from something far worse than a headache.

Monsieur Pamplemousse pricked two large potatoes

several times with a fork and placed them on a piece of folded paper towel to absorb the moisture, then put them directly on the floor of the microwave oven. He checked once again with the cook book – it was as well to make sure – he had heard tales of potatoes exploding in microwave ovens, spattering themselves all over the inside. Reassured, he set the timer to eleven minutes, pressed the start button, and stood back.

Nothing sinister happened, so he began checking the rest of the shopping with his list. Butter, eggs, parmesan cheese, *asperge*, flour, *baguette, saucisson d'Arles* . . .

Already he was feeling better. The episode in the *Cathédrale* seemed like a bad dream. Nevertheless, it had left him feeling shaken. Cooking would be good therapy.

The pinging of the timer brought it all back. He couldn't think what had come over him. Shouting out had been an act of sheer bravado: a momentary mental aberration. Telling anyone else about his actions would be embarrassing in the extreme. He certainly couldn't picture trying to explain to the local police what had happened. It made him blush even to think of it.

Taking the potatoes out of the oven, he halved them both and scooped out the middle from all four sections. Then he took a potato masher from the rack and beat the pulp until it was smooth. Adding around thirty grams of butter and an egg, he carried on beating. The heat of the potato caused the egg to cook slightly and helped thicken the mixture. Adding some flour, he carried on beating until it was firm enough not to stick to his fingers.

If there had been anyone else around in the cave he wouldn't have dreamed of behaving as he had. One thing was certain – it was the very last time he went on an expedition like that without Pommes Frites at his side. If

Pommes Frites had been there to protect him it would not have happened. He should never have agreed to their being parted in the first place. It had been a moment of weakness on his part and now he was regretting it. For all he knew Pommes Frites could be thinking the same thing. The sooner their relationship was restored to normal the better.

He weighed out sixty grams of the parmesan cheese, grated it and added it to the mixture, beating it again. Then he added some pepper and salt and a pinch of nutmeg.

Leaving the mixture to cool, Monsieur Pamplemousse began preparing his first course – boiled eggs with *asperge;* the eggs lightly done so that he could dip the tips of the *asperge* into the yolk – having first coated them with melted butter, of course – and naturally having seasoned the eggs with pepper and salt.

Another thing was certain. If it had been Brother Angelo hiding in the cave – and he couldn't for the moment see any other reason for the unprovoked assault – then almost certainly he would have been well and truly scared away.

The table laid, Monsieur Pamplemousse put a large saucepan of salted water on the hob to boil, then spread some flour generously over the working surface above the base unit cupboard. Having first checked that his mixture had cooled sufficiently, he took a handful and rolled it into a long, thin sausage about two cm across. With a sharp knife he cut the sausage into sections, each one as long as it was wide.

Dipping a fork into the flour, he set about flattening the pieces, working each one with the prongs until resembled a sea shell.

The thing was, if it had been Brother Angelo, and if he had taken flight, where would he have gone to?

Adding the shells to the boiling water, he turned down the heat and left them to simmer for ten minutes or so This was the tricky part; overcook them and they would become like curdled milk.

Perhaps it was as well Pommes Frites wasn't with him. He wouldn't take to all the preparations that were going into the meal. Waiting around for things to cook when he was hungry was not what he was best at.

Monsieur Pamplemousse wondered again about the things he had found in Brother Angelo's trailer. Daudet's *Letters from a Windmill in Provence* was an old English translation. It had been published in 1922 by a London firm – Arthur H. Stockwell. It looked as though it might well be a collector's item. If that were the case then Ron Pickles must have brought it with him. He certainly wouldn't have been able to buy it in Fontvieille. That suggested a more than passing interest in the subject.

The gnocchi had started to rise to the surface. Using a fish slice, Monsieur Pamplemousse removed the first batch from the water, allowing it to drain before arranging the shells in a buttered ceramic baking dish. Sprinkled with grated cheese and melted butter and baked in the oven until golden brown, they would, along with a green salad, be a perfect accompaniment to the *saucisson d'Arles.*

And if Brother Angelo had been hiding out in the *Cathé-drale,* was he also responsible for the various acts of sabotage on the lot? If so, why? For what purpose? Did he dislike Von Strudel so much? It couldn't be anything to do with money. When it came down to it, he must be getting paid a pretty hefty sum for doing very little.

As he put some more shells to boil, Monsieur Pample-mousse began to feel more relaxed; at least it had taken his mind off his headache. Rubbing the bruise with the back of a spoon had worked wonders. He poured himself a glass of wine, checked the cooking time for the asparagus, and set the microwave oven again. It was a whole new world. No liquid – cooking by weight – no loss of vitamins. He put the eggs on the hob to boil.

Doucette would not have approved of the pile of washing up in the sink. He had used up almost the entire armoury of saucepans, but then he usually did.

There was a knock at the door. It was not the sound he most wanted to hear.

'*Entrez.*' Monsieur Pamplemousse pressed the start button on the oven, then looked round.

It was Gilbert Beaseley.

It would have been churlish not to invite him in, but his heart sank nevertheless. He had been looking forward to eating on his own.

'*Ciao.*' Monsieur Pamplemousse's invitation was accepted with alacrity.

Beaseley looked around as he entered the kitchen. 'The Galloping Gourmet strikes again!' He peered in the saucepan. 'I see we're going all Italian.'

'*Gnocchi de pommes de terre* is a Provençal dish,' said Monsieur Pamplemousse. 'Even the name comes from this part of the world – "*inhocs*".'

'You learn something new every day. You're sure I'm not intruding?'

'On the contrary.' Putting a brave face on the situation, Monsieur Pamplemousse took two more eggs from the carton.

'You've heard about the business last night, of course?' Beaseley settled himself down in the dinette. 'I have to admit I slept through it all. I'm glad they didn't pick on my trailer. I suppose they must have been after souvenirs. I don't even know if there was anyone inside it or not.'

Monsieur Pamplemousse remained silent as he poured another glass of wine. He was perfectly happy to let the other make the running while he carried on with the cooking.

Beaseley took the glass from Monsieur Pamplemousse. 'You know what they're saying now? There's a rumour Ron's disappearance heralds the Second Coming. I suspect the Publicity Department of cashing in. They'll probably let it simmer away for a while on what they quaintly call the back boiler – dreadful expression – then they'll make an official announcement.

'Von Strudel is beside himself – his favourite position – "Dos zis mean ve hov to wait three days before ve see him again?"'

Monsieur Pamplemousse couldn't help smiling. It was a larger than life imitation, but true or not, he could picture it. The oven timer started to ping.

'You've no more news, I suppose?' said Beaseley.

Monsieur Pamplemousse made a grimace. 'I went back with Pommes Frites last night, but by the time we got to the cave it was too late. He picked up a scent inside the tomb, but it was impossible to follow – too many people had been trampling around. No doubt he has stored it away for future reference. All I got for my pains was a lecture from the *vétérinaire* for removing him without permission. He's supposed to stay in under observation for another day.'

'I expect the vet's lonely, poor chap,' said Beaseley. 'Apart from a few odd doves I doubt if he has any other patients.'

Monsieur Pamplemousse put a large knob of butter into the last remaining saucepan and ignited the gas. Then he removed the eggs from the saucepan and added two more before serving Beaseley. The *asperge* had lost none of its colour. One up to the microwave.

'It would be an odd twist of fate,' said Beaseley. 'If our hero really has undergone some kind of Heavenly metamorphosis.'

'Ron Pickles?'

'I must admit it isn't a name I would have chosen. Ron Pickles of Sheffield doesn't have quite the same ring to it as Jesus of Nazareth.

'The Anglican church has been making valiant efforts to be "with it" in recent years, but being "with it" is one thing . . . Ron Pickles reeks of desperation . . . Mind you, I don't trust Romans either. He could be in the pay of the Vatican.'

Watching the smoke rise from the butter as it began to melt, Monsieur Pamplemousse wondered whether or not to come clean about his morning adventure. He decided against the idea, at least until they were through the first course. Everything was happening at once, and the timing of the boiled eggs was critical to their enjoyment.

'Perhaps he has been spirited away.'

'Carted away more like it,' said Beaseley. 'Did you see the look on the face of some of those girls during the filming yesterday? Talk about wetting their knickers with excitement – those that had any on. Given half a chance they would have been up there with him.' He broke off a piece of *baguette* and spread butter over it. 'I say – this *asperge is* good. In England we like it white and thick. It comes from always wanting to cover things up.'

Monsieur Pamplemousse prepared the dish of gnocchi, sprinkled some grated cheese over the top, covered it with clingfilm and decided to take a chance on the oven timing.

He opened a bottle of red Domaine de Trèvallon from Eloi Durrbach. It was labelled Coteaux d'Aix en Provence, Les Baux. An anomaly of the French wine laws, since Aix and Les Baux were some hundred kilometres apart. Expecting it to taste of bauxite, he was pleasantly surprised.

'So you don't subscribe to the Second Coming theory?' asked Beaseley. 'On the third day and all that . . .'

Monsieur Pamplemousse shook his head. 'If I did I would have to say that Monsieur Pickles's sense of timing has deserted him.' It seemed a good moment to bring Beaseley up to date.

For once Beaseley heard him out without a single interruption.

'You think Ron's disappearance was engineered all by himself?' he said at last.

'I am sure of it.' Monsieur Pamplemousse rubbed the back of his head. 'Aided and abetted by someone who turned out the lights. It would only have taken him a second to get out of the cave by himself. The "rock" was only a prop. It weighed next to nothing.' He recalled calling Ron's name in the *Cathédrale.*' He paused. 'Since when I suspect he has been hiding out in the *Cathédrale d'Images.* That would explain why he made so many visits there and why his refrigerator was empty. He must have been building up a cache of supplies.'

'So our Ron is trying to opt out of everything,' mused Beaseley.

Monsieur Pamplemousse nodded. 'For whatever reason.'

'Who needs reasons?' Beaseley attacked the idea with enthusiasm. 'Oscar Wilde hit the nail on the head when he said that in this world there are only two tragedies. One is not getting what one wants. The other is getting it. Brother Angelo has had more than his share of getting what he wants – or wanted. He wouldn't be the first pop star to find it had all gone sour on him. It's not always the having that's fun – it's the getting. Imagine ending up with life being one long "farewell" tour – your fans growing older and older in front of your very eyes.'

The timer began to ping again as the oven switched itself off. Monsieur Pamplemousse removed the gnocchi. Golden brown they were not. Doucette's worst suspicions would have been confirmed. He turned the oven grill on to make amends and while he was waiting for it to heat up he sliced some *saucisson* into a thick Provençal pottery dish. By the time he had finished, the gnocchi had reached a satisfactory colour.

The *saucisson* had been air-dried for at least six months – or so the shopkeeper had assured him. Pork predominated – coarsely chopped, with hard back fat added, and the beef had been finely minced. It had been seasoned with garlic, ground black pepper and peppercorns.

'Delicious!' said Beaseley appreciatively. 'The poet Ponchon once wrote a work of some ninety-six lines in honour of a *saucisson d'Arles*. It sounded somewhat excessive. Now I understand why.' He dabbed at his lips with a paper napkin. 'How does anyone disappear?' he continued. 'I mean really disappear off the face of the earth.'

'You need to be dedicated. It isn't as easy as it might sound. We live in a sophisticated and increasingly computerised society. So many things are cross-referenced these days. So many people keep records.' Monsieur Pamplemousse pushed the dish towards Beaseley. 'First and foremost you need a new identity. That can be found in any churchyard. Every time there is a bad plane crash or a ship is lost at sea there are bodies which cannot be identified because officially they never existed. People don't really care who you are so long as you can prove you are who you say you are. If you plan to travel at all you will need a passport. If it is a stolen one you need to be sure it didn't belong to someone with a record. That can be arranged if you know the right people – at a price – but Brother Angelo could afford to pay.'

'How about things like bank accounts and credit cards?' asked Beaseley.

'Anyone can open a bank account. Credit cards are only a matter of time. Companies are only too anxious to dish them out these days. You would need to change your appearance. Again, that isn't too difficult. A new hairstyle, a moustache and some plain glasses can work wonders. In the long term there is always plastic surgery.

'It is easier if you are very poor or very rich. The average person needs to work and on the whole they tend to gravitate towards the things they know how to do. Eventually life catches up with them. Their details get thrown up on a computer screen somewhere and questions are asked.

'Loneliness can be a problem. It isn't always as easy as it sounds . . . forsaking all that has gone before. Family . . . friends.'

'I doubt if he will be alone,' said Beaseley. *'Cherchez la femme.* It may show me up as a ghastly old-fashioned fuddy-duddy, but I bet whoever has been helping him is a woman. Someone familiar enough with the set-up to know which plug to pull to cause the maximum effect.'

'Mangetout?'

'You must be joking. You've heard them together. She would be another reason for disappearing.'

'The Swedish *au pair*?'

Beaseley shook his head. 'She may be very beautiful – if you like that sort of thing, but she's a bit gloomy. Miss Iceberg herself. I don't think I've once seen her smile. If you ask me there's someone else on the horizon.'

Monsieur Pamplemousse was reminded of his night visitor. He would remember her scent for some time to come. A potpourri of a perfume. And she had certainly been no iceberg. He poured some more wine.

'One thing's certain' said Beaseley. 'If Brother Angelo has done a bunk for good his sales will rocket sky-high.'

'You think so? Surely there's nothing so dead as last year's pop record. Or last week's, come to that.'

'Death establishes a permanent enshrinement. There will be no more, so what is left becomes infinitely more precious. The bad is forgotten, the good lives on. Especially if he's done a bit of stockpiling. Think of all the Jim Reeves hits there were after he got killed. Sixteen years after his death he was still able to command a single in the top ten. And take Elvis Presley. He died in 1977 and he's still a thriving industry. His memory is perpetuated in every possible way you can think of. Graceland gets nearly three-quarters of a million visitors a year. It's second only to the White House as the most visited home in the United States. Each year they have a contest of look-alikes. There's a torchlight procession to his old home during Death Week. It's virtually unstoppable.'

'You're not suggesting Presley is still alive?' enquired Monsieur Pamplemousse.

'Hardly. But there are those who are only too willing to believe that he is. Anyway, alive or dead, the best investment a pop star can make for his family is to keep back a few tapes which can be "discovered" after he's gone. If Ron really has opted out and he's played his cards right he could live in comfort for the rest of his life.'

They sat in silence for a while, each busy with his own thoughts. Monsieur Pamplemousse drained his glass, then wiped his plate clean with the last of the bread. Taking a cucumber, he cut it into large slices and put them on a plate at the bottom of the oven. Then he switched the timer to four minutes. According to Barbara Kafka it would remove all the odours.

'May I offer you some dessert?'

Beaseley shook his head.

'I have some fresh peaches. Sliced in half and sprinkled with sugar and a little lemon juice . . . steeped in some Beaumes-de-Venise . . .'

'You're worse than Montgomery,' said Beaseley. 'Don't tempt me.'

'Café.'

'No, thank you. I must go. I have things to do. I've stayed too long as it is. I'm taking advantage of the natural break to do some work on my book. Besides, it isn't every day you find Les Baux closed to the public. It's too good an opportunity to be missed. I have reached the point in my narrative when Les Baux must have been at its best: a hundred years before Raymond de Turenne arrived on the scene. It's hard to picture it now, but in the thirteenth century it was a town of several thousand inhabitants; a highly formalised society – famous as a court of love – where troubadours composed passionate verses in praise of the ladies in return for a kiss and one of these.'

Feeling inside his jacket Beaseley produced a peacock's feather. 'One of nature's miracles. A thing of beauty – a joy for ever. My inspiration.'

He gave a bow. 'Good luck in your search for the truth. I will leave you with another thought for today: "If a man will begin with certainties he shall end in doubts, but if he will be content to begin with doubts he shall end in certainties." Not me, I'm afraid – Bacon.'

As Gilbert Beaseley disappeared through the door Monsieur Pamplemousse noticed for the first time that there were white marks on the back of his jacket. The kind of marks which might be acquired through leaning against a limestone wall? Not for the first time he decided that Beaseley was someone who needed watching. He had a disconcerting habit of playing his cards very close to his chest.

Long after the other had gone, Monsieur Pamplemousse sat lost in thought. One thing was certain. If it had been Brother Angelo in the *Cathédrale* he wouldn't have risked staying there. He would have moved elsewhere, possibly meeting up with his lady love at a pre-arranged *rendez-vous*.

Time and again he went through the other clues he had found in the trailer; Daudet's *Letters from a Windmill,* the tourist brochure for Fontvieille marking the Massif de la Sainte Baume in the guidebook, the book matches from the restaurant in Les Saintes-Maries-de-la-Mer. The three places formed a rough triangle on a map of the area . . . all were within relatively easy reach . . .

Halfway through tidying the kitchen the telephone rang. It was the *hospice*. The patient admitted in the early hours was asking to see him.

There was some confusion over their names. For some reason the girl at the other end had them transposed. It sounded urgent – more of a command than a request – so he didn't bother correcting her.

'*Oui*. Tell him I will be there as soon as possible . . .'

'*Oui*, that is true. He can be a little difficult . . .'

'*Oui, mademoiselle . . .*'

Glad of a diversion, Monsieur Pamplemousse reached for his car keys. It sounded as though the Director was beginning to feel better.

8
PATIENT PROBLEMS

The Director emitted a loud groan. 'Please do not think I am being ungrateful, Aristide, but I am hardly in the mood for *cerises* at the present moment.'

Monsieur Pamplemousse glanced around for a chair, but the room was sparsely furnished in the manner of other *hospices* he had visited over the years. Establishments where the kindness and dedication of the nuns who tended the sick necessarily took priority over the *meubles* department. Finding nothing suitable, he perched himself on the side of the bed.

'I am sorry, *Monsieur.*' He gazed at an embroidered figure of an angel hanging above the bedhead. 'It was difficult to know what to bring you. I had thought of flowers, but then it occurred to me that the pollen might bring on a sneezing fit, which I'm sure would be painful. Oranges are difficult to eat without getting sticky. You would probably not welcome the presence of biscuit crumbs between the sheets. Cherries seemed to be a good compromise. They are a clean fruit, easy to eat, and I am told the variety known as Bigarreau are particularly sweet and succulent at the moment . . .'

'I daresay,' the Director winced as Monsieur Pamplemousse reached across the bed in order to help himself from a brown paper bag and in so doing compressed the mattress causing it to rise on the side furthest away from

334

him. 'However, if you will forgive my saying so, food is not uppermost in my mind. I did not drive all the way down to Les Baux only to end up in a hospital bed watching you eat cherries.'

Monsieur Pamplemousse took the point. 'Molluscs are not at their best during the summer months, *Monsieur*, otherwise I would have brought you some oysters. The ancient Romans set great store on their healing powers. Who knows? A kilo or two might even bring about some restoration of life in that part of your anatomy which I am told bore the brunt of last night's attack.'

The Director gave a shudder. 'Oysters are the very last thing I need, Pamplemousse.' He motioned despondently towards a large mound in the centre of the bed. 'I doubt if I shall ever feel the need to eat one again.'

He sighed. 'What am I going to tell Chantal when we retire for the night? She is not a demanding person, but neither does she lack powers of observation. Rather the reverse. She will be the first to ask why I have need of a cage to support the bedclothes above my nether regions. I am told it may be several weeks before I can dispense with some form of protection. I need a story, Pamplemousse. I need a good one and I need it quickly.'

'You could say you had your mind on other things, *Monsieur* – the departure of some rare species of bird for cooler climes, perhaps – and you accidentally walked into a bollard. It would accord with your injuries.'

'In the middle of the Camargue?' said the Director gloomily.

Monsieur Pamplemousse gazed out of the window. The *hospice* was on the outskirts of Arles and the Director's room afforded a view across the Grand Rhône to the city itself. The Pont de Trinquetaille was packed with traffic;

lorries and cars nose to tail moving at a snail's pace. Arles was a notorious bottleneck. He could see the Amphitheatre in the distance and some way to the left of that the railway station.

He glanced back at the Director. 'It is strange to think, *Monsieur*, that we cannot be very far from the spot where Vincent Van Gogh cut off his ear in a fit of madness and presented it wrapped in paper to a prostitute called Rachel.'

The Director glared at him. 'That is a singularly unfortunate remark in the circumstances, Pamplemousse,' he boomed. 'I trust you are not suggesting I should follow his example. I must say that if the purpose of visiting the sick is to bring them courage and good cheer, then you are signally failing in your task.'

Monsieur Pamplemousse fell silent. He was doing his best, but when the Director was in one of his difficult moods he was an impossible man to please. He didn't envy the nurse on duty.

'I would have come sooner, *Monsieur*. However, when I telephoned early this morning I gathered you were in intensive care.'

'You gathered correctly,' growled the Director. 'I was in intensive pain as well. I am extremely lucky to be alive.'

Monsieur Pamplemousse reached across for some more cherries. They were too good to waste. 'I could hardly believe my eyes when I saw you go past my trailer last night. It was like watching a ship at sea. An ocean liner caught in a storm.

'Wave upon wave of undulating flesh passed by my window. A great tide of pubescent womanhood moving as one, moaning and groaning as though possessed of the devil. In the moonlight and with Les Baux silhouetted against the night sky, it reminded me of a Disney cartoon –

336

something from *Fantasia* perhaps; the inevitability of Mickey Mouse as *The Sorcerer's Apprentice* coupled with Moussorgski's *Night on a Bare Mountain*.' Monsieur Pamplemousse looked around for somewhere to place his accumulation of stalks and stones and drew a blank. He settled for the top of a bedside cupboard. 'It would have made a wonderful series of photographs, but unfortunately by the time I had reloaded my camera your trailer had disappeared from view.'

The Director stared at him. 'You were reloading your camera, Pamplemousse?'

'It needed faster film, Monsieur. Madame Grante would not have been pleased if she had found I had wasted all thirty-six exposures, as I undoubtedly would have done had I used the reel which was already in the camera. Besides, it was Kodacolor and the scene cried out for black and white.'

'At a time like that you were worrying about whether to use colour or monochrome?' The Director sank back on to his pillow. The strain was clearly telling on him. 'Did it not cross your mind, Pamplemousse, to come to my assistance?'

'Certainly, *Monsieur*. That was my very first thought. Then it occurred to me to wonder what one person could possibly do against so many.'

A shudder ran through the Director's frame. It was quickly suppressed. A look of pain crossed his face. 'Please do not remind me, Aristide. For as long as I live I shall remember the moment when the trailer door burst open and that drug-crazed, sex-starved mob entered.'

'With respect, *Monsieur*, they may have been high on drugs, but from all I have seen I doubt if they were starved of sex. Appetites whetted beyond their control, perhaps . . .'

'Allow me to be the judge of that, Pamplemousse,' boomed the Director. 'I can still feel their hot breath as they descended on me, shouting and screaming, tearing off their garments, casting them right, left and centre. Those lascivious lips, those hands, searching, all the time searching. Fortunately their sheer weight caused the vehicle to fall over on to its side and I was able to seek refuge beneath some kind of wall cabinet. It was not a moment too soon. My pyjama jacket was in shreds; the trousers had been ripped from my body. I cannot think what possessed them.'

Monsieur Pamplemousse contemplated the Director. All manner of possible replies jostled for position on the tip of his tongue. He suppressed them. It must have been a terrifying experience; one he would have had no wish to undergo himself. The nearest equivalent in his own experience had been the time in St Georges-sur- Lie when he had been attacked by the girls of the Drum and Fife Band led by Miss Sparkling Saumur, but that had been nothing by comparison. On the other hand, there was a corner of his mind which couldn't help but ponder other aspects of the affair. Why the Director? What possible reason could there have been? Could it have had to do with something he had eaten earlier that evening? Some ultra powerful aphrodisiac he had accidentally stumbled upon. Something peculiar to the region. Perhaps, whatever it was had combined with the heat and the night air. Had he added a dab or two of XS before retiring? The Director was reputed to be partial to such bedtime extravagances. If it had been a field trial then it had succeeded beyond its maker's wildest dreams.

Suddenly realising he was being watched, Monsieur Pamplemousse pulled himself together. Speculation as to the reason for the Director's sorry state was a waste of time at this stage. The fact of the matter was it had happened. Perhaps Beaseley was correct in his assumption that the fans had simply been after souvenirs. If that were the case finding an occupied bed in what they must have mistakenly assumed to be Brother Angelo's trailer would have seemed like a Heaven-sent bonus.

'Undoubtedly it was a horrifying experience, *Monsieur*. There must have been three or four hundred females, all of whom had clearly totally lost control of themselves. Their emotions must have reached a peak and then snapped like a ship's hawser strained to breaking point. There was no stopping them.'

'Four hundred and twenty-three, Pamplemousse.' The Director assumed the self-satisfied air of a company auditor putting the final touches to the firm's annual accounts after an exceptionally prosperous year.

Monsieur Pamplemousse gazed at his chief with admiration. 'You were counting, *Monsieur*? The *journaux* put it at over 500.'

'You know as well as I do they always exaggerate,' said the Director. 'Editors hate untidy figures. Give a journalist an odd sum and he will immediately round it off in an upward direction . . .' He broke off. 'Did I hear you use the word *journaux*?'

Monsieur Pamplemousse corrected himself. 'The *journal, Monsieur*. So far it has only appeared in a local paper. One of their reporters happened to be passing at the time. It was clearly something of a scoop for him and he made the most of it. I was hoping to bring you a copy but unfortunately the first edition has sold out.'

'This is terrible news, Aristide. Publicity is the last thing I wish for.'

'It will be hard to avoid, *Monsieur*. The activities of a film company are always good copy and given the temporary closure of Les Baux – which I am told has given rise to a great deal of local discontent- any incident such as the one last night will be seized upon.'

'Pamplemousse, I charge you with making certain it goes no further.'

Monsieur Pamplemousse looked dubious. 'I will do my best, *Monsieur*. But it is the kind of story *Paris Match* would give their eye teeth for. They are almost bound to pick it up. Besides, if news about Brother Angelo's disappearance has leaked out – as I am sure it will have by now – they will be hot-footing it here anyway.'

He looked the Director in the eye. ' I have no doubt the Paris boys are on a plane bound for Marseille at this very moment. Those that aren't will be on the TGV.'

'Then you must intervene. They must be stopped at all costs.'

'Short of sabotage, *Monsieur*, I doubt very much if that will be possible. There is an hourly service at peak periods.'

There was a knock on the door followed by a rustle of cloth as a nurse in nun's attire entered the room. Monsieur Pamplemousse rose to his feet as she came towards them holding a thermometer in her right hand. Brushing past him, she thrust one end into the Director's mouth.

'Monsieur Pamplemousse, you are very naughty. We can hear your voice right at the other end of the corridor.'

Monsieur Pamplemousse gazed at the girl's back. *'Mademoiselle*, I hardly think . . .'

He was about to remonstrate in no uncertain terms – if anyone had been raising his voice it had been the Director – but he broke off as a gurgling noise issued from the depths of the pillow. For a moment or two it looked as though his chief was about to have a fit. His head was rolling from side to side: his eyes were large and imploring.

A fit? Or was he trying to convey some kind of message? Monsieur Pamplemousse waited for the answer. He was glad help was at hand. There was something infinitely reassuring about the unflustered way the nurse was handling the matter. Had he been there on his own he would undoubtedly have pressed the emergency call button.

'There now! Just as I thought.' She removed the thermometer and looked at it with professional disapproval. Her worst suspicions confirmed, she entered the figure on a chart at the end of the bed. 'I do not want to hear another word, Monsieur Pamplemousse,' she said severely. 'Otherwise I shall have to tell the Mother Superior.'

Turning away from the bed, she assumed her addressing of visitors tone. *'Cinq minutes, Monsieur.* That is all. *Cinq minutes.* Not a second more.'

As the door closed behind her, Monsieur Pamplemousse stared at the Director.

'Monsieur . . .'

The Director placed a finger to his lips. 'You heard what the good lady said, Aristide. *Silence. Défence de parler.'*

'Monsieur. Why did she call you Pamplemousse?'

Monsieur Pamplemousse had to admit that the Director did have the grace to colour slightly.

'I was about to tell you, Aristide – just before the nurse came in. When I was admitted here last night I was delirious. I hardly knew what I was saying. The simple fact is that when they asked me for my details your name sprang to mind.'

'My name, Monsieur?' Monsieur Pamplemousse could still hardly believe his ears.

'I could scarcely give them my own. A man in my position has to watch out for these things, Aristide. Recognition would be disastrous. It would undermine the authority of *Le Guide;* an authority which I need hardly remind you has been painstakingly built up over the years. Our illustrious founder, Monsieur Hippolyte Duval, would turn in his grave. That apart, there is Chantal to be considered. She wouldn't give me a moment's peace ever again.'

Monsieur Pamplemousse stared at him.

'What about *my* peace, *Monsieur.* Supposing Doucette gets to hear?'

'She is used to your philanderings, Pamplemousse. It would come as no surprise. One more escapade is neither here nor there.'

Monsieur Pamplemousse reached for his hat.

Alarm was written across the Director's countenance. 'You are not going already?'

'You heard what the girl said, *Monsieur. Défence de parler.'*

'Please, Aristide . . . Stay a few minutes longer. There's a good *homme.* I have been thinking . . .'

'I, too, have been thinking,' said Monsieur Pamplemousse coldly. 'My thoughts tell me it is time I returned to Paris. My work here is done, if indeed it ever began. Such culinary advice as I was able to offer has been totally disregarded. No one is in the slightest bit interested. I was sent here under false pretences . . .'

'Aristide, I know you of old. Had I told you the real reason why I wanted you to come down here, imagine the fuss you would have made. You would have dreamed up all manner of excuses. The truth is, when, over dinner, I heard that subversive deeds were afoot, I volunteered your services on the spur of the moment. I should have consulted you first, of course, but the offer was accepted with gratitude. I then found myself on the horns of a dilemma. There was no going back.'

'We all have our problems, *Monsieur.*'

'Aristide, you cannot mean this. You cannot be serious. You cannot abandon me. At any moment the reporters may burst into this room. I am hardly in a state to defend myself. They will be like a pack of wolves. There will be photographers . . .'

'Are you suggesting, *Monsieur*, that I should by some means or other spirit you away?'

'You know about these things, Aristide. There must be somewhere I can hide . . . just for the time being . . . until I am able to walk again?'

The Director looked around him desperately, as if searching for inspiration. 'As I said a moment ago, I have been thinking . . . on your way back to Paris why don't you take your time. Pay a visit to Bocuse. Make a little detour via Troisgros at Roanne. But before that there are other three-Stock-Pot establishments *en route*. There is Pic at Valence. I need hardly tell you . . .'

Monsieur Pamplemousse had a feeling of *dèjá vu*. If it was shared by the Director, there was no outwardly visible sign. The conversation in his office only a few days earlier might never have taken place. He hesitated. Deep down, now that his feeling of indignation had subsided, he knew there was no question of his not coming to the rescue. On the other hand it would do no harm to let the chief ramble on for a while. It would be interesting to see what other goodies he would dream up.

'There is a little restaurant north of Orange you could visit. I called in there myself on the way down. The *patron* is known locally as the King of the truffles. His concoc-

343

tions, Aristide, are out of this world; omelettes which are *baveuse* in the *oeuf* department, but filled with great crunchy chunks of the noble fungus. He is also a compulsive buyer of wine from the Rhône valley. The only criticism one might level at him is that his list is too eclectic. It is overpowering in its vastness. It makes the choice difficult. But that is a fault on the right side. I would welcome your views.'

Monsieur Pamplemousse sighed. He knew when he was fighting a losing battle.

Sensing that capitulation was close at hand, the Director held out his hand. 'I knew you wouldn't let me down, Aristide.'

'Leave it with me, *Monsieur*. I will do my best.'

'I could not ask for more,' said the Director simply. 'And the troubles back at the location? You will look into those too?'

'I will look into those too, *Monsieur.*' He took the proffered hand. 'But first things first.'

They were only just in time. The door opened and the nurse entered. She looked at her watch. 'Your time is up, *Monsieur.*'

'I think possibly Monsieur . . . er . . . Pamplemousse needs his sheets changing.' It was hard to resist the temptation. 'He is very restless and he wants to look his best for the photographers when they arrive.'

'*Au revoir,* Aristide,' said the Director pointedly. 'I think you should hurry.'

'I shall be back, *Monsieur*. Rest assured, one way or another I shall return.'

'Tcchk! Tcchk!
'*Sacré bleu!*

344

'Mon Dieu! Mon Dieu!
'Un désastre formidable!'

Carefully removing a pair of rubber gloves, Monsieur Pamplemousse placed them on the bedside table alongside the cherry stones which he had abandoned earlier in the day. Out of the corner of his eye he could see the Director visibly blanching. Insofar as cold sweat was metaphorically able to mix with calcium carbonate, his face had gone a chalky white. Enough was enough.

Monsieur Pamplemousse was also only too well aware that his every move was being watched by others in the room, albeit with the reverence accorded to those whose knowledge and experience by definition far outshone that of his audience, but he needed to be careful. So far everything had gone according to plan; it would be a pity to over-play his hand.

It was early evening before he had arrived back at the *hospice*. Glancing up at his reflection in the rear view mirror as he drove in through the gates, he'd had to admit that the time he had spent at the make-up desk in his trailer had not been wasted. Unable to locate Anne-Marie, it had been very much a do-it-yourself job, but he looked – and felt – ten years younger. A thin layer of Mehron 26A Tan Glow make-up had changed his skin tone and formed the base for other titivations. No more than an inch of shadow applied midway between his cheek and jaw bones had changed the shape of his face. A thin line of collodion applied to his forehead suggested a past accident, repaired perhaps by another master surgeon. Parting his hair on the wrong side had worked wonders. His natural greyness now looked becomingly premature. Distinguished was a word which sprang to mind. Matching eyebrows and moustache provided the finishing touch.

Wardrobe had come up with a lightweight tropical suit and suitable accessories. Props had provided a pair of thick-rimmed plain glass spectacles. Both departments had been only too pleased to get their teeth into the problem – no questions asked. It helped break the monotony of waiting for something to happen. Work on the production had been brought to a temporary standstill. The local police had been much in evidence; taking statements, measuring wheel tracks, interviewing eyewitnesses. Brother Angelo was still nowhere to be found. The big test came when he found himself being interviewed for the second time in less than an hour by the same officer, who failed to recognise him.

Having parked his car as far away from the main entrance to the *hospice* as possible – apart from the fact that it wouldn't do for anyone to recognise it, a 2CV was hardly in keeping with his new role – he had taken the bull by the horns, relying on a peremptory manner to bluff his way through. Speed was the order of the day. 'Don't give the other side time to think,' was his motto.

With a white gown billowing out behind, a stethoscope hanging loose from one of its pockets, Monsieur Pample-mousse couldn't help but wonder if he wasn't overdoing things slightly. Would an eminent surgeon dress in such a manner? Wouldn't he be more likely to arrive immaculately attired and with a beautiful secretary in tow? But he needn't have worried. The only reason the red carpet hadn't been rolled out was because his arrival had taken everyone completely by surprise, which was as he'd intended. Had he forewarned the *hospice* he was coming, they might have tried looking him up in some medical *Who's Who*.

Using the Director's own name had been an added touch. Monsieur Leclercq of the 16th arrondissement produced the desired effect. Say no more. It was an area of Paris renowned for housing the *crème de la crème* of the medical profession. As an address, its very mention was an open sesame.

What he hadn't bargained on was the Director himself failing to penetrate his disguise. That needed to be rectified.

He turned away from the bed. 'This man must be operated on as soon as possible. Otherwise,' he made a suitable gesture to his audience. *'Amputé!'*

The Director's face went an even paler shade of white.

'Do not worry, *Monsieur*,' hissed Monsieur Pample-mousse.

'Do not worry!' repeated the Director. 'You use the word *amputé* about one of my most precious possessions and then you say "Do not worry". I demand a second opinion.'

Monsieur Pamplemousse's heart sank. 'The operation will need to be done in Paris,' he said, loudly and clearly for the Director's benefit. 'Away from here.'

'Amputé!' A man in evening dress who had clearly been called away from some important function turned to the Sister. 'Why was I not informed of this, Sister Agnes?'

'Monsieur . . .' The Sister was temporarily thrown off balance. 'It is the first I have heard . . .'

'Silence!' Hurriedly breaking into the conversation before it took a dangerous turn, Monsieur Pamplemousse hooked the hearing end of his stethoscope over the Director's ears. 'Keep very still, *Monsieur.'*

He turned to the others, 'An old trick. It keeps them occupied when delirium is setting in. Poor fellow. He is so overwrought he doesn't even recognise his old family surgeon, Monsieur Leclercq.'

Placing the business end to his lips he hissed the words 'It is I, Pamplemousse.' His words produced a satisfactory response. The Director gave a start and nearly fell out of bed. 'See, it works!'

'Now, you have some x-rays, I trust. Blood group confirmed? Measurements taken?'

The others exchanged glances. 'There has hardly been time, Monsieur Leclercq,' said Sister Agnes nervously. 'The doctor who has been attending Monsieur Pamplemousse is off duty and . . .'

'Tcchk! Tcchk!' Monsieur Pamplemousse was beginning to enjoy himself. 'I ask because it may be necessary to carry out a transplant.'

'A transplant! *Mon Dieu!*' A noticeable tremor of excitement ran round those present. One of the nurses crossed herself.

'You could carry out the operation here, *Monsieur.* Such an historic moment will help us gain valuable publicity for our *Amis du Hospice* fund-raising project. Doubtless you saw the board outside. If I may, I would like to be present while it takes place. Perhaps an article in the medical *journal* afterwards. With your permission, of course . . .'

'I am afraid that will not be possible,' said Monsieur Pamplemousse firmly. 'Utterly out of the question. To start with, the patient belongs to a rare blood group – *très, très rare.* Then there is the question of finding a suitable donor. Monsieur Pamplemousse is from the north. He is very particular about his lineage. He would not wish to be endowed with a Provençal attachment. Nor, I suspect, would Madame Pamplemousse be best pleased.

'I shall, of course, perform the operation myself. He must be transferred to Paris immediately.' Monsieur Pamplemousse looked at his watch. 'If he is not on his way within the hour I shall not be responsible for the consequences. The success rate, alas, is not high. Time is not on our side.'

Sister Agnes gave a tiny curtsy. '*Oui, Monsieur.* At once, *Monsieur. Je m'en occuperai.*'

'I trust you know what you are doing,' cried the Director as the others rushed out of the room leaving them on their own for the moment.

'*Monsieur,* have I ever let you down?'

'There is always a first time, Pamplemousse. Words like *amputé* and transplant should not be treated lightly. I fear the worst. I do not trust the medical profession. Did you see the look in that man's eyes? The one in evening dress. A frustrated butcher if ever I saw one. Doubtless he was attending a local bullfight. He cannot wait to get me on the slab.'

'Do not alarm yourself, *Monsieur.*' Monsieur Pample-mousse laid a soothing hand on the Director's shoulder. 'Everything is under control. I have arranged for you to be admitted to a private hospital in Paris. It is an establish-ment of the utmost discretion. They deal at government level with all manner of problems, so they are well used to the unusual.'

He felt inside the pocket of his gown and withdrew a small brown envelope. 'I have taken the liberty of purchasing a series of postcards particular to the region. They depict various delicacies – *soupe au pistou, boeuf en daube, salade noiçoise* . . . so they will not tie you down as to exactly where you are staying. If you care to inscribe them as though you are constantly on the move and address them to Madame Leclercq, I will see they are mailed at regular intervals. A short non-committal message or two along the lines of "Wish you were here", or "Regret severe local storms have disrupted lines of communication" will suffice. She need never know. In the meantime . . .'

The door was flung open.

'Monsieur Leclercq . . . there is a private ambulance leaving shortly for Paris . . . but it is meant for another patient.'

'Then you must commandeer it!'

'*Mais* . . . it is an emergency case. He has only just been admitted.'

'No "buts",' thundered Monsieur Pamplemousse. 'This is equally a matter of life and death. I shall hold you all personally responsible.' He held the door open. 'If nothing is done I shall inform the minister . . . heads will roll.'

Following Sister Agnes out into the corridor, Monsieur Pamplemousse viewed the scene with satisfaction. The normal cloistered calm had vanished. He couldn't remember when he'd last seen nuns running. The rustle of their habits sounded like a flock of frightened birds taking to the air.

A man encased from head to foot in plaster was being whisked on a trolley from one room to another. It must be the emergency Sister Agnes had spoken of, for he heard the bleep of someone being paged. It sounded urgent. Any momentary pangs of conscience were quickly stifled. In this day and age someone would surely find a solution to the problem.

Porters scurried to and fro. Somewhere in the distance he heard a telephone ringing. No one was bothering to answer it. It had all the ingredients of a television serial at its most chaotic. The only thing missing was Von Strudel shouting *'Dummkopf'* through his megaphone. Given his presence, the scenario would have been complete.

Monsieur Pamplemousse moved to one side as two more porters headed his way pushing a trolley. They disappeared into the Director's room. Moments later they emerged.

The Director managed a wave as he shot past. 'You are a good fellow, Aristide. I shall not forget this.'

Monsieur Pamplemousse waited just long enough to make sure his chief wasn't being wheeled towards the operating theatre, then he paid his respects to the sister.

'*Chère* Sister Agnes, please ensure Monsieur Pamplemousse is well looked after. And beware of answering any questions from *les journaux*. In return I will see your kindness and efficiency does not go unrewarded. A little contribution towards your fund, *peut-être?*'

It was the least the Director could do in the circumstances.

Back at base Monsieur Pamplemousse turned off just inside the main entrance and drove along a rutted pathway towards the scene of the Director's downfall. The trailer was still lying on its side. It looked sad and abandoned. Someone from wardrobe must have made a desultory attempt at retrieving the discarded garments, for they were laid out in neat piles on a trestle table awaiting collection. Using a window frame as a foothold he climbed up on top of the trailer. The door was lying open. He peered through the opening. The inside had been stripped bare. Any thoughts he might have had about retrieving the Director's belongings died a death. There weren't any. The souvenir hunters had picked it clean. He clambered unsteadily to his feet.

Closing the door was almost like putting the lid back on a coffin. There was an air of finality about it.

It had been an automatic gesture; akin to straightening the cutlery on an untidily laid table, no more. But as the door fell shut he stared at it. There, right in front of his eyes, was the answer to one of the questions uppermost in his mind. The name board screwed to the top of the door bore not the Director's name as he might have expected, but that of BROTHER ANGELO.

351

Monsieur Pamplemousse stared at it for several seconds while he absorbed the implications. It certainly explained why the Director had been so disorientated the previous evening and why the fans had descended on the trailer.

He knelt down and examined the name board more closely. The slots in the screws used to fasten it to the door showed distinct signs of having been tampered with. The metal was shining through in places where the layer of fresh paint had been penetrated.

Climbing back down off the roof, Monsieur Pamplemousse made his way back to his car. He was tempted to use the telephone and ring his chief to tell him the news. Then he thought better of it. The girl at the switchboard might well listen in. Given all that was going on he wouldn't have blamed her.

Switching on the engine, he drove slowly back towards his quarters, scanning the track on either side as he went. He had only gone a matter of some twenty metres or so when he saw what he was looking for. Something silver gleaming in the scrub to his right. It was the end of a long screwdriver. Monsieur Pamplemousse picked it up by the middle of the blade and wrapped the handle carefully in his handkerchief. Paint still adhered to the business end.

His immediate assumption was that someone had done a straight swap of the Director's name plate and Brother Angelo's, but as he drew near the site he realised others had been tampered with too. His own name plate was now attached to the door of Mangetout's trailer. It was no wonder the Director had gone there by mistake. Familiarity bred contempt and the old hands probably never even bothered to look for their names any more. Why should they? Monsieur Pamplemousse had to admit he had stopped doing so himself. It had never occurred to him to check the name plate on his own door, any more than he had bothered to check the name on Brother Angelo's trailer when he'd broken into it. To compound the problem, when he reached Pommes Frites' trailer he discovered it bore the name of Gilbert Beaseley.

Someone had taped a message to the door. 'Hope I have done the right thing. Am a little confused.' It bore an illegible signature.

Monsieur Pamplemousse tapped on the door and waited a moment before trying the handle. It opened to his touch.

The expression on Pommes Frites' face when he saw who his visitor was made his previous performance by the Ark pale into insignificance. Unalloyed joy radiated from every pore as he jumped to his feet, scattering bowls of food and water in all directions.

Monsieur Pamplemousse responded in like vein. Words were unnecessary. Recriminations would have been unthinkable; worse than the endless post-mortem of two bridge players raking over past mistakes. What had been done was in the past, and not up for discussion. A touch, a gesture, a lick, the wagging of a tail, a lingering pat, they said it all. Master and hound were as one again.

That fact clearly established, Pommes Frites stretched and wagged his tail in anticipation as he followed his master out of the trailer and back towards their rightful home. The signs were unmistakable. Clearly, there was work to be done.

9

DID HE FALL OR
WAS HE PUSHED?

Monsieur Pamplemousse set off with Pommes Frites shortly after breakfast the following morning. It was time he put his money where his thoughts lay. To 'put up, or shut up' as the Americans would say.

It was good to be together again. Together and on the open road. Pommes Frites patently felt the same way. You could tell by the way he was sitting. If Pommes Frites didn't want to go somewhere, then he always left Monsieur Pamplemousse in no doubt as to his feelings. Driving a 2CV with some fifty kilos or so of solid flesh leaning the wrong way every time you turned a corner was extremely tiring, not to say hazardous. Today he was behaving like a seasoned pillion passenger on the back of a motorcycle; swaying with the movement rather than against it.

With the canvas roof rolled back and the roar of the slip-stream in their ears, life was as it should be; the horizon free for the moment of any unpleasant blemishes, the world their oyster.

Leaving Les Baux behind them, Monsieur Pample-mousse headed towards Fontvieille, anxious to put his theory to the test.

His feeling of euphoria was short-lived. The harsh world of reality soon made its presence felt. It was Sunday traffic at its worst. Caught behind a slow-moving coachload of schoolchildren, he turned on the radio. There was music, followed by a news bulletin: a catalogue of international woes. After the headlines came the local items. Pride of place was given to the latest happenings at the film location, but there was no mention of the Director. Sister Agnes must have taken his little talk to heart. Brother Angelo's mysterious disappearance, now officially admitted, dominated the talk. Speculation as to its possible religious significance was growing.

Monsieur Pamplemousse wondered idly if Beaseley had his radio on. He doubted it. When he'd tried ringing the other's number before leaving there had been no reply. Quite likely he was out early gathering material for his book.

There was an interview with a local Cure who cast cold water on the very idea of a Second Coming. God, he implied, moved in mysterious ways, but there were limits even to His degree of tolerance. Enlisting the aid of a pop star – an English one at that – was one of them. On the spot interviews with various locals produced a wide variation of views. Clearly there were those who would like to believe the worst – or the best, according to one's standpoint.

At least the Director was back in Paris by now. A second telephone call had confirmed his arrival there in the early hours of that morning.

Any hopes Monsieur Pamplemousse might have entertained about losing the coach in Fontvieille were quickly dashed. As they approached some traffic lights in the centre of the village the driver signalled a left turn. Monsieur Pamplemousse followed suit. Small faces gazed out of the rear window at Pommes Frites as they were tailed up a long pine-shaded avenue leading out of the village and on to the D33, then left again into a vast and crowded car park. There they waved goodbye as the coach peeled off and disappeared in a cloud of dust.

The picture in the guidebook which accompanied the description of the windmill where Alphonse Daudet was reputed to have drawn the inspiration for his stories showed a circular stone building with a black pointed roof standing in splendid isolation on top of a small hill to the south of the village. A cypress tree framed the left side of the picture, whilst a solitary goat to its right directed the viewer's eye towards the great wooden sails of the mill itself. The tips of two small patches of white cloud in the top corners of the picture added symmetry, breaking up an otherwise azure blue sky. There was not a human being in sight. It was a peaceful scene, one which any writer would have yearned for. An ideal spot for a lover's meeting.

As Monsieur Pamplemousse drew in between two coaches, one taking on a load of old-age pensioners, the other in the act of filling the vacuum left by the departure of another, it struck him that the guidebook's picture was either a very old photograph or whoever was responsible had been singularly fortunate in his choice of days. There were people as far as the eye could see, people preparing for a picnic, people playing games, people taking pictures of other people. The hill on which the windmill stood was alive with antlike figures. There was no sign of the goat. It must have long since given up in disgust.

Monsieur Pamplemousse decided to follow its example. Without even bothering to get out of his car, he bade farewell to the Moulin de Daudet and headed back the way they had come, resolutely turning left in the village on to the road to Arles.

Despite his momentary disappointment, it was what detection was all about; the piecing together of unrelated scraps of information – discarding one, picking up another, like pieces in a jigsaw puzzle. Completing the final picture was often a matter of trial and error. That and painstaking application. If the ticket stubs to the *Cathédrale* had turned up trumps there was always a possibility one of the other clues might do likewise.

A member of an animal rights group was holding forth on the radio, speaking on behalf of the South East Asian civet, prized for its overpowering odour of narcissus and much used by the perfume industry as a fixer and blender, but when questioned about Brother Angelo's disappearance he denied all knowledge.

A flower grower from Grasse declared that even if it wasn't the Second Coming, it was still an act of God. Revenge on the profiteers in Paris who kept forcing down prices and depriving people of their livelihood.

Arles was stiflingly hot and the traffic was at a standstill. It was a classic man-made bottleneck. Posters advertised a week's programme of bullfighting, which couldn't help matters. The city looked full of sightseers. Cafés and restaurants lining the main through-road were already crowded. The holiday season was well underway.

A little way out of Arles he turned off the main road in order to make a detour round the Étang de Vaccarès.

The Camargue was as he remembered it – vast and flat; all 800 square kilometres of it. Driving past beds of reeds and rushes, he could already taste the salt in the air. There were pine trees shaped like parasols, acres of furze bushes, and rice fields everywhere; it was the big new industry. Thick cypress hedges acted as windbreaks. *Promenades à Cheval* signs proliferated; so much for the famous wild horses.

They passed a little cottage with a wooden sabot hanging by the front door. In the old days it would have been ready to receive an anonymous token of friendship from any passer-by who felt so inclined – an egg, a posy of flowers, an orange; now it had most likely been put there simply as a tourist attraction. There were roses in the garden, growing to a height undreamed of further north.

Discounting all the wild theories on the radio, the inescapable fact was that Ron Pickles, alias Brother Angelo, had disappeared without trace. The more he thought about it, the more he went over his conversation with Beaseley, which had helped crystallise his own thoughts, the more he felt sure he was right. Apart from Beaseley, he had passed on his suspicions to no one. But knowing something deep down inside was a world away from proving it to be true.

The vast Étang came into view. It wasn't hard to imagine the furore the film company must have caused when they turned up intending to part it. At certain times of the year they might have got more than they bargained for. According to the guidebook, waves could reach a height of a metre or more.

He spotted a whitewashed, thatched *gardien's cabane* nestling amongst some tamarisk trees. Built with a rounded rear and a tiny opening at the front to provide shelter from the Mistral, it would be equipped with a fireplace and everything needed to hold out for days at a time. In theory it would be an ideal hiding place for anyone on the run, but in practice the reverse would almost certainly be true. The Camargue was still a relatively unpopulated area. Anything the slightest bit out of the ordinary would be spotted immediately.

A brick-red patch in the water resolved itself into a group of flamingoes. One leg tucked beneath their plumage, they stood erect on their remaining limb as they busied themselves over an early lunch. Beaks plunged deep into the mud in search of worms and insect larvae and whatever else of interest might be lurking beneath the surface.

Monsieur Pamplemousse brought his attention back to Ron's disappearance. He had lain awake most of the night turning the problem over and over in his mind. It seemed to him that Beaseley's theory of *cherchez la femme* was the most likely. Ron must have had an accomplice and given his reputation it was more than likely to be female.

It certainly wasn't his agent. He was going around giving a passable imitation of the man who had lost the goose that laid the golden egg, and his fears sounded genuine.

And if Ron had fled the *Cathédrale*, where would he have gone to? Presumably somewhere not very far away. He'd left it too late to try and leave the country – at least for the time being. From all the coverage he had received everybody would be on the lookout for him.

If that were the case, then it would need to be some- where pre-planned where he could meet up with his girl Friday when the coast was clear.

Daudet's windmill had been a disappointment, that he had to admit. Browsing through the guidebook at three o'clock in the morning it had looked an ideal rendezvous for a romantic meeting.

A buzzard on a reconnaissance mission flew high over- head, keeping a watchful eye on the passing scene. The flamingoes took to the air in a perfect V-formation.

Monsieur Pamplemousse glanced at his watch, wondering if he had time to stop and take a picture, but it was gone eleven-thirty. By rights they should be in Les Saintes-Maries-de-la-Mer.

At least they were making better time than Van Gogh. One June day in 1889 it had taken the painter five hours to make the journey by *diligence* from Arles. Including stops,

359

Monsieur Pamplemousse in his *Deux Chevaux* had taken just under an hour. There was one great difference. After his journey Van Gogh was able to write to his brother, 'I walked one night along the deserted beach by the sea . . . It was beautiful.'

The pleasure of walking along a deserted beach was one which they were clearly not destined to share. Monsieur Pamplemousse's heart sank as he caught sight of an arrow pointing to an out-of-town car park. Ignoring the sign, he took a chance and followed one marked *Centre Ville*. Luck was with him. He found an empty space on a pedestrian crossing, and from there fought his way down towards the sea front and the old fortified church, built to commemorate the landing of Mary Magdalene after she had been cast adrift from the Holy Land. It was number two on his itinerary.

Place de l'Église was full of gypsies; the girls, dark-eyed and proud, pushed their way in front of the passers-by, almost daring them on pain of unmentionable future disasters to say no to having their fortune told. Any one of them, hearing his story, would probably have told him he was wasting his time. Anywhere less suitable for a clandestine meeting would be hard to imagine. He left Pommes Frites to wait while he went inside the church.

The one-franc coin Michelin advised him to have ready to feed into a coin operated light switch was redundant. The church was packed. There was nothing for it but to join the shuffling crowd of half-naked sightseers waving their video cameras to and fro like so many hosepipes.

It was hard to tell what they were thinking: a pause to see the fresh water well inside the nave at the far end, down into the crypt for a momentary glimpse of the statue of Sarah, patron saint of the gypsies, up again past a side altar with its model of the legendary boat, and suddenly he was outside again, inexorably ejected like the cork from a champagne bottle.

Pommes Frites had a faraway look in his eyes. He could have been dreaming once again of a penthouse kennel in Beverly Hills, or shopping at Cartier for a diamond encrusted collar. Monsieur Pamplemousse gave him a consoling pat. Mary Magdalene would have sympathised. She would have turned round and gone straight back to Palestine. Although in truth Pomme Frites' preoccupation had more to do with a gnawing feeling in his stomach than with his immediate surroundings.

The Cinema Le Camargue down by the harbour was showing an old Von Strudel film. A children's carousel on the other side of the road was doing a better trade.

It was as they were making their way slowly back to the car along an avenue Frédéric Mistral awash with souvenir shops, bars, cafes and restaurants, that Monsieur Pamplemousse remembered the matchbox he'd been carrying in his pocket. There was no point in leaving Les Saintes-Maries-de-la-Mer without exploring all the possibilities.

Le Croissant d'Or turned out to be a Chinese restaurant. It was a card of sorts, but not exactly the one he'd been expecting. Hardly the ace of trumps.

After the blinding sunlight, the inside looked distinctly gloomy. Even the bamboo had been painted black. A bead curtain made of old Coca Cola crown tops separated the kitchen from the main eating area. An unseen loudspeaker was emitting strains of what sounded like an oriental version for Chinese wood block and crash cymbals of 'I Did it My Way'.

Monsieur Pamplemousse chose a pavement table. Perhaps Ron, brought up on a diet of Chinese take aways in his native Sheffield, had been drawn to the restaurant on a wave of nostalgia – or desperation. He was beginning to feel that way himself.

Pommes Frites eyed his bowl of bean-shoots with a look of distaste bordering on downright suspicion; aware perhaps, with that extrasensory perception given to canines, that in other circumstances, in other climes, he might well have found himself featuring on the menu as an integral part of lunch 'C' – (six *personnes min.*). It was not what he'd had in mind while he'd been waiting outside the church.

Lunch was a hurried affair – the Chinese habit of bringing everything at once was not without its merits, but even so, by the time they had finished the restaurant was full. Monsieur Pamplemousse called for *l'addition* and mentally crossed it off his list.

Leaving Les Saintes-Maries-de-la-Mer by a back road, he headed for the car ferry near the mouth of the Rhône. It would be better than driving back to Arles and risking getting snarled up in the traffic again.

It was not the best idea he had ever had. There was a long queue of like-minded drivers for the double-ended, drive on drive off boat, and it was late afternoon before they eventually arrived at their last port of call. Set high up in the steep northern face of La Sainte-Baume Massif, it was the cave where Mary Magdalene was reputed to have spent her last thirty-three years, and the one remaining place marked in Ron's guidebook.

As he parked his car, Monsieur Pamplemousse recognised the coach he'd followed into Fontvieille earlier in the day.

From where he stood it was impossible to see beyond the first hundred metres or so of the stony path which led up to the cave. It disappeared into a forest of huge trees – beech and lime and maple – rising majestically out of an undergrowth thick with holly and ivy.

He consulted *Michelin*. They quoted an hour on foot there and back. Another way of putting it was more likely to be an upward trudge of three quarters of an hour plus fifteen minutes to come back down again.

Glad of a chance to stretch his legs, Pommes Frites ran on ahead as they set off up the path. The first of the kamikaze mosquitos arrived almost at once. They were followed by a swarm of madly persistent flies. Halfway up they met an old lady sitting on a rock, awaiting the return of her family who were making the final assault. Monsieur Pamplemousse was sorely tempted to join her. Pommes Frites paused long enough to slake his thirst from a fresh water spring.

The path began doubling back on itself concertina fashion. Voices assailed them from all sides as schoolteachers dressed in suitable shorts led their chattering flocks on what was probably an oft-repeated end-of-term outing.

Steps carved into the sheer rockface came into view, followed by a door leading to the Sanctuary. There were signs asking for silence; others were marked NO FLASH and CHIENS INTERDITS. None were having much effect.

Predictably, it was a repeat of everything that had gone before. The inside of the vast semi-circular cave was packed with visitors. It was cold and it looked as though it was permanently wet. The only dry place visible in the flickering light from the candles was in a cavity behind the altar. It contained a recumbent statue commemorating the thirty-three years Mary Magdalene had spent there in solitude.

Monsieur Pamplemousse paid his respects and left. Ignoring a souvenir shop run by the Dominicans, he rejoined Pommes Frites on the balcony. The view from a thousand metres up was magnificent; the mountains in the far distance had a mauve haze from the fields of lavender. But he wasn't there for the view.

As an exercise in detection it had been a total disaster. In truth, romantic notions arrived at under cover of darkness seldom lived up to their promise next day. A feeling of dejection came over Monsieur Pamplemousse as he made his way down the steps, past a bronze Calvary and out through the gate to begin their downward trek. It had been a totally wasted expedition.

Taking it slowly to avoid catching up with a crowd of schoolchildren, he found himself wondering how the Director was getting on.

'As well as could be expected,' according to the Sister. That probably meant he was feeling sorry for himself. If he knew he'd been the innocent victim of a practical joke he would have felt even more upset. Or was it a joke? One of Von Strudel's 'bugginks'. Swapping two name boards might have been someone's idea of a bit of harmless fun. Moving four around was taking a joke a little too far. Six smacked of some deeper reason.

At least his chief was safely tucked up in a mosquito-free bed. He didn't know how lucky he was.

Monsieur Pamplemousse suddenly felt cut off from things. Paris seemed a long way away, remote and eminently desirable, even though half the population would have fled to the sea.

Perhaps by the time he and Pommes Frites got back to Les Baux there would be some news. Ron might even have reappeared. Maybe it was all a publicity stunt; a gigantic

Bible-inspired hoax. If that were so his time in hiding must be almost up.

Alone in his trailer, the memory of his night-time visitor still disturbingly fresh in his mind, it had been all too easy to arrive at a romantic answer. Beaseley would have embroidered it in cinematic terms; music reaching a climax as the two lovers walked towards each other in long shot before meeting in a passionate embrace. Cut to BCU. Hold for the final chords. Dissolve. Credits superimposed over a shot of the windmill.

Monsieur Pamplemousse stopped dead in his tracks as he realised there was a fatal flaw in his reasoning. He was allowing his heart to rule his head.

The girl who had entered Brother Angelo's trailer the night he was there must have been a regular visitor. She'd had a key and she knew her way around in the dark. Presumably she hadn't even bothered checking the name on the door. What was more, she hadn't been at all taken aback to find the bed occupied. Her immediate reaction had been one of pleasurable surprise rather than shock – her clothes had been discarded and she had climbed into bed without a second's hesitation – until she realised all too late the occupant wasn't who she'd expected it to be, when she'd fled like a frightened rabbit. The inescapable conclusion was that it must have been someone who was not only on intimate terms with Brother Angelo, but knew he was still in the area; hence the lack of surprise at finding him there.

If that were so, lovers' trysts as such were probably the last thing on their minds. Whoever it was would most likely stay put until the unit broke up rather than arouse suspicion.

Monsieur Pamplemousse's feeling of depression mounted as he and Pommes Frites climbed into his car and they set off on the homeward journey. Depression combined with a vague feeling of unease that was hard to rationalise.

The news on the radio was mostly about traffic jams, and even via the autoroute, dusk was already gathering by the time they reached Les Baux and checked in at the gate. Monsieur Pamplemousse drove straight to his quarters, parked the car, and did what he should have done at the beginning of the day; what he certainly would have done had his mind not been full of romantic notions. He took the screwdriver out of a drawer where he had left it and offered it to Pommes Frites. Pommes Frites gave the handle a thoughtful sniff, registered the information and fed it into his computer. Recognition dawned almost immediately. He looked enquiringly at his master.

'So?' he appeared to be saying, 'what are we waiting for?'

Monsieur Pamplemousse responded by opening the door of his trailer and standing clear.

Pommes Frites paused for a moment on the top step, then he set off at a steady pace with Monsieur Pample-mousse hard on his heels.

They went past each of the other trailers in turn with hardly a second's pause. First the front row and then in and out of the ones which were scattered behind. It wasn't until he had finished his second confirmatory tour of inspection that Pommes Frites came to a halt and sat waiting for further instructions. Monsieur Pamplemousse had to confess to a feeling of disappointment as he registered the name on the door. It was not what he had expected to see. Either Pommes Frites had done the unheard-of thing and made a mistake, or yet another of his theories had bitten the dust.

He was about to retrieve the screwdriver when he heard his name being called and turned to see Montgomery – Von Strudel's chef – hurrying towards him.

'Monsieur Pamplemousse. Monsieur Pamplemousse, I have been looking for you everywhere. Have you not heard?'

Monsieur Pamplemousse gave a non-committal grunt. 'Pommes Frites and I have been away all day. Something has happened?'

'Monsieur Beaseley. His body has been found at the foot of the cliff.'

'The cliff? What cliff?'

'The one where the old castle once stood. The highest point in Les Baux.'

Monsieur Pamplemousse felt slightly sick. It was the spot where the sadistic Raymond de Turenne had made after-dinner sport of watching prisoners being hurled to their death – not far from the cave where Brother Angelo had vanished. Beaseley would have fallen more than 250 metres on to the rocks below. Death would have been instantaneous, but the moments before must have seemed endless.

'He has been identified?'

'There is no doubt.' Bernard hesitated. 'We shall miss his practical jokes. His whoopee cushions, his toads in the bed . . .'

Monsieur Pamplemousse gave a wry smile. 'His exploding stoves . . . his sand in the camera . . . his *savon d'agneau* when they were filming the Last Supper . . .'

Montgomery shook his head. 'No, those things were not the work of Monsieur Beaseley. There was no real harm in him. He once told me he caught the habit when he worked in a joke factory. Someone else must have been responsible. Someone who wanted to delay the production.'

He wiped his hands in a cloth. 'I must go. Herr Strudel will be looking for me. But I thought you should know.'

'*Merci.*' Monsieur Pamplemousse felt infinitely sad. It didn't seem possible. As always, there were so many things left unsaid; so many questions he should have asked. Now it was too late.

At least Beaseley had lived to see his name written in large letters on the door of a Hollywood-style trailer. It was fame of a kind, the next best thing to having it up in lights. But then, so had he; so had the Director.

Suddenly, he realised what he was thinking. He must be getting old – or tired – tired by all the driving.

The door Pommes Frites had led him to certainly bore the Director's name, but assuming no one had restored the sign boards to normal, the trailer was the one which had belonged to Brother Angelo.

If Pommes Frites had got it right, then it raised all sorts of questions. Following Montgomery's line of thought about the more bizarre acts of sabotage, why would Brother Angelo wish to delay the completion date?

And if he was becoming more and more desperate – desperate enough to have lashed out in the *Cathedrale* when he thought he'd been cornered, could he – either accidentally or on purpose – have been responsible for Beaseley's death?

Monsieur Pamplemousse's feeling of elation was short-lived. It was all pure conjecture on his part; conjecture based on circumstantial evidence. None of it would stand up in court for a second.

What had Beaseley's last words to him been? 'If a man will begin with certainties he shall end in doubt, but if he will be content to begin with doubts he shall end in certainties.'

Doubts Monsieur Pamplemousse had plenty of, but although certainties were beginning to take shape, they were still very thin on the ground. None of them took him the slightest bit further forward in the most important factor of all: locating the missing Brother Angelo, without whom nothing could be proved anyway.

10
THE RESURRECTION

It ended as it had begun, in Parc Monceau in the 8th *arrondissement* of Paris. Almost three months had elapsed since Monsieur Pamplemousse's last visit. Paris was back at work, and in a way it was both a voyage of nostalgia and a treat for Pommes Frites.

Work of a kind was the reason why Monsieur Pamplemousse found himself one autumn morning strolling in leisurely fashion down the avenue Montaigne accompanied by the Director. Each of them was carrying a black imitation-leather valise bearing the motif XS in gold letters on the side, for they had been to a private screening of the perfume commercial prior to its release.

After the vintage Krug champagne, the speeches, the overpowering chicness of beautiful hostesses, the plethora of congratulations – everyone received their share of praise, from the head of the perfume company to the commissionaire on duty at the projection studio – it was good to be outside again breathing comparatively fresh air. Names like Dior, Vuitton and Jean-Louis Schrerrer dripped expensively off buildings on either side of the tree-lined avenue.

'A triumph, would you not say, Pamplemousse?'

'Immaculate, *Monsieur*. Miraculous in its way.'

'I understand plaudits from various religious bodies around the world are arriving hourly. Doubtless you noticed there was a sprinkling of purple cassocks present this morning. It is amazing what can be achieved with judicious editing.'

Monsieur Pamplemousse had to agree. The proof of the pudding was in the eating and the end result was a work of art. Tasteful. Quite surprisingly moving in places. It was hard to picture anyone taking offence. A *Palme d'Or* at next year's Festival of Commercials was assured.

Pommes Frites' big moment came fairly early on during the flood. Seen in tight close-up, the expression on his face as he watched the Ark disappearing into the horizon drew a spontaneous round of applause. There was hardly a dry eye in the house.

Monsieur Pamplemousse found himself wondering what the reaction would have been had the audience witnessed the true cause of Pommes Frites' consternation – the collapse of the *papier mâché* palm tree.

'At least we can say we were in a film directed by Von Strudel,' said the Director, breaking into his thoughts.

'Along with Mangetout . . .'

'. . . and Brother Angelo.'

'You didn't think the make-up was a little over the top?' asked the Director anxiously.

'I think it was exactly right, *Monsieur*. And the lighting was superb. As for the casting – it was brilliant in its way. There was a kind of spiritual quality about his performance which was quite the reverse of all one had feared. And the fact that he disappeared before the final scene didn't matter at all. They must have amassed so much material in the earlier shots every eventuality was covered. Most of it was in close-up anyway, and the long shots were so brief you would never know it was a stand-in. Perhaps Eisenstein was right. One doesn't need actors . . .'

The Director clucked impatiently. 'I wasn't referring to Brother Angelo, Pamplemousse. I was thinking of my own appearance; the moment, albeit brief, when I was caught in the eye of the camera. You noted it, of course?'

The Director was clearly excited at having seen himself preserved on celluloid. No doubt for many weeks to come there would be breaks in the conversation at dinner parties while guests were forced to watch television commercials between courses.

'Although I say it myself, it is not hard to spot me.'

Hardly surprising, thought Monsieur Pamplemousse, since the Director was the only one looking towards the camera. He wasn't actually waving, but like the classic Hitchcock shot of the man who kept staring straight ahead at Wimbledon when all those around him were following the ball, once seen there was no taking your eyes off him. It was a wonder they had left it in. Perhaps they thought it added a touch of mystery. Speaking for himself, Monsieur Pamplemousse was glad his merging with the crowd had been rather more successful. All the same, the Director was right. They could have ended up like so many thousands of others – as out-takes on the cutting-room floor.

'I once played Robespierre in a school play,' mused the Director. 'Did you know he invented *mayonnaise?*'

'It was kitchen-sink drama, *Monsieur?*' asked Monsieur Pamplemousse innocently.

The Director glanced at him suspiciously. 'No, it was not, Pamplemousse,' he said grufffly. 'It was set at the time of the revolution. I mention it in passing merely as a matter of interest.'

They walked together in silence for a moment or two. A van bearing the letters XS on its side passed them.

'That was a bad business at Les Baux after I left,' said the Director. 'What do you think happened to that poor fellow? Lost his footing, I suppose.'

Monsieur Pamplemousse gave a non-committal grunt. It was a subject he still didn't feel like discussing.

'And what about Brother Angelo? They never found a body. No one ever claimed responsibility. I am glad the "Second Coming" theory was thoroughly discredited. That would not have been good news.'

'It served its purpose,' said Monsieur Pamplemousse. 'Things could hardly have worked out better for the perfume company. All that free publicity for XS has acted as a teaser for the real thing.'

The Director gave him a sideways glance. 'Are you suggesting it was a put-up job?'

Monsieur Pamplemousse shook his head. 'Certainly not on the part of the perfume manufacturers. Nor the film company.'

'What then? If you are suggesting Brother Angelo spirited himself away, I do not see how he could have done it. The whole of the police force were looking for him at one point. The *journaux* . . .'

'One knows it is not possible to make an elephant vanish into thin air, *Monsieur*, but magicians do it every day. In his own way, with his stage act, Ron Pickles was something of an illusionist. He knew it was all a matter of timing. That, and some kind of distraction which would cause attention to be diverted elsewhere at the *moment critique.*'

'The turning off of the lights . . .'

'*Exactement.* For a few seconds everyone was looking everywhere but at the mouth of the cave. It was all he would have needed.'

'But why give up a successful career?' said the Director.

'The death – or in this case the disappearance – of an artist creates an entirely new set of values. Suddenly everybody realises the well has dried up, so the remaining water becomes more and more precious. If someone is lucky enough to find a hidden cache, their fortune is assured. Suppose one were to stumble across a collection of paintings by Monet. Or even a few sketches . . . a Mozart symphony . . .'

'They are hardly in the same category, Aristide.'

'Perhaps not in your eyes, *Monsieur*, but tastes vary. It is over twenty years since Jim Morrison died in a Paris bath from a heart attack brought on by drugs and alcohol but his tomb in the Père Lachaise cemetery is rarely without its circle of worshippers. They would give anything for some tangible reminder.'

'Surely it is still preferable to be free to go anywhere one cares to choose rather than to renounce everything?'

Monsieur Pamplemousse was suddenly reminded of Beaseley's quotation.

'In this world there are only two tragedies, *Monsieur*. One is not getting what you want. The other is getting it.'

'That is a very shrewd remark, Aristide.'

'Unfortunately, *Monsieur*, an Irish writer thought of it first – before he, too, ended up in the Père Lachaise.'

They reached the point where the Director had parked his car.

'I haven't thanked you properly for coming to my assistance, Aristide. I don't know what I would have done without you.'

'There is no need to thank me, *Monsieur*. I only did what I thought was right at the time. I am glad it all worked out.'

While the Director felt for his keys, Monsieur Pample-mousse posed a question he had been dying to ask. 'You have had no problems *chez* Leclercq?'

'All is quiet on the distaff side,' said the Director. 'Ominously so, I thought for a while, but there is no knowing with women. So far I do not think Chantal has even noticed the extent of my indisposition. If she has, then she has passed no comment. She accepted my story without hesitation.'

'Your story, *Monsieur?*'

'The one about walking into a bollard. Once again, I have to thank you, Aristide. I simply transferred the location to Marseille. It struck me as being rather more believable. I'm sure it happens there all the time to drunken *matelots* reeling back to their vessels after dark.'

Monsieur Pamplemousse found himself hoping the Director hadn't embroidered his tale too much; something he was apt to do at times. He might well find himself in for a rough time at a later date when his wife discovered he had taken part in a perfume commercial. Questions were bound to be asked.

'And you, *Monsieur*. You are feeling better?'

'Much better, thank you, Aristide. As you can see, I am able to do without crutches for days at a time. Only when there is rain in the air do I feel certain twinges. I have been giving a lot of thought to the question of a transplant. Not serious consideration, you understand – who knows what problems might be unleashed? But it has kept me awake a good deal. The imagination has run riot.

'One thing is very certain, Aristide. Misfortunes of any kind have a sobering effect. None more so than in the world of medicine. It is always possible to see people worse off than oneself.'

'That is true of hospitals everywhere, *Monsieur.*'

'I wasn't thinking so much of the hospital,' said the Director. 'Although, as you said at the time, there are a lot of unusual cases there. It is incredible the things that some people in the highest echelons get up to. I could hardly believe my eyes – or my ears.

'No, I was thinking more of the poor man who shared the ambulance with me on my journey to Paris. Even now, I shudder to think what could possibly have happened to him. It made my own troubles seem minor by comparison. Swathed in bandages from head to foot like an Egyptian mummy. He didn't utter a word all the way there. Several times I tried to engage him in conversation in the hope of lightening his burden, but he seemed not to wish to talk.

'The nurse with him was equally reticent. It was strange. I could have sworn I'd seen her somewhere before. She pretended not to speak any known tongue, although she seemed to communicate very readily with the driver when we reached their destination. There was a dreadful commotion as they entered the building – something to do with getting the stretcher jammed in the lift doors. All hell broke lose. There was a crash and I heard a bleeper going as someone called for assistance. The *concierge* was either asleep or on holiday along with the rest of Paris. One can't rely on anything these days.'

Monsieur Pamplemousse, who had been listening with only half an ear, suddenly stopped in his tracks.

'Where did this happen, *Monsieur*? Here – in Paris?'

'Somewhere in the 8th *arrondissement.*'

'But you do not know exactly where?'

'Pamplemousse, I was in no fit state to take note of details, nor did I greatly care where we were. It was bad enough having to make a diversion in the first place. It was somewhere near the Parc Monceau, that is all I know. I remember glancing out of the window as we drove past the old toll house at the northern entrance and thinking not much further to go. What with all that and some wretched child crying incessantly I had a most unpleasant journey.'

'And you say you thought you had seen the nurse somewhere before?' persisted Monsieur Pamplemousse. 'Was it in the *hospice?*'

The Director shook his head. 'No. I have been through them all in my mind, one by one, and it was no one there. I think it must have been on the film set. She was very like one of the staff. I looked around at the showing but no one came to mind.'

Monsieur Pamplemousse fell silent for a moment. Something clicked in his mind. Reaching into his carrier bag he felt amongst folders filled with 20 cm x 25 cm glossy colour stills and several immaculately wrapped sample packs of soaps and perfume, until he came across what he was looking for. Removing an A4 size brochure, he flipped through it until he came across the picture he wanted.

'Was this the person, *Monsieur?*'

The Director stared at the photograph. 'You know I believe you could be right, Pamplemousse. She looked different in her working clothes, of course. And the girl in the ambulance had blonde hair . . . but I remember the green eyes . . . they were very distinctive.'

'*Merci, Monsieur.*'

Monsieur Pamplemousse felt a sudden surge of excitement.

The Director hesitated and then, realising he would get no further, abruptly changed the subject.

'I hope you had a happier journey back to Paris. You followed up my suggestions?'

'*Oui, Monsieur.* The restaurant you spoke of north of Orange was all you said it would be.'

'Remember also, Aristide, that it was not the truffle season. I must arrange for you to pay another visit now that October is here.'

'*Merci, Monsieur.*'

'And the *cuisine* at Pic?'

'As generous as ever.'

'That is good to hear. How about Bocuse?'

'He was there in person. He actually turned my *poulet* on its spit with his own hand.'

'A signal honour, Pamplemousse.'

'Poetry in motion, *Monsieur.*'

'I trust he did not . . .'

'*Non, Monsieur.* He did not realise I was from *Le Guide.* He simply happened to be going past. It was a purely reflex action.'

'I shall look forward to reading your report, Aristide.' Sensing a certain restlessness in his companion, the Director glanced at his watch. 'How time flies. It is nearly lunchtime already. I fear I have an appointment, otherwise . . .'

'I understand, *Monsieur.* But thank you.'

The Director glanced uneasily at Pommes Frites. Pommes Frites had been kept busy at the reception making his paw-mark on scraps of paper with the aid of an ink pad provided by a thoughtful PRO. There were still faint marks visible on the pavement where he had been walking.

'Can I give you both a lift to your car?'

'We walked, *Monsieur.* It was a lovely morning.'

'Walked? From Montmartre?' The Director coupled relief with a certain awe at the thought. 'I must say I envy your stamina, Pamplemousse.'

Monsieur Pamplemousse felt equally relieved as the Director climbed into his car and waved goodbye. He suddenly wanted to be alone with his thoughts.

Pommes Frites followed him across the Champs Elysees at the Rond Point. At the far end, beyond the Arc de Triomphe, clouds were beginning to roll in from the west. The sun which had been shining brightly not half an hour earlier now had a watery feel to it. Monsieur Pamplemousse gave an involuntary shiver. In less than two months' time the gardens surrounding the fountains on either side of him would be planted out with fir trees, all sprayed a seasonal white.

He could have kicked himself. Fancy not recognising the sound of Brother Angelo's bleeper that evening at the *hospice*. True, he'd had his mind on other things, but all the same . . .

He paused, as he always did, to admire the display in the window of the *chocolatier* a little way along the avenue Franklin D. Roosevelt. He would soon have to think about Christmas shopping. Doucette's favourites were the chocolate trees. He always bought her one as a 'surprise', although more often than not she couldn't bring herself to start on it until long after the holiday.

It took him exactly eighteen minutes to walk from the *chocolatier* to the Parc Monceau. He could have done it in fourteen, but Pommes Frites made several stops on the way.

Entering the park by the south gate, they encountered a stream of office workers heading in the opposite direction in search of lunch-time sustenance. A few of the hardier ones had already commandeered an empty bench and were tucking into sandwiches.

The joggers were out in force. Beds had been cleared of their summer plants and there were piles of newly swept leaves everywhere.

Through some gaps in the trees to his right he spotted the ubiquitous group of statuesque figures doing their Tai Chi exercises. A scattering of lovers braved the elements in sheltered nooks and corners.

Monsieur Pamplemousse picked an empty bench at a point near the centre of the park where the two main paths crossed. He settled himself down and began sorting through the contents of his bag, spreading the various items out on the bench in the hope that it might deter others from joining him. Pommes Frites stationed himself firmly at the other end of the bench, neatly obscuring a CHIENS INTERDITS sign.

All around the trees were changing colour. Behind him the *carrousel* was already covered for the winter, and the last few roses of summer looked as though they hadn't long to go.

Some children went past on tricycles. They were followed by a procession of *voitures d'enfant,* their occupants muffled against the autumnal weather. Heavily encased arms and legs stuck out at unlikely angles. If it were true to say that anyone who sat outside the Café de la Paix would eventually end up seeing the whole world go past, it certainly felt as though an afternoon spent sitting in the Parc Monceau must afford a glimpse of most of the children in the 8th *arrondissement.* It was simply a question of waiting, and Monsieur Pamplemousse had time at his disposal.

The press office had certainly gone to town. The brochure was a no-expense-spared work of art. The margins were as large as the bottles of XS were small.

There was a brief history of the company, with a run-down of all their successes. Failures, of which there had probably been many, didn't get a mention.

A rare photograph of Monsieur Parmentier headed an article on the subject of the science of perfume; mostly to do with the ingredients which had gone into the making of XS. Musk from the deer which roam the Atlas and Himalayan mountains. Ambergris from the intestines of whales. Civet from Asia, Africa and the East Indies. Cinnamon from Ceylon and Southern India for the American market. Other raw materials came from Egypt, India and Madagascar.

Von Strudel had a whole section to himself. There was a résumé of his credits over the years. It was an impressive list. Some films, like *The Babylon Years,* he remembered seeing as a young man; others he had to admit to never having seen, although they were still shown in art cinemas from time to time. Doubtless after the commercial appeared there would be a retrospective Strudel season at the Musée du Cinéma in the Palais de Chaillot.

He looked long and hard at the photograph of Anne-Marie, the key make-up artist. It would figure. According to the notes, she had worked on various pop videos and was credited with having suggested Brother Angelo for his role in the commercial. It must all have been planned a long time ago. Things were beginning to fit into place. Anyone wanting a change of personality would have expert advice permanently to hand.

Presumably it had been Anne-Marie who had visited the trailer that night. He wondered if she had any idea who the mysterious occupant of the bed was.

There were pen portraits of the others involved. The designer; the lighting cameraman; the sound supervisor; wardrobe; there was even a brief mention of Gilbert Beaseley.

Monsieur Pamplemousse closed his eyes, transporting himself back in his thoughts to that first morning when he had met them all in the viewing theatre. And now Beaseley was dead. In his heart of hearts he knew he couldn't let the matter rest there. If he hadn't, albeit unwittingly, flushed Brother Angelo out of his hiding place Beaseley might still be alive. But was Ron Pickles capable of murder? By then he might well have been desperate enough. And had Beaseley been in the *Cathédrale* that morning, also hot on the trail of Brother Angelo? It would account for the telltale traces of white on his jacket. Perhaps he had left as soon as he realised Monsieur Pamplemousse was there too.

Brother Angelo must have engineered the flight to Paris with Anne-Marie long before the filming began. He would have needed someone who could transform his appearance; someone French who could cope with all the problems of getting him admitted to hospital and arranging for an ambulance to take him to Paris – no doubt there had been another suitable contribution to the *hospice* fund. Someone who could also arrange a place for them to go when they got there. Perhaps it was a case of being wise after the event, but thinking back there had been certain signs; something about the way they behaved together – the way Anne-Marie had removed the strand of hair from Brother Angelo's shoulder that day; not the automatic gesture of a professional at work, but of a lover. Now that he had a name and a face it was suddenly much easier to picture it all.

As for the various acts of sabotage, they were presumably made in an effort to delay the end of the production. It probably suited his purpose to make his flight to Paris when the city was as quiet as possible. There would be fewer questions asked. Changing the names round on the trailers must have been a precaution against being invaded by prying fans: a highly necessary one as things turned out.

It was late in the afternoon when Monsieur Pamplemousse felt a tug on Pommes Frites' leash. He let go of it immediately and Pommes Frites was away. Pricking up his ears, nose at the ready, he hastened towards a young girl with a pushchair.

Calling out in a way which he knew would have no effect whatsoever, Monsieur Pamplemousse followed on behind. As he drew near the girl he raised his hat.

'Pardon, Mademoiselle.'

He'd been half expecting it to be the Swedish *au pair*, but the girl spoke with an English accent. Again that figured. Ron would feel more at home with someone from his own country.

'Forgive me.'

'That's all right.' She seemed relieved to find someone who spoke her native tongue.

Never fully at ease with very small children, Monsieur Pamplemousse bent down to tickle the child's nose. It was hard to tell whether it was a boy or a girl, it was so protected against the elements.

'Fuck off!' Monsieur Pamplemousse jumped back as if he had been shot.

'That's very naughty. You know you mustn't say that.' The girl delivered a half-hearted smack on her charge. It had about as much chance of penetrating the thick clothing as a wet dish cloth.

'Oh, dear. I am sorry.' She blushed. 'She's a dear little thing really, but she just can't help herself. It's funny how children always pick up the worst. I shan't be sorry when she's had her operation.'

'There is something wrong?'

383

'She's going in next week to have some sort of bleeper thing fitted.' The girl looked round as though she was suddenly afraid of being overheard.

'Her father suffered from exactly the same thing and he had it done. She's lucky. Being bilingual could have been a problem, but they can programme it for more than one language now.'

'Coprophalia,' said Monsieur Pamplemousse, finding the word he had been searching for.

'Fancy you knowing that!' exclaimed the girl. 'I'd never heard of it before I got this job. I'm not sure I would have taken it if I had known. On the other hand, he couldn't be nicer and he thinks the world of his daughter. He sings to her every evening before she goes to bed.'

Monsieur Pamplemousse gazed down at the child. Dark, innocent-looking eyes gazed up at him. Her hair was a mass of black ringlets. Angelic was the word which immediately sprang to mind. He was tempted to reach down and give her another pat, but he thought better of it.

'Is she very like her father?'

'Not really. He's got fair hair. I don't know about the eyes – he always wears dark glasses.'

'And the mother?'

'I haven't met the real mother. They live apart. He never mentions her. But the woman he lives with is very nice. She used to be in films.'

'Would I know her name?'

'I doubt it. She was something on the technical side.'

Monsieur Pamplemousse was tempted to ask more, but already he was in danger of sounding over-inquisitive.

He raised his hat again. 'Forgive me, I am keeping you.'

'That's all right. We must be getting back home anyway. It was nice having someone to talk to.'

As the girl went on her way she turned to wave, then removed something from a basket at the back of the pushchair which she gave to the child. A moment later a small hand was raised. It was clutching a long, multi-coloured object which it began to wave in unison with the *au pair*.

Monsieur Pamplemousse stood transfixed, hardly able to believe his eyes. It was Exhibit 'A': the answer to all his questions.

For a split second he was tempted to run after them. Then he thought better of it.

Reaching down as though pretending to fondle Pommes Frites, he gently undid the strap on his collar, then he uttered a brief command. It was all that was needed.

Secure in the knowledge that Pommes Frites would not be back until the task of trailing his quarry to their destination had been satisfactorily completed, he returned to the bench to wait and to cogitate on what he had just seen.

'For *dîner*,' said Doucette, 'I have some ham from the Ardennes.'

'On the bone?'

'*Naturellement.*'

'Thickly sliced?'

'Just as you like it.'

Monsieur Pamplemousse heaved a sigh of contentment. Pommes Frites registered ten on his wagometer. It was good to be back home and in the warm.

'With it there is *purée de pommes de terre*, a little *salad verte* and some *salad de tomates*. After all your gourmandising this morning, and with Pommes Frites still being off lamb, I thought you might prefer something simple.'

'The simple things of life,' said Monsieur Pamplemousse, 'are often the best.'

'I have also opened that tin of olives you brought back from Les Baux. They look delicious.'

'Monsieur Arnaud is something of a perfectionist. I am told the black ones are kept in salt for at least three months – sometimes six until he is sure they are absolutely ready. The rest- the exact combination of herbs and sunflower oil – is a secret.'

'They look expensive,' said Madame Pamplemousse.

'You get what you pay for in this world, *Couscous*,' said Monsieur Pamplemousse.

As Doucette left the room he crossed to the hi-fi, inserted a cassette, then picked up the day's *journal* and settled down in an armchair. Pommes Frites took up his favourite position – on the rug at his master's feet. Contentment reigned.

Perhaps that was why Brother Angelo had visited Fontvieille – not to see Daudet's windmill at all, but to buy some olives. Olives in Fontvieille; a Chinese meal in Les Saintes-Maries-de-la-Mer; a picnic in the Massif de La Sainte-Baume; sometimes it didn't pay to look for too deep a meaning in things.

Monsieur Pamplemousse glanced up from the *journal* as Doucette bustled back into the room carrying the olives in an open dish. 'I think, *Couscous*,' he said, 'we are shortly due for the Second Coming; a resurrection in the 8th *arrondissement.*'

'Really, Aristide,' said Madame Pamplemousse impatiently, 'you do come out with the strangest things at times.'

'Don't say I didn't warn you when it happens.'

It wouldn't perhaps merit a plaque, like the one in the Parc Monceau commemorating the landing of the first parachutist, but it would be a fitting end to all that had happened.

'What is that noise?' Madame Pamplemousse glanced towards the hifi.

Monsieur Pamplemousse held up the empty cassette case. 'It is the best of Brother Angelo.'

'If that's the best of Brother Angelo I would hate to hear the worst,' said Madame Pamplemousse. 'I don't know what the neighbours will think.' She turned down the volume. 'It doesn't sound like you at all.'

'I treated myself to it on the way home,' said Monsieur Pamplemousse. 'It is number one on the charts. The man in the store told me a whole lot of unreleased recordings have been found. Enough to keep the market going for several years.'

'It is a pity Brother Angelo won't be around to enjoy the proceeds,' said Madame Pamplemouse.

'I am not entirely sure that is true.'

While his wife bustled around laying the table, he gave her a brief run-down on all that had happened during the day.

'But surely Brother Angelo already has another identity?' said Doucette in her down-to-earth fashion. 'Until all the fuss has died down can he not simply become plain Monsieur Pickles again? He has not really committed a crime.'

'Therein lies the problem,' said Monsieur Pamplemousse, 'I suspect that is just what he has done. He may not have meant to. It may simply have been an accident in the heat of the moment, but . . .'

'You don't mean you suspect him of being responsible for that man . . .'

'Monsieur Beaseley?'

'. . . Monsieur Beaseley's death? How can you be sure?'

'Something I saw less than an hour ago in the Parc Monceau.'

Doucette looked at him enquiringly.

'If you really wish to know, *Couscous,* it was a peacock's feather.'

'And that is enough to prove a man guilty of murder?'

'It could be more than enough. That will be for a jury to decide.'

Innocent or guilty? The outcome would depend on whether Brother Angelo was tried in France or in England. If it was the former he would have to prove his innocence. If it were the latter the authorities would have to prove his guilt.

'If there is one thing certain in this world, *Couscous,* it is that nothing is certain.

'I think possibly Monsieur Beaseley came upon Brother Angelo by accident. Perhaps he was hiding out up in a deserted part of the old town, waiting for nightfall. Or Beaseley may even have followed him there. There was more to him than he let on and he was something of a nosy parker.

'If it was the latter, he may have confronted Brother Angelo. There was a struggle and in the course of it Beaseley fell to his death.

'That he was carrying a peacock's feather at the time I know, because he showed it to me before he said goodbye. It is extremely unlikely that Brother Angelo would have picked it up at the spot where Beaseley landed. The obvious alternative is that he picked it up after their argument and later gave it to his daughter.

'Did he fall, or was he pushed? Who knows?'

'What do you think, Aristide?'

'I think,' said Monsieur Pamplemousse, 'there are times when I am glad I am no longer in the *Sûreté*. It is for other people to reach such conclusions.'

Doucette opened the sample bottle of XS and smelled it. 'All that fuss for a tiny bottle of perfume.'

'The smaller the package,' said Monsieur Pamplemousse, 'the more expensive it is. Do you like it?'

'I am not sure it is you.'

'I am not sure,' said Monsieur Pamplemousse, 'that it is intended to be. It is altogether too complicated for my taste.

'I also think it is time I opened the wine and we have *dîner*. The ham will spoil if it is left too long.'

Pommes Frites pricked up his ears. As a 'nose' in his own right, he had decided views on the subject of smells. Had he been asked to venture an opinion he would have had to agree with his master; in the end the simple things in life were best.

When it came to scents, you could keep your XS. In his humble opinion there were few things to equal the aroma from a good *jambon*.

Had he been able to read Pommes Frites' thoughts, Monsieur Pamplemousse might also have put forward a strong case for the bottle of Beaune Clos des Ursules he was in the act of opening. It was from Louis Jadot and the bouquet reminded him of black cherries.

It would be a good marriage, the ham and the wine; a natural combination which rendered mere words redundant, like master and hound they simply went well together.

Monsieur Pamplemousse Takes the Train

Contents

1
NIGHT TRAIN FROM ROME

Monsieur Pamplemousse spotted the hat first: a splash of red bobbing about amongst all the dark suits and overcoats entering *binario* 21 of Rome's Stazione Termini. He couldn't resist taking a quick photograph. The light was not all that it might have been and he held his breath while he pressed the shutter. It would either work or it wouldn't. If it did it might make a good cover picture for *L'Escargot, Le Guide's* staff magazine: a change from the usual gourmet offerings.

He had forgotten how soberly people tended to dress in Italy; dark colours predominated. In much the same way he had been taken by surprise, as he had been in the past, when he arrived in Rome the previous afternoon and caught sight of the suburban balconies festooned with laundry hanging out to dry. If it wasn't laundry it would be people anxious to chat with their neighbours. In some ways it was as unlike Paris as it was possible to be. Parisians tended to keep themselves to themselves.

Steadying himself against the side of the waiting train, he pressed the shutter release once more for luck.

The girl was accompanied by two nuns in long grey habits, one on either side of her. From a distance it was almost like prisoner and escort, although there the resemblance ended. The nuns had their heads covered by black headdresses. It was hard to tell what, if anything, lay beneath them. Most policewomen in Rome seemed to wear their hair provocatively long, way below shoulder-length. Again, quite unlike their Parisian counterparts.

As the party drew near he moved forward to greet them, conscious that the eyes of the sleeping-car conductor were not the only ones following his progress down the platform. An American couple in the next compartment to his – a grey-haired man and his vastly overweight wife – peered out through their open door. Wisely, Pommes Frites, worn out after all the walking they had done during the past twenty-four hours, elected to stay on the train.

Raising his hat, Monsieur Pamplemousse mustered the little Italian he knew: not much more than the basic pleasantries – '*Buona sera. Per favore. Grazie. Prego.*' The nice thing about the language was that you could always make things up and the natives seemed to understand. 'Si, *signorina. Je suis il signor* Pamplemousse. May I take your valise?'

The girl handed it to him gratefully. As befitted a relative of the Director, it felt expensive. Not what one might have pictured of the average convent girl going away for the half-term break. It also weighed a ton. He could see why she was glad to get rid of it.

'I am Caterina.' She spoke French with hardly a trace of an accent, although the intonation gave away her Italian origins. That, and the dark, expressive eyes.

'My first guess was correct.'

She laughed as she followed his glance towards the accompanying nuns. Their faces remained expressionless. It struck Monsieur Pamplemousse that he was being quietly vetted. He must have passed muster, for a moment later, after a barely perceptible exchange of glances, one of them held out her hand. It felt soft and warm to the touch. He wondered why he should be so surprised. It occurred to him that he had never held a nun's hand before. It was withdrawn almost immediately, as though she were reading his thoughts.

'I trust you will both have a pleasant journey, Monsieur Pamplemousse.'

'*Arrivederci. Ciao.* I will take good care of her.' He found himself launching into another series of basic pleasantries, bowing his way out of the encounter as the two women issued last-minute instructions to the girl; more warnings than advice he fancied. From the tone of their voices it sounded as though Paris was beyond redemption: a place of perpetual sin.

'Phew!' Leading the way back up the *quai* he felt the girl relax. The face beneath the hat looked wide-eyed and innocent, as pale as the faces of the nuns had been, but the lips and the slight flare to the nostrils suggested she had a wayward streak too; not someone to be trifled with if you got in her way. Black hair peeped out from beneath the wide brim of the hat. Undoing her top coat, she revealed a dark blue skirt reaching to below her knees, and a matching jacket over a starched white blouse.

Reaching the door to their coach, he waited patiently while the conductor collected the girl's passport and examined her ticket, ticking off her name against his list of reservations. He handed her a customs declaration form and then stood back to allow them access. The American couple were clearly talking about them, trying to work out the relationship.

'Is it possible to make a reservation for the dining-car?'

'There is no dining-car, *signore.*'

'No dining-car?' repeated Monsieur Pamplemousse. 'But . . .'

He gazed at the conductor. It would be useless trying to explain that the main purpose of his travelling on the train in the first place was to report on the catering facilities. Useless, and against all the rules under which Inspectors working for *Le Guide* were expected to operate.

'There is a buffet car, *signore*, where they do a hot dish. It is three coaches down. But they do not take reservations. I will fetch you some mineral water if you like – once everyone has boarded.'

'*Merci. Merci beaucoup.*' Monsieur Pamplemousse resorted to his native tongue. He couldn't trust himself to deliver the right degree of sarcasm in Italian. It would probably be wasted in any language.

With a heavy heart he set off down the corridor, pointing out his own sleeping compartment as they went past.

Pommes Frites opened one eye and gazed benevolently, if noncommittally at his master's latest acquisition.

The girl paused and reached down to pat his head. 'You should have ordered two bottles of mineral water. Never mind, we'll see if we can get you a doggy bag from the buffet car.'

Pommes Frites returned her gaze with loving eyes. Clearly he was dealing with a person who knew the way to a dog's heart.

Monsieur Pamplemousse suddenly warmed to her too. He doubted Pommes Frites' response at being presented with the remains of someone else's meal wrapped up in silver foil when he, too, had most likely been looking forward to dining in style. However, it was the thought that mattered.

'That is a nice idea, but it will not be necessary. Pommes Frites will have to take his place in the queue like everyone else.'

'He travels with you everywhere?'

'Everywhere,' said Monsieur Pamplemousse firmly. Carrying on up the corridor until they reached the girl's compartment, he placed her *valise* on the seat.

'I take it you would like to try the buffet car?'

'You bet. I'm starving.'

'The train leaves at nineteen ten. Shall I give you a call at, say, eight o'clock?'

'Seven forty-five sounds even nicer.'

'Seven forty-five,' said Monsieur Pamplemousse. *'Arrivederci.'*

'A tout à l'heure, monsieur.'

Retracing his steps, Monsieur Pamplemousse entered his own compartment. Catching sight of the American couple watching his movements via a reflection in the corridor window, he closed the door and settled back to scan through the various *Compagnia Wagon-Lits Italia* brochures contained in a rack above the toilet cupboard.

There being no restaurant car was little short of a disaster. A sign of the times if ever there was one. The Director would be furious when he heard. Or would he?

Monsieur Pamplemousse gazed out of the carriage window with unseeing eyes. The train in the adjoining *quai* was just leaving, but he scarcely registered the fact.

Wasn't the whole situation typical of the tortuous way in which things at *Le Guide* were so often arranged? The simple truth was, the Director hated being put in the position of having to ask a direct favour of a subordinate. It was always a case of taking a circuitous route up and down the byways and round the houses before entering his chosen destination via the back door.

If only he had come straight out with it and said: 'Pamplemousse, I want you to do me a very special favour.

My wife, Chantal, has a *petite cousine* who is attending a convent school near Rome. She is coming to stay with us for the half term. She will be travelling to Paris on the night express and one reads such strange things these days. I may be old-fashioned, but a young girl by herself . . . Unfortunately both my wife and I are otherwise engaged. I am up to my eyes in work overseeing the preparation of next year's *Guide* . . . Chantal has to go to Digne to attend the funeral of an old aunt who has just died . . . perhaps you wouldn't mind escorting her?'

That would have been easily understandable.

Instead of which it had been: 'Pamplemousse, I have been giving the affairs of *Le Guide* a great deal of thought over the past few weeks and it seems to me that it is time we extended our horizons. We should not remain stationary, but we should move forward. Air travel is but one area we have neglected in the past. Railways are another. Perhaps we should also have a section devoted to the great trains of Europe . . . *Par exemple* . . . PAUSE . . . *par exemple* the night train from Rome to Paris . . . I believe it is called the Palatino. With this in mind I have made arrangements for you to do some preliminary fieldwork. Oh, and *en passant* it just so happens that a relative of Chantal's will be travelling on the same train . . .'

He must have got someone to check the arrangements, but it simply wouldn't have occurred to him to come straight out with the simple truth: 'I'm afraid it is not quite like the old days, Pamplemousse. There is no longer a restaurant car as such. It is a self-service buffet car, but I am told the *plat du jour* is always heated.'

As had happened so many times in the past, Monsieur Pamplemousse had been caught napping. Halfway through the Director's discourse – the point where he had opened a second bottle of Gosset champagne (the Grand Millésime Rosé '82!) – he had even found himself coming up with other ideas. Cruise liners might be a rich field to research – Truffert would be a good candidate for the task – he had spent some time in the merchant navy. Then there were converted canal barges in the Midi catering for small groups of holidaymakers – that would suit Guilot – he liked the quiet life. And why stop there? Loudier was getting on in years. Why not 'Meals on Wheels for the Elderly' before he finally retired? Come to that, eating in a dining-car was a form of 'Meals on Wheels' – why not send Loudier instead?

The Director had not been amused by the suggestion.

Almost imperceptibly the train began to move. They were barely out of the station when there was a knock on the door. It was the conductor with his mineral water: *Effervescente naturale.*

Pommes Frites gazed mournfully at the bubbles as his master poured some water into a dish. Bubbles tickled his nose and it was not what he was used to. Monsieur Pamplemousse heaved a sigh. Something told him he was in for a bad night. He opened the door before the atmosphere became too oppressive.

And at the end of it all, where was he? Sitting in an overnight train heading back to Paris, acting as nursemaid to a sixteen-year-old.

Sixteen? That is what the Director had said, and there was no reason to disbelieve him. She seemed pleasant enough. But what did you talk about to a sixteen-year-old convent girl? Perhaps it was just as well he didn't have to sit through a long-drawn-out meal.

Wouldn't it also be true to say that it was a way of getting Monsieur Pamplemousse's services for free? Madame

401

Grante in Accounts might suspect the worst when she checked his expenses, but she wouldn't be able to prove anything.

Anyway, who was he, Pamplemousse, to argue? Looked at in another light, it was an unexpected bonus. Travelling aboard a trans-European express still had an aura of romance about it. He glanced around the cabin. The quality of the workmanship and the solidity of the wood and the metal fittings reflected the lavishness of a bygone age. It might lack the smoothness of the TGV, but it was certainly a pleasant change from the hours he normally spent crouched over the wheel of his 2CV.

Rome had been another bonus. Arriving late the previous afternoon, he'd had time to explore the city. It was bathed in a golden light and stank of petrol fumes. Along with hordes of others he had paid his respects to the Church of San Pietro, seen and marvelled at the ceiling of the Sistine Chapel, walked beside the Tiber – dusty and disappointing compared with the Seine, gazed at the view across the rooftops from the balcony above the Piazza del Popolo, walked in the Borghese Gardens – counting the number of broken off organs on the statues in the Pincio area – breaking them off was apparently a popular local sport – sat on the Spanish Steps; in short, he had done all the things a good tourist should do and in a remarkably short space of time. Art Buchwald's four-minute Louvre wasn't in it. Above all he had eaten well. Now, like Pommes Frites, he was feeling worn out.

A motherly woman bustled down the corridor ringing a handbell to indicate the buffet car was open. It was another reminder of more gracious times; a pleasant change from the ubiquitous hidden loudspeakers bombarding passengers with endless announcements.

Closing the door again he unpacked his suitcase and after a quick wash and shave, made his way down the corridor to collect the Director's *petite cousine*.

Engrossed in his own thoughts, he was totally unprepared for the sight which met his eyes as the door was opened in response to his knock. It literally took his breath away and for a second or two he thought he had picked on the wrong compartment. Even Pommes Frites looked taken aback. Clearly he was searching his memory, trying to pin down where he had seen the girl before.

'You should have warned me.' Monsieur Pamplemousse gazed at the elegant figure standing before him, trying hard to make the adjustment: a quantum leap from the schoolgirl he'd escorted along the *quai* less than an hour ago to a *soignée* young lady of the world; a dramatic mixture of striking understatement.

'You approve?' Moistened lips parted in a smile which revealed the whitest teeth he had ever seen. Liquid blue eyes gazed into his. There was a momentary heady waft of perfume as she pirouetted gracefully on one high heel – a vision of loveliness; hair, released from the confines of the school hat, now hung loosely about her shoulders, a fashionably short, dark red dress revealed silk-clad legs which under other circumstances he would have been hard-put not to linger over. Her skin was firm and smooth.

The total transformation took him a moment or two to get used to. Everything about the girl had miraculously changed. She even looked taller. Her neck seemed longer, perhaps because the low-cut line of the dress was emphasised by a small gold cross hanging from a chain. Two small diamonds, one in each ear, matched a larger diamond in the centre of the cross. Make-up underlined the fullness of her lips; her cheeks were now the colour of a warm peach. Her figure . . .

Monsieur Pamplemousse pulled himself together. 'I think,' he said gruffly, 'it is time we ate.'

It struck him as he led the way along the corridor, that had the nuns been following on behind they would have been searching beneath their gowns for bottles of *sal volatile*.

Half expecting the buffet car to be crowded, Monsieur Pamplemousse was relieved to find there were still a number of vacant tables. All the same, he was conscious of the stares from other occupants as they made their entrance. Seating the girl at a table which was still reasonably isolated, and leaving Pommes Frites in charge to ensure it remained that way, he gathered up three trays and slid them in line along a counter beneath a row of stainless steel shelves and compartments, picking up cutlery and anything else that struck his fancy as he went along. It was assembly-line catering.

He recognised the woman who had gone past his compartment earlier ringing the bell. She was presiding over a cash desk at the end of the small queue. Orders for the main course were dispatched in ringing tones through an open doorway to her right. A framed colour illustration of a *steak garni* was fixed to the side of the carriage opposite the kitchen. He wondered if it was there for the benefit of the public or the chef. Time would tell.

Monsieur Pamplemousse called out his order, then waited patiently while those in front of him shuffled forward. A polyglot clientèle, both in speech and dress; jeans and open-necked shirts predominated, with here and there a more formal suit. There were exchanges in Italian, German, Swedish and English.

'Can't think where they're all going to at this time of night!' his old Mother would have said, using the tone of voice she reserved for those occasions when she mixed deep-felt suspicion with impatience at being kept waiting.

He wondered what she would have thought of Caterina. He felt sure she would have warmed to her. It would be hard not to. 'Nice, but not too nice,' would have been her summing up.

'*Oh, lá! lá!*' Seeing Monsieur Pamplemousse struggling with the trays, the Madame in charge abandoned her till for a moment while she helped him back to his seat, fussing over him like a mother hen. It was a little piece of French territory on wheels, presided over by someone who had it all organised. Paper serviettes were spirited out of thin air. Clucking heralded the arrival of the condiments. *Bon appétits* floated down the carriage as she returned to her post.

'I think you have made a conquest,' said Caterina.

'Not as many as you have,' said Monsieur Pamplemousse, glancing round the coach. 'Besides, I think she is glad to hear someone speaking her own language. I doubt if she approves of other tongues.' He poured two glasses of Côtes-du-Rhône.

'You do not mind *vin rouge?*'

'I do not mind *vin* anything,' said Caterina.

She looked around at the other diners. 'It isn't quite what I expected. Do you think I'm overdoing things? Nobody else seems to have bothered to dress.'

'You are looking absolutely ravishing,' said Monsieur Pamplemousse. 'That is no crime. I doubt if there is a girl here who does not envy you, nor a man who would not wish to ride off with you on his white charger.'

Suddenly aware that another passenger seated on the opposite side of the coach was listening intently to their conversation, Monsieur Pamplemousse glanced across and looked the other up and down. Having registered pointed black shoes, polished until you could see your face in them, and what he could only describe as an old-fashioned dark pin-striped suit – he couldn't quite say why it struck him as old-fashioned, perhaps it was the cut, or the over-wide stripes – a white silk shirt, pencil moustache, thick black hair, brilliantined and brushed back – it somehow went with the suit – he formed what was probably a wholly irrational dislike of the man. 'Il Blobbo' would be a good name for him. The fingernails of the left hand, which was holding a small glass of colourless liquid – it could have been Grappa – looked freshly manicured. Eye contact was rendered impossible by virtue of a pair of impenetrably dark Bausch & Lomb glasses.

Monsieur Pamplemousse was irresistibly reminded of the famous anti-Nixon campaign slogan 'Would you buy a second-hand car from this man?'. The answer in the present case was most emphatically 'no'. From the studiedly insolent way in which the other took his time before seeking shelter behind a copy of *La Stampa*, it was clear that the feeling was mutual, although he hoped it was for a different reason.

'Pardon?' He suddenly realised the girl was talking to him.

'I said, *grazie*. It is always nice to have compliments.'

Caterina eyed Monsieur Pamplemousse curiously as he produced a notebook from under the table. 'It is true, then, that you eat for a living?'

'Don't we all,' said Monsieur Pamplemousse, 'in our different ways?'

'So what will you say about this?'

Monsieur Pamplemousse regarded his plate, then applied his knife to the steak. 'I shall say that the meat is of good quality and that it has been cooked as I asked it to be. It is pink in the middle and juicy – not dried out. The *pommes frites* could be crisper; they have been kept a little too long. The *petits pois,* which might have been disappointing, are surprisingly good. They have the right amount of sweetness. The French beans . . . *comme ci, comme ça . . .'* He shrugged.

'I also have to ask myself the question: would I feel the same way if we were eating in a restaurant instead of hurtling through the night at over one hundred kilometres an hour?' He was tempted to add 'together with a young and undeniably beautiful girl', but it might have sounded too *gauche,* particularly with others around.

'Normally when I am working I eat by myself so that I am not distracted. Unlike taking a photograph of a distant mountain, where it is possible to add a tree or a shrub to give foreground interest. It is easier to be analytical when you eat alone.'

'I am sorry if I am a distraction. I have never been called "foreground interest" before.' It was said with a smile.

'I forgive you.' Monsieur Pamplemousse broke off to add a few more notes. 'For my taste, there are too many vegetables. They are probably trying to make it look like value for money.

'And you? What do you think?' he asked.

'I think,' said Caterina, 'I think it is all very wonderful. I can't tell you what it feels like to be free.'

Monsieur Pamplemousse gazed at her. What was it the poet Lemierre had once said? 'Even when a bird is walking, we sense that it has wings.' perhaps it went with being brought up in a convent school. When the door to the outside world was opened the inmates often grasped their new-found freedom with both hands.

'Be careful it does not go to your head.'

'But that is exactly what should happen,' said Caterina. 'It is like champagne. Where else should it go?'

Monsieur Pamplemousse could think of a dozen answers, but rather than risk getting into deep water he changed the subject.

'What do you plan to do when you leave school?'

'I shall become a model. I get all the magazines.'

It accounted for the weight of her valise. He wondered where she kept them hidden back at the convent. Under the mattress? It was exceedingly doubtful they would be approved reading.

'It is a hard life,' said Monsieur Pamplemousse. 'For every one who reaches the top of the ladder there are hundreds – thousands – who have to content themselves with clinging to the first few rungs. It is also a comparatively short one. Age has no mercy.'

'That makes it all the more of a challenge,' said Caterina simply. 'For those who do make it, there is a fortune waiting. A top model doing the circuits can easily earn $10,000 a show just for marching down a catwalk. Naomi Campbell started out at fifteen. She walked into the offices of *Elle* and sold herself on the strength of a portfolio of photographs. By the time she was twenty-one she had a million in the bank.'

'At that rate,' said Monsieur Pamplemousse drily, 'by the time you are that age you will be able to retire and open up a *boutique* . . . a chain of *boutiques*. You could have one in Rome, another in Paris, one in London . . . another in New York.'

'Why run a shop when you can be paid more to open one for somebody else?'

Monsieur Pamplemousse gazed at her. She had it all worked out. He also had a feeling she was holding back in some way. It all sounded a little too glib. It wasn't just his imagination – his years in the *Sûreté* had given him a sixth sense in such matters. Her eyes were focused on his, and yet the overall effect was that of a television personality reading someone else's lines from an auto- cue. He couldn't help but wonder why.

'Be careful you do not become like a Dugong.'

Caterina looked at him inquiringly.

'A Dugong,' said Monsieur Pamplemousse, 'is a fish which inhabits the Indian Ocean. It reaches a length of four metres and attains a weight of some 700 kilograms. Leather, ivory and oil are obtained from it, and as if that were not enough, its flesh is considered very edible. In almost all respects you could say it is a very successful fish, consequently it is in great demand. So much so that it has completely disappeared from some areas where it once thrived.'

'I shall be careful,' said Caterina simply.

'And your parents? What do they think?'

The girl pulled a face. 'Papa will go mad. If he had his way he would keep me behind walls for the rest of my life. There would be no choice.'

A clattering of china from somewhere below the table broke into their conversation.

'I know one who enjoyed the meal.' Monsieur Pamplemousse wiped his own plate clean with the last of the bread. He pointed to the tray.

'On a more mundane level, right now you have a choice. There is a carton of yoghurt or there is *clafoutis*. It is a fruit-filled pastry from Limousin – made with black cherries.'

The girl's eyes dwelt longingly on the *clafoutis*. 'May I? Would you mind?' Monsieur Pamplemousse put away his notebook. There wasn't much you could say about a yoghurt that hadn't already been said.

'I know what you are thinking. You are thinking if I am to be a model I shouldn't be eating this. But I am lucky . . . I burn it up. See . . .' Reaching across the table she half rose and struck a pose.

Monsieur Pamplemousse hesitated. 'Would you mind if I took your photograph? It would be nice to look back on.'

'I would like that too.'

'In that case I will fetch my camera.'

Monsieur Pamplemousse began the hazardous journey back to his compartment, battling with the sliding doors as the train swayed from side to side. The conductor was putting the finishing touches to making up his bed when he arrived. It took longer than he had anticipated, and he occupied his time reloading the camera with black and white film.

By the time he got back, the dining-car had begun to fill. Someone else was sitting at the table previously occupied by the man with the dark glasses. He reached his own table at the same time as a party of English. They eyed the empty plates.

'Nobody sitting here.' It was a statement rather than a question. The speaker scarcely waited for an answer before unloading his tray.

Monsieur Pamplemousse made a grimace in Caterina's direction. It had been a wasted journey. Now was not the moment for taking pictures. Conscious once again of eyes watching their progress, he led the way out of the car.

It was the girl's idea to make use of his compartment.

Not that Monsieur Pamplemousse wished to blame her in any way, of course. He had been a willing partner; but in retrospect and for the record . . .

410

Having got the attendant to unlock the door, and seeing that Caterina was waiting expectantly, it seemed like a good idea when she suggested it.

She posed easily and without a trace of embarrassment, throwing her head back as she sat on the bed so that her hair cascaded down over her shoulders like an inky-dark mountain stream. Her lips parted as she undid the top button of her dress. She would be equally at home on a cat-walk or in an Italian rice field. Silvana Mangano in *Bitter Rice?* Sophia Loren in *Black Orchid?* It was wrong to compare. Comparisons were odious. She was her own person.

Focusing on her eyes, Monsieur Pamplemousse stepped back into the corridor trying to frame the picture. As he did so, he glanced round to see if he was being watched. It was not quite what he'd had in mind. He wondered if the girl's reflection could be seen by the couple in the next compartment. Clearly, from the rapt expression on their faces, the answer was *oui*.

As the first flash went off the woman pursed her lips. It struck him that she looked like an outsize version of Madame Grante. Probably, like Madame Grante, she went through life voicing silent disapproval. She nudged her husband as the girl took up another position and Monsieur Pamplemousse fired off a second flash. At least she was getting value for money out of her journey. It probably confirmed her worst suspicions of 'the Continentals'.

Monsieur Pamplemousse took some more pictures and then came to the end of the reel. 'I will send them to you when they are ready.'

'Papa may not approve.' Caterina thought for a moment and then felt in her handbag. 'I will leave you an address.' She tore a piece of paper from a small pad and wrote on it.

Not to be outdone, Monsieur Pamplemousse reached for his wallet. 'Here is my card. It has my telephone number in case there is a problem. I will get the films processed as quickly as possible – before the end of your holiday.'

'You are very kind.' She stood and suddenly leaned forward. 'Thank you for looking after me so well.'

Monsieur Pamplemousse was totally unprepared for the kiss which followed, still less for its nature. The merest double brushing of lips upon cheek, starting with the right and ending with the left, as in Paris or Lyon, he could have taken in his stride. Intuition coupled with reflexes honed to perfection over the years would have enabled him to cope with regional variations; the Ardèche habit of starting on the left and adding a third, or even the Midi method, where four was the preferred number.

Brillat-Savarin, in his learned and often amusing work, *The Physiology of Taste,* devoted a section to the tongue's place in the natural scheme of things. It was a subject dear to the good doctor's heart. Having waxed lyrical on such matters as the number of papillae on the tongue's surface and the amount of saliva furnished by the inside of the cheeks when the two made contact, he then divided the sensation of taste into *direct, complete,* and *reflective.*

Caterina's kiss was both direct and complete, and it was in reflective mood that Monsieur Pamplemousse hovered in his doorway. Like a schoolboy reeling from his first encounter with the opposite sex, he watched her progress down the corridor.

When she reached her compartment she turned and gave a final wave before disappearing inside. Monsieur Pamplemousse returned it weakly. As he did so he caught sight of the conductor, now safely ensconced in his tiny office at the far end of the coach, a position which enabled him to keep a watchful eye on the comings and goings in his domain. He didn't actually utter the words *'Mamma mia!'*, but the look on his face said it all: a total lack of comprehension that a man could spend an evening with such a beautiful girl and yet sleep with a bloodhound. It was, thought Monsieur Pamplemousse, a typical Italian attitude.

Retreating into his own compartment, he closed the door and sat on the bed gazing out into the darkness. It was still warm from where she had sat. Recognising the symptoms, Pommes Frites gave his master a despairing look, followed by a deep sigh. It was the kind of sigh a dog emits when it realises it could be in for a bad night.

Monsieur Pamplemousse ignored the interruption. Had not the learned Brillat-Savarin's researches also brought to light certain other facts concerning tongues? Fish had to make do with a simple moveable bone; birds a membranous cartilage. Pommes Frites was as other four-legged creatures, his tongue lacked the power of circulatory motion. Once Pommes Frites' tongue had been given the go-ahead it went straight to its target, veering neither to the right nor to the left. Food scarcely touched the side of his mouth. Reminders that he should chew every mouthful at least thirty times would have been a waste of breath. Osculation was a pleasure denied him.

Monsieur Pamplemousse closed his eyes. Circulatory motion of a brief but undeniably sensuous and exploratory nature had been apparent in every second of Caterina's kiss.

There was a rustle of linen as Pommes Frites climbed up beside him. He pointedly turned round several times, then fell heavily into a heap in the middle of the bed, forcing his master into a corner.

It was Monsieur Pamplemousse's turn to sigh. Having expressed his feelings in no uncertain manner, he went out into the corridor and beckoned to the conductor.

The man took his time over the paperwork he was engaged in. Then, with an exaggerated gesture, he put down his pen and came to see what was required of him.

'Would it be possible to make up an extra bed?'

There was an intake of breath. 'The *signore's* reservation is for a *singolo.*'

'*Oui,*' said Monsieur Pamplemousse patiently. '*Maintenant I* would like *un doppio.*'

Silence reigned.

'*Per favore?*' He pointed to Pommes Frites. '*Per il cane.* For the dog.'

'*Per il cane?*' The man looked him straight in the eye.

Monsieur Pamplemousse reached for his wallet again.

'*Si, signore. Pronto.*'

Communication established at long last, Monsieur Pamplemousse watched from the corridor while the operation was carried out swiftly and with practised ease.

'*Il cane* – he will be able to climb the ladder, *signore?*'

'I shall be taking the top bunk,' said Monsieur Pamplemousse.

'*Si signore.*' As the conductor emerged, Monsieur Pamplemousse slipped him some folded notes.

'*Grazie, signore.*' The exchange didn't pass unnoticed by the couple in the next compartment. Clearly they feared the worst.

It was as he retreated into the compartment that Monsieur Pamplemousse caught sight of his reflection in the mirror over the cupboard and noticed the lipstick. He pulled down the blind, slowly undressed, then climbed the ladder to the top bunk.

Tired though he was, sleep eluded him for a while. He had to admit to himself that he found the thought of the girl preparing for bed in her compartment further down the coach strangely disturbing.

He started going over the encounter in his mind, trying to recapture the moment. Caterina's lips, full and inviting, had felt but a foretaste of what lay within and beyond. The experience had been at one and the same time both innocent and yet intensely pleasurable; investigative and exploratory, as natural and unforced as a rosebud bursting forth in spring. He wondered if everyone received the same treatment. Probably. It would be flattering his own ego to think otherwise.

The next thing Monsieur Pamplemousse knew it was morning. He looked at his watch. It showed seven-forty. Hearing the sound of the train changing pitch, he peered round the side of the blind and saw they were passing through Dijon. They must have stopped somewhere during the night, for they were now travelling in the opposite direction.

There was a clear blue sky overhead and the hilly countryside beyond the city was white with frost. Mistletoe grew in profusion on avenues of leafless trees. There was no sign of life anywhere; no people, no animals.

He washed and dressed quickly, swaying with the motion of the train as it gathered speed. It felt as though they were making up for lost time.

Breakfast arrived promptly at eight o'clock on a plastic compartmentalised tray. While the conductor folded up the bunks and restored things to normal, Monsieur Pamplemousse led Pommes Frites outside. He was just in time to see the man he had silently crossed swords with in the dining car the night before disappear along the corridor

415

towards the front of the train. Il Blobbo, as he'd mentally christened him!

The couple next door were exactly as he had last seen them. He wondered idly if they had been sitting up all night. Perhaps the woman was too large for her bunk, or perhaps they had read about the spate of robberies that were reported to have been taking place on sleeper trains from Italy and weren't taking any chances.

Back in his compartment, Monsieur Pamplemousse settled down and began analysing the breakfast. The chief wasn't going to get away with things that easily. A lengthy report wouldn't come amiss.

Espresso coffee in a china cup. Two small packets of *sucre*. Tinned *jus d'ananas*. Bel Paese cheese. A packet containing two thin slices of Dr Jaus *Roggenvollkornbrot* bread – the exact composition of which was translated into Italian, French, English and Spanish. It sounded unappealing in all five languages, but turned out to have a pleasant taste all its own. It went well with the cheese. A bread roll, also done up in plastic. A small pack of butter. A honey-flavoured confection made of naturally leavened cake shaped like a ringed donut. It was called *La ciambellina* and it was both warm and delicious. A packet of *Pan Brace San Carlo* toast. A hygienically wrapped plastic knife and spoon.

Busy with his own thoughts, Pommes Frites crunched noisily at the toast while his master wrote.

Soon after nine-thirty the attendant returned with his passport. Monsieur Pamplemousse was tempted to call on the girl, but decided he would give her a little longer. She would come to him if she needed anything. He wondered how she would be dressed. The demure convent girl or the woman of the world ready to take Paris in her stride?

416

Perhaps she would surprise him once again and appear in something totally different.

He would know soon enough. All the same, on his way back from the toilet at the end of the coach, he couldn't resist knocking on her door.

'It is nearly time.'

He thought he detected an answering call, but there was a sudden upsurge of noise as they roared through a station – it looked like Melun – and he couldn't be certain.

Thirty minutes later, when there was still no sign of the girl, Monsieur Pamplemousse decided to try again. Signalling Pommes Frites to stand guard over their belongings, he went out into the corridor. But he had left it too late. The train was slowing down for its final approach into the Gare de Lyon and he found his way blocked by the Americans: the woman overseeing her husband, who was struggling with a positive mountain of luggage. There was no possible way past, and certainly no hint in the woman's eyes that she might under any circumstances give way before the train had come to a complete stop.

With rather less than his usual good grace, Monsieur Pamplemousse abandoned his attempt to get past. Having collected his belongings, he took his turn in alighting from the train and waited patiently on the *quai* for the girl to appear.

He waited in vain. Patience gradually gave way to mental drumming as one by one the other passengers emerged and still there was no sign of her. It wasn't as though she had a lot of luggage. He tried not to think of the queue for the taxis. Any advantage they might have gained by being in one of the forward coaches was entirely lost.

Sensing Pommes Frites' growing restiveness, Monsieur Pamplemousse glanced round and spotted Il Blobbo again –

hovering at the end of the *quai* nearest the main concourse. He was with another man; a look-alike in dress if not in stature. Shorter and fatter, less dapper perhaps, but wearing an equally expensive looking black overcoat and matching fedora hat. As a duo, Monsieur Pamplemousse mentally bracketed them as a pair of high-class undertakers, although since they were both carrying violin cases he assumed they must be musicians.

They appeared to be intercepting some girls who were coming off the train. None of them were any older than Caterina, and since they were wearing red hats similar to the one she had arrived in, he assumed they must be from the same school. One or two stopped to hold a brief conversation, but most shook their heads and hurried on their way.

As the two men saw him looking in their direction they turned and moved off, melting into the already thinning crowd heading towards the exit.

'*Il signore* has forgotten something?'

The conductor held out an arm, barring Monsieur Pamplemousse's progress as the last of the passengers disembarked and he made to climb back on board.

'Not forgotten . . . left. The *signorina.*'

'The *signorina?*' The man looked at him blankly. 'But the *signorina* has already gone. She left as soon as we arrived.'

He waved his clip-board vaguely in the air. 'She went further along the train . . . she wished to be near the door . . . she was in a hurry. *Molto presto! Molto presto!*'

2
MURDER MOST FOUL

The view as they crossed the Seine by the Pont d'Austerlitz did nothing to raise Monsieur Pamplemousse's spirits. Paris was noticeably colder than Rome. The temperature must have dropped several degrees while they had been away. The water, dark and metallic under the leaden sky, looked deceptively calm; a heavily laden barge travelling upstream was having to fight its way against the current. A moth-eaten spaniel occupying the front passenger seat of the taxi eyed Pommes Frites dispassionately in the rear-view mirror. It received a blank stare in return.

As their driver turned right and accelerated along the Quai Saint Bernard, Monsieur Pamplemousse found himself automatically glancing into other taxis, wondering if he might catch sight of the girl. It was a forlorn hope, but she could have been delayed for some reason.

He felt aggrieved. Aggrieved and somehow let down. Flat was the word. He tried to tell himself that there was no reason in the world why she should have waited for him. Nothing except common courtesy; a commodity which seemed to be getting rarer and rarer in this day and age. It wasn't that he expected any thanks for his trouble, and admittedly he hadn't said he would be escorting her beyond the Gare de Lyon once they reached Paris. The girl wasn't a mind reader; she had no reason to know he was going into the office anyway to collect his car. But she might at least have had the decency to say *adieu*. A wave would have been better than nothing. A kiss blown from the end of the *quai:* something to file away in his memory.

So much for the brief flirtation of the night before. It would teach him not to romanticise. There was no fool like an old fool.

On reflection, Monsieur Pamplemousse was in no particular hurry to get to the office. The last thing he wanted to do was arrive ahead of her and perhaps bump into the Director waiting on the steps. In the circumstances, it would be an embarrassment. But as always when speed was not of the essence, the lights were green all the way and they reached the Esplanade des Invalides in record time.

The vast area was unusually devoid of tourists. The few people abroad had their hands in their pockets, coat collars turned up. The boules players had not yet put in an appearance.

Monsieur Pamplemousse stopped the driver in the rue Fabert, a little short of their destination, ostensibly in order to let Pommes Frites out for a walk. In truth, he wanted to get rid of his *valise* before putting in an appearance at the office. He wasn't in the mood to answer a barrage of questions. A quick in-and-out was the order of the day.

After his long journey, Pommes Frites looked perfectly content to be left to his own devices while his master disappeared into the depths of the underground car park bearing their luggage.

He was still waiting patiently by the same bench ten minutes later when Monsieur Pamplemousse returned, having deposited his films in the art department for Trigaux to process.

By eleven-twenty they were on their way, and shortly before midday Monsieur Pamplemousse was unlocking the door to his apartment in rue Girardon.

As he opened it he could hear the phone ringing, but by the time he had removed his overcoat it had stopped. Pommes Frites made his way into the kitchen and glanced hopefully at his food bowl, but clearly there was no-one at home. The sound of lapping water filled the air.

Monsieur Pamplemousse was about to open the French windows to let in some air when he spied a note propped against a bowl of flowers in the centre of the dining-room table.

It was from Doucette saying she had gone to Melun for the day to see her sister Agathe, who was feeling poorly again. Without either of them realising it, they had probably passed each other that morning travelling in opposite directions. Doucette would have taken the local train from the Gare de Lyon. There was a picnic lunch in the refrigerator. The salad dressing was in a jar on the top shelf. There was also some fresh cheese and some strawberry *barquettes*. Agathe said she had a lot to tell her so she might be late back.

Monsieur Pamplemousse absorbed the news with mixed feelings. He was beginning to feel hard done by, as though the world had suddenly turned against him. It would have been nice to have been greeted by something other than a note about a cold collation; the smell of a stew simmering on the stove, perhaps, or a *coq au vin* in the making. Even the pungent whiff of some freshly brewed *café* would have been better than nothing. He had even brought back some fresh truffles from Italy; not the white variety from Piedmont, which Doucette didn't really consider proper, but ironically some imported black ones from France, large, succulent and earthy, each separately wrapped in tissue and packed in an airtight plastic container. They would keep, but not for very long.

On the other hand, matters could have been worse. It was Friday; the day when Agathe was wont to cook *tripe à la mode de Caen*, under the mistaken belief that all you had to do was line a casserole with onions and carrots, shove in a kilogram or so of tripe, along with a calf's foot and the rest of the ingredients, leave it all to simmer for about ten hours and something magical would happen. It never did; not when he was there anyway. More often than not something went wrong. Either Agathe didn't add enough water, or else she didn't seal the pastry top completely tight. Once she even forgot to turn the oven on.

Going into the kitchen, Monsieur Pamplemousse encountered Pommes Frites coming out. An empty bowl pushed to the centre of the floor made clear his feelings.

A walk was indicated. A walk as far as the Place de Clichy. Pommes Frites could work up an appetite chasing a few stray cats in the Cimetière de Montmartre and afterwards they would indulge themselves with a leisurely lunch at, say, Le Maquis in the rue Caulaincourt.

Pommes Frites registered approval as his master picked up the telephone and booked a table. It was a sign that things were returning to normal. Basic decisions were being made.

Some three and a half hours were to pass before they returned home, tired but happy.

Monsieur Pamplemousse took off his shoes and lay back on the bed. What was the word he had used in *Le Guide* to categorise the food in the restaurant? *Copieuse?* He saw no reason to recommend a change in his next report. And *cuisine bourgeoise* was the only way to describe a meal which began with *feuilleté au roquefort* – the mountain of cheese still bubbling away in its casing of flaky pastry – followed by *gigot d'agneau rôti* with *pommes Lyonnaise;* the portions of leg of lamb so generous there was scarcely room left on his plate for the potatoes (on reflection, that had been an error of judgement on his part – following cheese in pastry with cheese in potatoes). Sadly, he had been forced to refuse the *plateau de fromage* in order to leave room for the *tarte sablée aux framboises.*

He closed his eyes in order to contemplate it the better. Pommes Frites' snores from the foot of the bed said it all. If Stock Pots were *Le Guide*'s symbol of excellence, snores were Pommes Frites'. So, too, in a matter of moments were those of his master.

Monsieur Pamplemousse woke to the sound of the phone ringing. He looked at his watch and saw to his horror that it registered seventeen-fifteen. It was not possible. It could not be.

It was not only possible. It was, according to the Director's secretary, a matter of some urgency.

Monsieur Pamplemousse tried to focus his attention on what she was saying. Having a whole bottle of Côtes-du-Rhône-Villages to himself had been a mistake. His head was throbbing.

'Monsieur Pamplemousse . . . it is Véronique. Forgive my troubling you. I know you must be tired after your journey . . . but I wonder if you can possibly help?

'I tried several times to get you. *Monsieur le Directeur* wishes to know what the problem is. . .'

'Problem? What problem?' Monsieur Pamplemousse tried to concentrate on what was being said.

'*Monsieur le Directeur is* reluctant to telephone Rome for fear of causing unnecessary alarm, but he wondered if perhaps there was a mix-up at the other end . . .'

'A mix-up?' Monsieur Pamplemousse forced himself into a sitting position. 'Are you saying his *petite cousine is* not with you?'

'*Monsieur le Directeur* waited on the steps for over an hour this morning. When she didn't appear we tried telephoning you, but there was no reply so we thought perhaps the train had been delayed. It was only when we found out that it had arrived on time that we began to get worried.'

'May I speak with the Director himself?' Monsieur Pamplemousse was suddenly wide awake, all his senses working overtime.

'I am afraid that is not possible, Monsieur Pamplemousse. He is with Sister. He fears he may have caught a chill. It is very cold for this time of year and Rambaud had the main doors open . . .'

'Then tell him I will phone as soon as possible.'

'I will see if I can put you through . . .'

'*Non.* I am going out now.'

'But, Monsieur Pamplemousse . . .'

'*A tout à l'heure,* Véronique. Thank you for calling.'

'Monsieur Pamplemousse . . .' Veronique sounded worried.

'What is it?'

'*Monsieur le Directeur* would not wish for any publicity. Only as a last resort, you understand?'

'*Oui,* Véronique. *Je comprends.*'

Monsieur Pamplemousse replaced the receiver with rather more force than he had intended. He understood only too well. Véronique was only doing as she was told, but it was typical of the Director that in a moment of crisis his first thought should be one of fear at being on the receiving end of any kind of adverse publicity. If ever there was a case for telephoning around, this was it. Well, they would have to see. First things first.

He hurried into the bathroom in order to freshen up with some cold water and in a matter of minutes, with Pommes Frites sitting beside him, he was at the wheel of his 2CV heading down the boulevard Magenta in the general direction of the Gare de Lyon.

As yet, he had no clear idea in his head as to why he was going there, or what he would do when they arrived. It was a matter of instinct – of past experience – going back to square one and starting again; much as an electrical repairman might handle a piece of faulty equipment. Check all external connections to make sure they were correct and move on from there. Tedious and painstaking it might be, but more often than not it was what produced results in the end.

Square one was the Gare de Lyon. It was hard to picture, but for all he knew Caterina might still be waiting there, panic having set in when she found herself lost in a strange city. Despite her outward self-confidence, she was still only a schoolgirl, and a schoolgirl with very little experience of the outside world at that. The *gare*, with its multitude of layers, each one teeming with travellers indifferent to anyone's problems but their own, was about as far removed from the cloistered calm of a convent as it was possible to imagine. She could have met with an accident, or been knocked down and suffered a loss of memory – stranger things had been known. The possibilities were endless. Mugged? Heaven forbid! He would never hear the last of it.

In any event, it would be a start. For the moment he refused to allow thoughts of anything more serious to enter his mind. The explanation, when it came, would probably turn out to be something quite mundane.

It was the height of the evening rush hour and traffic was heavy; the reverse of his morning journey. Every junction had its hold-up. Lorries fighting their way into the city, cars fighting their way out, with no quarter given on either side. Autobuses exerting their priority over other traffic – the drivers with their telephones at the ready in case a total *impasse* was reached.

Finding somewhere to park his *deux chevaux* was yet another problem. It took him something over ten minutes before he found a suitable gap in a side street behind the *gare*. As they made their way towards the entrance the clock in the belfry above the Big Ben bar showed midday on one face, on another four-twenty. The architect, Marius Toudoire, would not have been pleased. Monsieur Pample-mousse looked at his watch. It said eighteen-fifteen.

Inside the station, he set off on a quick voyage of explo-ration, retracing much the same path he had followed that morning. As before, he soon gave it up as a bad job. There were innumerable places Caterina could still be without having left the building. The Gare de Lyon was vast, and it had grown larger still since its integration with the RER high-speed underground system. It would take for ever to search all the different levels thoroughly, particularly with so many people milling around.

Monsieur Pamplemousse returned to the main concourse serving the *Grandes Lignes* and looked around and up in search of inspiration. It came almost immediately in the shape of the Departures board.

Scanning it for want of something better to do, he regis-tered the fact that the train they had travelled up on – the Palatino – was scheduled to leave for Rome in less than half an hour's time. At eighteen-forty-nine to be precise. *Quai* 'J'. It was not beyond the bounds of possibility that the same staff would be manning it for the return journey. Most of them would be going home.

The train was already in the *quai*. Looking slightly old-fashioned amongst the chic orange and grey livery of the TGVs, it still managed to exude an air of quiet superiority; of the way things *should* be done. Inside the first-class compartments people were unpacking their bags; hanging suits and dresses on to hooks; others had already drawn their blinds. Several coaches along, Monsieur Pamplemousse saw a familiar figure in brown clutching a clip-board.

As they drew near there was a glint of recognition. An official hand reached out for his ticket.

Monsieur Pamplemousse shook his head. 'We are not travelling.' He decided to plunge straight in. For the moment there was a lull. Quite possibly it wouldn't last very long. 'I was wondering if I might ask you a few questions?'

'Questions, *signore?*' There was the faintest change of expression on the conductor's face.

Before it had time to harden, Monsieur Pamplemousse felt for his wallet. It was becoming an expensive operation.

'Last night I travelled up from Rome with a girl . . .'

'*Si, signore.*' The man's face lit up again. 'I remember her well . . .' He sought for the right words. '*the bella figura!*'

'It was my intention to escort her to her destination,' said Monsieur Pamplemousse. 'But somehow in the rush we missed each other. You may remember. I looked for her at the front of the *quai*, but . . .'

'But she got off further down the train, *signore.*'

'Further *down* the train?' Monsieur Pamplemousse looked at the man in amazement. 'You mean she didn't go towards the front?'

427

'She said she was in a hurry and I told her to leave nearer the middle. I explained to her that it is often quicker. There are exits all the way along the *quai*. Also it is often easier for taxis. There is another rank at the back of the *gare*. Everyone makes for the front.'

Monsieur Pamplemousse looked aggrieved. 'Why did you not tell me that when I spoke to you yesterday morning?'

'You did not ask me, *signore*. As I remember it you simply asked me if I had seen her.'

The man hesitated. 'I think she was trying to avoid someone. That is why she wished to leave as quickly as possible.'

Monsieur Pamplemousse pondered the remark. Was it possible that Caterina had not wanted to see him? His pride took a momentary fall.

As though reading his thoughts, the conductor shook his head emphatically. 'No, *signore*. Not you. There was someone else. Another person.' He hesitated as a couple drew near, the woman pushing a trolley laden with luggage, the man comparing the number on their tickets with the one on the carriage. An electric trolley driven by a bearded porter wove its way past them.

Realising he was running out of time and that he was still holding his wallet, Monsieur Pamplemousse made to open it. 'This other person. Was it a man?'

The conductor covered the wallet with his clip-board. 'It is not necessary, *signore*.' He hesitated again, looking over his shoulder as though not wanting to be overheard. 'Come back in a little while. When the rush has died down. We can talk then.'

Accepting the man at his word, Monsieur Pamplemousse was about to set off back down the *quai* towards the main concourse when he spied one of the secondary exits. Acting on an impulse, he made his way down some stairs and found himself in a vast marble concourse on a lower level.

It was true what the conductor had said. Arrowed TAXIS signs pointed beyond the shops towards an exit at the rear of the building. Ambling after his master,

Pommes Frites paused at the top of the stairs and stared back at the train as though some nameless unhappiness had entered his soul.

But he paused in vain, for Monsieur Pamplemousse had his mind on other things. The Director for a start. He made for a row of telephones tucked away in a corner near the foot of the stairs and searched for his *télécarte*. It was time he checked in. For all he knew, Caterina might have turned up by now and he could be wasting his time.

It was a felicitous thought, but one that alas was not to be borne out in fact. The Director's first words set the tone of the conversation. It was worse than Monsieur Pamplemousse had feared. Total disbelief emanated from every nuance of every word.

'Pamplemousse, would you mind repeating your last utterance. I feel I may have misheard you.'

Monsieur Pamplemousse decided to play for time.

'I said, *Monsieur*, that conversation is a little difficult on account of the ambient noise level in the *gare*.' Even as he spoke, he was conscious of the fact that compared with the hustle and bustle of the main concourse, he had actually stumbled on an oasis of relative quiet. He wished now he had stayed put; it would have made matters a little easier.

Catching sight of the lugubrious expression on Pommes Frites' face as he hung on his master's every word, Monsieur Pamplemousse buried himself deeper still into the screened telephone booth, tightening his grip on the receiver as he did so. Pursing his lips, he went into his 'departure of the Orient Express for sunnier climes' routine. It always went down well with his colleagues, although to be truthful he only ever performed it towards the ending of an evening, when everyone else was suitably primed, not to say well oiled. A man at the adjoining telephone stopped talking for a moment in order to listen, then said something into the receiver.

Monsieur Pamplemousse ignored it. Clearly his own audience at the other end of the line was in a less receptive mood. Disenchantment set in almost immediately. Hardly had he completed his interpretation of a *chef de train* blowing a warning blast on his whistle than there was an explosion in his left ear which was little short of being on the threshold of pain.

'Pamplemousse! I have had a particularly trying day. I do not wish to listen to the kind of charade you trot out every year at the staff outing. Furthermore, the last steam train left the Gare de Lyon over forty years ago. Will you please answer my question. Did I or did I not hear you say you have lost Caterina? I trust my ears deceived me.'

Monsieur Pamplemousse took a deep breath. 'I said I couldn't find her, *Monsieur.*'

'That is splitting hairs, Pamplemousse!' barked the Director. 'What have you done with her?'

Ignoring the unfairness of the question, Monsieur Pamplemousse essayed a run-down of his end of the story. There was nothing like setting out the facts in detail to another person to help crystallise one's own thoughts.

'I have done nothing with her, *Monsieur.* I took *petit déjeuner* early as I wished to be alone in order to write up my notes so that they would be ready for you at the earliest possible moment. Apropos of which, I may say the catering

430

facilities were not quite as they were described to me. Alas, the days of *le grand wagon salle à manger* are no longer with us. The buffet car is admirable in its way, but one might as well be eating in a Jumbo jet. There is no longer a silver service. The salt and pepper comes in little plastic packets. . .'

'This is dreadful news, Pamplemousse.'

'It is a sign of the times, *Monsieur.*'

'I was referring to *ma petite cousine,* Caterina,' said the Director. 'Did she not join you for *petit déjeuner?*'

'No, *Monsieur,* she did not. We both took breakfast in our respective compartments. It was brought round on a tray by the conductor. When we were getting near Paris I knocked loudly on Caterina's door to warn her. I am almost certain I heard her call out to thank me. That being so, I fully expected to see her ready and waiting as we entered the *gare,* but there was no sign.

'Unfortunately my own departure was delayed for several minutes by an extremely large American lady with a great many *valises.* Even Pommes Frites couldn't get past. I suspect she was being deliberately difficult.

'When I finally managed to alight I was told by the conductor that Caterina had made her way to another coach shortly before I appeared. I assumed he meant nearer the front, but I have just learned I was mistaken. Since when I haven't seen her.'

'I say again, Pamplemousse, this is dreadful news. I charged you with her safe keeping. You have failed to carry out my orders.'

'With respect, *Monsieur,* that is not entirely correct. You merely suggested that as I was investigating the catering facilities on the Palatino and as *by chance* your *petite cousine* happened to be travelling on the same train, we

431

could keep each other company. Caterina is no longer a child, *Monsieur*. Furthermore, I must remind you I am employed by *Le Guide* as an Inspector of hotels and catering establishments, not as a nursemaid. I assume you are not suggesting I should have shared Caterina's sleeping compartment. There is no other way I could have kept my eyes on her all the time. Unless, of course, you wanted me to camp out in the corridor. There are little fold-down seats. I could have sat on one of those all night. Madame Grante would have been pleased. It would have saved *Le Guide* a considerable sum.'

There was a moment's silence before the Director spoke again.

'Forgive me, Aristide. I am overwrought.'

Monsieur Pamplemousse relaxed. The apology sounded genuine enough. The chief always grew a bit edgy towards publication day.

'I must admit to feeling a little put out that she hadn't even waited to say goodbye, *Monsieur*. I put it down to the forgetfulness of the young. Forgetfulness coupled with the excitement of the occasion. I assumed she was making her way straight to your office.'

'What time did the train arrive?'

'Ten-nineteen, *Monsieur*. It was two minutes late. There was a slight air of restiveness everywhere. Watches were being consulted. I have never seen the *gare* so crowded on a Saturday morning. It was a seething mass of schoolchildren going on their skiing holidays. I had to fight my way through. I tried mounting the grand staircase leading to *Le Train Bleu* restaurant, but I encountered a certain amount of resistance. Pommes Frites was dying to obey the call of nature by then and not unnaturally when he saw the Christmas trees he took advantage of them. I became involved in an argument with one of the waiters who was cleaning the stairs and that delayed matters still further . . .'

'Christmas trees?' barked the Director. 'In March?'

'*Exactement, Monsieur.* I trust the whole thing will be removed at the end of the skiing season. It is an eyesore.'

'They used to serve the best dry martini in Paris,' said the Director dreamily. 'The barman merely showed the label on the vermouth bottle to the gin.'

'It is possible, *Monsieur,* that he still does,' said Monsieur Pamplemousse.

Taking advantage of the change in the conversation he tried to maintain the hopeful note he had struck.

'It is the usual syndrome when someone is late, *Monsieur.* First there is irritation. Then one becomes cross. Crossness gives way to worry. Finally, when they do arrive, there is relief; relief mixed with guilt at ever having doubted them. It is early days to get one's *culottes* in a twist. There could be a dozen reasons why Caterina is late. She may have met an old friend, or she may have decided to do some shopping before she came to see you.'

'It is not my *culottes* I am worried about, Pamplemousse,' said the Director meaningly. 'We are talking about the *culottes* of a young girl who has spent much of her life in a convent. We all know what that means.'

'We do, *Monsieur?*'

'It is a highly charged atmosphere, Pamplemousse. Sex is always uppermost in the mind of the pupils. Couple that with a sense of guilt instilled at an early age by the Sisters and you have a sure-fire recipe for trouble. The nearest comparison which springs to mind is that of a piece of dry tinderwood awaiting the striking of the first match.'

'My knowledge of convent life, *Monsieur, is* limited. I know only those things I have heard at second or even third hand.'

'Me too, Pamplemousse. Me too. But as a boy my imagination was much exercised by a book called *The Dreadful Disclosures of Maria Monk.* It was required "under the desk" reading at the *lycée.*'

'Surely things have changed since that was written, *Monsieur?*'

'I think not, Aristide. I think not. Only in matters of detail. The book is probably part of the National Curriculum now, but I strongly suspect lascivious thoughts are still rife in the minds of those attending such establishments – fed as they are on a diet of fish.'

'We ordered steak for dinner last night, *Monsieur. . .*'

'The damage is done, Pamplemousse,' said the Director impatiently, 'It is a well-known fact that those whose diet consists largely of fish procreate like the proverbial *lapins.* It is the presence of so much phosphorus. Take any fishing community in the world. Notwithstanding the fact that many of the men-folk are away for long periods of time, the birth-rate is invariably above the national average. That is why I fear your comment on twisted *culottes* was singularly misplaced.'

Monsieur Pamplemousse remained silent for a moment or two. He was beginning to wish he had never used the phrase. The Director was fond of throwing in statements one longed to disprove. Apart from which, it was hardly the time to let fall the fact that the last time he had seen Caterina he doubted if her *culottes* were of a type to have passed muster at her convent's weekly knicker inspection, let alone have sufficient material in their construction to allow for much in the way of twisting.

He looked at his watch. It showed eighteen-thirty-five. 'If you will forgive me, *Monsieur*, I must go. I have been questioning the conductor of the Palatino. He may have some vital information.'

Even as he spoke, Monsieur Pamplemousse realised he hadn't the slightest idea what Caterina had been wearing. Her school outfit or something a little more chic?

'If I draw a blank I will telephone the police. Although I doubt if they will do very much at this stage other than circulate a description.'

There was a sharp intake of breath at the other end of the line. 'That is the very last thing you must do, Pamplemousse.'

'But, *Monsieur*. . .'

'No *buts*, Pamplemousse. I cannot explain matters over the telephone – there are certain complications. Continue your present inquiries by all means, but I suggest that as soon as they are complete you return to Headquarters, *tout de suite*. I will await your arrival.'

'But, *Monsieur*. . .'

'*Immédiatement!*'

Monsieur Pamplemousse replaced the receiver and removed his *télécarte*.

Quite understandably, the chief had sounded worried. But there had been something else as well: overtones of some deeper emotion; for want of a better word, a distinct note of apprehension – apprehension bordering on panic.

Monsieur Pamplemousse's own fears, which until that moment had lain dormant, perhaps if he was completely honest with himself, had been deliberately swept under the carpet, now surfaced. His pace quickened as he led the way back up the stairs.

As though infected by the same sense of urgency, Pommes Frites ran on ahead and was waiting by the Palatino as his master emerged from the stairway.

Monsieur Pamplemousse looked for the conductor, but he was nowhere to be seen. Assuming the man was inside the coach making last-minute preparations for the train's departure, he made his way along the *quai* peering in through the windows. But he drew a blank. Unfamiliar faces stared back at him, as though resenting the intrusion of a peeping tom. It was vexing to say the least.

With a feeling of impatience he boarded the train and looked inside the little office at the end of the coach. It was empty. There was a clip-board and a small pile of ticket stubs on the table. Alongside it was a tray with some bottles of mineral water, several glasses and an opener.

He checked the nearby toilet and once again drew a blank. A passenger standing in the corridor waving a last goodbye to someone outside eyed him curiously.

'*Le chef de train,*' said Monsieur Pamplemousse. 'The conductor. I was looking for him.'

The man gave a shrug. 'I'm sorry. I don't know. He was here earlier.' He resumed his waving, more urgently this time.

Monsieur Pamplemousse looked at his watch. It was time he left. It would be the final straw if he found himself trapped on board. Dijon was probably the first stop.

Calling Pommes Frites to follow, he made a less than dignified exit on to the *quai*. They were only just in time. The two-minute warning of the train's imminent departure was already being made over the loudspeakers. First in French, then in English, then in Italian.

Those on the *quai* who had come to see their nearest and dearest safely on their way stood back a little as the

436

hands on the clock above the stairs moved inexorably closer to departure time. There was the faintest jolt from the Palatino as it prepared to leave. Somewhere towards the front came the sound of a whistle being blown and moments later, as the second hand reached the vertical, the train began to move.

Impatience gave way to frustration and a sense of failure as Monsieur Pamplemousse watched the coaches glide past, gradually gathering speed. The engine that had brought the train into the *quai* followed on at a respectful distance, perhaps some twenty or thirty metres or so behind, the driver clearly anxious to return to his depot.

As it went past Monsieur Pamplemousse turned and began walking slowly back up the *quai* towards the main concourse. It was infuriating. The conductor must have been deliberately avoiding him. There was no other explanation. And for what reason? Perhaps they should have stayed on board after all until the man put in an appearance.

He was so engrossed in his thoughts he was totally unaware of what was going on around him.

At last, sensing that for some reason best known to himself, Pommes Frites was trying to attract his attention, he glanced up impatiently and was just in time to see a shadowy figure in a dark overcoat ducking beneath a gap between two coaches of a stationary train waiting alongside the adjoining *quai*.

Even from the back, there was something familiar about the person, but before he had time to call out, that train, too, began to move. It gave him quite a turn, for he felt sure the man must have been caught by it before he had a chance to scramble clear.

Monsieur Pamplemousse stood rooted to the spot for a moment, half expecting to see the worst as the last of the carriages went past, but instead all that remained was an almost empty *quai*. Whoever it was must have escaped by the skin of his teeth and made a bolt for it.

Gradually he became aware of yet another distraction; voices coming from further up his own *quai*, near to where he had been standing only minutes before.

Turning round, he saw that the engine which had brought the Palatino into the *gare* had ground to a halt alongside a small group of officials. He recognised the bearded porter among them. They were staring down at something on the line.

With a growing sense of foreboding, Monsieur Pample-mousse made his way back up the *quai*. As he drew near the group he followed the direction of their gaze and saw a figure in brown sitting in the gap between the two tracks. It was the conductor from the Palatino.

He looked for all the world as though he were taking part in a game of cards. From the total lack of expression in the eyes he could have been playing a hand of poker. Only the decorated head of a silver hat pin protruding from his right ear and a small trickle of blood running down behind his collar proclaimed the truth. The pointed end of the pin must have entered his brain. Death would have been both instantaneous and soundless.

Alongside the man lay a pair of dark glasses, one lens of which was smashed as though it had been trampled under-foot.

Monsieur Pamplemousse gazed at the motionless figure for several seconds, trying to absorb the fact and the meaning behind it, before he turned and began retracing his steps along the *quai*, slowly at first, then with gathering speed.

Mindful of the Director's warning, and conscious that others were watching his movements, he called Pommes

Frites to heel as they drew level with an exit and as though obeying a sudden whim, stopped abruptly and led the way quickly down the steps, feeling for his car keys as he went.

Reaching the lower level rather quicker than he had on the previous occasion, Monsieur Pamplemousse threw dignity to the wind and broke into a run. There were times when discretion was the better part of valour, and this was undoubtedly one of them.

3
OUT ON A LIMB

Le Guide's headquarters was ablaze with light. Everyone was working late. It was the busy time of the year.

Rambaud – who rarely emerged from his gate-keeper's office when there was an 'r' in the month – had stationed himself outside the main entrance. He wore a scarf round his neck to keep warm. The large wooden doors, as discreet in their way as the entrance to a London club, unadorned by anything so plebeian as a nameplate and normally kept closed to the outside world, were wide open. When he caught sight of Monsieur Pamplemousse's car approaching Rambaud stood to one side and signalled him to enter. It was an unheard of occurrence. Normally parking space in the inner courtyard was for VIPs only, the sole exception being a carefully marked area set aside for *Monsieur le Directeur* near the entrance to his private elevator.

One of the girls in reception was waiting for them by the lift. Rambaud must have given prior warning of their arrival, for she was holding the door open in readiness.

'Merci.'

As Monsieur Pamplemousse entered the lift the girl handed him, a large, official-looking brown envelope. It bore the Art Department's emblem. If Trigaux had done his stuff with the films it might well come in useful.

They were whisked up to the seventh floor without stopping once. As the doors slid open he saw Véronique, the

Director's secretary, standing outside. She led the way along the thickly carpeted corridor.

'How was Rome?'

'Warmer than here,' said Monsieur Pamplemousse. 'The children were mostly in costume. They were throwing confetti everywhere. It was the last big festival before Lent.'

'And the food? Did you eat well?' Clearly the subject of the Director's *cousine* was not up for discussion.

'On the first evening I had *culatello di zibello*. It is a *prosciutto* made from a knuckle of ham which has been aged, then soaked in sparkling red Lambrusco. It was possibly the most beautiful ham I have ever tasted; so soft it almost melted in the mouth. I followed that with *tortellini alla panna*. It was a speciality of the house and it was served covered with thinly sliced truffles. The taste comes back to me every time I think of it.'

He followed Véronique into her outer office and waited while she pressed a buzzer.

'Yesterday for *déjeuner* I ordered baked baby lamb with rosemary. It was accompanied by a green salad and it was so good Pommes Frites had a second helping. He made short work of the bones as well.'

Véronique opened her desk drawer and took out an imaginary violin which she began to play.

'Work, work, all the time work. It must be unbearably hard at times.'

Monsieur Pamplemousse put on his injured look. 'On both occasions the wine was of the most ordinary. The house *vino rosso*, which came in a glass jug. The information may come in useful if we ever do an Italian edition of *Le Guide.*'

Veronique stopped playing. 'Pigs might fly.' She tried buzzing the Director again. There was still no response.

441

'I should go on in. And watch out – I think *Monsieur le Directeur* is in one of his moods.'

Unexpectedly, despite the cold, the Director was standing outside on his balcony gazing into space. He looked in sober mood as he turned to greet his subordinate.

'Aristide, you are the last person in the world I would have wished this to happen to.' He gave a shiver as he came back into his office, closing the French windows behind him.

'But, *Monsieur*, it is I who should feel badly about the whole thing. Even now it is hard to say how it came about.'

Avoiding Monsieur Pamplemousse's gaze, the Director motioned him to sit, then crossed to the far side of the room. He looked as though he had aged ten years.

'Let me get you a drink.'

Catching sight of the portrait of Monsieur Hippolyte Duval, founder of *Le Guide*, it struck Monsieur Pamplemousse that for once he, too, seemed to be avoiding his gaze. Normally, those magnetic ice-blue eyes, captured in oils by the artist at the turn of the century, followed visitors everywhere they went in the room; there was no escaping them. Now, they seemed to be gazing into the middle distance. It must have been an optical illusion for as soon as the Director opened the door to his drinks cupboard and the light came on the feeling disappeared.

'A little white wine, *Monsieur*. A glass of Muscadet, perhaps?' He suddenly realised how thirsty he felt.

'Why not have something stronger?' The Director reached for a bottle of cognac. 'A glass of my Roullet *Très Rare Hors d'Age – numero vingt-six*, perhaps? Everyone should have at least one glass before they die.'

Monsieur Pamplemousse pretended not to have noticed the last remark. Véronique was right. The chief was in a downcast mood and no mistake. Stifling any kind of response, he watched while a more than generous measure was poured. Clearly something was afoot. Even Pommes Frites shifted uneasily as he recognised the signs.

Putting a brave face on matters, Monsieur Pamplemousse tried to turn the conversation in a happier direction.

'Should you ever choose to embark on an Italian edition of *Le Guide, Monsieur*, you may like to know that we had an excellent *dîner* in Rome the night before last. It was in a little family restaurant called Colline Emiliane, not far from the Piazza Barbarini . . .'

'I doubt, Pamplemousse, if any of us will be venturing on to Italian soil for some time to come,' said the Director gloomily.

He held out a large, balloon-shaped glass. Monsieur Pamplemousse took it reverently with both hands, warming the contents before lifting it to his nose. He was rewarded by a superbly rich and opulent bouquet.

'Perhaps,' said the Director, seating himself behind his desk, 'I should begin at the beginning.'

'It is always a good place to start, *Monsieur.*'

'The name Caterina, Pamplemousse, is derived from a Greek word meaning pure. I don't know what impressions you may have formed, but I think you must agree that if ever the choice of a name was inappropriate it has to be that with which Chantal's *petite cousine* was christened.'

Even if Monsieur Pamplemousse had been inclined to answer, he wasn't given the chance.

'She has always led a sheltered existence,' continued the Director. 'Her formative years were spent on her parents' estate. She was never allowed outside its four walls. They have always guarded her chastity. She is an only daughter,

443

her mother's pride and joy, the *pomme* of Uncle Rocco's *oeil*, and when she began to show unmistakable signs of maturity she was dispatched to a convent for safe keeping.

'As things turned out it was a disastrous move. Desires held in check all those years blossomed as they emerged from beneath the metaphorical bed-clothes. Loins which hitherto had only been exercised in the picking of orange blossom, were girded before being unleashed on an ill-prepared world. It must have been somewhat akin to Mount Vesuvius erupting after a particularly hot summer. Imagine her parents' distress when, after only a week in her new surroundings, she was asked to leave.'

'All young girls are high-spirited, *Monsieur*. Perhaps she found the regime too strict. Was it a Jesuit establishment?'

'This was not a simple case of high spirits, Pample-mousse. She pushed the Mother Superior into the swim-ming pool. Having been caught behind the changing rooms *in flagrante delicto* with a young gardener, she was trying to make good her escape when she was intercepted. Unfor-tunately the encounter took place near the deep end of the pool, and as swimming had not been part of the curriculum when the Mother Superior was a child it nearly ended in disaster. Nuns' garments weigh exceedingly heavy when they are steeped in water.'

'Is that so, *Monsieur*?'

The Director chose to ignore the interruption. 'Cate-rina was judged to be a corrupting influence on the other girls in her class,' he continued. 'She was told to pack her belongings and her parents were sent for. But Uncle Rocco, who has connections with the Vatican, persuaded the powers that be to change their minds. As a result they now have one of the finest tennis courts that money can buy.'

'And the gardener, *Monsieur*? What happened to him?'

The Director shrugged. 'He was never seen again. But that was no problem. I am told that even though they pay only the minimum rates there is always a sizeable queue of applicants for the post. But that is a thing of the past. The nuns have learned their lesson and they are paying the price with backs bent over the hoe.'

'But with respect, *Monsieur*, we are living in the latter half of the twentieth . . .'

'Correction, Pamplemousse. We may be living in the latter half of the twentieth century, but not everyone recognises that fact, still less do they allow others to enjoy the benefits that go with it. Some people – particularly those who are used to living in a relatively closed community – set great store by what they consider to be their "property". They guard it assiduously. That is the case with Uncle Rocco and his daughter and that is why I entrusted you with the mission.

'Anticipating her safe arrival, our own gardeners have been briefed. Warnings have been issued. The pool has been drained. And now . . .'

'I wish you had told me all this earlier, *Monsieur*. To be forewarned is to be forearmed.'

'You are not the only one, Pamplemousse. You are not the only one. My wife and I discussed the matter at great length and in the end Chantal felt the least said the better. We did not wish to worry you unduly.'

Monsieur Pamplemousse sipped his brandy thoughtfully. 'I still do not understand, *Monsieur*, why you are so against calling in the police. Surely, a discreet word in the right quarters . . .'

'That is out of the question, Pamplemousse. Utterly out of the question. Uncle Rocco is impatient with authority. In his eyes there are no "right" quarters. He is a law unto himself. We shall need to mobilise our own forces – and quickly. Speed is of the essence. He will be awaiting a call to hear that all is well and there is a limit to the number of excuses I can find when he asks to speak to his daughter. The sound of a departing steam train, however well executed, will cut little ice in the circumstances.'

'But, surely, *Monsieur* . . .'

'There is no "surely" about it, Pamplemousse. Chantal's Uncle Rocco is a very powerful person and Chantal is his favourite niece. He is also by nature the sort of person who at the slightest whim would pick up a telephone and erase her from his memory with no more thought than he would put to telling the captain of one of his merchant ships to alter course for the Azores. He is also, I may say, perfectly capable of erasing others from his memory too.'

And from his will, thought Monsieur Pamplemousse. That had to be it: the reason for his boss's unhappiness. The more some people had, the more they wanted.

'Life will not be worth living once he gets to hear what has occurred,' said the Director.

'But what can he do, *Monsieur*? He may be powerful in the world of shipping, and I agree that he has good reason to be upset . . . but here in Paris . . .'

The Director dithered for a moment or two, making a show of tidying his desk before replying. 'Uncle Rocco's interests are not entirely confined to maritime matters, Pamplemousse,' he said at last. 'He is involved in many things. He has his fingers in a multitude of pies. Buying and selling . . . the construction business . . . his tentacles are like those of an octopus and they stretch far beyond the confines of the island where he lives. He has connections everywhere.'

446

'He lives on an island, *Monsieur?*' The word 'tentacles' coupled with that of 'island' caused faint warning bells to start sounding in the back of Monsieur Pamplemousse's head. 'I assumed he lived somewhere near Rome.'

'Did I say that?' asked the Director innocently.

'No, *Monsieur*, you did not. I merely assumed . . .'

Draining his glass, the Director rose and crossed to the French windows, where he stood gazing out across Paris. The golden dome of St Louis des Invalides gleamed dully in the cloud-filtered sunset. Much further away and to its left, the equally distinctive dome of the Sacré Coeur on the heights of Montmartre seemed nearer than usual; a hint, perhaps, that rain was on the way.

But Monsieur Pamplemousse noticed none of these things. His thoughts were concentrated on more immediate matters. The Director's behaviour for a start; his wife Chantal's unexpected absence – they all began to add up. He had a sudden mental picture of the conductor's body sitting where it had been placed on the railway track. At the time the method of killing had seemed extraordinarily bizarre, now he wasn't so sure.

'What was the name of the island where Caterina spent her childhood, *Monsieur?*'

The Director waved one hand vaguely in a westerly direction. 'Corsica, Sardinia . . . there are so many . . . I really cannot remember which one.'

'Were you to be gifted with extraordinarily long sight,' persisted Monsieur Pamplemousse, 'could you, from where you are standing, *Monsieur*, perhaps see beyond Corsica, and beyond Sardinia, to an island known as Sicily?'

'Sicily!' There was barely a split second's hesitation, but it was more than sufficient. 'That was it. Thank you, Pamplemousse. It all comes back to me now. An interesting island, steeped in history. First colonised by man towards the end of the Ice Age. Occupied for a time, according to Greek mythology, by a race of one-eyed cyclopean giants of cannibalistic propensities. There was also the Barbarian period; the Byzantine period; the Arab period . . .'

'The Cosa Nostra period?' broke in Monsieur Pamplemousse. 'Which began shortly after Garibaldi drove out the last of the Bourbon kings and which has been active ever since.'

'Sicily has always been a turbulent isle,' said the Director evasively, turning his back on the outside world. 'Greeks, Romans, Barbarians, the Emperors of Byzantium, the Arabs, the Normans and the Germans; they have all occupied it at various times.

'Over the centuries the inhabitants have had more than their fair share of troubles, and it is perhaps not surprising that they have turned to those who are prepared to help. Two thousand years of foreign occupation and despotic rule have also taught them to keep their mouths shut. I need hardly remind you, Aristide, that "Cosa Nostra" means "our affair".'

The Director raised his hand as he saw Monsieur Pamplemousse was about to interject.

'Please don't misunderstand me. I am not for one moment saying the Mafia is a force for good – quite the reverse. Their motivation is simply one of greed. Where there is easy money to be made, that is where you will find them. They rule by fear and once you are a member there is only one way out – feet first.

'Having said that, there have been times when the State has been undeniably bad; hopelessly out of touch with the needs of its people and seemingly indifferent to their fate. There are those – mostly poor peasants, who in times past have felt abandoned by their government – who might say that life would be infinitely less happy and secure without the protection of the Uncle Caputos of this world. I would not like to sit in judgement of that belief. There, but for the Grace of God, Aristide, go I.'

'Caputo?' Monsieur Pamplemousse gave a start. 'But, did you not say, *Monsieur*, that the name of your wife's uncle is Rocco?'

The Director brushed aside the remark. 'It is merely a nickname. A childish appellation Chantal bestowed on him when she was small. Her Uncle Rocco is not, I fear, a very good loser. Sometimes, when they were playing together and he found things weren't going his way he would bring the game to an abrupt end – either by sending her off to play hide and seek and then never going after her, or else by pretending to shoot her, saying "Right, Chantal, your time is up – you are *caputo.*" She has never forgotten the fact. Over the years it became something of a joke in the family.'

Monsieur Pamplemousse digested the information slowly and carefully.

'And when he is not playing games, *Monsieur*, what does Uncle Caputo do then?'

'This and that,' said the Director vaguely. 'I understand he plays a prominent role in the Sicilian laundry business. He is highly thought of in ecclesiastical circles.'

'You mean – he takes in the Vatican's washing?'

The Director glared at Monsieur Pamplemousse. 'You know perfectly well what I mean, Pamplemousse. Chantal's Uncle Caputo happens to enjoy a good relationship with a certain dignitary in the church, an official holding high office whose duties take him to the mainland from time to time. This person is not averse to lining his cassock with whatever he is given, in return for enjoying the many benefits concomitant with travelling first class, not the least of which is that of having extra space between the seats. It is a happy arrangement on both sides.'

'Would it be true to say, *Monsieur*, that within your own family circle Il Signor Rocco is more of a Godfather than an uncle?'

The Director gazed unhappily at Monsieur Pamplemousse. 'If you insist on my spelling it out, Pamplemousse, I am saying that Chantal's Uncle Rocco is an important member of the Cosa Nostra and as such he commands respect. People cross swords with him at their peril. He does not live in an unnumbered house in an unnamed street on the island of Sicily for nothing.'

'In what other directions do Uncle Rocco's tentacles travel, *Monsieur*?'

'He was very much into cigarettes at one time. A container-load is worth a great deal and is easily disposed of – especially if you happen to control all the machines which dispense them. Currently, I understand he is very much interested in caviar. It is a matter of bartering. The Russian Mafia, such as it is, will do anything for foreign currency. I am told that if you hail a taxi in Moscow the first question the driver asks is not where are you going, but how you wish to pay? If you say roubles, then he goes on his way leaving you stranded.

'Forty francs' worth of Beluga caviare at source is worth the equivalent of 20,000 francs in Rome and corruption abounds.

'Kidnapping, protection, extortion, loan sharking . . . all the usual things. All, that is, except gambling and prostitution. It is against the principles of the Sicilian Cosa Nostra to be involved in either – they leave that to their American counterparts. Gambling indicates a weakness which they

450

have no wish to exploit lest they themselves get tainted in the process, and for a Sicilian, living on a woman's earnings is dishonourable.

'As a man of honour, that is one of the principal reasons why Uncle Caputo is so protective of his only daughter. To date he has always kept her free from the gaze of other men. Letting her come to stay in Paris only came about as a result of much pleading on her part and an undertaking on ours that we would never let her out of our sight. On pain, Pamplemousse, of certain anatomical modifications to our persons as yet hardly touched on by the medical *journaux* should we fail in our task.'

'If that is the case, *Monsieur*, why did you agree to have her to stay?'

'Why do you pay your income tax, Aristide? Certainly not because you do not wish to hurt the feelings of those in power by declining.'

'Would it not have been better to have gone to Rome yourself ?'

The Director raised his hands. 'Work, Aristide, work! It never goes away. Having said that, I cannot tell you the guilt I feel at having placed you in this onerous position. I wouldn't have wished it on my worst enemy.

'Once Uncle Caputo learns what has happened he will lose no time in tracking you down. Whatever happens we must find Caterina first. At least we know what we are looking for. There can't be many girls in convent school uniform loose in Paris. It can only be a matter of time.'

'Aah!' It was Monsieur Pamplemousse's turn to drain his glass. 'We may have a problem there, *Monsieur*. It depends what she is wearing. It could be either one of two extremes.'

He picked up the envelope the receptionist had given him and carefully unwound the string fastening the flap.

Trigaux had certainly excelled himself. It was packed with glossy 20 cm x 25 cm prints. He must have dropped everything. Perhaps the subject matter had appealed to him.

'These are some photographs I took on the journey.'

Removing them, he flipped through the pile. Most of the earlier ones were of Pommes Frites: Pommes Frites gazing out of the hotel window; Pommes Frites chasing a Roman pigeon; Pommes Frites waiting patiently outside the Vatican, looking as though he might be hoping for an audience with the Pope.

The photographs he was searching for were at the end of the pile. Apart from the colour prints of those taken inside the Termini at Rome, where he could have done with a faster film, they looked sharp enough. The ones taken on the train were on black and white stock and bore all the hallmarks of a flash photograph; hard shadows, lack of facial tones, but they were pleasing nevertheless. Although he said it himself, they wouldn't have disgraced the pages of many a fashion magazine.

'These are the snaps I was looking for, *Monsieur*. As you will see, they show two different sides of your niece – before and after as it were.'

The Director sat bolt upright in his chair. 'Before and after what, Pamplemousse?' he exclaimed. 'What are you trying to tell me?'

It was Monsieur Pamplemousse's turn to ignore the interruption. 'The first two were taken when your *petite cousine* arrived at *la gare, Monsieur*. The rest were taken on the Palatino after she had changed for *dîner*.' As he glanced at the photographs, the remaining colour drained from the Director's face.

'This is terrible, Pamplemousse. Much worse than I believed possible. I would hardly call them *snaps*.'

'They were intended as a surprise, *Monsieur.*'

'They are more than that, Pamplemousse. They are a severe shock. I can hardly believe my eyes.'

'I have to admit I was somewhat taken aback myself, *Monsieur.* It was a total transformation.'

'Where were the later pictures taken, Pamplemousse?'

'She was sitting on the bed in my compartment.'

The Director clutched the side of his chair. 'I feared as much.'

'There is no cause for alarm, *Monsieur.* I can assure you it is not how it looks. The door was open at all times. The compartments are very small and I had to stand in the corridor in order to achieve a pleasing composition. There was an American couple in the one next to mine. I remember the first flash made them jump. There is also the conductor. He made up a bed for Pommes Frites and received a handsome *pourboire* for his trouble . . .'

Monsieur Pamplemousse's voice trailed away. The conductor was one witness he would never be able to call on. He wondered if he should tell the Director what had happened to the man, then thought better of it.

'Pamplemousse, this story must never, ever reach the ears of others.'

'Least of all the Mother Superior?' hazarded Monsieur Pamplemousse.

'It is not the Mother Superior I am worried about,' said the Director. 'It is Uncle Rocco.'

'There is no earthly reason why he should ever know, *Monsieur.*'

'What if the person operating the processing machine took a fancy to the pictures and had copies made?'

'I hardly think that is likely, *Monsieur.*' Trigaux's last words to him had been 'Don't tell the chief – he's having a purge on home processing. Madame Grante's been getting at him.' He couldn't let him down.

'You do not know, Pamplemousse. You do not know. It is not beyond the bounds of possibility that the concessionaires are already paying some form of protection money – "insurance" against unforeseen dilution of their chemicals en route from the factory. Not necessarily to Uncle Caputo – it is not his territory – but to the member of another family.'

'This is France, *Monsieur*, not Sicily.'

The Director looked less than convinced. 'I trust these are the only pictures you took? You are not hiding anything?'

'What are you suggesting, *Monsieur*? You surely don't think . . . Caterina is young enough to be my daughter – my granddaughter even. What I have told you is the simple truth.'

'The truth is seldom simple, Aristide, and it often has as many faces as there are those involved. I do not doubt your version of the affair, or that your intentions were entirely honourable. Doubtless, if you asked Caterina for her opinion, she would see it in an entirely different light.

'However, what you or I think is immaterial. It is what Uncle Rocco thinks that matters. I am simply placing myself in his shoes. Shoes, Pamplemousse, purchased from Salvatore Ferragamo in Florence and polished with the blood of those who have offended him along the way; burnished until they could have seen their own faces in them had they still been alive to do so, and always assuming they would have wished to see their faces after he had finished with them.

'I know the way his mind works. There you are in Rome, meeting his only beloved daughter – a girl still at convent

454

school. Within an hour you have persuaded her to dress in a manner which would not have passed unnoticed on the stage of the *Folies Bergère*. You then take her to the buffet car and ply her with drink.'

'It would have seemed churlish not to have offered her any liquid refreshment, *Monsieur*. I felt sure you would wish me to.'

'There are other beverages, Pamplemousse. Some form of Cola might have been preferable in the circumstances.'

Monsieur Pamplemousse felt for his notebook. 'I kept a strict record, *Monsieur* . . .'

The Director raised his hand. 'Wait, I have not yet finished. I am merely seeing things through Uncle Rocco's eyes. Having plied his only daughter with drink, you take her back to your compartment and there you persuade her to pose in a most provocative manner. Shortly afterwards you ask the attendant to make up another bed, offering the lame excuse that it is for your dog. On your own admission you offered the man a sum of money, presumably to make sure his lips were sealed. Doubtless the same couple who were startled by your flash witnessed you doing that too.

'Try convincing Uncle Rocco it was all done in pure innocence. You will soon see why he deserves the nickname "Caputo" .'

'It shows a great lack of faith in his daughter, *Monsieur*.'

'It shows a great lack of faith in human nature, Pamplemousse, but where he comes from faith in human nature lies thinly on the ground, usually surmounted by a cross to show where it died. Uncle Rocco's reasoning would be that it is not simply a case of Caterina exchanging her dark blue bloomers with double gussets for frilly garments of a more provocative kind. If you think what that prospect does to others, think what it must also do to the wearer. A wearer, moreover, who

455

is doubtless still suffering from having once already reached out to pluck the forbidden fruit, only to feel it literally slip from her grasp. Whatever the outcome of this sad affair, the fact remains that in his eyes you have condemned her to eternal damnation and there is no going back.

'Now, to cap everything, you have lost her and she is all alone in a strange city. The heady rush of Parisian air in her nostrils may well have brought on an attack of amnesia, leaving her unable to make up her mind which way to turn. I need hardly remind you, Pamplemousse, that the streets of Paris are filled with those who will be only too willing to guide her.'

Gloom settled over the Director again. 'You know what this means, of course?'

Monsieur Pamplemousse shook his head.

'You must go to ground, Pamplemousse, possibly never to emerge.'

'But why me, *Monsieur?*'

'Because, Pamplemousse, as soon as Uncle Rocco hears the news you will be seen as the prime suspect and he will go for the jugular.'

'But, *Monsieur,* I have already said I can explain everything . . .'

'Explanations,' said the Director heavily, 'do not come easy when you are standing at the bottom of the Seine wearing nothing but a pair of concrete boots. "Thinks balloons" will emerge as bubbles. You see now why I said we cannot possibly go to the police. No-one must know what has happened. I will stay here and man the fort, staving off all questions to the best of my ability.

'Your only hope – your only salvation – lies in finding Caterina with all possible speed. In the meantime you must make yourself as scarce as possible.'

It didn't escape Monsieur Pamplemousse's notice that the two tasks were not exactly compatible, nor did he fail to observe that the Director was already distancing himself from the affair. The word 'you' was starting to appear with alarming regularity.

'I will instruct Véronique to light a candle for you in the church of St Pierre du Gros Caillou.' As the Director picked up the phone, he felt in his pocket, then he appeared to change his mind. 'I shall also warn Chantal not to return to Paris until I give her the all-clear. I suggest you make similar arrangements with your own wife.'

While he was talking, the Director turned and crossed once again to his French windows, there to gaze silently at the lowering sky. It was a clear signal, if one were needed, that conversation was at an end.

Imbued with a sense of impending doom, Monsieur Pamplemousse made his way slowly out of the room, closely followed by Pommes Frites, his tail hanging at a suitably recumbent angle.

Véronique was already taking the Director's call. '*Oui, Monsieur*, I will make sure it is carried out straight away. *Oui, Monsieur*, I will arrange for a candle to be lit. The ten-franc size? *Oui*, I will take it out of petty cash.'

As Monsieur Pamplemousse passed her desk she placed her other hand over the mouthpiece of the receiver. She looked in a state of shock.

'*Monsieur* . . . I had no idea . . .'

'It happens . . .' Monsieur Pamplemousse didn't know what to say.

Véronique looked as though she would either burst into tears at any moment or start organising a collection on his behalf. Either way it was no time to linger.

As he left the building Monsieur Pamplemousse paused, unsure for the moment which way to go; whether to take his car or walk for a while. Suddenly feeling very alone, he looked round to make sure Pommes Frites was still with him. He also couldn't help but wonder how long a ten-franc candle normally lasted. A day? Two days? Knowing the ways of the Vatican, probably a lot less. To the best of his knowledge the church of St Pierre du Gros Caillou was used by Ukrainians, but at least it was fairly near the office.

It didn't add to his peace of mind that on the way out he had called in at the Operations room: that sacred part of the building where, day and night, uniformed girls armed with long poles kept constant vigil on the whereabouts of all the Inspectors, manoeuvring their personal figurines around a table-top map of France with croupier-like efficiency as they up-dated their every movement.

His own figurine had already been relegated to a parking bay near the back; somewhere on the outskirts of Lille.

4
THE SEARCH BEGINS

A feeling of *déjà vu* came over Monsieur Pamplemousse as he arrived back at his apartment. The telephone was ringing again. This time he decided to ignore it. If it was the Director with more prophecies of doom he didn't wish to know. If it was anyone else they could wait. First things first. Number one priority was a stiff drink. Brillat-Savarin had never spoken a truer word when he said that man is the only creature who drinks when he is not thirsty.

He poured himself a large cognac. After the earlier Roullet it tasted like firewater. *Très Rare Hors d'Age* was not what it was all about. When all this was over – *if* it was ever over- he would remind the Director that a bottle of his favourite cognac wouldn't look out of place in the drinks cabinet *chez* Pamplemousse. In the circumstances it was the least Monsieur Leclercq could do.

After a moment or two Monsieur Pamplemousse reached for the telephone and dialled a Melun number. He drew the short straw. Doucette's sister answered.

'Agathe. How are you?' He immediately regretted asking. Agathe was the kind of person whose health one didn't enquire after. It was her favourite subject. Visits to the doctor were seldom undertaken without her taking along a wall chart showing all the organs of the female body – in full colour.

459

Cupping the receiver under his left ear, Monsieur Pample-mousse reached for the envelope he had brought back from the office and emptied the contents on to the table. Spreading the photographs out across its surface, he began sorting through them, putting the earlier ones – mostly of Pommes Frites – to one side in order to concentrate his attention on the last reel. He had said it before and he would say it again – Trigaux had done a good job. It was easy to see why. The Director's *petite cousine* must have made a pleasant change from endless shots showing the outside of hotels.

There was no doubt Caterina was beautiful. She had a haunting quality. She would go places, of that he was sure. There was a determined look in her eyes. But wasn't there something else as well? Another, deeper layer. A vulnera-bility perhaps, or an innocence? Perhaps in the end she was a flawed beauty? It was hard to say which element lay just beneath the surface and which was on top. The various sides of her character seemed inextricably mixed up; each one trying to fight its way out. But wasn't that the case with most teenagers?

And had there not been, in that brief moment when she had suddenly and unexpectedly kissed him in the train, an exchange of something else again? It had nothing to do with giving or taking, or of expecting anything in return. It had simply been a brief and uncomplicated moment of truth; the sharing of a secret, as with a brother and sister. Or perhaps more appositely in this case, between father and daughter. A bond had been forged, like the wiping of a pin-prick of blood on to the paper image of a saint in a Mafia initiation ceremony, and he knew that whatever happened, if Caterina were in trouble he would go to her aid without question.

'*Chérie.*' Monsieur Pamplemousse suddenly realised Doucette was talking to him. It was a good thing videophones were still a thing of the future. 'Have you been trying to get me? A moment ago . . . ?

'*Non*? I simply wondered, that is all. The phone was ringing when I came in . . .

'*Non.* I have been at the office. Pommes Frites and I had a good *déjeuner.* Too much . . . I am afraid we went to sleep afterwards. I would have telephoned before, but something urgent has cropped up at work. It always happens near publication time.'

Monsieur Pamplemousse hesitated, wondering how best to frame what he wanted to say. In the event the problem was solved without his having to say a word. Doucette was the one who sounded worried; more on his behalf than her own.

'*Couscous,* of course I do not mind if you stay the night. Stay for as long as you wish. I shall be busy for the rest of the week . . .'

He hoped he hadn't sounded too relieved, too anxious to fall in with her plans. Doucette had a keen ear for undue emphasis; the unnecessary underlining of words in what was intended to be taken merely as a casual remark. Out of context, such utterances didn't always stand up to close analysis. Her next question realised his worst fears.

'*Monsieur le Directeur's petite cousine?* Poof! She is but a child.'

Monsieur Pamplemousse cast his eyes around the room and settled on a photograph of his sister-in-law. 'I fear nature has not been kind to her, *Couscous.* She is grossly overweight and much given to complaining.'

'Oh dear, Aristide, did you have a very tedious time?' Doucette sounded contrite. He must have struck a sympathetic chord. No doubt she was suffering too.

'I would rather not talk about it, *chérie* . . .

'*Oui.* I will telephone in the morning. I may know more

of what is happening then. *Monsieur le Directeur* is up to his eyes at present.

'You, too. Sleep well!'

Monsieur Pamplemousse replaced the receiver rather quicker than he had intended. He hoped it hadn't sounded too abrupt. He sat for a moment or two lost in thought. It was good that Doucette had opted to stay with her sister. It was one less thing to worry about. Judging from the tone of the conversation, if Agathe had any say in the matter – which she undoubtedly would – he might be on his own for several days.

His mind returned to the events at the Gare de Lyon. How was it that the man on the Palatino had been there too? Had he also been looking for Caterina? Even more to the point – had he been responsible for the death of the conductor? The more he turned the matter over in his mind, the more certain Monsieur Pamplemousse felt it was a self-answering question. The evidence was purely circumstantial, of course – it wouldn't stand up for a second in a court of law. But it was too much of a coincidence for there to be any other explanation.

But why? What possible reason could there have been for murder? It couldn't have been a premeditated act.

He rose to his feet and crossed to the French windows. Opening them, he went out on to the small balcony which ran the length of the building. Ciné 13 on the corner of rue Junot must be holding a private screening, for there were people in evening dress gathered outside. He could hear their chatter and the occasional shrill laugh. A pair of lovers stopped to watch, probably hoping to catch a glimpse of someone famous.

Across to its left, beyond the old Moulin de la Galette and further down the hill, he could see the large shape of the Cimetière de Montmartre, where he and Pommes Frites

462

had walked earlier in the day; an island of darkness now, submerged in a sea of twinkling lights. The resident population of cats would be on the prowl by now, safe from the likes of Pommes Frites.

To its left, the sky was illuminated by the glow from the Place de Clichy; an amalgam of multi-coloured neon signs and light from restaurants and cinemas, criss-crossed by headlights from a never-ending stream of traffic flowing in all directions. The view across the rooftops was one of his favourites – at any time of the day or night. But night-time brought its own magic, glossing over some of the less salubrious aspects of the area.

On the lower slopes of Montmartre – the one-time hill of windmills – the hookers would be out in force, watched over by their pimps. *Racoleurs* would be trying to entice likely-looking candidates into the strip joints in order to make their percentage on the grossly overpriced drinks. Concierges in the rue de Douai would be handing out 'short-time keys' on a strictly cash in advance basis.

In the far distance, beyond Place de Clichy, he could make out the Eiffel Tower, and to its right the Arc de Triomphe. Beyond that lay the whole of western France, and then the Mediterranean. And beyond that again, lay Sicily with its strange medieval, closed-in society from which there was no escape, and its family feuds which bubbled away over the centuries, occasionally erupting like a volcano into unbelievably savage and bloody acts of revenge. Sicily, with its code of *omertà* – its conspiracy of silence – a code enforced in the old days by sawn-off shotguns, and nowadays by the short-barrelled .38 or Magnum .357 armed with exploding bullets.

Sicily and Uncle Caputo. The name, in the circumstances, sounded more fitting than Rocco.

And now, somewhere in amongst the teeming mass of humanity that went to make up Paris, was Uncle Caputo's daughter, alone and unprotected. The Director was right. If anything happened to Caterina he, Aristide Pamplemousse, would be held responsible.

Retribution would be a foregone conclusion; swift in its execution – terrible in its method. Monsieur Pamplemousse had no wish to end his days trussed-up like a goat in the boot of a car, legs doubled back behind him, feet lashed together with the other end of the rope tied round his neck. If he didn't die by self-strangulation, he would be shot in the back of the head prior to being fed to the pigs, or liquefied in a barrel of acid which would later be poured down a drain. When the Mafia used the words like 'erase' or 'remove' they weren't joking. They called it the 'white death'.

He might, of course, be left to simmer for a while. Since it was a question of someone else's territory, a contract would have to be negotiated, and that in turn would be followed by weeks of never leaving the apartment without wondering whether it was for the last time. Until the day came when he got careless . . .

A flash of unseasonable lightning lit up the sky towards the eastern outskirts of Paris, momentarily silhouetting the massive skyscrapers of La Défence.

Monsieur Pamplemousse shivered as he turned to go back inside. Finding Caterina had to be number one priority and time was not on his side. As he closed the French windows he heard the sound of thunder rolling away in the distance.

Crossing to the hi-fi he slipped a tape into the cassette player: *Ellington and Friends.* The soothing strains of Mood Indigo filled the room. He poured himself another cognac. It was a time for firewater; a time for action.

Pull yourself together, Pamplemousse. Facts. You are not entirely without facts. You must marshal them. Put them into some kind of order. Seating himself at the table once again, he reached for his pen and began writing on the back of Trigaux's envelope – making out a list, as he so often did at such times, of the pros and cons. It helped concentrate his thoughts.

You have acquired a little knowledge of the girl. You spent one entire meal with her and you have been privileged to talk with her in a way that perhaps few others have, and to learn something about her.

You know she has ambitions to be a model. Presumably that is the real reason why she wished to come to Paris. But why Paris? Why not Rome? Rome would be too close to home. From all she had said, *papà* would certainly not approve. And now that he knew *papà's* identity he could well understand her fears.

Assuming for the moment that she had set off of her own accord, where would she head for? Where would she start? One of the big model agencies? One of the well-known fashion photographers? Perhaps, like the girl she had mentioned – Naomi something – Campbell? – at the door of some glossy magazine.

Hoping for inspiration, Monsieur Pamplemousse picked up the telephone directory and began flipping through the pages. He quickly abandoned the idea. There were model agencies galore. Photographers occupied several pages. He looked up *journaux*. There were so many he didn't know where to begin. He would need help to go through them all. If he followed that line of thought he would have to go knocking on a great many doors.

But then so would Caterina. Almost certainly she would start at the top. In that respect at least she would have a head start. Clearly she knew exactly what was what in matters of fashion. His own knowledge – at least as far as women's wear was concerned – could have been written on the back of a postage stamp. It was another world.

On the other hand, he did have her likeness. Not an end of term school photograph – although in a sense he had that too – but one which showed a totally different side to her. One which any agency or dress designer would recognise immediately if she had paid them a call.

Working his way back through the pile in chronological order he reached the ones taken in the Stazione Termini in Rome. Suddenly he paused.

Opening up his issue case from *Le Guide,* he took out a magnifying glass and focused on a picture showing a general view of the main concourse. Luckily it was one he had taken before boarding the train – almost the last of a reel of colour film. After that he had changed to black and white and it might have escaped his attention.

Immediately in front of the departure board there was a small, red triangular telephone booth – one of a number dotted about the area. As with Caterina's hat, it stood out amongst the surrounding tones of black and grey like a sore thumb. Occupying a booth nearest to the lens was the ubiquitous Il Blobbo. He had a receiver to his ear, but clearly he was more interested in watching the passing crowd than in whoever it was he was talking to; if, indeed, he was carrying on a conversation at all. The thin-rimmed dark glasses were what gave him away. The same dark glasses he had last seen lying on the track alongside the conductor in *quai* 'J' at the Gare de Lyon.

It confirmed his worst fears.

What was it the Director had said? 'I need hardly remind you, Pamplemousse, that the streets of Paris are filled with those who will be only too willing to guide her . . .'

Supposing it hadn't started in the streets of Paris. Supposing it had begun much earlier. On the night train from Rome, *par exemple?*

The more he thought about it, the more convinced Monsieur Pamplemousse became that he was right. It would also account for Caterina's reserve on the subject when she had been talking to him. Women – girls – tough though they could be in many respects, could also be surprisingly naïve at times. Perhaps 'trusting' was a better word. You only had to read the *journaux.* Perhaps it had to do with wish-fulfilment. Caterina's desire to become a model might well have outweighed her common sense.

One thing was certain. If it was the man on the Palatino there was no knowing where she might end up. It certainly wouldn't be on the catwalk at a fashion show. He wouldn't have trusted the man any further than he could have thrown him, and subsequent events seemed to bear that out.

Crossing to the cassette player, Monsieur Pamplemousse stopped the tape and slipped it back into its case. 'Sophisticated Lady' was hardly a suitable refrain in the circumstances.

He picked up the telephone.

Despite his promise to the Director, there were times when you needed the help of the professionals, and this was one of them. Without giving away his true reason for asking, there would be no harm in putting out a few feelers.

He dialled the number of the *Sûret é* and asked to be put through to his old department.

Luck was with him. Ex-colleague and and friend, Jacques, was working late.

'Aristide! *Comment ça va?'*

'*Bien, merici. Et vous?'*

Jacques sounded pleased to be interrupted. He regaled Monsieur Pamplemousse with a list of reasons before getting down to routine inquiries.

'Doucette?' Monsieur Pamplemousse hesitated. 'She is well. She is staying with her sister in Melun for a few days.' Now that he had the floor, so to speak, he looked for a way to justify his reason for calling.

'I was wondering if you can help me. I am doing an article on prostitution for the staff magazine . . .

'*Oui*, I know *Le Guide is* to do with food, but there are other appetites which often go hand in hand . . .

'*Non,* I would rather not talk to anyone in the Vice Squad for the moment.

'*Non,* nor anyone in the Brigade for the Repression of Pimping. In my day they did not have such a body.' Having lit the fuse, he paused for Jacques to begin. He hadn't long to wait. Clearly it was a subject close to his heart.

'The vice squad is run by a woman these days. Mme Martine Monteuil: ex-drug squad with the smashing of a Chinese heroin racket to her credit before she became Paris's only female police *commissaire*. I wouldn't like to get on the wrong side of her.'

Monsieur Pamplemousse could almost sense Jacques looking apprehensively over his shoulder. He had read about Mme Monteuil. Elegance personified. The Hermès scarf; the fashionably short skirt; the classic quilted Chanel shoulder-bag housing not a powder compact, but a .357 Magnum. By all accounts she was ready to use it, too.

'Mind you,' said Jacques, 'if you want my opinion, at the end of the day she's on to a losing battle. You don't always have the sympathy of the hierarchy behind you, let alone the public. The rue St Denis without its women would be like cheese without wine, and most of them are a mine of information. Remember the last big raid there?'

Monsieur Pamplemousse did. In addition to a varied selection of pimps, prostitutes and clients, the police had netted three of their own senior officers, all of whom had claimed they were involved in secret undercover operations. Under the bedcover operations more like it.

'You're right in your equation,' said Jacques. 'There are two things that are always going to be in demand – food and sex. And when you really get down to it people can go without food for a long time. Prostitution is the only business in France that doesn't shut down for August. Close down one area in Paris and it soon opens up again in another.'

'So what's new?' asked Monsieur Pamplemousse.

Jacques considered the question for all of three seconds. 'Not much has really changed since your time. Shifting Les Halles out to Rungis caused a big upheaval, as you can imagine. Taxis are out – the girls have taken to waiting at the exits to the *Périphérique* with their *caravanettes*. Most of the old *hôtels de passe* have been shut down, and there's even a trade union now: the Association d'Action et de Défense des Prostitutées they call it.'

'How about brothels?'

'Well, as you know, prostitution is still legal – provided you aren't caught moving while you tout for custom. Brothels aren't, so those who run them go to great lengths to trade under another name – they're much more discreet these days. They're called *clandés* and most of them have a little plaque by the door saying "Villa –" or "*Résidence* whatever". There was a case in the 15th not long ago. A certain Mme Zabbel set up a charity for what she called the "Association for Happy Animals". Her first big mistake was putting a brass plate up outside her house announcing the fact. All the kids and old ladies in the neighbourhood turned up with stray pets they'd come across. Her second mistake was going on television – one of the vice squad recognised her as someone he'd arrested years before for the same thing. . .'

'Any other areas I need to know about?'

'Minitels are the "in" thing nowadays. There's no need to go out any more – you just tap out the options on a screen. The PTT are making a fortune, but nobody gets them for living off immoral earnings. There was even a case of a call-girl operation being run on a church computer under the guise of a share-dealing service . . .

'Of course, if you're doing an article on vice you can't leave out the gay bars and clubs – the rue Sainte-Anne is lined with them. Or there are the *boîtes à partouze* – the clubs for mass sex – there's one on the rue de Chazelle. Massage parlours, escort services – you name it.

'Then there's the Bois de Boulogne, but that's been cleaned up ever since the boys from the Salubrité du Bois de Boulogne moved in. At one time you could hardly move at night for all the *travelos* – transvestites, transsexuals out walking their dogs hoping to rake in enough dough to pay for a sex change operation in Morocco – not to mention the ones who'd turned up to watch.'

Monsieur Pamplemousse suppressed a smile. That was one area he wouldn't have to bother with. He felt sure Caterina would be perfectly happy to stay the way nature had intended her to be, thank you very much.

'How about the pimps themselves?' He broke in while he had the chance. Jacques sounded as though he had settled down for the rest of the evening.

'They're having a harder time. The Eric Botey's of this world – remember him? He used to run that chain of hotels

470

in Pigalle – they've mostly gone. The ones that are left go in for real estate – renting "studios" they call it, at prices only someone on the game could afford. On top of that they use hot-dog salesmen with their street barrows to keep an eye on the comings and goings – just so they don't lose out on their percentage. They don't miss a trick – if you'll pardon the pun.'

'Where would the youngest and newest girls be found?'

Monsieur Pamplemousse thought he detected a slight hesitation at the other end. 'Luxury or cheap? *Comme ci – comme ça*. Avenue Foch or rue de la Goutte-d'Or? It depends on what you want. There are always new ones arriving. Look round any main-line station.'

'How about the trains themselves?' Monsieur Pamplemousse broke in again.

'I haven't come across it, but it wouldn't surprise me. Since I did an attachment to the vice squad nothing surprises me. It might be a good way of picking out likely candidates without running the risk of being jumped on.'

'The sort of girl I am looking for,' said Monsieur Pamplemousse, 'would be young, still at school – a Catholic girls' school – she would have blue eyes, dark hair . . .'

'*Oh, là, là!*' A whistle assailed his left ear. 'She could name her own price. If you go up the social ladder a rung or two then things work in a different way. At the top there are always people willing and able to pay for the best. It depends on what your tastes are.'

'I am not asking how much,' said Monsieur Pamplemousse. 'I am simply asking where?'

'Money no object, eh? Things must be good in the restaurant business. Is it the seven-year itch?'

'Hardly. I have been married twenty-eight years.'

'The very worst. That's the four-times factor. You must have got it badly.'

471

'Now look here. .

'How long did you say Doucette's away for? I must say you don't waste any time.'

Monsieur Pamplemousse took a deep breath while he counted up to ten. Talk about giving a dog a bad name. Any moment now he would be reminded of the affair at the *Folies* – the scandal that had forced his early retirement. No doubt the number of girls credited with being involved had risen with the years.

'If you want my advice, old man, you'll stick at home with a good book. It's much safer these days.'

Sensing that Jacques was about to terminate the conversation, Monsieur Pamplemousse tried another tack.

'Before you go,' he said, 'there was a murder at the Gare de Lyon earlier this evening . . . I think I may be able to help.'

'We already have a description of the man we want,' said Jacques. 'Middle-aged. Height around 170, maybe 175 centimetres. Weight around 100 kilograms. Small moustache. Fresh complexion. Wearing an overcoat and a brown hat – or it may have been black.'

'Or green?' suggested Monsieur Pamplemousse. 'Or red?'

'I know, I know,' said Jacques. 'But he had a large dog with him. That may help. They're making up an identikit picture of the man right now. I'm waiting for it to be sent up.'

'And the dog?' asked Monsieur Pamplemousse drily. 'Are they doing one of him too?'

'The consensus of opinion is that it was a Great Dane.'

'The real culprit,' said Monsieur Pamplemousse, 'was totally unlike the person you describe. I can provide you with a photograph, if you like – in colour.'

472

It did the trick. Jacques was suddenly all ears.

'You were there?'

'As it happens . . . by sheer coincidence .ₓ. .

'*Oui*. I will be at the Quai des Orfèvres as soon as possible.'

Monsieur Pamplemousse had hardly replaced the receiver when the phone rang again. This time he answered it.

'*Allo. Allo. Qui est la?*' There was a moment's silence. In the background he could hear the sound of traffic and an engine revving, as though the driver was anxious to be on his way. Then, whoever was making the call hung up.

Monsieur Pamplemousse sat staring at the instrument for a moment or two, wondering if his caller would try again. Then he got up and wandered round the apartment, automatically straightening a picture here, aligning a row of books along the edge of a shelf there, thumbing through some old *journaux*.

Pommes Frites followed him with his eyes. He knew the signs of old. His master had a problem and there wouldn't be much rest until he had solved it. He wondered what it was this time.

Having turned out the light, Monsieur Pamplemousse opened the French windows again and went outside on to the balcony. Pommes Frites padded silently after him and peered through the grille of the iron balustrade. Suddenly he stiffened and a low growl issued from the depths of his stomach.

Monsieur Pamplemousse registered the fact. It was a note of warning; a signal that something was bothering him. He followed the direction of Pommes Frites' gaze along the street, but there was nothing to be seen. Rue Girardon was unusually empty, perhaps because of the passing storm. A car swept past and turned into rue Junot. The cobblestones glistened in the headlamps and there was a hiss from the tyres. It must have been raining hard while he had been inside.

Another flash of lightning lit up the street, and he saw a man approaching alongside the gardens opposite. He was wearing a dark overcoat and he was breathing heavily as though he had just completed the long climb up the steps from rue Caulaincourt. The thunder was nearer this time: almost overhead. As the sound died away the man stopped beneath a lamp and glanced up – either at the sky or at the apartment block – it was hard to say which.

Monsieur Pamplemousse stepped back into the shadows to await developments. Was he letting his imagination run away with him, or was it not the third time that day he had seen the man? And had the last occasion not been at the Gare de Lyon, moments after the Palatino had left for Rome?

Clearly, from the way he was reacting, Pommes Frites thought so too, and he was rarely wrong about such matters.

And if that were the case. . . If that were the case it meant the man hadn't been at the *gare* by accident. The possibility that someone might be tailing him hadn't crossed Monsieur Pamplemousse's mind at the time – either in the taxi to the office or on the journey home. Nor had it when he responded to the Director's call. His mind had been so busy with other things, he had paid little or no attention to the traffic behind.

There was another possibility, of course. He had given Caterina a card with his home address. Could she have passed it on – either voluntarily or for some other more sinister reason?

Putting a finger to his mouth for Pommes Frites' benefit, Monsieur Pamplemousse retreated slowly into the living-room and once he was inside, drew the curtains on all the windows. Only after he had made absolutely certain there were no cracks where the folds met did he turn on the light.

Then he rang the Quai des Orfèvres and asked for Jacques.

'On second thoughts, would it be possible for you to come here?

'You know what it's like in Montmartre at night. You take your car out and you lose your parking space until early next morning.'

It was a truthful statement of fact. If he omitted to say that he had an arrangement with the owners of the block next door which gave him off-street parking facilities, that was simply because it was something he wished to keep to himself for the time being.

Jacques sounded pleased to have an excuse to get out of the office for a while. He bucked up even more when asked if he felt hungry.

'I was about to go to the canteen!'

Making his way into the kitchen, Monsieur Pample-mousse opened the refrigerator door. The food Doucette had left was sitting in its polythene wrapping. So was the small package of truffles he'd brought back from Italy.

Allowing for clearing up his desk and issuing orders for a car, it would be at least twenty minutes before Jacques reached him. Fresh truffles were best eaten as soon as possible. It would be a shame if he allowed them to spoil.

Twenty minutes later Monsieur Pamplemousse tested the potatoes with a sharp-pointed knife. It slid in easily. Draining the water into the sink, he replaced the saucepan on the hob for a second or two to dry out the remains of the liquid before turning off the gas. Then he dropped several small knobs of butter on to the potatoes and as they started to melt, added a little milk, followed by a sprinkling of black pepper and some grated nutmeg. He began mashing the contents of the saucepan with a fork; gently, for he wanted to preserve a slight coarseness rather than end up with *pommes purèe*. He was in the middle of the operation when he heard the sound of an approaching siren coming up rue Junot from the direction of Clichy.

Emptying the mixture on to a board, he picked up a palette knife and quickly moulded the potato into four generous-sized portions. Removing the truffles from the glass of cognac where they had been resting, he reached for a *mandoline* and began slicing them thinly and cleanly until they covered the top of all four cakes. The smell which rose as the heat from the potatoes permeated the truffles was earthy and good; like no other smell in the world.

He was only just in time. As he reached for the pepper pot again the buzzer on the entry-phone sounded and there was a crackle followed by a metallic voice over the intercom. Putting the plates under a gentle grill to keep warm, Monsieur Pamplemousse acknowledged the call, pressed the lock release button for the downstairs door and poured two glasses of wine from an opened bottle of Guigal '78 Côte Rotie 'Brune et Blonde'. It was the last but one in a case he'd bought *en primeur* when it became available – one of Bernard's bargain offers. Fortunately for his colleagues Bernard had never entirely severed his earlier connections with the wine trade. Long may it remain that way!

The sound of the lift coming to a halt in the corridor outside the apartment and then footsteps, followed by the strident noise of the door buzzer, sent Pommes Frites hurrying to the entrance hall. He stood waiting expectantly, his body taut and ready for action.

Following on behind, Monsieur Pamplemousse placed his hand on the door knob and was about to slip the catch when some sixth sense, honed razor sharp through years in the force, caused him to pause. He flashed a brief signal with his eyes to Pommes Frites. It was received and understood in a flash.

'Attaquez! Attaquez!'

Shouting out the words, Monsieur Pamplemousse flung open the door and flattened himself against the wall as some 50 kilos of unstoppable muscle, bone and flesh shot past him into the hall. There followed a brief, but satisfactory crash, and then silence.

5
CATCH 22

'*Merde!* What was all that about?' Jacques looked aggrieved, as well he might. Having had what felt like a lump of living, breathing concrete suddenly land on his chest when he least expected it was no laughing matter. It was a case of Greek meeting Greek, for Jacques was no lightweight. Pommes Frites was looking distinctly sorry for himself too.

Monsieur Pamplemousse tried to pass it off. 'It doesn't do to take chances these days. You said so yourself.'

'That was different.' Jacques glanced around for somewhere to hang his hat. As he did so he spotted a clothes' brush.

Keeping a respectful distance from Pommes Frites, who was clearly only waiting for an opportunity to lick him better, he followed Monsieur Pamplemousse into the living room, tidying himself up as he went.

'It's not like you to be jumpy. Does everyone get the same treatment?'

'Come, I will show you why.' Monsieur Pamplemousse went through the routine of turning out the lights and drawing the curtains back. He opened the French windows and led the way out on to the balcony. Anxious to make amends, Pommes Frites pushed his way to the front and peered down at the street. His tail dropped several degrees as it registered disappointment.

Monsieur Pamplemousse looked first towards the far corner of the tiny square Marcel Aymè. It was the obvious place to stand if anyone wanted to keep an eye on the comings and goings of the apartment block, for it was possible to see along both sides, but there was no one around. The crowd outside the cinema had long since dispersed.

The other streets in the surrounding area looked unusually deserted for a Friday night; he drew a blank in all directions. The storm must have driven everyone away. The only sign of anything untoward was a white car parked facing the wrong way on the other side of the road. Even without the blue light attached to the roof it wouldn't have been hard to guess who it belonged to.

'Well? I hope you didn't make me come all the way across Paris simply to admire the view?' Jacques sounded as though insult had been added to injury.

'I think perhaps it was a mistake to use the siren.'

Jacques shrugged. 'They always do in *Miami Vice*. Besides, you made it sound urgent.'

'They do lots of strange things in *Miami Vice*,' said Monsieur Pamplemousse gruffly. All the same, he took the point. It was catching. No-one in the force went anywhere these days without a siren. In his time it had been a case of 'softly, softly, catchee monkey'.

Ushering Jacques back into the apartment, he drew the curtains and felt for the light switch. He wasn't an illusionist; staring into the night wouldn't make anyone appear if they weren't there to begin with – or were making sure they were nowhere to be seen. All the same, it was disappointing.

'Pour yourself some wine.' Monsieur Pamplemousse motioned Jacques to take a seat at the table while he hurried out into the kitchen.

'Don't tell me . . .' The smell as he opened the warming compartment of the oven must have penetrated into the other room, for he heard the other's voice.

'Diamonds of the kitchen!' Jacques eyed the plates as Monsieur Pamplemousse returned. 'I can't remember when I last had any. Certainly not so as you can't see what's underneath.'

'It is the only way,' said Monsieur Pamplemousse simply. 'Let us not waste time. They've been kept hanging about too long already.'

'Whose fault is that?' Jacques smacked his lips. 'There's nothing like a good peasant dish to round off the day. When I was a boy we had them every Sunday. Truffle omelette before the main course. In those days it was easier to find the truffles than the eggs. Now look at the price.'

'F3,800 francs a kilo in Fauchon,' said Monsieur Pamplemousse.

'Everything's F3,800 francs a kilo in Fauchon.' Jacques raised his glass and gave an appreciative sniff.

'How the poor do live!'

The truffles were still beautifully fresh and crunchy; the Côte Rotie a perfect match. In its own way, it was equally earthy; powerful as the Rhône valley itself, with a fruity, fig-like flavour, combined with a wonderfully dry finish.

For a moment or two they ate and drank in silence. It would have been sacrilege to do anything else.

'So, what can you tell me about the stiff at the Gare de Lyon?' Jacques wiped his plate clean as a whistle, glanced hopefully towards the kitchen, then helped himself to some more wine.

Monsieur Pamplemousse pushed the photograph he had taken of the main concourse at the Stazione Termini across the table.

'That's your man. I would stake my life on it.' He indicated the telephone kiosk with his forefinger. 'The one with the dark glasses.'

Jacques stared at it dubiously. 'You're sure it's not a fly?'

Monsieur Pamplemousse rose from the table and returned a moment later with the magnifying glass. 'Try that.'

Pushing aside his wine glass with a certain amount of reluctance, Jacques picked up the photograph and held it to the light. Then he felt inside his jacket and withdrew a folded sheet of A4 paper and made a show of comparing the two.

Glancing over the other's shoulder, Monsieur Pamplemousse was relieved to see the identikit picture bore only a superficial resemblance to himself, or at least the way he saw himself. Far be it for him to say so, but any self-respecting judge would have sentenced the man depicted in the made-up picture to five years' hard on sight. Even so, he didn't doubt the phone would start ringing at the Quai des Orfèvres once the likeness was circulated. It always did.

The drawing of Pommes Frites was inset into a square at the bottom of the page. Apart from having four feet and a tail, it was like no dog he had ever seen before. It wasn't altogether surprising that Jacques hadn't made the connection as yet, although that was perhaps only a matter of time. The people who had furnished the original description probably hadn't seen it either. Corrections would be made. Who knew what strange mutation they would end up with?

Jacques looked up. 'Any idea what the motive could have been?'

Monsieur Pamplemousse raised his hands to Heaven in a gesture of mute ignorance.

'Do you have the negative?'

'No problem.' Monsieur Pamplemousse looked inside the envelope. They were neatly packaged in a transparent

481

envelope. 'I'll let you have it before you go.' The lab wouldn't thank him if he got truffled fingerprints all over it

Jacques took another look at the print. 'It's not much to go on. It might be anyone in a crowd.'

'You could add height around 167 centimetres. Weight approximately 60 kilograms. Natty dresser. Dark suit – old-fashioned style. Expensive haircut. Manicured nails . . .'

'What is he? Some kind of gigolo?'

'*Non.*' Monsieur Pamplemousse shook his head. 'Anything but. I would say he's simply someone who spends a lot of time sitting in a barber's chair watching the world go by.'

'The dark glasses don't help. If he's got any sense he'll give up wearing them for a while.'

'I'm sure he already has.' Monsieur Pamplemousse took the opportunity to pour some more wine.

'You mean – the ones on the track? Bausch & Lomb?'

Monsieur Pamplemousse nodded. 'He is also left-handed.'

Jacques glanced up. 'You seem to know a lot about him.'

'That's about it. Except, I happen to know he is still around.'

'You've seen him since?'

'Outside the block – just after we talked on the phone.'

'Why on earth didn't you tell me?'

'Because . . .' Monsieur Pamplemousse shrugged. He was rapidly reaching the point where any further explanations might become difficult, not to say embarrassing.

'So what happened?'

Monsieur Pamplemousse launched into a brief rundown of the journey back from Rome with the Director's *petite cousine* and his return visit to the Gare de Lyon. In part, it helped crystallise his own thoughts and get them into perspective.

Not unexpectedly, Jacques wasn't slow to spot the deliberate mistake.

'Why did I go back there?' Monsieur Pamplemousse repeated the question, playing for time.

'You heard me. Don't tell me you've taken up train-spotting in your old age!'

'I mislaid something.' even to his ears it sounded lame.

'The office of the Service des Objets Trouvés is in the main building,' said Jacques, 'not on *quai* "J". Come off it.'

'All right,' growled Monsieur Pamplemousse. 'Some*one.*'

Jacques stared at him. 'Don't tell me! Not the girl you were supposed to be looking after?'

Monsieur Pamplemousse pushed the pictures of Caterina across the table. 'That's her.'

'Did you take these?' Jacques let out another whistle, longer this time, a mixture of surprise, envy and admiration. 'I thought you said she was still at school.' He tapped his teeth with the end of a pen. It had, recalled Monsieur Pamplemousse, been a source of irritation in the old days.

'So she is.' Sorting through the pile he found the one of Caterina arriving with the two nuns.

'Talk about before and after.' Jacques gave the second photograph a cursory glance and then returned to the pictures taken on the train.

'I'm surprised at you. Losing someone like that doesn't come under the heading of being careless – it's downright criminal; a chargeable offence. If you let me have the negs along with the other I'll get some more prints done straight away.'

Monsieur Pamplemousse shook his head. 'I'm afraid that is not possible.'

'Never mind. I'll get copies made of these. The sooner they're circulated the better.'

'You misunderstand me. When I said it is not possible, I meant simply that. I cannot let you have either the photographs or the negatives. They may fall into the wrong hands.'

'Fall into the wrong hands?' Jacques stared at him. 'You realise what you're saying?'

'I have made a promise that I would not tell the police,' said Monsieur Pamplemousse. 'At least, not for the time being.'

'A promise to whom? The family?'

'You could say that.' Monsieur Pamplemousse refused to let himself be drawn. 'You will have to accept my word that there are very good reasons.'

'Blackmail? Someone demanding a ransom? You know as well as I do we've got ways of dealing with that kind of thing. You only have to say the word.'

Monsieur Pamplemousse shook his head.

'Vice? Porno movies? Is that why you were asking all those questions earlier on?'

'If you start by thinking the worst,' said Monsieur Pamplemousse, 'anything else has to be better.'

'True. Well, I'll tell you something. If it has got anything to do with any of that and someone has got hold of her, they're not going to let go in a hurry. Anyway, what makes you think along those lines?'

'She is young, pretty, ambitious. She wants to be a model. She made it clear to me that she wishes to escape from her present life.'

'You mean she may have met up with someone like Madame Claude. Remember her?'

Monsieur Pamplemousse certainly did. In the 1970s Madame Claude had run one of the most fashionable and successful brothels of all time. Heads of state, royalty, millionaires, were said to have paid anything up to 10,000 francs a time for a one-night stand with the 'companion' of their choice.

'There could be worse fates,' said Jacques. 'If you recall, she chose the girls well – mostly out-of-work dancers or models. And she looked after them- bought their clothes, supervised their make-up, their hair, their lingerie, educated them, arranged for plastic surgery where necessary. Considering the number who went on to marry well, they couldn't really grumble. It was better than going to a finishing school as far as most of them were concerned. Every time you open one of the glossy *journaux* there they are, staring out at you.'

'That is hardly the point,' said Monsieur Pamplemousse. 'I agree there might be worse fates, but I would still be held responsible.'

'How about her parents? Have they been told?'

'I was hoping that wouldn't be necessary.' Monsieur Pamplemousse hastily tried to change the subject. 'Are there any Madame Claudes around these days?'

'There will always be Madame Claudes,' said Jacques. 'At 25 per cent commission off the top it wasn't bad going while it lasted. In the end, if you remember, the tax collector presented her with a bill of 10,000,000 Francs and she fled to America where she opened up a cake shop. When that failed she tried to make a come-back, but Martine Monteuil got her. Good old Martine.'

'The Brigade for the Repression of Pimping strikes again.'

'Who says she was pimping? Most of the girls were only too pleased to be working for her. At least it's not like it was in the old days. Remember the Corsicans just after the war? If any of the girls played up rough they used to rub coarse

485

sugar into their faces. It played havoc with the make-up before it festered. Nowadays pimps are more discreet. They realise the value of not despoiling the goose that lays the golden eggs; they make sure any major disfigurement takes place where it isn't likely to be seen until it's too late.'

Monsieur Pamplemousse began to wonder if he had done the right thing in asking for Jacques' advice.

'So the answer to my question is no, you don't know of anything similar going on?'

'Not that I've heard of. Mind you, that doesn't mean to say it doesn't exist. Discretion is the name of the game in that kind of operation. Half the government would be out of a job if it weren't. Heads would roll. If you like I'll put out some feelers when I get back to the office. Give you a ring.'

'*Merci.*'

Jacques took one last look at the photographs of Caterina before returning them. 'And you think the man who was responsible for the murder at the Gare de Lyon – if he was responsible – has something to do with this girl's disappearance?'

'I think she was desperately trying to avoid him, put it that way.'

'So, if we find our man he may in turn lead you to the girl.'

'Exactly.'

'A real game of cat and mouse.' Jacques went back to the original photograph. 'It makes a change from *cherchez la femme* – although I know which I'd rather do. Care to swap?'

Monsieur Pamplemousse shook his head. He didn't feel much like joking.

'I don't blame you,' said Jacques. 'It isn't a lot to go on. Dark glasses work both ways. They may act as a good cover-up, but they also attract attention. What did he look like without them?'

'Thin-faced. A bit of a Charles Aznavour look-alike. I didn't get that close a view.'

'That's something, anyway.' Jacques took out his notebook.

'How about fingerprints?' asked Monsieur Pample-mousse. 'Anything on the glasses?'

'Fat chance. The frames were too thin.'

'Weapon?'

'He would have held the crown in the ball of his hand. Anything on the business end would have been wiped off when it penetrated.'

'How about trying another source?'

Jacques gave a deep sigh. 'Another source!' he repeated. 'What other source? Where? Are you holding out on me, Aristide?'

'Earlier this evening,' said Monsieur Pamplemousse, 'I received a telephone call. A hang up. If it was who I think it was, it must have been made from a call-box somewhere near here. I could hear an engine ticking over – it could have been a number 80 *autobus* waiting at the lights. They have a particular sound to them. In which case I suggest it might be worth checking the phones in the boxes down by the Place Constant Pecqueur . . . there's a group of three on this side of the road – nearly opposite the steps leading up from the Lamarck-Culaincourt Metro. . .'

Without waiting for him to finish Jacques reached for the phone.

While he was talking, Monsieur Pamplemousse cleared away the dishes and looked in the refrigerator to see what there was in the way of cheese.

He unwrapped a small wheel of Coulommiers and a wedge of Roquefort, still half-covered in its silver foil, and put them both on to a plate. There were two strawberry *barquettes*. Doucette must be psychic.

If he wasn't careful Jacques would start asking some awkward questions. Or, worse still, others would start asking Jacques awkward questions, and then the fat would really be in the fire.

Pommes Frites loitered in the doorway looking hopeful. It was long past his usual dinner time. Monsieur Pamplemousse obliged with a bowlful of biscuits and the remains of some stew he found in a plastic container. Then he returned to the other room.

Jacques looked up. 'They're on their way.'

The Coulommiers had a distinct Brie-like tang to it; the Roquefort felt firm and smooth as he unwrapped the foil. Monsieur Pamplemousse poured the last of the wine.

'It tastes of sheep.' Jacques pointed to the Roquefort. It was the kind of grudging back-handed compliment a man from the Rhône valley would pay to a cheese from another *département* of France. It didn't stop him cutting a second slice.

Having polished off the cheese and drained his glass, he disposed of a *barquette* and then looked at his watch. 'I must go. Thanks to you, I've got work to do.'

'I'll come down with you – I could do with some fresh air.' Monsieur Pamplemousse took Pommes Frites' lead down from its hook and ushered Jacques out into the hall.

Instinctively leaving the light on, he double-locked the door behind him.

The lift was still where Jacques had left it. Half the occupants in the block had probably gone away for the weekend, the rest were most likely eating out and wouldn't be back until late. It was always the same on a Friday night.

A feeling of loneliness swept over Monsieur Pamplemousse as the enormity of the task ahead of him struck home.

Pommes Frites automatically stationed himself just inside the lift, breaking the ray of light to stop the doors closing before his master arrived.

'Look,' said Jacques, as Monsieur Pamplemousse joined him. 'I'll see what I can do – no questions asked. But I can't promise a lot. The old grapevine is in need of a bit of a watering at the moment. It's like I said earlier – cleaning things up is all very well, but it's really a case of sweeping the dirt under the carpet – it doesn't go away. In the meantime valuable sources of information have dried up. You'd probably do just as well putting out some feelers in the right quarters yourself.'

'*Merci.*' Jacques' words only served to underline Monsieur Pamplemousse's current mood.

As they made their way through the main hall on the ground floor, he glanced through the perspex front of his mailbox. He hadn't bothered clearing it when he arrived back earlier in the day and it looked full.

No doubt it was the usual collection of junk; he could list most of it by heart. A selection of cards from various organisations giving numbers to ring in an emergency – everything from a leaking washing- machine to lost keys. Boucheries Roger would be having yet another *promotion*. Halfway down the pile he spotted a copy of *Paris-Le Journal* – the free monthly guide to what was happening in the city. On the very top there was a large coloured brochure – most likely from the *super marché* in rue Marcadet. There would be nothing that couldn't wait.

'Thanks for the hospitality. I'll phone you tomorrow if I have any news.' Jacques slammed his car into reverse, executed a commendable half turn considering the width of the road, then roared off down rue Junot, tyres squealing as he took the bend, heading towards rue Caulaincourt and the telephone kiosks. As his tail lights disappeared from view Monsieur Pamplemousse heard a siren, then it faded away into the distance, deflected by the buildings, and everything went quiet.

The *parc* opposite his apartment was closed and he led the way down the road towards the steps leading down to rue Caulaincourt, pausing a couple of times on the way while Pommes Frites obeyed the call of nature.

If the worst came to the worst they would have to move elsewhere, of course. At least for the time being. Possibly, if he failed to find Caterina, it might mean leaving Paris for good. The Mafia never forgave – or forgot. Doucette would be heartbroken. So would he for that matter. Ambitions to become a member of the Boules de Montmartre team after he retired would remain unfulfilled.

Monsieur Pamplemousse decided against taking a short cut along the alleyway to his left which ran through to the back of the *parc*. It was narrow, with no escape routes on either side, and there was no point in taking unnecessary risks.

He stood for a moment at the top of the steps. Beyond the cobbled area at the bottom he could see a small crowd of spectators gathered round the kiosks – no doubt some of them were chafing at the bit because they wanted to make a call; most would have simply come to stare. There were a couple of squad cars parked nearby, their blue lights winking. The one facing the wrong way probably belonged to Jacques. A flash gun went off. They must be recording the fingerprints *in situ* as a precaution. Latent prints tended to go off quickly when the weather was cold. After that they would wait for the engineers to arrive in order to remove the actual phones so that they could work in comfort. Anyone who wanted to use them would be in for a long wait.

But if they left their apartment, where would they go? Would anywhere be safe? Despite the efforts of many, the Mafia still wielded a power which in many parts of the world reached into all corners of life. To be a Godfather was akin to being a feudal lord in ancient times. Their power was absolute. Upsetting them could provoke terminal arrangements.

Not wishing to get involved in the goings on in the *Place*, Monsieur Pamplemousse turned right and headed up the hill towards the Sacré-Coeur.

An occasional car drifted slowly past in the opposite direction, those at the wheel looking in vain for somewhere to park. At one point he took shelter in the narrow space between two vehicles as the last *Montmartrobus* of the evening swept down the hill towards him, the lights from its windows casting strange shadows on the ivy covered stone wall to his right. It was almost empty.

As the bus disappeared round a corner at the bottom, Monsieur Pamplemousse took the precaution of moving out into the middle of the road. He had read somewhere that in Italy there was a Mafia murder every ten hours. In America it was probably a lot more. In France? He had no wish to become a statistic in someone's crime report.

Pommes Frites had no such qualms. Glad to be out after being cooped up all the evening, he ran on ahead, reporting back every so often that all was well.

Monsieur Pamplemousse's thoughts went back to the murder at the Gare de Lyon. Had he just happened on it? He couldn't rid himself of the feeling that for some reason or other he might have been a direct cause.

491

The conductor was the only person able to shed any light on the subject; possibly the only one apart from himself able to identify the man on the train. If the news of Caterina's disappearance did leak out he would have been one of the first to be questioned. Better to eliminate any problems before they occurred. The very fact of Monsieur Pamplemousse returning to question the man must have been bad news.

But why had the murderer followed him back there? Monsieur Pamplemousse had a sudden thought. Supposing the reverse were true. Supposing the man – and his accomplice, whoever he was, were hoping *he* would lead them to Caterina. They must know by now that he had no idea where she was either? If that were the case, then for the time being at least, he would be safe. It was a Catch-22 situation and no mistake. If the news reached Sicily that Caterina was missing his number would be up. If he found her the same might apply.

The Place de Tertre was, as always, alive with tourists: noisy, colourful, like the setting from an operetta. Tables spilled out on to terrace and pavement alike; others filled the middle of the square. Surrounding it, artists' easels supporting ubiquitous pictures of wide-eyed street urchins, or cartoon dogs relieving themselves on walls and lamp-posts to the delight of their colleagues, vied for space alongside others depicting the surrounding landmarks. People sat under acetylene lights having their likeness sketched in charcoal or their silhouette cut out in black paper. Music in the French idiom gushed forth from dimly lit restaurants. Waiters in their white aprons bustled to and fro serving those hardy enough to dine outside beneath the trees.

Squeezing past a *commis* waiter carrying an ice-bucket in one hand and balancing a heavily laden tray with the other, Monsieur Pamplemousse was reminded for some unaccountable reason of a trick question his old school mistress, Mademoiselle Antoinette, was fond of asking new pupils: 'Which freezes first, a bowl of boiling water or a bowl of cold water?'

Very few ever got it right. Most newcomers automatically plumped for what seemed the obvious answer; the bowl of cold water. They did so on the grounds that it 'stood to reason, of course'. The old hands looked superior as they grinned at each other.

He could still see the triumphant gleam in the mistress's eye as she pointed out there was no 'of course' about it, and that in life, 'reason' often flew out of the window.

'What reason? Where?' she would say, looking under her chair.

The explanation was simple enough. Under most circumstances the bowl of boiling water will turn to ice first. Why? Because it will give off steam and some of the water will evaporate, so that in the end there will be a smaller volume of water left to freeze.

Monsieur Pamplemousse carried on with the rest of his walk in an even more thoughtful mood than he had when he started. There was something odd about what was happening; something which didn't quite gel. Was it possible that he, too, was guilty somewhere along the line of letting reason fly out of the window?

The cobbled street was slippery after the rain, and he kept to the path, pausing every now and then to let a car go past. One way and another he wasn't sorry to get back to the Place Marcel Aymé.

If Il Blobbo was still watching the block, he was nowhere in sight. Monsieur Pamplemousse reached for his keys as he entered.

He hesitated as he passed the mail-box, and as he did so he noticed a small, white card on top of the pile. It hadn't been there when he went out, of that he was certain.

Opening the door, he reached inside and removed a plain postcard. It had his name on it, written in black ink – no address. It must have been slipped into the box while they were out. He turned the card over.

On the back someone had drawn a crude picture of a coffin.

6
THE OLDEST PROFESSION

'Pamplemousse! I fear I have bad news. I did not sleep at all well last night. . .'

Monsieur Pamplemousse stared at the telephone receiver in disbelief. Was it possible? Had the Director really woken him up simply to announce that he hadn't had his full quota of rest? Was there no limit to the chief's self-centredness? Indignation welled up inside him. Responses had to be choked back for fear he might say something he would afterwards regret.

He looked at his bedside clock and then relented slightly. It was almost nine-thirty. He must have slept like a log. Although it wasn't altogether surprising after all that had happened the day before, such a thing hadn't happened in years. Doucette must be wondering why he hadn't phoned.

Controlling his emotions with difficulty, Monsieur Pamplemousse held his fire in order to allow Monsieur Leclercq time to continue with a resumé of cause and effect. He hadn't long to wait.

'There is worse to come, Pamplemousse.'

'Worse, *Monsieur?*' Monsieur Pamplemousse made a half-hearted attempt to keep the sarcasm from his voice. 'The hot water was running slightly cold, *peut-être?* Your morning *croissant* was perhaps not quite as fresh as it might have been? The *jus d'orange* a trifle acid?'

A hissing sound indicated that the Director was using his car telephone, so any immediate response was obliterated. As the car emerged from the other side of the tunnel or whatever else it was that had conspired to interrupt their conversation, it became apparent that he was on to another tack, and from his dolorous tones it was clearly one which was causing him considerable alarm.

'. . . pened this morning, Aristide. I received a postcard through the mail. . .'

Monsieur Pamplemousse experienced a momentary pang of conscience. 'Not bad news from Madame Leclercq, I trust?'

'No, Pamplemousse. Much, much worse. The message was in graphic form. The card bore a simple motif; that of a *bière*. A black *bière!*'

'A coffin?' Suddenly all ears, Monsieur Pamplemousse struggled into a sitting position. This was indeed bad news. He tried to strike a cheerful note. 'Perhaps it was a local *entrepreneur* mortician in Viroflay seeking extra business, *Monsieur*? Times are hard.'

'Times are never hard in the funeral business, Pamplemousse,' said the Director gloomily. 'Certainly not as far as the Mafia are concerned. In Italy they make sure business is booming.'

'But this is France, *Monsieur.*'

The Director was not to be consoled. 'If it is a genuine offer of service,' he continued, 'why did the company not append their name and address? Besides it had been hastily drawn by someone using a felt-tipped pen. No, I detect the hand of the Cosa Nostra. It is part of their tradition. They always warn their intended victim so that he knows exactly where he stands – or falls – and meets his death fully aware of who is responsible. It is what is known as '"job satisfaction"'. Otherwise, when their victims are hit in the back by a bullet, they may die thinking it is only a passing sportsman with an unsteady aim.'

'But why you, *Monsieur*? You said yourself that if anything happened to Caterina the blame would fall squarely on my shoulders.'

'That was Thursday, Aristide. Since then I, too, have burned my boats. Yesterday evening Chantal's Uncle Caputo telephoned to ask after his daughter. On the spur of the moment I concocted a story about her arrival and all the things we have done together. First the Eiffel Tower, then the Musée d'Orsay, followed by a trip on a *bateau mouche* and hot *chocolat* at Angelina's. I must say, I became so fired with the whole thing I almost began to believe it myself. When he asked to speak to her I told him that she was tired out after all her exertions and that we had insisted on her going to bed early.'

'Was he not satisfied, *Monsieur*? It sounds perfectly reasonable to me.' Monsieur Pamplemousse seized the opportunity to climb out of bed and slip into his dressing gown.

'Unfortunately, Aristide, I then took a leaf out of your book. I pretended I was taking the telephone upstairs to her room. I think you would have been pleased with my efforts. I made great play with the fact that the guest room is on an upper floor and that due to the age of the building the second flight of stairs is unusually steep. Breathing heavily, I knocked on a nearby bureau to simulate the sound of tapping on a bedroom door. I then essayed the squeak of an unoiled hinge followed by a series of random snores to show how deeply Caterina was sleeping after her day out.'

Monsieur Pamplemousse held the receiver away from his ear as a sound like that of a wailing banshee emerged. His spirits fell on the Director's behalf. Knowing the chief's habit of going over the top once he had the bit between his teeth, it was more than possible that Uncle Caputo's suspicions had been roused.

'Was that it, *Monsieur?*'

'No, Pamplemousse, it was not.' The Director sounded shaken. 'It was another automobile coming in the opposite direction. I fear my concentration lapsed for a moment. As, indeed, it did yesterday evening.'

'What happened, *Monsieur?*'

'Flushed with success, I opened the window and imitated the mating call of a Mallard duck.'

'And?'

'The Mallard, Pamplemousse, is a *oiseau* which at this time of the year goes into eclipse. Neither duck nor drake is anywhere to be seen. Both are resting in the reeds. The male, having lost his flight quills – probably through having given way once too often to his carnal desires – is waiting for them to grow again. The female, exhausted by constant egg laying, remains at his side.'

Monsieur Pamplemousse resisted the temptation to ask if Uncle Caputo would be likely to know that fact. Clearly, the Director was in no mood for speculation.

'The die is cast, Aristide. I am now in it as deeply as your good self. There is only one consolation. There is a Sicilian saying: *"Uomo avvisato, mezzo salvato"* – a man who is warned is halfway to being saved. However, you can see why sleep eluded me, and why Caterina's early and safe recovery is of the essence . . .'

'Uncle Caputo can hardly have sent the card, *Monsieur.* He wouldn't have had time. I posted Doucette a card in Rome three days ago and that has yet to arrive.'

'Paris is but a telephone call away, Pamplemousse.

Doubtless the Cosa Nostra have reciprocal mailing arrangements with their opposite number in France. The Mafia is organised on military lines. Each Godfather is like a general – responsible for his own territory. However, they have watertight methods of communication; their own codes.'

'But . . .'

'But what, Pamplemousse?'

'It doesn't make sense, *Monsieur*. Even if Uncle Caputo found your performance less than convincing, something else must have happened to arouse his suspicions. What could it have been?'

'I cannot answer that question, Pamplemousse. All I know is that the Mafia moves swiftly. Decisions are always instant and to the point. There is no dithering.'

'Unless . . .'

'Unless what, Pamplemousse?'

'Nothing, *Monsieur*. . .'

'Well, Pamplemousse,' said the Director severely, 'I trust that your deliberations on nothingness bear fruit within the very near future. Otherwise, I fear for both our lives . . . not to mention the lives of our nearest and dearest.'

Monsieur Pamplemousse was saved any further interrogation as the Director's voice was engulfed by a wave of static. He waited a moment or two in case reception improved, then replaced the receiver and made his way towards the bathroom.

The news that the Director had also received a card bearing a picture of a coffin came as something of a surprise. Instinct told him that no matter how efficient the Mafia's lines of communication were, it could hardly have been sent by Uncle Caputo, or even at his instigation. But if Uncle Caputo hadn't sent it, who else would have done? And why? It would have to be someone who knew Caterina was missing. It would also need to be someone who was armed with a lot of information; the Director's home address outside Paris for a start – unless, of course, he had been followed too, but that suggested a whole army of people on instant call.

Lying back in the bath, Monsieur Pamplemousse's thoughts returned to events at the Gare de Lyon. The man on the Palatino had certainly been met by someone when he arrived in Paris – either that, or the two had travelled up separately on the same train. But if it went beyond that, if there were a number of other people involved, why had Il Blobbo turned up outside his apartment block the night before? Why hadn't someone else been given the job? It would have made more sense.

Pommes Frites, who looked as though he had been up for some while, came out from under the table as his master entered the kitchen.

Monsieur Pamplemousse returned his greeting absent-mindedly as he put some coffee on to brew, then he sliced the remains of the previous day's *baguette* and put it in the toaster while he made himself a glass of fresh orange juice.

He should have asked the Director if his postcard had borne a stamp, or whether, like his own, it had been slipped in by someone amongst the rest of the mail.

Worries about Caterina, already tempered with fears about his own and Doucette's future, now included anxiety on the Director's behalf.

He gazed out of the kitchen window. At this time of the day, before the tour buses arrived, Montmartre was a haven of peace and quiet, much as it had been when Utrillo was alive and committed so much of it to canvas. In their time, Toulouse-Lautrec, Degas and Renoir had been inspired by their surroundings, too.

The storm had passed and the water he could see glistening in the sunshine as it ran down the gutters carrying all before it, came from underground pumps, not from the sky, which was blue and cloudless. Pigeons and sparrows carried out their morning ablutions. A few early-morning photographers were out and about.

'You had better make the most of it!' As he poured himself some coffee, Monsieur Pamplemousse couldn't help but wonder how much longer he and Doucette would be there to enjoy the view.

The apartment had become theirs soon after they were married. It was at a time when prices were low and they had just come into a little money after Doucette's father died. Such good fortune wouldn't happen twice. Marcel Aymé, the writer, was living there when they first moved in. They had seen him many times. A statue fashioned after a character from one of his books – *Le Passe-Muraille* – about a man who discovered he could walk through walls, had been made part of a real wall outside the building, and the *Place* itself had been named after him. The composer and conductor, Inchelbrect, had been another neighbour.

A smell of burning brought Monsieur Pamplemousse back to earth. He pressed a button to switch off the toaster, then buttered the slices and gave one to Pommes Frites while he consumed the rest standing up.

They could, of course, stay with friends for a while. He had lain awake the night before, going through various possibilities in his mind, rejecting them one by one. In the end he could only think of Doucette's sister in Melun. The thought depressed him. Anyway, he told himself it wouldn't be fair to involve anyone else.

One thing was very certain. They wouldn't be going anywhere at all unless he did something and did it quickly.

Pouring a second cup of coffee, he went into the livingroom and picked up a copy of *Le Guide*. Flipping through the pages until he found the section he wanted, he reached for the telephone. It was early days, but it was worth a try. The Director wouldn't be able to hold Chantal's Uncle Caputo at bay for very long before the latter began to smell a rat, if he hadn't already.

On the principle that there was nothing like starting at the top, Monsieur Pamplemousse dialled the number for the first hotel listed under GRAND LUXE ET TRADITION and asked to be put through to the *concierge*.

Using an assumed voice, for no reason he could logically have justified, he pretended to be telephoning on behalf of a very important foreign dignitary.

'I cannot mention his name. Discretion is paramount, you understand? He requires a suite and accommodation for his entourage . . .' Times were hard in the hotel business and there was no harm in holding out a carrot or two. 'He is also in need of someone to entertain him. A young lady of an amiable disposition.'

'When would this be for, *Monsieur*?' From the tone of the man's voice he might have been asking for an extra lump of sugar to be sent up to accompany his *café*.

'*Tout de suite*. He is arriving in Paris shortly and he is not a patient man. He will be wishing to relax after his long journey. He has a *penchant* for young Italian virgins . . .'

'*Puceaux Italiennes*?' It was the equivalent of two lumps.

'One would do,' said Monsieur Pamplemousse. 'Preferably convent educated and under seventeen, with dark hair. Money is no object. You know of an agent who could arrange for such things?'

The *concierge* lowered his voice. He knew of several likely candidates, but in his opinion they could all be sued under the trade descriptions act, particularly if *Monsieur's* client spoke Italian.

'It stands to reason, *Monsieur*. It is a once-only situation. It is like a car – once it leaves the showroom it is second-hand. If the *Monsieur* you represent would care to lower his standards a little . . . perhaps something with a low mileage on the clock?' The motoring metaphor had clearly been used before.

'My client is not accustomed to second best,' said Monsieur Pamplemousse severely. 'I would need to speak to your agent in person.'

No, that would not be possible. However, all things were open to negotiation . . . If *Monsieur* cared to make an appointment . . .

Monsieur Pamplemousse thanked the *concierge* for his trouble and hung up. He marked the entry in *Le Guide* with a cross. It might be worth bearing in mind for future reference.

At least the man had been honest, which was more than could be said for the next two.

'*Pas de problème, Monsieur,*' was the immediate response. They seemed surprised that he was bothering to ask, as though they had immediate access to an inexhaustible supply of young Italian virgins.

Lowering his sights slightly, Monsieur Pamplemousse set about tackling THE HÔTELS GRAND CONFORT. The first on the list, a small but discreet establishment with an unusually high ratio of suites to rooms, sounded hopeful to begin with. After asking him to *attendez* for a moment, the person on the other end – he suspected it was the manager – had the call transferred to another line. He then asked Monsieur Pamplemousse if he would mind repeating his request in more specific terms. The man sounded slightly guarded, as though he were not the only one listening in to the conversation. Monsieur Pamplemousse put down the receiver.

It was not a promising beginning. It only served to underline the enormity of his task. In the old days he would have delegated it to a subordinate.

He flipped through *Le Guide* again. Some twenty or so pages of hotels were listed. It would require a whole team of helpers on the job.

He wondered about giving the office a call – Loudier was an expert on Paris – he might have some ideas. Maybe he should have come clean with Jacques after all and told him the whole story. The trouble was it wouldn't stop there, and then the fat would really be in the fire and no mistake.

The phone rang. He reached for the receiver. Talk of the devil!

'I've been trying to get you for the last ten minutes!' Jacques sounded put out, as people always did when the person they wanted to speak to was engaged.

'Our man's put in an appearance.'

The proprietorial use of the word 'our' didn't escape Monsieur Pamplemousse's notice.

'You won't believe this, but he went into a security shop soon after nine o'clock this morning and bought up their entire stock of solar-powered security lights – the sort that switch on automatically if anyone comes within range of the infra-red beam.'

'How on earth did you get to know that?'

'It's run by someone who used to be in the Department – probably after your time – name of Frèche – *Crème Frèche* we used to call him. Anyway, he got fed up with advising people about what to do *after* they'd been broken into. He was for ever putting business into the hands of other people and not getting any thanks for his trouble, so he handed in his badge and set up on his own account.'

'Why did he tell you?' asked Monsieur Pamplemousse.

'Because . . . and here's the funny part . . . it was a case of the biter bit. The man left without paying. You know what he said?'

'Tell me.'

'He wasn't into buying retail.'

Monsieur Pamplemousse couldn't help laughing. It wasn't funny, but . . .

'He simply admired the windows,' continued Jacques. 'Said what a pity it would be if they got broken, glass being expensive, and the cost of replacement being what it is these days. Also it wouldn't look good in a shop specialising in security. To have it happen more than once might well result in a great loss of trade. Then they walked out with all twelve units. Imagine!'

'They?'

'There was another man with him. Short. Stocky. Swarthy looking. Frèche felt he knew him from somewhere.'

'And you're sure the first man was the one I told you about?'

'A blow-up of your photo is on its way to Frèche right now, but the description fits. Besides, he spoke with an Italian accent. They both did.'

'What on earth would they want with twelve solar-powered burglar alarms?'

'Who knows? Unless it's for something entirely unconnected with the present problem. I asked Frèche and he came up with the suggestion that they might be using them to trigger off some kind of explosion. Apparently he's seen the idea written up in an American magazine. Rather a nifty thought. It doesn't require much imagination to think what would happen if you replaced the light with an ignition device and some semtex. The beauty of it is that being solar-powered you wouldn't need any external wiring.'

Monsieur Pamplemousse considered the proposition for a moment, but he couldn't for the life of him see where it might lead to.

'How about the telephone kiosk?' he asked. 'Any luck there?'

'Ah . . . that's something else again. The fingerprint boys are still working on that. But thanks to you, they've struck a rich seam. Two breaking and enterings. Three sex offenders. A known heavy-breather. One with a record for armed robbery as long as your arm – or, to put it another way, by rights he *should* have a record as long as your arm, but apart from a spell inside for attempted murder we've never been able to pin anything on him. We should try it more often.'

'No other leads?'

'Give us a chance – it's not eleven o'clock yet.'

Monsieur Pamplemousse glanced at his watch. He had lost all track of time.

'Anything else I can do?' asked Jacques.

'Nothing . . . No, wait . . . Do you think you could ask around the local taxi companies? Allo Taxi operates around here. They're on 42-00-67-87, or there's G7 – they're on 47-39-33-33. See if they had a request from someone wanting to travel outside Paris late last night. South-west of the city – out towards Viroflay. If they don't turn up trumps you could try Taxis Bleus. After that I guess it's the car hire companies. They must have got some transport from somewhere. Unless, of course . . .'

'Well?'

It occurred to Monsieur Pamplemousse that the second man might have driven up from Italy.

'It could have a Rome number plate.'

'Thanks a heap!'

Despite his protest, Jacques was clearly beginning to enjoy the whole operation. 'I'm off to see Frèche. For two pins I'd set up in business myself. You know what they say – "If you can't beat 'em, join 'em". *Bonne chance.*'

'Bonne chance!'

Monsieur Pamplemousse sat for a moment or two sipping his coffee. Good luck was something he would need in abundance if he was to make any progress. Telephoning round the hotels had been something of a non-starter, but at least it had got his brain working. Perhaps it was time he did some field work – spread the word around a bit. A walk with Pommes Frites wouldn't come amiss. It would do them both good, and it would also be an opportunity to kill two birds with one stone; a chance to put plan 'B' into action.

It was very rare that he ventured on to the Boulevard Clichy these days, but unless things had drastically changed since his day, the 'girls' started early – especially the ones who could stand inspection by daylight – and even quite a few who couldn't.

From the top of the long flight of stone steps which ran down from the *Place* in front of the Sacré-Coeur he could see balloon sellers in the Square Willette far below; a splash of colour against the background of grey stone buildings. Behind him the tourists were out in force; the steps in front of the Sacré-Coeur itself were littered with them. He wondered if Il Blobbo was anywhere amongst them. Il Blobbo, or his friend. He certainly wasn't going to give them the satisfaction of looking.

In one of the streets off the Boulevard Clichy, just around the corner from the Moulin Rouge, he had his first encounter.

'*Un petit cadeau, Monsieur*?' Things hadn't changed. In the old days, when he had been in the force, it had always been a request for '*un petit cadeau*' – 'a little gift' – never a downright demand for money.

'I am looking for someone new . . .

'Funny you should say that, dear.' The woman turned to a friend lounging inside a doorway and winked. 'It's my very first time out.'

'Someone . . . *very* new,' said Monsieur Pamplemousse politely. 'I mean *new* new.'

'You'll be lucky.' The welcoming smile disappeared.

'Who is looking after you? Is there someone I could talk to?' Monsieur Pamplemousse glanced through the doorway beyond the second woman towards a dimly lit flight of uncarpeted stairs. A smell of disinfectant, lust and disillusionment filled the air. There was the sound of running water from one of the upper floors; probably from a bidet.

'What's it to you?'

'It would be worth your while. . .' Monsieur Pamplemousse felt inside his jacket. 'I am doing an article . . .'

'Piss off,' said the second woman. '*Fiche le camp!* And take your dog with you. I've met your sort before.'

'Perhaps he could do with a quick *passe?*' said the first one. 'Not stuck up like his master.' She reached down and gave Pommes Frites a pat. 'How about it, *chérie?*'

'Doesn't know a good offer when he sees one,' said the second woman, as Pommes Frites backed away, showing his teeth. Releasing him from his leash, Monsieur Pamplemousse gave up the conversation and carried on up the hill.

It wasn't a good start. The occupants of a *Montmartrobus* eyed him with interest as it went past. He hoped there was no-one travelling on it who knew him.

Biding his time while he tried to sum up the situation, Pommes Frites followed on behind at a discreet distance. Straining his ears, he managed to catch several key phrases which emerged during the few brief conversations his master had on the way.

Unfamiliar words like 'quickie' seemed to predominate, followed by gestures which he couldn't recall having come across on any of his training courses.

Much as he loved and respected his master, the thought crossed Pommes Frites' mind more than once that Monsieur Pamplemousse's tastes seemed to have slipped; plummeted was a word he might have used had it formed part of his vocabulary. Translated into his own terms, if the first two women were anything to go by, most of them didn't look as though they were worth more than a passing sniff, if that. Nor were they dressed in a style which would have met with Madame Pamplemousse's unqualified approval. Leather trousers, pink tights and jackets unzipped to the waist didn't normally form part of her wardrobe.

On the other hand, having said that, his master seemed perfectly capable of resisting any temptations thrust in his way, even to the point of enduring coarse laughter and jibes which clearly related to his manhood. It was all very strange.

Seeing a large, ginger-haired woman dressed in thigh boots and not much else, who seemed to be making lunges with a whip at anyone who came within reach, Pommes Frites moved out into the road. As he did so he became aware of a car moving slowly up the hill behind them. Its four occupants, three men and a woman, were all in uniform, and all – including the driver – were glued to the windows.

A group of four *péripatéciennes* standing in a doorway enjoying a quiet smoke saw it too and immediately froze.

Unaware of what was going on, Monsieur Pamplemousse tried to engage the women in conversation. His blandishments were unsuccessful. They might have been turned to stone for all the notice they took.

'Is this man annoying you?' He heard a voice behind him.

'You are aware of the word *drageur, Monsieur?*' A second voice joined in.

Monsieur Pamplemousse turned and stared at the officers. 'Are you accusing me of accosting women?' he protested.

'We have been watching you. It's a bit early in the day to be out "trawling" isn't it?'

'What's the matter?' asked the policewoman. 'Couldn't you sleep?'

'What if I couldn't?' demanded Monsieur Pamplemousse. 'That is no business of yours.'

'There have been complaints.'

'Who has complained? Where? You have witnesses?'

The group exchanged glances.

'Witnesses?' said one of the gendarmes. 'What's he talking about?'

'Don't get cross, *Monsieur*,' said the policewoman, ogling him. 'I go off men who get cross.'

Monsieur Pamplemousse glared at her. Resisting the temptation to say that if she was the last person on earth she would be so lucky, he sought instead to encapsulate the words in a look of contempt as he blew her a kiss.

'Attempting to importune a policewoman,' said the leader. 'That is a serious offence.'

'Harassment of the opposite sex,' broke in a second. 'That is also an offence these days.'

'It seems to me,' said Monsieur Pamplemousse, 'that I am the one who is being harassed.'

The number three piped up. '*Monsieur* is also doubtless aware that it is against the law in Paris to take a dog out without a lead?'

'A law,' said Monsieur Pamplemousse, 'which is never enforced.'

'Never?' The officer in charge held out his hand. '*La carte d'identité, Monsieur. S'il vous plaît.*'

Monsieur Pamplemousse knew better than to argue. It wouldn't help matters that Pommes Frites had just been relieving his boredom by doing a *pipi* on the rear wheel of the police car. Circumstantial evidence, it was true, for he was now looking in a shop window as though such an act would never cross his mind in a million years. All the same, he could have chosen a better time and place.

He felt in his pocket. He had already caught a faint gleam of recognition in the officer's eyes. Once he saw the name on his card the game would be up. There would be nudges and winks. Cracks about his past record; the affair at the *Folies;* his enforced early retirement.

He was right.

'Pamplemousse!' The man's face lit up. 'Of course! Pamplemousse of the *Sûreté.*'

Monsieur Pamplemousse decided to take a chance.

'*Exactement*! He nodded meaningly towards the four women, who were still frozen in their original pose.

'Please pay my respects to Madame Commissaire Martine Monteuil. Tell her my report is almost complete. It

511

will be on her desk shortly – always provided, of course, I do not receive too many interruptions.

'I take it she has not changed? As I remember her, she does not suffer fools gladly. The Vice Squad has not been the same since she arrived on the scene. I hope I can tell her how helpful you have been in assisting me in my researches. All four of you.'

It worked. Returning the salutes, Monsieur Pamplemousse called Pommes Frites to heel and made his way on up the hill with all possible speed. He wondered how long it would be before the others remembered that Madame Monteuil had arrived long after his retirement.

One thing was certain. He would have to give Montmartre a miss for the time being.

Perhaps it was time he put plan 'C' into action. What was it Jacques had said earlier? 'If you can't beat 'em, join 'em.' It would be his last chance to make direct contact with those in the know.

But it would have to be later, after dark, when there was less chance of being recognised. The one thing he couldn't risk at the moment was being arrested. That would put an end to all his plans.

And it would have to be without Pommes Frites. Regrettably, they must not been seen together again for a while. From now on he would be on his own.

Quite how or when or why he had hit on plan 'C' was not a question uppermost in Monsieur Pamplemousse's mind as he parked his car near the Boulevard St Denis soon after dark that evening. Later on it would be, and later on, as it happened, wasn't as far away as he anticipated.

As he made his way towards that part of the Boulevard St Denis which lies to the south of the métro station, or as

512

purists might have it, the point which marks the old city limits, indicated by the fact that beyond it the rue St Denis becomes the rue Faubourg St Denis – *faubourg* meaning 'suburb' – he had to confess to a feeling of excitement; the particular kind of excitement that can only come from doing a naughty deed after dark in a naughty world.

It was a feeling which grew with every step he took. Naughtiness, dressed in its party clothes, was lurking in every shop doorway and on every street corner. Not that any of it reached out to take him in its arms; rather the reverse, in fact. Shadowy figures drew back as they saw him approach.

It was a long time since Monsieur Pamplemousse had been in the area by day, let alone at night; still less on a Friday evening. As he remembered it, the bottom half – the end nearest the Seine – was mostly porno-movies and air-conditioned lesbian double acts. The top end was where all the action used to be, and by the sound of it things hadn't changed. There was a feeling of revelry in the air. He could hear whistles being blown. Shrill blasts rent the air, followed by cheers and counter cheers. It suited his purpose admirably. Any worries he might have had about attracting attention on his own account soon disappeared.

It was as he turned a corner into the rue St Denis that Monsieur Pamplemousse caught the full force of a fire hose on his chest. It knocked him sideways, propelling him inexorably into something which felt warm, soft, perfumed, and splendidly suited to cushion his fall. But his moment of respite was all too brief. Having taken stock of his sodden state, the owner of the *doudons* he was clasping uttered an apposite oath and sent him spinning on his way again.

From that moment on everything became a blur; a confused montage of black stockings and fish-net tights, of

513

gendarmes with batons drawn, and of fighting, screaming girls in leotards, lace panties, leather, or simply total nakedness beneath fur coats thrown open to the elements.

Monsieur Pamplemousse also registered a group of strange hairy creatures in skirts, uttering wild barbaric shouts and grunts, the like of which he had never before encountered in the whole of his career.

At least it answered Jacques' question as to where the *travelos* had gone – from the Bois de Boulogne to the Boulevard St Denis.

Monsieur Pamplemousse was in the act of bending down to tie up his shoe-lace while he took stock of the situation, when he heard a guttural cry from somewhere near at hand. Before he had a chance to take evasive action, what felt like the claws of a small but powerful mechanical digger reached up from behind, groping as it came. As it made contact with his person it tightened its grip in no uncertain manner.

A cry of mingled rage, disgust and disappointment followed, but by then Monsieur Pamplemousse had all but passed out. He was vaguely aware of helping hands lifting him to his feet, half carrying him, half dragging him along the street, then he flew through the air and joined an assorted pile of other bodies in a van, where he lay gasping for breath like a stranded whale cast ashore after being caught in an Atlantic storm.

7
THE MORNING AFTER

Monsieur Pamplemousse woke to the harsh, metallic sound of a key turning in a lock and an iron gate being swung open. He felt cold, hungry and he had a splitting headache. He also perceived a dull ache in his private parts, which was hardly surprising considering what they had been through. He regretted now having left Pommes Frites at home. Pommes Frites would have stood up for him, administering punishment in like manner, but with compound interest. The unknown assailant who had grasped Monsieur Pamplemousse where it hurt most, would have felt the full measure of Pommes Frites' wrath encapsulated in molars which, in their time, had caused many an adversary to tremble in his boots. Nor would he have let go in a hurry.

Waving aside the token breakfast offering, Monsieur Pamplemousse asked once again to be allowed to use the telephone.

The request granted, he was led up a flight of stone stairs. His entry into the charge room was greeted by a cacophony of whistles and cat-calls from a large holding cage opposite the main desk. The population seemed to have swelled far beyond its maximum capacity level since he had last seen it. It was like a scene from the Snake Pit; Brueghel gone mad. Worse even, if that were possible, than the episode in the rue St Denis the night before; although at the time that had seemed bad enough.

Monsieur Pamplemousse gazed at the occupants of the cage, some barely able to stand, clutching the bars for support, others lying on the floor out for the count, their spreadeagled hairy legs protruding at odd angles from their skirts as though long since abandoned by their owners. In a far corner a small group were crouched over a communal bowl, their heads clutched in their hands.

He turned to the inspector behind the desk. It was someone he hadn't seen before. The early morning shift must have taken over. 'You have had a busy time.' It was a statement rather than a question and as such met with a non-committal grunt.

'Brazilians over here for the operation?' hazarded Monsieur Pamplemousse. 'Animaux,' growled the officer. 'It is worse than the zoo. You are lucky you got here early and had a cell to yourself. Some of us had to sit here all night looking at them.' He shook his wrist in time-honoured fashion.

'So who are they? Where are they from? Don't tell me the "B" team from Mars are playing an away match?'

From the look on the man's face it felt as though he could be getting warm.

'*Les écossais.* Scotsmen. They are over for the Rugby International. It is the big match of the season today. With supporters like that who needs a ball?'

'Who, indeed?' Suddenly it all became clear. What a night to have picked! Monsieur Pamplemousse gazed round at them. 'They won't see the game.'

'*Non!*' The inspector could hardly conceal his pleasure at the thought as he handed Monsieur Pamplemousse the telephone. 'It is the same every year. They come – they get drunk – they miss the match – they go home again. Not that there is any doubt as to who will win. The matter is one of pure *formalité.*'

'If it is like that before the match, think what it will be like tonight!'

Monsieur Pamplemousse dialled the Director's home number for the umpteenth time and then stood back, half expecting to hear the engaged signal, as had happened the last half dozen or so times during the night when he had tried. He caught the eye of the inspector looking at him.

'Haven't I seen you before?'

'Possibly.' Monsieur Pamplemousse turned away. He had no wish to be quizzed on the subject of his past. Once word got around that old Pamplemousse of the *Sûreté* was in the nick he would never hear the last of it.

He received several blown kisses from the occupants of the cage for his pains.

'*Allo Allo*! Is anybody there?' It sounded like a wrong number.

'*Pardon. Excusez-' moi* . . .'

'Pamplemousse! Thank goodness it is you.' The voice suddenly became recognisable, as though a sock had been removed from the speaker's mouth.

'I have been trying to telephone you, *Monsieur,* but each time you were engaged . . .'

'Not engaged, Pamplemousse . . . in hiding! I took the precaution of leaving the receiver off the hook in case there was another call from Sicily. Where have you been?' The Director contrived to make it sound as though the fault lay entirely with his subordinate.

'It is not so much where I have *been, Monsieur,* as where I still am. That is the reason why I have been trying to contact you.'

'You have news of Caterina?'

Monsieur Pamplemousse glanced round at the inspector, who was making play of filling in a report form. Clearly it wasn't receiving his undivided attention.

He cupped a hand over the mouthpiece. 'It is hard to say, *Monsieur.*'

'Why is that, Pamplemousse?' The Director's booming voice came through loud and clear. 'Are you not alone? Is someone else listening in to our conversation?'

As Monsieur Pamplemousse bent over the counter someone opened the door leading to the street and he felt a draught of cold air sweeping up behind him. It provoked another round of whistles, cat-calls and what were clearly, from the accompanying gestures through the bars, obscene Celtic remarks being directed at his nether regions from the occupants of the cage.

'Pamplemousse, what is that noise I hear?' barked the Director. 'It sounds like something out of *Grand Guignol. Is* someone being attacked?'

'It is nothing, *Monsieur.* It is simply that my frock has a large tear down the back . . . I am being given the once-over by a group of Scotsmen who are the worse for drink . . .'

'Did I hear you use the word frock, Pamplemousse?' The Director sounded in a state of shock.

'*Oui, Monsieur.* I can explain everything, but for the moment my hands are tied . . .'

'Give me your address,' barked the Director. 'If, indeed, you are in a fit state to know it. I will arrange for a dispatch rider to deliver you a knife as soon as possible . . .'

'*Monsieur*, I can explain.'

'There is no need to, Pamplemousse,' said the Director coldly. 'Provided it does not bring opprobrium on *Le Guide*, what you do in your spare time is no concern of mine, although I must confess there are times when your extra-mural bedroom activities leave me at a loss for words.

'Bondage is something I have never been able to understand. Neither is sado-masochism. I admire your tenacity in leaving no stone unturned when you are hot on the scent, but there are limits. I fail to see what you hope to gain by these esoteric avenues of investigation, other than to satisfy some bizarre twist in your character in the process.'

'*Monsieur,* I am telephoning you because I am in urgent need of some string-pulling. . .'

Monsieur Pamplemousse winced as a crack like a pistol shot nearly shattered his ear-drum. It sounded as though the Director might be striking his telephone on a particularly solid item of furniture. It said much for the makers that the handset still worked. If anything, the quality seemed to have improved.

'Things go from bad to worse, Pamplemousse. How dare you try and involve me in your sordid bedroom games! Were it not for the exceptionally good turn you have done me, I would be sorely tempted to leave you to stew in your own juice for a while. As it is, I will do what I can, but it will not be easy. Today is Saturday and most of my contacts in the higher echelons of authority will have left Paris for the weekend. However, before I do anything, I must come and see you in order to apprise myself at first hand of the salient facts . . .'

'That will not be necessary, *Monsieur.*' Monsieur Pamplemousse closed his ears to all around and spoke coldly and clearly into the telephone. 'The salient facts, as you call them, are quite simple. Firstly, I am not in the habit of indulging in bondage, or in sado-masochism. Nor, for that matter, are my hands tied to any bedposts. It was a metaphor I used on the spur of the moment in order to describe my present situation. I am in a *gendarmerie* in the 2nd *arrondissement* and I am in urgent need of some string-pulling in order to secure my release. How I came to be here in the first place is something I will explain to you later, but for the time being every second spent arguing is a second wasted at a time when each and every one is precious. Secondly, either you wish me to continue with my task, or you do not.'

'Pamplemousse . . .'

'I am in a *gendarmerie* in the 2nd *arrondissement,*' repeated Monsieur Pamplemousse. 'A word in the ear of the examining magistrate, *peut-être?* Otherwise . . .'

'Aristide . . .'

Monsieur Pamplemousse replaced the receiver. He hesitated, wondering whether to try his luck and ask if he might be allowed an extra telephone call in order to get a message through to Jacques, but he decided against it. The desk officer was all ears. Word would spread like wildfire. Besides, the *gendarmerie* had enough problems on its hands without his adding to them.

As it happened Monsieur Pamplemousse had hardly got back to his cell, a matter of ten or fifteen minutes at the most- although it could have been more, he had lost all feeling for time since he had been deprived of his watch the night before – when he received another summons.

'You're in luck,' said a *gardien,* as he opened the cell door. 'You must have friends in high places. Someone has been talking to someone.'

Maddening though the Director could be at times, Monsieur Pamplemousse couldn't help but feel grateful for his 'connections'. On this occasion he really had excelled himself, breaking all previous records.

'Sign here.' The inspector gave Monsieur Pamplemousse an odd look as he spread an assortment of belongings across the counter.

Anxious to be on his way as quickly as possible, Monsieur Pamplemousse did as he was bidden and swept the articles into a large brown paper bag without even bothering to check them.

'Why?' The officer looked him up and down sadly, then shook his head. 'What possible reason?'

Monsieur Pamplemousse felt tempted to say that it had seemed like a good idea at the time, but he thought better of it. It was the kind of remark that was open to misinterpretation.

'It happens when there is a full moon,' he said. 'I can't help myself.' The simple explanations were often the best. At least they avoided a lot of tedious explanations.

'I've got an uncle like that.' A *gendarme* pecking away at an ancient typewriter near the back of the room looked up. 'About the same age as you. He can't help it either.'

'I could lend you a skirt if you like,' said a woman colleague.

'That will not be necessary,' said Monsieur Pamplemousse stiffly.

The inspector nodded towards the cage. 'It must be worse where that lot come from. Especially when there's a full moon.'

The walk back to his car was not a happy one for Monsieur Pamplemousse. The Boulevard de Bonne Nouvelle was crowded with people heading west to do their shopping, but at least his car was still astride the pedestrian crossing where he had left it.

He drove the rest of the way home crouching as low as he could behind the dashboard. From a distance there were times when it looked as though there was nobody at the wheel at all; a fact which didn't pass unnoticed by several alert members of the Paris police force, who duly reported the phenomenon.

Pommes Frites greeted his master in somewhat muted fashion; a mixture of relief at seeing him again, coupled with anxiety at what might befall him next; joy tempered with fear that he might be too late to rescue him from whatever fate had in store. Tail-wagging was sincere but tentative.

Seeing that his friend and mentor clearly had other things on his mind, Monsieur Pamplemousse put two and two together and led him to the lift, where he pressed the button for the ground floor. Pommes Frites was well able to look after himself when he got downstairs, but to make doubly sure Monsieur Pamplemousse rang the *concierge* to let him know he was on his way.

It wasn't until he went into the bathroom and caught sight of his reflection in the mirror that he realised for the first time the full extent of the damage he had suffered. It was no wonder Pommes Frites had looked worried.

His make-up was, to put it mildly, no longer in pristine condition. Lipstick, eyeshadow and rouge had run in all directions, and the foundation cream had certainly not been improved by a night's growth of beard. His face bore a remarkable resemblance to an early map of the Camargue marshlands. As for Doucette's frock; it looked like something the cat had brought in.

Monsieur Pamplemousse lay in the bath for a long time, growing gloomier and gloomier as he took stock of the situation. He was rapidly running out of ideas, and he was no nearer finding Caterina than when he had started. Short of going against the Director's wishes and bringing in the authorities, he didn't know which way to turn. And if he did that, Heaven alone knew where it would all end. The fat would be in the fire and no mistake.

Half an hour later, dressed and ready to face the world again, he started going through his belongings to make sure everything was there. His Cross pen, his Cupillard Rième watch – both of which he would have been mortified to lose – were safe and sound. The contents of his wallet looked intact – he must have held on to Doucette's handbag like grim death during the fracas. Emptying the contents on to the dining-room table – keys, *télécarte* and various other odds and ends, he came across a small sealed envelope bearing his name. The flap was tightly sealed down and he had to slit it open with the tip of his pen. Inside, there was a card. It bore the name of an Italian restaurant called Mamma Mia's, in the 2nd *arrondissement*.

Someone had scrawled a message across the card: ASK FOR MARIA. Alongside it there was an arrow pointing towards the right-hand edge. He turned the card over. On the back the same hand had written the day's date and a time – '19.30'.

Monsieur Pamplemousse gazed at it for a moment. Somewhere in the back of his head the name Mamma Mia rang a faint bell.

He picked up his copy of *Le Guide* and thumbed through the Paris section devoted to the 2nd *arrondissement*, but there was no mention of the restaurant. It was hardly surprising. Checking the address again on a map, he saw it was in the north-eastern section – not very far, in fact, from where he had left his car the night before: hardly a fertile eating area.

He jumped as the phone rang.

'*Allo.*'

523

'Pamplemousse!' It was the Director.

'*Monsieur!* I cannot thank you enough.'

'There is no need. I have to admit straight away, your release had nothing whatsoever to do with any efforts on my behalf. In fact I telephoned the station where you were being held to let you know that it was as I feared – most of my contacts are out of Paris for the weekend and that it might take some time, when they informed me you had already left.'

'That is very strange, *Monsieur.*'

'Very,' said the Director drily. 'The inference was that someone on high has been leaned on. It certainly had nothing to do with me.'

Monsieur Pamplemousse absorbed the fact. If it wasn't the Director, who could it have possibly been?

'Regardless of who was responsible, Aristide, it is good news. I am sorry if I flew off the handle this morning – especially after the exceptionally good turn you did me. I have been thinking about it since then . . .' He broke off. 'Are you listening, Pamplemousse?'

'*Oui, Monsieur.*' Monsieur Pamplemousse sounded puzzled. 'It was something you said a moment ago . . . about my doing you a good turn . . . You used the word *exceptionelle.*'

'Modest as ever, Pamplemousse. You are a strange mixture and no mistake. One moment you indulge in practices which would bring a blush to a raven's cheeks, the next moment you hide your light under a bushel. I refer of course to your kind act in arranging for the overnight installation of what I can only call an early warning system. There are lights over every door. From where I am standing I can see at least three. I trust you will bill *Le Guide* direct . . . I will see to it that Madame Grante in Accounts gives it her approval . . . I must

524

also ask you to pass on my thanks to the workmen. They must have worked swiftly and silently. I didn't hear a thing.'

'*Monsieur* . . .' Monsieur Pamplemousse tried hard to keep the note of alarm from his voice. 'Where are you speaking from?'

'I am on my way downstairs, Pamplemousse. I wish to carry out a closer inspection of your arrangements. So far I have only seen them from my bedroom window.'

'What is the weather like, *Monsieur*? Is the sky very blue?'

'It is indeed, Pamplemousse. The sun is almost over the tree tops. After all the rain, we are in for a perfect day. Spring is here at last.'

'*Monsieur*, you must not, under any circumstances, set foot outside your house until I have given the "all clear". Furthermore, you must warn anyone who approaches – the mailman – the gardener – not to come anywhere near . . .'

'Why in Heaven's name?' boomed the Director. 'I cannot be incarcerated in my own house like this, Pamplemousse. I have important work to do . . .'

'Because, *Monsieur*, the "arrangements" as you call them, have nothing whatsoever to do with me. Furthermore, I have good reason to believe the lights contain high explosive . . .'

'High explosive?' repeated the Director. 'Is this some kind of joke . . .'

'No, *Monsieur*. I assure you, it is deadly serious.'

During the silence which followed, Monsieur Pamplemousse took the opportunity to go through his wallet, checking the contents with his free hand.

'What shall I do, Aristide?'

'I can only suggest you pray for rain, *Monsieur*. I will try and obtain a copy of the instruction manual, but as the devices are solar-powered I fear it may need a long spell of inclement weather before the batteries lose their charge. I will also check with the weather bureau.

'At least you are safe from attack. The device will work both ways. Short of using a helicopter, not even the Mafia can get anywhere near.'

'That is true, Aristide.' The Director sounded slightly mollified. 'You know, I hadn't thought of that.'

'It is the Mob's favourite form of murder,' said Monsieur Pamplemousse. 'Remember the "pineapples" in the Twenties.'

'No, Pamplemousse, I do not remember the "pineapples" in the Twenties. And I do wish you wouldn't keep using the word "murder". It makes me nervous.'

Monsieur Pamplemousse placed the receiver under his chin. While they were talking he had suddenly stumbled across an item he had completely forgotten about.

'Later, *Monsieur,*' he said. 'I will telephone you later.'

'Pamplemousse . . .'

Monsieur Pamplemousse replaced the receiver, then he picked up the piece of paper on which Caterina had written her forwarding address. It was the same as that for Mamma Mia's. He compared the handwriting with that on the card, but it was totally different.

The telephone rang again, but he ignored it. It was the first glimmer of a breakthrough and he wanted time to think. His mind was racing with possibilities, none of which seemed to make any kind of sense.

It was only then that he realised Pommes Frites still hadn't returned from his walk.

Monsieur Pamplemousse turned into the rue Jardis and drove slowly along it until he saw the address he was looking for. It was sandwiched between a store specialising in costume jewellery and another stacked to the ceiling with bales of dress material.

By day the whole area would be a seething mass of humanity, the pavements awash with men struggling to manipulate trolleys piled high with cardboard boxes; the traffic almost permanently grid-locked. It was a wonder any business got done at all. Now it was relatively quiet and peaceful.

The street was narrow and strictly one-way, with room for parking on one side only; a rule enforced by iron posts set in the pavement. Having passed a vacant space almost opposite the restaurant, he managed to find another some 20 or so metres further along.

Backing in to it, Monsieur Pamplemousse switched off his lights and checked the time on his watch – nineteen-twenty. He hadn't been aware of another car on his tail but seeing he was early it was worth waiting a few minutes, just to make doubly sure.

Mamma Mia's was in one of the less salubrious parts of the 2nd *arrondissement*; an area packed with sweat shops catering for the rag trade. In a game of Monopoly, landing on it would not under any circumstances have constituted a stroke of good fortune. Building a hotel on the site would have been an act of desperation on the part of the unlucky thrower of the dice. On the other hand during the daytime it must enjoy a near monopoly in providing food for the workers – if they were allowed that much time off.

There were net curtains at the windows and the lights were on inside, but there was no sign of anyone either coming or going. The woodwork looked as though it could have done with a lick of paint, as indeed could most of the other buildings round and about.

The few people abroad wore a furtive air, as though they spent their lives waiting for the tap on the shoulder. An old woman shuffled past pushing a pram. She stopped by a pile of garbage just beyond the restaurant and poked at it with a stick for a moment or tvo before going on her way, her hopes unfulfilled.

Monsieur Pamplemousse waited until the hands on his watch said exactly nineteen-thirty, then he climbed out of his car, locked the door and crossed over the street, wondering what to expect, but prepared for the worst.

To his surprise, the restaurant was almost full. In his experience Italians usually didn't begin eating until much later in the evening, whereas most of the occupants of Mamma Mia's looked as though they were already halfway through their meal.

As he closed the door a man he took to be the *patron* came forward to greet him.

'*Monsieur* has a reservation?'

'The name is Pamplemousse.'

The man's face lit up. 'Ah, *signore*. We are expecting you.' He led the way towards a row of three small tables placed in front of a *banquette* seat which ran along the fabric-covered wall of an alcove near the window. It faced the back of the small entrance lobby, so the whole area was relatively isolated from the rest of the room. Preparations had clearly been made for his arrival, for all three tables carried a *Reservé* sign and the chairs which normally would have faced the *banquette* had been removed.

Taking away the middle sign, the *patron* pulled the table out so that Monsieur Pamplemousse could seat himself.

'You are expecting others?'

The man shook his head. 'It is so that you will not be disturbed.' He put a finger to his lips. '*Molto tranquillo.*'

528

Suddenly realising how hungry he was, Monsieur Pamplemousse looked around as he settled down. Taste buds began to throb as he unfurled a napkin and tucked it inside his collar. The atmosphere felt warm and inviting. There were propitious signs everywhere. People were eating with obvious pleasure. From the kitchen there came the sound of a woman's voice singing an aria from *Madame Butterfly*. He wondered if it was Mamma Mia herself. A happy chef was a good chef.

On the matchboarded wall opposite him there was a large mirror decorated with an advertisement for Cinzano. Framed pictures of past customers and other memorabilia covered the wall on either side of it.

A bottle of Sicilian wine arrived on his table, along with a long glass containing some sticks of wrapped *grissini*.

'Tell me,' said Monsieur Pamplemousse. 'Who is Maria? Will she be joining me?'

'Later, *signore*.' The *patron* pointed towards the kitchen. 'For the moment she is busy. It is Saturday night. In the meantime she says you must eat and enjoy yourself.'

'She is your wife?'

'*Si, signore*.' Monsieur Pamplemousse looked for the menu but the owner held up his hand in protest.

'*Signore*, for you, she is preparing *spaghetti all' acciuga in salsa d'arancia* – spaghetti with orange and anchovy sauce. It is all home made.' Lip-smacking was accompanied by the classic finger and thumb to the mouth gesture. '*Molto buono.*'

'Home made . . . on the premises?' In his experience 'home made' was often a euphemism for a superior brand of factory prepared food.

'*Signore!* Reproach was evident in the *patron*'s eyes.

Monsieur Pamplemousse expressed sorrow that such a thought should have entered his mind.

'Then, tonight, we have *ossobuco*. It is served with *risotto.*'

'*Risotto milanese?* With saffron and Parmesan cheese?'

The owner nodded with pleasure.

'And the *ossobuco* . . . it comes with the long thin spoon for extracting the very last of the bone marrow?'

'The "tax agent"? *Si, signore.*'

Monsieur Pamplemousse beamed back at him. It was a genuine little corner of Italy and no mistake. He reached for his notebook, then thought better of it. He might need all his powers of concentration. No matter. Perhaps when it was all over he would pay the restaurant a return visit.

He was tempted to ask if the owner's wife was in any way related to Uncle Caputo. It was possible. If such were the case she might even know the Director's wife. That would explain why there was no mention of the establishment in *Le Guide*. The Director would fall over backwards rather than be accused of nepotism by any of his rivals.

'Maria will join you later. . .' The *patron* was about to leave when he suddenly broke off and stared towards the window, almost as though he had seen a ghost.

Following the direction of his gaze, Monsieur Pamplemousse felt his own heart miss a beat. Scarcely a metre away from him two faces were peering into the restaurant through a gap in the curtains. Even without the dark glasses one of them was clearly recognisable as the man on the train. His eyes were dark, steely grey and totally expressionless.

As they disappeared from view the owner crossed himself and hurried to the door, returning a moment later followed by the two men. As they headed towards

Monsieur Pamplemousse's corner, he made a halfhearted attempt to bar their way.

'*Signore.* The tables in the window are reserved.'

'*Grazie.*' The shorter of the two men pushed past him, picked up the two *Reservé* notices and tossed them on to the floor. An uneasy silence descended on the restaurant.

Il Blobbo, the long, thin one, seated himself on Monsieur Pamplemousse's right and spoke first.

'How are things in the funeral business?' he asked.

The short, fat one laughed as he seated himself on the other side. It was not a pleasant sound.

Glancing at his reflection in the mirror, Monsieur Pamplemousse saw only too well what was meant by the remark. He also caught sight of something silver sticking out of Il Blobbo's top pocket. It looked like the end of a hat pin.

Gradually the chatter in the main body of the room started up again, but as he sat very still, waiting for his *spaghetti al'acciuga* to arrive, Monsieur Pamplemousse realised that the singing in the kitchen had stopped.

8
IN THE SOUP

Monsieur Pamplemousse was still waiting for his first course some twenty minutes later. All he had to show for his pains was a plateful of crumbs and some screwed-up paper left over from the supply of *grissini*.

He made the final stick last as long as possible; which was more than could be said for the bottle of wine. It was one of the newer, lighter Sicilian blends, unclassified for lack of ancestry. Pleasant enough, but as the picture beneath the name suggested, it was meant to be quaffed along with the food of the region, not drunk purely and simply as an *apéritif*. Food of any region would have been a welcome bonus.

He eyed a symbolic loaf of the local bread which occupied a place of honour on the counter. It was shaped like a three-breasted woman. He wondered what would happen if he went across and broke one of them off to assuage his hunger. Would it cease to be a symbol of prosperity?

It was good to find a restaurateur who had pride in his origins, but as time passed he couldn't help wondering if the connection went deeper than that. Perhaps not as a 'soldier' who had been through the ceremony and was on a percentage – he would need to have committed a murder for that, and he didn't look the type – but perhaps as an unpaid 'associate'; someone with a 'connection'. If that were the case he couldn't expect any help from that direction.

More than once Monsieur Pamplemousse tried to catch the owner's attention, but he was clearly avoiding that end of the room. As soon as there was the slightest sign of a hand being raised he rushed out into the kitchen. Once, Monsieur Pamplemousse saw what he took to be Mamma Mia herself staring straight at him through the hatch. It was hard to tell what she was thinking. Her expression was a mixture of frustration and consternation, and when he caught her eye she, too, crossed herself.

Shortly afterwards a small boy he took to be a member of the family emerged and passed through the restaurant. He returned a few minutes later armed with a large packet partly concealed beneath his jacket. It was impossible to see what was written on the side. Perhaps he had been out for his own supper?

Monsieur Pamplemousse's hunger pangs grew worse as he watched the others around him tuck in to their food. Mounds of pasta melted away before his gaze; plates were wiped clean with large chunks of bread. One party in a far corner of the room even had the gall to return a dish of *pollo ripieno alle noci* only half eaten. The walnut stuffing, according to the host, had overwhelmed the delicate taste of the chicken. Apologies were profuse. They were allowed another choice and it arrived within minutes.

The men on either side of him had been served almost straight away by a young waitress; a comely, if taciturn girl, who apparently suffered badly from a disease common to her calling. Galloping myopia. She reached past Monsieur Pamplemousse as though he didn't exist.

The thin one, the one on the train – Il Blobbo, ate his bowl of *ravioli* slowly and with precision, savouring each and every mouthful as though he had all the time in the world. The short, fat one gobbled his down noisily, as though there were no tomorrow. Both methods were a form of torture.

Apart from their opening remark, neither had uttered a word during the whole time they had been there. The chill which had entered the establishment on their arrival gradually permeated the room, communicating itself from table to table like a slow-moving cloud of dry ice.

'Why are you here?' Monsieur Pamplemousse broke the silence.

'Because we are hungry.' Once again it was the thin one who spoke first.

'*Si. Abbiamo molto fame.*' *His* companion showed a mouthful of pasta. A dribble of olive oil landed on his tie and began to spread.

'Does your friend always speak with his mouth full?' asked Monsieur Pamplemousse.

The first man allowed himself the ghost of a smile.

Monsieur Pamplemousse tried again. 'What have you done with the girl?'

Both men stopped eating and stared at him as though he had said something totally outrageous. He watched their reflection in the mirror as they exchanged a quick glance.

The fat one nudged the other. 'You know something? He's a joker. He could be flavour of the month.'

'You realise I could call for help.'

The man he had christened Il Blobbo reached for a bottle of Pellegrino. He poured the water slowly and carefully into his glass.

'But you won't.'

Something about the total arrogance of the man suddenly made Monsieur Pamplemousse's gorge rise.

'So, what is keeping you? Why don't you get on with it? Do you enjoy playing games?'

His outburst fell on stony ground. Neither man paid him the slightest attention. They just carried on eating.

Monsieur Pamplemousse went back to examining his empty wine bottle, wondering about the possibility of making a break for it. The thin one was right, of course. Hemmed in as he was between the two of them, he wouldn't get out from behind the table, let alone reach the door. It was a game of cat and mouse. He glanced around the restaurant. One thing was certain. He wouldn't receive much help from the other occupants either. And why should he expect any? They were mostly locals, out for a quiet night with their family. They wouldn't want to be involved.

Perhaps it was a case of being wise after the event, or accepting what should have been obvious from the start, but seeing the two men together at close quarters, they both had their origins written all over them. Hoodlums in black suits. It was a sort of uniform, the kind of clothing other people kept for weddings and funerals: almost like a badge of office. The Mafia was nothing if not conservative.

But if what the Director had said were true – that there was nothing more dishonourable for a member of the Cosa Nostra than to be involved in prostitution – and his own limited experience confirmed the fact, then what were they up to? Why were they in Paris?

Their arrogance came naturally to them, but was it not overlaid with something else? Once again, he found himself searching for the right word. Unease? Fear? Despite their outward show of indifference, they were definitely on edge about something. The fat one's nails were bitten almost to the quick. Monsieur Pamplemousse decided to have another go.

'Don't tell me you have no idea where the girl is either? Is that why you have been following me?'

It was number two's turn to speak first. He looked at his partner and winked.

'No flies on his nose, eh?'

The thought made him laugh so much he nearly choked. It gave Monsieur Pamplemousse no small pleasure to see the man's tie land in his pasta.

He decided that perhaps the best thing to do was sit back and see what happened. If he waited long enough he might even get served.

'Encore!' Seeing the waitress approaching his side of the room, Monsieur Pamplemousse pointed to the bottle.

Settling back in his seat again, he happened to glance towards the window and as he did so he caught a momentary glimpse of something black and wet pressed against the outside of the glass. It took all his self-control not to register the fact. At first sight it looked not unlike one of the truffles he had brought back from Italy; a *tuber melanosporum* from Périgord, rather than the Piedmont variety, but there the resemblance ended.

It struck Monsieur Pamplemousse that Pommes Frites – for there was no doubt in his mind as to the ownership of what at second glance was clearly a nose – wore his enigmatic expression. Their eyes met for a fraction of a second and there wasn't the faintest flicker of recognition. The fact didn't bother him unduly, for he knew Pommes Frites was too well trained to give the game away. All the same, it would have been nice to have some reaction. A reassuring bang on the restaurant door with a paw perhaps, or even a faint howl of sympathy from further along the street wouldn't have come amiss in the circumstances.

But Monsieur Pamplemousse waited in vain. There was no indication that Pommes Frites had the slightest intention of joining him. Perhaps, unlike his master, he had managed to grab a bite to eat somewhere, or perhaps he simply didn't fancy what was on the menu; Pommes Frites had never been deeply into pasta. As it was, he had simply disappeared into the night. One moment he was there, the next moment he wasn't. To all intents and purposes the brief incident might never have taken place.

Nevertheless, the sight gave Monsieur Pamplemousse cause for hope. At least he wasn't entirely on his own. He also knew that whatever else happened, Pommes Frites wouldn't let him down. Doubtless he had his own very good reasons for holding his fire.

As a summing-up, it would have pleased Pommes Frites had he been there to share it, for it would have confirmed the rightness of his decision to become the follower rather than the followed; a role for which he was admirably suited.

Pommes Frites' thought processes might have been slow, but nobody could say they weren't thorough. Having, over a period of time, weighed all the facts at his disposal, adding a tiny morsel here, removing another one there, the scales of his computer-like brain had come down heavily on the debit side, and the brief glimpse he'd had of the scene inside the restaurant confirmed his worst fears.

Not for the first time in their long relationship, he found himself entertaining fears about his master's sanity. Hobnobbing with villains was one thing, but actually sitting down to eat with them was something else again.

After such a long and concentrated spell of hard thinking, it was good to be seeing a bit of action again. Time had passed all too slowly since Monsieur Pamplemousse had let him out of the apartment that morning. The first half an hour or so he had spent doing the rounds. Doors opened for him, as they always did; the lady in the *boulangerie* had given him a *croissant* – yesterday's baking if he was any judge, although he was hardly in a position to complain; the man in the *boucherie* had found him a few scraps of beef and veal; but after that there was nothing much else to do except wait patiently in the gardens opposite for his master to make the next move.

That it had all started during the train journey to Paris was beyond doubt. That it had to do with the girl Monsieur Pamplemousse had met was equally obvious. It was an all too familiar pattern of events; the kind of mathematical equation he knew off by heart. Monsieur Pamplemousse + girl = trouble.

From the moment they had stepped off the train things had gone from bad to worse. All in all, Pommes Frites wasn't surprised Madame Pamplemousse appeared to have left home. The only good thing about it was that she hadn't been around to see the state his master had been in when he arrived back that morning – *having been out all night!* Nor had she seen her dress. If she had seen her dress with its tear all the way down the back there would have been hell to pay. Pommes Frites could picture the scene, although he tried very hard not to.

Then there were the baddies. Pommes Frites could tell a baddie from a kilometre away.

Part of his early training with the *Sûreté* had been to sniff them out. It had been one of the easier parts of his induction course and he had passed it with flying colours. Baddies always had a particular odour about them; you could smell them coming before they even turned a corner. The fact that Monsieur Pamplemousse was at that moment sandwiched between two examples of the very worst kind only served to intensify Pommes Frites' resolve. One way and another, for reasons best known to himself, his master had decided to 'go it alone', but that, to Pommes Frites' way of thinking, didn't necessarily mean he shouldn't be around to keep an eye on things, ready to act the moment he was needed.

That moment appeared to have arrived.

The same Saturday evening traffic that had helped him follow his master's 2CV all the way down from Montmartre now worked against him, slowing him down when all he wanted was to reach his destination with all possible speed. Tourists, wandering aimlessly along the pavement in twos and threes, attracted by the lights and the sound of music from Les Halles, conspired to impede his progress. Some even went out of their way to try and stop him.

Tiring of his constant battle against the odds, Pommes Frites took a sharp turn off the boulevard Sebastopol into the rue de Turbigo and entered the underground network of high speed one-way roads which ran below the Forum. Ignoring the hooting of passing motorists, he hugged the side of the tunnel and emerged a few minutes later opposite the Pont Neuf, where he seized the chance to draw breath while waiting for the traffic lights to change in his favour. On familiar territory at long last, it was possible to relax for a moment or two.

Once he had crossed the Seine and reached the safety of the Ile de la Cité, Pommes Frites trotted to the far side, opposite the Left Bank, and then headed off at a brisk pace along the Quai des Orfèvres, confident in his own mind that when he reached his destination his reception would, as always, be welcoming.

His confidence was not misplaced. Seeing him approach, one of the *gendarmes* on duty emerged from his perspex sentry box and saluted. Then he gave an inquiring look.

Clearly, if Pommes Frites saw fit to arrive on a Saturday night minus his master, something must be very much amiss.

If the reception being accorded to Pommes Frites at the Headquarters of the Paris *Sûreté* came under the heading of 'welcomes, hearty', the same could not be said of the manner in which Monsieur Pamplemousse greeted the arrival at long last of his first course. To say he radiated disappointment would have been to put it mildly.

From the reverential manner in which the owner of the restaurant had borne the food to his table, it looked as though he had been entrusted with some rare and exquisite ambrosial offering contained in a dish made of the most precious and fragile Limoges porcelain imaginable. Monsieur Pamplemousse's taste buds, already on triple time, braced themselves for something special indeed, the spilling of which would have incurred not just the wrath of Mamma Mia, who was anxiously watching her spouse's every movement through the hatch, but the anger of the Gods themselves.

He glared at the china bowl which had been set before him. 'I did not order this,' he exclaimed. 'There must be some mistake.'

'It is a *very* special dish, *signore*. For you. It *is pastino in brodo* – a speciality of the house.'

'There is nothing remotely special about alphabet soup,' growled Monsieur Pamplemousse, 'in this house or in any other. For children, perhaps. But for a fully grown, extremely hungry adult – an adult moreover, who has been promised *spaghetti all'acciuga in salsa d'arancia*, then it is very ordinary!' He looked around the restaurant. 'And if, as you say, it is a speciality of the house, why has no one else ordered it?'

Grasping a spoon, he emphasised each and every point with a jab at the contents of the bowl, causing the liquid to swirl up and engulf the pasta letters until they formed a tangled heap in the centre.

'*Mamma mia!*' The owner clasped his head in both hands, raising his eyes to Heaven.

'Please offer her my apologies,' said Monsieur Pamplemousse, mindful of the fact that it might be wise not to upset the kitchen staff too much, for fear they might try and get their own back later in the meal (Guilot swore he had once witnessed an irate chef in Marseille doing unspeakable things to some *bouillabaisse* destined for a customer who had complained about the quality of his first course), 'but tell her I shall wait for the dish you first recommended.'

'Not Mamma Mia, my wife,' said the owner unhappily. 'Just *Mamma mia!*' For some reason he seemed to be losing command of his French. There were beads of perspiration on his forehead.

He glanced apprehensively over his shoulder towards the hatch. From somewhere beyond it there came an impatient clattering of pans. It struck Monsieur Pamplemousse that they were being handled with a considerable amount of undue force. Others in the room sensed it too and looked round to see what was going on.

'Isa good. You try.' Taking Monsieur Pamplemousse's fork, the owner began disentangling the letters, arranging them into a more becoming pattern. Seizing the opportunity, the waitress brought another opened bottle of wine and filled the glass.

Monsieur Pamplemousse relaxed. The Italians did many strange things with pasta, but this had to be the limit. Having said that, hunger began to get the better of him. He picked up the spoon again.

'It is made with the best *pastino, signore.*'

'From a box?' said Monsieur Pamplemousse dryly. He realised now what the boy must have been carrying. At least he hadn't been given a child's portion.

He tried a spoonful. It was rather better than he had expected. If the basic component – the *pastino* – was factory made, the other ingredients tasted as though they were fresh from the market; vegetables and red beans, tomatoes, celery . . . some *pesto*. He began to warm to the idea.

As a small boy he had once been taken as a treat to Madame Barattero's Hôtel du Midi in Lamastre. It had been a family occasion, a celebration of some kind- the reason escaped him – but what he remembered most about it was not the *pain d'écrevisses* for which the restaurant was famous, but the fact that Madame Barattero in person had presented him with a dish all to himself. For his special benefit, letters had been added to the broth from a *pot au feu*. It was the first time he had ever come across such a thing, and the first time he realised that food – even in such a revered establishment as the Hôtel du Midi – could be fun. It had sown the seeds for what he was destined to become in later life. Much to everyone's delight he had picked out the words MERCI BEAUCOUP and as a reward had been allowed some red wine out of a glass which was almost too big for him to hold in both hands; the largest he had ever seen at that time.

Lost in a wave of nostalgia, Monsieur Pamplemousse began playing around with the letters, laying them out one by one along the rim of the bowl.

In no time at all he had formed the word GRANDE.

It gave him a certain amount of added pleasure that his actions were clearly causing irritation on either side of him.

The two men were watching his efforts with ill-disguised contempt.

'Does he have nothing better to do?'

'Perhaps he thinks we will grow tired of waiting?'

Monsieur Pamplemousse ignored both the comments and the wave of garlic that accompanied them. He was enjoying himself. Clearly, immediate company excepted, he was giving pleasure to others as well. Every so often the owner beamed at him through the hatch, giving the thumbs-up sign whenever their eyes met. Once he was even joined by his wife, who echoed his satisfaction with a nod and a beatific smile. Monsieur Pamplemousse warmed to the couple. You could say what you liked about the Italians, they really appreciated the simple things in life.

After some ten minutes or so he ended up with LU GRANDE MALAISE. It wasn' t, perhaps, quite as good as MERCI BEAUCOUP, and his old school teacher would have had something to say about the definite article, but at least it used up another letter and as a definition it summed up his present feelings to a tee: unease, discomfort, unrest.

Spooning up the remaining letters, Monsieur Pamplemousse disposed of them before tucking into the broth. The deed was automatic; it was the Capricorn in him. Neatness came naturally.

The *pastino* felt hard and unyielding, as though it had been baked in an oven. He was glad to have got it out of the way.

Looking up, he realised the owner had joined him. Disappointment, perhaps even a hint of alarm was writ large over the man's face as he gazed down at the half empty bowl.

'There is something wrong?' inquired Monsieur Pamplemousse.

'*Non, non, signore.* Nothing that can not be put right. It is like a game. The permutations are endless. Messages can be made.' Reaching over, the owner began rearranging the letters of the word GRANDE to form DANGER. Then he attacked the others, ending up with ALLE U MA IS.

Monsieur Pamplemousse stared at the result of the manoeuvrings. In the circumstances DANGER seemed a somewhat redundant word: a case of stating the glaringly obvious. As for the rest . . .

'What kind of message is ALLE U MA IS? he demanded. 'I do not wish to sound complacent, but I feel my arrangement was infinitely preferable. I agree the genders left a lot to be desired, but that is a minor point. At least it made sense . . .'

He broke off as the owner began poking a finger in what was left of his soup.

'You have lost something?' he inquired apprehensively. 'A cuff-link perhaps? A collar stud?'

The man looked puzzled. 'There should be some more *pastino, signore.*'

'An "R", a "Z", I think,' said Monsieur Pamplemousse. 'A couple of "A"s – plus a couple of figures – I have forgotten what they all were. It so happens that I have eaten them, but I fail to see . . .'

'You have eaten them? *Christabella, Santa Maria*! The owner gazed at him in horror. '*Signore!* You not supposed to eat the *pastino.*'

'*Faut pas manger le pastino?*' repeated Monsieur Pamplemousse in a loud voice. 'What kind of a restaurant is it where the *patron* tells you not to eat the food? I see now why there is no mention of your establishment in *Le Guide*. Why should I not eat it?'

'Because, *signore* . . .' Conscious that in the wake of Monsieur Pamplemousse's outburst the other diners –

particularly the ones in closest proximity – were hanging on his every word, the owner desperately groped for the right phrase, 'because eating is like music, it is like listening to a symphony. Every note has its place – every quaver – every semi-quaver – remove but one tiny element and you spoil the whole; the message is lost. In this case the message was in the *pastino.'*

Something about the way the man was staring at him, enunciating each and every word with the utmost clarity, caused Monsieur Pamplemousse to stifle the retort he had on the tip of his tongue. *Alors on a compris!* The penny suddenly dropped.

'The message was in the *pastino?'* he repeated.

'*Si, signore.* In the *pastino.'* The relief on the patron's face was like a burst of sunshine after a storm. He mopped his brow. 'It needs to be savoured, and thought about, and acted upon.'

'In that case,' said Monsieur Pamplemousse, 'perhaps you should bring me another bowl?'

'*Si, signore. Pronto. Immédiatement.* At once.' He bustled off in the direction of the kitchen only to return almost immediately with a face as long as a stick of grissini.

Monsieur Pamplemousse said it for him.

'You have no more soup?'

The man nodded his head miserably. 'It is all gone – and the shop will be closed.'

'That makes it very difficult for you.'

'*Impossible, signore.'*

In desperation, Monsieur Pamplemousse half rose and glanced towards a sign saying TOILET over a door beyond the kitchen.

Following his thoughts, the two men on either side of him did likewise.

Once again Monsieur Pamplemousse regretted the absence of Pommes Frites. At least Pommes Frites would have stood guard outside the door, stopping the others from following him inside. There might be a window he could climb through, or a chance to pick up some kind of message *en route*. Anything would be an improvement on his present situation. As it was, the two men were watching him like a hawk.

He sat down again. They had him by the short and curlies and no mistake.

'How about the *ossobuco?*' he asked the owner.

'*Si, signore.* I will bring it.' The man shrugged. It was a gesture of defeat.

Monsieur Pamplemousse was made of sterner, more imaginative stuff. Wild ideas of messages inscribed on the bottom of the plate entered his mind. He wondered if the paint would come off with the heat, and if so would it spoil the *ossobuco*. The ink from a felt-tipped pen most certainly would.

Inspiration struck. Thoughts of *ossobuco* reminded him of Pommes Frites and that in turn combined to trigger off a third possibility.

'No!' he exclaimed. 'I have changed my mind. I have had enough. I would not eat here again if I found myself starving to death in the middle of the Sahara desert. The food here is fit only for my dog.'

The owner looked at him as though he had taken leave of his senses. 'But, *signore . . .*'

'I will pay for the rest of the meal,' said Monsieur Pamplemousse slowly and distinctly, 'but I would like to take it home in un *petit sac pour mon chien:* a doggy-bag.'

'Ah! *Sì!*' After a moment's hesitation the owner's face lit up again. '*Sì, sì, signore!* I understand.' Removing the remains of the first course, he disappeared in the direction of the kitchen.

Avoiding the gaze of the men on either side of him, Monsieur Pamplemousse poured himself another glass of wine.

He hadn't long to wait. The prospect of his imminent departure acted as a spur to the speed and quality of the service. He hardly had time to dispose of his wine before the owner reappeared clutching a plastic carrier bag. It felt warm to the touch.

Leave-taking formalities were reduced to a minimum. Offers to pay the bill were waved to one side. The waitress appeared with his coat, holding it open for him as he squeezed his way out from behind the table.

With cries of *'ciao'*, *'buona notte'* and *'buona fortuna'* ringing in his ears, Monsieur Pamplemousse left Mamma Mia's, closely followed by the two men. Ignoring their presence, he made his way up the street to where his car was parked. The men's car – a black Chevrolet – was parked almost opposite the restaurant. The fat one climbed into the driving seat, started the engine and reached over to open the passenger door so that Il Blobbo could join him.

Monsieur Pamplemousse went through a pantomime of searching for his keys, then switching on his side-lights and traffic indicators. He made equally heavy weather of extricating his car from its parking space, playing for time as he tried to decide what to do next. Size was on his side; when it came to manoeuvrability his 2CV would win against the other's Chevrolet any day, but once they reached the main boulevards he wouldn't stand an earthly. He turned the rear-view mirror at an angle so that it afforded a clear view of what was going on behind him.

Suddenly, he saw what he had been praying for-lights from an approaching car nosing its way slowly along the narrow street, the driver clearly looking for somewhere to park. Seeing a car was about to leave, he accelerated past the Chevrolet, then pulled up a few metres behind Monsieur Pamplemousse, effectively blocking the way for anyone who might be following.

Monsieur Pamplemousse seized his chance. Switching on the main beams, he put his right foot flat down on the floorboards and wrenched the steering wheel to the left. Clearing one of the iron bollards on the opposite side of the street by a matter of millimetres, he wrenched the wheel to the right again. With a shriek of protesting metal the car bounced off the edge of the kerb and, weaving from side to side, hurtled on its way. Braking sharply at the end, the *deux chevaux* rocked as he made a sharp right turn, then it miraculously righted itself.

In his wake he could hear the sound of blaring horns. It was a very satisfactory noise. The driver of the car wanting to make use of his space looked the kind of person who would take great delight in being as bloody-minded as possible if he were pushed too far.

Following a similar, but parallel, route to the one Pommes Frites had taken earlier in the evening, Monsieur Pamplemousse slowed down to a more leisurely pace. Seeing some traffic lights at red in front of him, he took the first turning right and doubled back into the rabbit warren of streets which made up that corner of Paris.

He was only just in time. As he pulled up behind a lorry making a late-night delivery, he glanced over his shoulder and saw a black Chevrolet shoot past the end of the street. For once he almost wished he drove something slightly less conspicuous than his 2CV. If it had been his pursuers and they were looking the right way they must have seen him. He would be thoroughly boxed in, with no chance of escape.

On the principle of taking no chances, Monsieur Pamplemousse slammed his car into reverse and shot back the way he had come.

Regardless of oncoming traffic swerving to avoid both him and each other, ignoring other drivers hooting and gesticulating at his seemingly imbecilic behaviour, he crossed the busy boulevard Sebastopol at speed.

Reverting to his head level with the dashboard mode of driving, he carried on until he found a suitable turning, then he made good his escape. Only then, as he slowed down to open the side window and let in a welcome draught of cold air, did he realise he was sweating like a pig.

On the corner of rue de Turbigo a *gendarme* reached for his portable radio.

'It is the phantom *Deux Chevaux* again!'

'*C'est la vie!*' That was the way it went. Sometimes you spent hours doing nothing. Then everything happened at once. First a driverless car going backwards up a main artery. Then, even as he spoke, he saw another one approaching. It was doing exactly the same thing – only this time he could see both driver and passenger.

The second car had a Rome registration, so what else could you expect? Fortunately he was able to give the girl at the other end both sets of numbers.

9
CATCH 22 BIS

Monsieur Pamplemousse replaced the telephone handset and stood for a moment or two staring out of the kiosk, lost in thought.

The conversation had been short and to the point. As short and to the point in its way, as had been the message contained in the doggy bag. Wrapped in silver foil to protect it from the *ossobuco* and with the missing letters inserted, it had spelled out the words: DANGER: ALLEZ AU MARAIS. Underneath it there was an address in the Place des Vosges.

It was yet another case of reason flying out the window. The Marais was the last area of Paris where he would have chosen to look: the Place des Vosges at that! Unarguably, with its central fountain and its carefully tended symmetrical gardens, it was one of the most beautiful squares in Paris. The perfectly proportioned town houses surrounding it on all four sides, with their arched stone arcades at ground level and their dormer windows and steeply pitched slate roofs above, gave it an air of discreet respectability. It was hard to picture 'goings on' behind the elegant red-brick façades of the upper storeys. Or was it? Perhaps that same air of respectability would add a certain *cachet*. It would undoubtedly up the prices!

Below the message telling him where to go there was a hastily scrawled telephone number: first the 19 code for

International, then 39 for Italy, followed by a Sicilian number, with instructions to dial it at 20.00 precisely.

A woman had answered, almost before the first ring was completed. She must have had her hand poised on the receiver. She had spoken quickly and clearly, and from her manner and tone of voice Monsieur Pamplemousse formed the opinion that she was in fear of being overheard. It had sounded like a cry from the heart, an act of desperation on the part of someone who had swallowed her pride and knew there was no going back.

Conscious of all that, and aware that after his long conversation with the Director when he had telephoned from the Gare de Lyon there weren't many units left on his *télécarte,* he had listened and taken careful note, interjecting only when it was absolutely necessary.

'Were you responsible for "springing" me after I was arrested?' he inquired.

'You are the only one I can turn to or trust. Caterina has spoken of you to my cousin at the restaurant, who phoned me.'

It was said as though it had been the simplest problem in the world, but he couldn't help wondering how she had got to hear of his plight so quickly. It was no time to go into details.

'Mamma Mia is your cousin?'

'Maria is my cousin. I would not wish either her or her husband to be involved any more than they have been already.'

'How can you be sure that what you have told me is true?'

'Because Caterina is my daughter, and I know her perhaps better than she knows herself. Besides, I am a woman and I am from Sicily. Women in Sicily are told nothing, yet we know everything.

'It has always been so. Our men have protected us. Their wife, their family, it is the most important thing in their life. They say they know what is best.'

'I, too, have someone who is dear to me and who is often told nothing, but who knows all,' said Monsieur Pamplemousse, in an effort to establish a common bond.

'It is not the same,' said the woman. 'Believe me, it is not the same. Your wife has her freedom. In Sicily that is not so.

'In Sicily, the men can do as they please provided they are not found out. But things are changing slowly. Women here are starting to rebel. They want to go out into the world too.

'I have always had everything I could possibly wish for in the way of money . . . clothes . . . everything except freedom. That is the most precious thing of all, and that is what I want for Caterina.'

'But it has to be used wisely?'

'Exactly. It is not good to run before you can walk. That is why I need your help. You must do whatever it costs.'

'There is no price, *signora*. I will simply do my best. That is all I can do.'

'*Grazie.* I will tell you . . .' She was in the middle of speaking again when there was a click and the line went dead. It was the moment of truth and no mistake.

Monsieur Pamplemousse climbed back into his 2CV and switched on the engine. Heading south and using back streets as far as possible, he drove slowly through the relatively deserted 3rd *arrondissement* while he considered his next move.

Despite the modest pace at which he was travelling, or perhaps because of it, his progress didn't go unreported. Space in the airwaves above Paris soon became at a premium.

552

Finally abandoning his car in a side street near the rue des Francs-Bourgeois Rivoli – the main thoroughfare leading into the Place des Vosges – Monsieur Pamplemousse set off on foot. He felt less conspicuous that way. He hadn't gone very far before he realised the wisdom of his move. As he drew near the *place* he was nearly run down by a car reversing at speed. He only just managed to jump clear in time.

'*Poule!* Where do you think you are going?'

'*Voilà! Les Flics.*' The driver had his window wound down. He looked anxiously over his shoulder as he drove on his way, more concerned for his own well-being than for any passing pedestrians who were foolish enough to walk in the road. It was asking for trouble.

Where he had just been, a group of *gendarmes* were flagging down the traffic, peering into car windows, scrutinising the occupants.

Monsieur Pamplemousse stood for a moment in a shop doorway while he considered the matter. Perhaps they were expecting more trouble after the International, or maybe there was some kind of 'happening' in the Place de la Bastille. The former was hardly likely – it was too much off the beaten track – the latter was too far away.

Playing it by ear, he backtracked and made a short detour towards the rue de Rivoli, entering the Place des Vosges through a side street. On the way he passed three long grey buses filled with CRS riot police. There were two *gendarmes* standing inside the archway at the entrance to the square, but they paid him scant attention. They were far more interested in the solitary occupant of a large Mercedes trying to leave. The car had a CD plate and the man was protesting in no uncertain terms.

The restaurant Coconnas to his right was full. Light streamed from its windows and he could see waiters hurrying about their business, but beyond it, towards the house where Victor Hugo had once lived and worked, there was a patch of relative darkness. Some way beyond that again, Monsieur Pamplemousse found the number he was looking for. There was a modern coded entry-lock, but it must have been disconnected, for when he pushed against the huge wooden door it swung open easily and he found himself entering a small, paved court-yard.

Approaching an ornate front door, he pressed an unla-belled bell push let into the wall beneath one of a pair of wrought-iron lamps.

The door was opened almost immediately by a young girl. She was wearing school clothes – a gym slip and blouse. If the intention had been to conceal what little else she might be wearing underneath, both garments were several sizes too small. Her cheeks were heavily rouged and she carried a hockey stick. There was music playing in the background and he could hear the clink of glasses and the sound of laughter coming from a room nearby.

'I wish to speak to the *"Madame"*.'

'Do you have an invitation?'

'Non.'

The girl hesitated. 'I'm dreadfully sorry . . .' She spoke with a cultivated English accent.

'It is I who am sorry,' said Monsieur Pamplemousse firmly. 'The *"Madame"*, *s'il vous plaît.'*

After a moment's hesitation the girl led him towards a flight of wide, richly carpeted stairs. Monsieur Pample-mousse reflected that it was interesting the difference clothes and subdued lighting made to a person. Dressed the way she was, she didn't look more than fourteen or fifteen

554

years old. As they mounted the first few stairs, he averted his gaze, glancing instead through an open door to his right. He registered all he needed to know.

What was it President Mitterrand had once said? 'If Ministers resigned because of their peccadillos I would lose half my cabinet overnight.' It looked as though the other half might be in imminent danger too. He recognised several well-known faces from other walks of life.

The girl tried several doors on the first landing. The first two were locked. Someone was attempting to play the hornpipe on an accordion behind one, the sound of rattling chains came from the second room.

'My name's Deirdre, by the way,' said the girl. She tried another door. 'Third time lucky!'

'*Sacré bleu!* Following her into the room, Monsieur Pamplemousse narrowly escaped being struck on the head by a naked man swinging upside down on a trapeze. A girl kneeling on a bed in the centre of the room looked round. 'Shut the door, Deirdre. There's a draught.'

'*C'est impossible!*' Monsieur Pamplemousse stared at the scene.

'Nothing is impossible with Ernestine,' said Deirdre. 'She's Hungarian. Her parents owned a travelling circus. They were always on the move. Would you like to have a go? It's super fun.'

'*Non, merci,*' said Monsieur Pamplemousse hastily. 'I am afraid I do not have a head for heights.'

'How about the banisters?' Deirdre, who seemed to have a penchant for *non sequiturs*, licked her lips and ran her hands down the highly polished surface. 'You can get up quite a speed if you start from the top.'

Monsieur Pamplemousse winced. He was still feeling the effects of his outing the night before.

'I am not sure I would know what to do when I got to the bottom,' he said.

Deirdre giggled. 'It's easy when you know how.' She hitched up her skirt. 'Don't worry. I'll show you.'

'Is there no pleasure in simplicity any more?' asked Monsieur Pamplemousse. 'Besides, when I said I am in a hurry, I meant just that.'

He stood back to allow another girl free passage. It struck him that she didn't take as much advantage of his move as she might have done. She was sucking something nameless on the end of a stick and as she squeezed past him he smelt aniseed; aniseed and what could have been Chanel 19. It was a strangely disturbing combination.

The room the first girl took him to was at the front of the building. It was lavishly furnished in the style of the period. Whoever lived in the house must be wealthy beyond most people's wildest dreams. Thick wooden beams supporting the high ceilings were ornately inlaid with other woods. From the central beam there hung a sizeable unlit chandelier.

Deirdre glanced up. 'Would you like a "freebie" while you're waiting?'

'I am in a hurry,' said Monsieur Pamplemousse.

'A "quickie" then?'

'There comes a time in a man's life,' said Monsieur Pamplemousse with a sigh, 'when the word "quickie" betrays a certain degree of optimism.'

'I don't mind waiting.'

'Please. There is no time to lose.'

For one awful moment he thought she was going to cry, then the door closed behind her.

Left on his own at long last, Monsieur Pamplemousse crossed to the window and parted the curtains slightly. If anything, police activity was on the increase. More *gendarmes* were now stationed just inside the arcade on the west side, where they were able to keep an eye on traffic entering the square. The only other way in, except on foot, was through an archway directly opposite the one he had just used. From a policing point of view the layout of the square couldn't have been better. There were just two ways in – from the north and from the west, and two ways out – to the east and to the south.

'What are you doing here?'

He turned at the sound of a voice. 'I think I might ask you the same question.'

'I presume you know the truth – otherwise you wouldn't be here.'

Monsieur Pamplemousse gazed long and hard at Caterina. In the glow of the soft pink light from table lamps scattered about the room she looked positively ravishing. Even more so, he had to admit, than when he had last seen her on the train. She was wearing an ivory coloured dress of a simplicity which only came when expense was no object. With her hair up, she had an air of authority beyond her years. It made him feel momentarily sad.

He motioned her to sit. It was no time for beating about the bush.

'I have just had a long conversation with your *mamma*. She applauds what you have done, but now she wants you to come home. If you stay it will lead to nothing but unhappiness, to tragedy even; to a war within the "family" itself.'

'I am sorry. It is too late.'

'You realise your *papà* will be forced to kill you.'

'Me?' Caterina laughed, but it was clear a chill had entered into her. 'That is not possible. He would never do such a thing.' For the first time she avoided his gaze.

'He would have no choice,' said Monsieur Pample-mousse. 'He is bound by the code of the Cosa Nostra. He has been "baptised"; he has sworn an oath, he has under-gone the ritual, mixing the blood of his trigger finger with the blood of others. You of all people should know, from that moment on the Mafia Family took – precedence over his own, even if it means killing his only daughter. That is the rule. It is a total requirement and there is no escaping the fact. He would demand it of others, and he would expect them to obey the rule without question. Therefore, as a Man of Honour, he cannot possibly escape it himself.

'You have committed one of the worst sins of all – a whole series, in fact. You have disobeyed his orders, and what you are doing is something that in itself will bring disgrace.'

Monsieur Pamplemousse's thoughts went back to the conversation he'd had with Caterina's mother and a ques-tion he had posed: 'Why are you telling me all this?'

'Because I want Caterina back and I want the explana-tions – the pressure – to come from someone else. If this thing leaks out it will kill her father.'

He sat down beside Caterina and placed a hand on hers. 'You must close down. Now. This moment.'

'But I can't. It is the opening night.'

'Then it must also, I fear, be the closing night. Apart from anything else, from what I have seen in the very short time I have been here, you have managed to accumulate enough "names" to promote the biggest scandal that has hit France for many years.'

'What if I refuse? You cannot make me.'

'You are right. I cannot make you. But if you go ahead, then just as surely as night follows day, you will be respon-sible for the death of your father. Even if he goes against his own code – the code of the Cosa Nostra – and if others let that be, which is unlikely, he will be unable to stand the disgrace. A daughter who disobeys his commands? A daughter who runs away without permission to do her own thing? A daughter who opens a bordello in Paris?

'You know what they would say? They would say he was no better than a pimp. A pimp, living on his daughter's earnings. For someone with his background there could be no greater insult.'

It was, thought Monsieur Pamplemousse, yet another case of Catch 22 with a vengeance. Catch 22bis.

'But can it not wait? Until the end of this evening at least. I cannot go back on my promises . . .'

'Promises to whom? The worst that can happen is that you will leave behind a lot of unsatisfied customers; unsatisfied in the truest sense of the word. They will probably take it out on their subordinates in the morning, but so what?'

Caterina shrugged, then she looked around. 'It has been a lot of work for nothing. What do you think of it all?'

'Banisters will never be the same again,' said Monsieur Pamplemousse. 'It has also given me a whole new perspective on lollipops.'

'No, seriously.'

'Seriously . . .' Monsieur Pamplemousse crossed to the window again and parted the thick curtains. 'Look!'

He raised his hands as Caterina joined him. 'It is not of my doing, believe me.'

'Then who?'

'I do not know. It is of no consequence. We are dealing in facts. And the fact is, unless we leave now you will be in serious trouble, and so shall I. They will throw the book at me.'

Monsieur Pamplemousse looked at her curiously. 'You ask me what I think. I think you have done much in a very short time. In some respects I am lost in admiration.'

'It was very easy really. The house is empty. It belongs to a member of my family – an uncle. Mamma spoke of him many times. He is out of the country.'

'And the girls? How many are there?'

'Fifteen.'

'*Fifteen!* Where do they all come from?'

'That was the least of the problems. You forget – I attend a convent school.'

Monsieur Pamplemousse suppressed a whistle. No wonder the place threatened to be such an instant success. It must be quite unique in the annals of *maisons de débauches.*

'Do you realise the risk you are running? There are other ways of proving yourself. You have your whole life before you. It is pointless to gain your freedom only to lose it again. Besides, remember what happened to the Dugong . . . there is such a thing as being too successful.'

While he was talking, he ushered Caterina out of the room. 'Round up the rest of the girls – as quickly and as quietly as possible. Tell them to get dressed. I will see you outside.'

Giving her no time to argue, Monsieur Pamplemousse hastened down the stairs and let himself out into the arcade.

He looked to his right and then to his left, trying to decide what to do for the best. Shadowy figures made their way round the perimeter of the *Place,* but now he was on ground level again it all looked relatively quiet. Only the stationary headlamps from waiting cars and vans on the north side gave a clue to the activity that was going on. By their light he could see passers-by being asked for their *cartes d'identité.*

Fifteen girls! Sixteen, if you included Caterina – and he had no intention of leaving without her. Even in small groups they would never make it without being stopped. It was like a war-time operation. No one was being spared.

Monsieur Pamplemousse's attention was momentarily diverted by a burst of flash guns further along on his side of the *place.* A party of Japanese tourists, streaming out of a *café,* were boarding a parked coach through a door in its side, taking photographs of each other as they went. Photographs of each other and . . . Monsieur Pample- mousse gave a start.

To his astonishment he saw Pommes Frites posing along- side one member of the group. Not so much directing oper- ations, but clearly taking an active interest in what was going on. He had an extraordinary capacity for putting in an appearance when it was least expected. It was quite uncanny.

Whether it was the flashlights, or simply a case of built-in extrasensory perception was hard to say, but Pommes Frites caught sight of Monsieur Pamplemousse at almost exactly the same moment, and came bounding towards him full of the joy of his discovery.

He looked pleased with himself, as well he might, since in his way he was partly responsible for bringing together and coordinating the forces not only of those who were looking for his master, but those who, coincidentally, were even now about to home in on the clandestine activities in the Place des Vosges. For all its outward aloofness, the Marais was like a village. News travelled fast.

That the two events were not necessarily compatible didn't cross Pommes Frites' mind as he exchanged greetings with his master. As far as he was concerned, their meeting up was sufficient in itself.

'Wait.' Seeing the door open behind him, Monsieur Pamplemousse signalled both Pommes Frites and Caterina to stay where they were.

Brushing past the last of the Japanese tourists, he approached the front of the coach and tapped on the door. Receiving no response, he slid it open. The driver was laid back, feet on the dashboard, a cigarette dangling from his mouth.

Waving his *Guide* pass with an authority learned in the Sûreté and developed over years of dealing with some of Paris's worst criminal elements, who thought they knew all the answers, Monsieur Pamplemousse glared at the man. His first thought had been that they might all beg a lift, but something told him he wouldn't get very far with that idea. He decided to try another tack.

'Do you see anything strange about the way you are parked, *Monsieur?*'

The driver didn't even bother to remove the cigarette. '*Non.* Why should I? This is where I always park.'

'Half on the pavement? In an area where coaches are expressly forbidden to park?'

'*Oui.*' The man made play of looking out of his window. 'What would you have me do – stay in the rue des Francs-Bourgeois and cause an *impasse?*'

Monsieur Pamplemousse jerked a thumb over his shoulder. 'Out,' he barked, dropping any pretence at politeness. 'I am booking you for illegal parking. Furthermore, I am also booking you for causing an obstruction and for being in charge of an unsafe vehicle.'

'Unsafe?' Brushing ash from his jacket, the driver clambered out of the coach and joined Monsieur Pamplemousse on the pavement. 'It is brand new. It was delivered from the factory only two weeks ago. It has two toilets, a bar, video, air-conditioning, walk-in luggage space, tinted windows.'

Monsieur Pamplemousse withdrew his notebook from the concealed fold in his trousers and flipped it open. 'A flat tyre on the nearside rear wheel.'

The man kicked it. 'I have no flat tyre.'

Monsieur Pamplemousse removed his Cross ballpoint pen from an inside pocket, gave the barrel a quick twist, and then applied the pointed end to a valve. There was a satisfying hiss of escaping air. Fortunately for his purpose the wheel was one of a pair. The coach would still be driveable.

'*Merde!*' Leaving the man gazing disbelievingly at his tyre, Monsieur Pamplemousse strolled in leisurely fashion round to the back of the vehicle. He was beginning to enjoy himself. It was quite like old times. 'One defective rear light.'

'*Morbleu!*' bellowed the man as he joined him. 'That is nonsense! Look at them!'

Monsieur Pamplemousse lifted his foot. There was a crash of splintering plastic and the light went out. He turned to a new page.

'Telling lies. Arguing with those in authority. I wouldn't be in your shoes. Wait till I get you back to the station. The Squad for the Protection of Tourists may have other ideas.'

Having carefully made sure none of the police were looking his way, Monsieur Pamplemousse mimed waving to an imaginary colleague, going through a routine of whistle blowing and holding a telephone to his ear. As an *encore* he made a throat-cutting gesture followed by the classic sign for 'at the double'.

Out of the corner of his eye he saw Pommes Frites watching his every movement. The worried expression had returned. Clearly, he was of the opinion that his master was suffering from another relapse; possibly permanent this time.

'Look here . . .' Unbelievably the *salaud* was still attempting to bluster his way out.

Monsieur Pamplemousse pointed towards the rue de Rivoli. 'Waiting there are three van loads of CRS. One more peep out of you, my friend, and I shall hand you over. They have been doing nothing all day and they will enjoy a little diversion; a chance to flex their muscles. It will be like feeding time at the zoo. They are not gentlemen like me.'

It did the trick, as he knew it would.

With considerable ill grace, the driver reached for his wallet.

Monsieur Pamplemousse grabbed hold of the man's jacket lapels and slammed him against the side of the coach. His action triggered off another series of photographs, this time from inside the vehicle. White faces pressed against the inside of the glass as they waited for their flash-guns to recharge.

'*Imbecile!*' He took the note from the man and slipped it into his trouser pocket. 'Never do that in the open. People will think the worst.'

He pointed to the *café*. 'Wait in there. I will see what I can do, but I warn you – 100 francs will not go very far.'

As the man disappeared, Monsieur Pamplemousse turned and waved to Caterina. 'Quick! Get everyone into the coach.'

Ignoring the flood of girls pouring out of the house, he went round to the front and climbed into the driving seat. Compared with his 2CV it was the ultimate in sophistication; more like the cockpit of a jumbo jet. He made a stab at some switches. The windscreen washer came on, the sound of soft music filled the air, and the interior lights went out. A murmur of oriental approval rose from behind.

'Where are you taking us?' Caterina boarded the coach and slid the door shut behind her.

'Where do you think?' asked Monsieur Pamplemousse. 'To the Gare de Lyon.'

He peered at the controls and made another stab at starting the engine. This time he struck lucky. It roared into life.

As they moved off, Pommes Frites stationed himself behind the windscreen alongside his master and Caterina picked up a microphone. She switched it on. 'What would you like me to say?'

'Anything,' said Monsieur Pamplemousse. 'How about "The safety instructions are in the back of the seat in front of you" or "Be careful when you open the overhead luggage compartments. Heavy objects might fall out"? No-one is going to know any different.'

Seeing the exit he was heading for was temporarily blocked, he made a snap decision to go round the Place des Vosges a second time. Apart from anything else, it would give him a chance to familiarise himself with the controls. He mopped his brow. The interior of the coach was like an oven.

'Try turning off the heating,' hissed Caterina. 'The Marais,' she continued, for the benefit of those behind, 'is a maze of squares, many of which in time begin to look exactly the same.'

'Tell the girls to lie down,' said Monsieur Pamplemousse, as he completed his circuit and began making a second approach. 'Whatever happens they must not be seen.'

Caterina switched off the microphone. 'I do not think that will be necessary.'

Something about the wistful tone of her voice made Monsieur Pamplemousse look round. He saw what she meant. Feet rather than heads protruded above the top of the seats. His knowledge of Japanese was non-existent, but what little sound he could hear above the music seemed to be registering pleasure rather than complaints.

As they turned the corner leading to the eastern exit of the square, he gave a loud blast on the horn and slid open his window.

'S'il vous plaît, monsieur. S'il vous plaît.'

The *gendarme* nearest the coach tapped on one of the windows, registered an inscrutable face staring back at him, and having received a blinding flash straight in the eyes for his pains, uttered an oath and hastily waved them on.

Monsieur Pamplemousse breathed a sigh of relief as he accelerated away. At least he would have more room to manoeuvre once they reached the safety of the boulevard Beaumarchais. The possibility of their becoming inextricably jammed between a couple of bollards, or worse still, wedged in one of the many arcades had never been far from his mind.

It was as they joined the never-ending stream of traffic circulating round the central column in the Place de la Bastille – the very moment when he needed all his concentration – that Caterina suddenly broke off from her commentary and shrieked a warning into the microphone. It was accompanied by a loud growl from Pommes Frites as he launched himself into space.

Monsieur Pamplemousse braked sharply. Aware of a commotion going on behind him, but surrounded on all sides by fast-moving traffic, he accelerated again, switching off his mind to all but the task in hand as he jockeyed for position in order to enter the rue de Lyon before the lights changed.

At one point he felt a draught of cold air down the back of his neck, and heard renewed squeals of brakes behind them, but by then he was long past caring. Never had the lights above the Gare de Lyon seemed more welcoming.

Ignoring rumbles of discontent from waiting taxi drivers, he parked the coach as close to the main entrance as it was possible to get and climbed out of his seat.

'Wait here.'

The clock in the tower still couldn't make up its mind as whether it was midday or four-twenty. His own watch said twenty-one thirty-seven. He dashed into the station and was outside again by twenty-one thirty-nine. Caterina was waiting for him by the open door of the coach.

'There is a train to Rome leaving at twenty-two hundred hours. You will need to change at Milan. Hurry – there isn't much time.'

'Have you enough money?' Monsieur Pamplemousse looked inside the coach. It was a redundant question. Large quantities of notes seemed to be changing hands all round.

'You were wonderful,' said Caterina. *'Papà* would have been proud of you.'

'Merci.' It struck Monsieur Pamplemousse as a dubious compliment, but he suddenly realised the tour leader was trying to address him.

'Excuse, please . . . *s'il vous plaît.'*

'What is it?' asked Monsieur Pamplemousse impatiently. He seemed fated not to say a proper goodbye to Caterina.

'Hope we did right thing with strangers in coach.'

Monsieur Pamplemousse stared at the man in bewilderment. 'Strangers? What strangers? Where?'

'Two men dressed in black. Not part of tour. All right now. They gone.'

'Gone?' repeated Monsieur Pamplemousse.

'We make them offer they cannot refuse.' For a split second the semblance of a smile crossed the other's face.

'What happened?'

'They refuse offer. Great shame.' The man made a throat-cutting gesture.

'But where are they?' repeated Monsieur Pamplemousse impatiently.

The tour leader made a gesture towards the back of the coach. 'Make use of emergency exit. Much traffic in Paris this time of night. Especially round what you call Place Bastille. They will not bother you again.'

Looking back down the centre aisle, Monsieur Pamplemousse realised to his horror that the *Issue de Secours* window was wide open. It was no wonder he had felt a draught down the back of his neck. Inscrutable faces gazed back at him and cameras were raised yet again. There was a series of flashes. First one, then another. It was followed by a whole barrage.

'We have saying in Japan – "It is good when man's deeds express his thoughts." We take quick vote and our thoughts all as one. By same token, sometimes best to be saying nothing afterwards.'

'The Japanese have much wisdom,' said Monsieur Pamplemousse. 'I have already forgotten our conversation.'

'Family are happy for you.'

'The *Family*? You do not mean . . .'

'No, not what you are thinking. Not the *Yakuza* – not Japanese Mafia. Family of brothers from company sports club. We all black belts. It is our reward for highest output ever – one week in your wonderful city. Already we have seen *Folies Bergère,* Lido, Moulin Rouge and many night spots. This part, with lovely young hostesses best of all. Come as big surprise – not included in itinerary. Round things off and no mistake.'

The tour leader handed Monsieur Pamplemousse a hat. It felt heavy.

'We offer many thanks in gratitude. Have no need of loose change any more.

'Staff of Nagihuku return to lathes happy men. Output go up.

'Best part of holiday. Better holiday than last year – three weeks in Saigon. Men wonder what will happen to them next year.'

At a given signal, cameras flashed again and there was a polite round of applause.

Monsieur Pamplemousse acknowledged it with a bow.

As he did so a feeling of guilt came over him. 'Were you planning to visit any other nightspots?'

'No. We all worn out. Only nightspot we visit now is bed.' Again there was a flicker of a smile. 'Leave for Japan by early flight in morning.'

'I will telephone the *café*,' said Monsieur Pamplemousse, 'and arrange for the driver to return you to your hotel.'

'All good things come to end,' said the tour leader. 'But we return home with good memories.'

'You must take care of them,' said Monsieur Pamplemousse. 'In France, we have a saying: *Les bons souvenirs sont des bijoux perdus* – Good memories are lost jewels.'

He looked towards the station entrance, but Caterina and her friends had long since disappeared.

'Nice girl,' said the man.

'Very,' said Monsieur Pamplemousse.

10
LE TRAIN BLEU

Monsieur Pamplemousse paused at the foot of the marble staircase leading up to Le Restaurant Train Bleu. He hesitated, wondering whether or not to take the plunge. The tables and chairs outside the *brasserie* on the main concourse below the restaurant were crowded with people aware of trains to catch. The *Grande Salle* would be a much more leisurely affair. The other diners would mostly be there for the food, not because they were going anywhere. Pommes Frites decided for him. He bounded on ahead as though the matter were a foregone conclusion.

'*Deux personne, Monsieur?*' One of several black-suited *maîtres d'hôtel* came forward and took in the situation at a glance.

'Is it possible to have a table in the window? One with a view of the *quai.*'

The man made a sucking noise through his teeth.

Monsieur Pamplemousse did something he had never, ever done before and probably never would again – the Chief would throw a fit if he knew – but he suddenly felt too tired to care. Besides, without making heavy weather of it, he wanted to be absolutely certain Caterina was carrying out his wishes.

'*Le Guide* would consider it a great favour.'

It did the trick. It wouldn't make any difference to the

outcome of his report, of course, and anyway he would meet that hurdle when it came.

An elderly waiter arrived with the menu, then a young *commis* brought a bread roll. The first waiter somehow went with the restaurant. But then, looking around, so did most of the staff. Much more so than the *Echiré* butter, wrapped in gold foil.

Monsieur Pamplemousse gazed out of the window. He hadn't long to wait. A crocodile of demure looking school-girls appeared from somewhere out of the depths and wound its way towards a waiting train. Whoever was hearing confession on the morrow was in for a busy time.

Was it his imagination or did the girl at the head of the file turn and look up? He would have given anything to have had his Leitz Trinovids with him so that he could bring the whole thing into sharp focus. He resisted the temptation to rush down the stairs and say a last goodbye. Not with others around. Caterina probably wouldn't thank him for it.

The first waiter reappeared with pad and pencil at the ready. He looked as though he was anxious to get home and rest his feet.

'It is sad when they have to go away, *Monsieur.*'

'Very sad,' said Monsieur Pamplemousse.

'*Mademoiselle is* going far?'

'To Rome. Possibly beyond.'

'Beyond Rome!' The man made it sound like a journey to the moon.

Perhaps realising the fact, he gave a sigh. 'It is nothing nowadays. In my day, Lyon and the Mediterranean seemed far away and magical. Then there were trains with romantic names like Mistral; in July the *quais* would be full of wives going south for the long summer holidays – or to their lovers. Husbands would wave goodbye and go back to their offices and their mistresses until August came.'

'It is hard to picture now,' said Monsieur Pamplemousse. 'The young go everywhere. It is the modern way.'

'Everything is the same – like *Eurosucre*,' said the waiter. 'We, too, have been modernised. The new kitchens are . . . *poof!*' He waved towards the service area. 'What shall I say? It is like comparing a luxury coach with a 2CV.'

'That, of course, depends on the driver,' said Monsieur Pamplemousse. 'Some are adept at both.' He picked up the menu and made a pretence of studying it.

The waiter leaned over to help. 'I can recommend the *assiette gourmande "Train Bleu", Monsieur. Foie gras, melon, saumon fumé, rillette de saumon, salade.*

'Afterwards, perhaps I might suggest fresh leg of lamb roasted the *Forézienne* way, with mushrooms and diced potatoes sauté in butter and truffles. It has always been a speciality of the restaurant.'

Truffles again! Monsieur Pamplemousse gladly surrendered the decision-making to another. Compared with the ones he had eaten the other evening they would be only a token gesture -discarded peelings probably, but nonetheless welcome for that. From now on he would always think of Caterina when he ate them. Perhaps he should have asked her mother to pay him in 'black diamonds'? A whole lorry load! Except he knew he was being facetious.

'And to drink, *Monsieur*?'

Monsieur Pamplemousse turned the menu over and consulted the wine list on the back.

'A Côte Rotie "Les Jumelles".' He had more or less begun with a Côte Rotie; it would be fitting to end with one. Although, once again, he doubted if it would equal his own bottle. At least he would be able to give it his full attention this time round.

'*Parfait!*' The waiter beamed his approval . 'An excellent choice, *Monsieur*. You will not be disappointed.' He spoke with the authority of one who seldom drank anything else.

'*Monsieur* would like some water?'

'An *eau de Vichy*,' said Monsieur Pamplemousse. 'It will be good for my digestion.' He was tempted to ask for one of the Director's dry martinis, but he thought better of it and ordered a Kir instead.

'*Vin blanc, Monsieur,* or *Royale?*'

'*Royale.* No, on second thoughts, leave out the cassis. Make it a straight champagne.' Why not? He was suddenly feeling very flat and the champagne would give him a lift.

As the waiter disappeared, Monsieur Pamplemousse reached for his notebook. It was back to work again.

He looked around at the setting. Built at the time of the Paris Exhibition of 1900 and now classed as a national monument, the whole restaurant was a memorial to the carefree life of *la Belle Époque;* overwhelming in its extravagant decadence. The Baroque gilded pillars supporting the vaulted ceilings were a riot of rococo, scantily clad, Rubenesque female figures – not a straight line among them. The ceiling itself and the surrounding walls, all newly restored, had been covered by artists of the day with murals depicting romantic scenes of the times: men wearing straw hats and women in long, frilly dresses, or views which might be seen from the windows of Train Bleu itself by those who were taking the route to the sun and the Côte d'Azur.

Everything about it was sumptuous. The rich, buttoned leather *banquettes* and dark red hanging drapes, the chairs and the tables with their spotless white linen cloths, the vast chandeliers overhead, the ornate coat stands surmounted by lamps, the heavy polished brass, all served to remind those using the restaurant of a bygone age. Eating in Le Train Bleu was as much an architectural as a gastronomic experience. *Le Guide's* symbols would be stretched to their limit.

Monsieur Pamplemousse suddenly became aware of a shadow materialising beside him and he felt a kiss on the back of his neck. It sent shivers down his spine.

'I must run,' said Caterina. 'It is only to say thank you.'

'Thank *you*,' said Monsieur Pamplemousse. 'And *bonne chance* – whatever you do – wherever you go.'

'I will write!'

'That would be nice,' said Monsieur Pamplemousse. But he knew she wouldn't, and it might be just as well.

The waiter arrived back carrying a bottle of wine.

'*Monsieur's* daughter?'

Monsieur Pamplemousse shook his head. 'Not even a Goddaughter . . . I'm afraid.' He almost added 'yet' as an afterthought.

'Aaah!' It was the long drawn out response of one who had seen many things in his time. 'Young men have visions, *Monsieur.* Old men have dreams.' He withdrew the cork, sniffed it briefly, and with an air of approval placed it in a dish alongside the bottle, pocketing the foil. Then he poured a little of the wine, swirled it round the glass, and placed it back on the table.

'*Monsieur?*'

It was, thought Monsieur Pamplemousse, arguably the best Côte Rotie he had ever tasted. Soft, heady, assertive and surprisingly mature for its age, with plenty of body, fruity. . . But then, didn't that go to prove his long-held theory: wine, a living thing, tasted of many things besides the grapes that went into its making, not least being the company you kept and all that went with it.

He placed the hat he had been given on the table in front of him.

'You may keep the change,' he said grandly. 'In the meantime, please look after the table. We shall be back in a moment.'

If they hurried he would be just in time to wave the Palatino goodbye.

'You were very restless in your sleep last night, Aristide,' said Madame Pamplemousse. 'Was it something you had for dinner?'

'No, *Couscous*,' said Monsieur Pamplemousse. 'If anything it was something I didn't have.'

'Did you miss me while I was away?'

'Of course I did, Doucette. I always do. You know that. The apartment is very quiet without you.'

'I tried to telephone you several times, but it was either engaged or there was no answer.'

That summed up the last few days to a tee.

Madame Pamplemousse concentrated on dusting a picture near the window. 'You didn't eat half the things I left you.'

Monsieur Pamplemousse resisted the temptation to say, 'But I ate the other half.' He changed the subject instead. 'How is Agathe?' It would be good for ten minutes at least. Agathe would complain if she had nothing to complain about.

He had arrived home late the previous evening to find Doucette already in bed and asleep. Climbing in beside her, his mind swarming with all the things that had happened during the day, he had fully expected to lie awake for hours.

Instead of which he had fallen asleep almost as soon as his head touched the pillow, and he was only now beginning to come out of it.

'That man I was telling you about is still there.' Madame Pamplemousse was in the middle of listing her sister's woes when she broke off and stared out of the window.

Prowling round the apartment, looking to see if he had left anything lying about which might be hard to explain – a photograph of Caterina, *par exemple*, or the remains of dinner for two, Monsieur Pamplemousse paused.

'What man?'

'The one I was telling you about at breakfast,' said Madame Pamplemousse impatiently. 'The one on crutches. You don't listen to a word I say sometimes.' She opened the door to the balcony in order to get a better view.

'He's hardly moved since I first saw him, although that's not surprising. Poor man. How he manages to play anything at all with his legs in plaster and his head all bandaged up like it is, I don't know. I suppose he's a musician. He wouldn't be carrying a violin case otherwise.'

She glanced back over her shoulder. 'He keeps looking up this way. Is it someone you know, Aristide?'

'Let me see.' Monsieur Pamplemousse made his way to the balcony. Pommes Frites hurried after him. His hackles rose and he emitted a low growl as he followed the direction of his master's gaze to the street below.

'Aristide!' cried Madame Pamplemousse. 'Where are you going?'

'Out!' said Monsieur Pamplemousse briefly. He looked round for assistance, but Pommes Frites was way ahead of him. When they reached the ground floor he flew out of the lift, and only the fact that the main entrance door was closed prevented him from taking action there and then.

'*Attendez, s'il vous plaît.*' Signalling Pommes Frites to remain where he was for the time being, Monsieur Pamplemousse strode across the rue Girardon to where the man was hovering.

Attack being the best form of defence, he went in with all guns blazing.

'*Salaud!*

'*Cochon* of a macaroni-eating peasant!

'*Allez! Allez!*

'I never wish to see you again . . . *jamais* . . . never!'

All the frustration and fears of the preceding few days erupted.

'And furthermore, when you have your plaster removed tell them to throw away your clothes as well. They offend me.

'You are nothing but a no-good cheap-skate bully of a crook masquerading in a Caraceni suit.

'You are a *maquereau* – a pimp! You are worse than that – you are a failed pimp!'

Each time he thought of something new, Monsieur Pamplemousse emphasised it with a stabbing motion of his right forefinger.

To his surprise, the man suddenly toppled over backwards. As he hit the road his left hand shot towards his top pocket, but Pommes Frites was there before him.

Monsieur Pamplemousse deftly removed a four-inch hat pin and placed the pointed end against the man's ear. 'I could, you know.'

'But you won't.'

'Don't push me,' said Monsieur Pamplemousse in disgust. 'Just don't push me. And I wouldn't stay there if I were you. The *Montmartrobus is* overdue and the driver will be making up time. You are likely to end up as nothing but a bump in the road.'

'*Signore* – all I wanted was to say *grazie* . . .'

'*Grazie?*' Monsieur Pamplemousse paused for breath. 'You wish to thank me? Thank me for what?'

'For finding the girl. We were in charge of her safe-keeping. Think what would have happened to us if we had failed.'

Monsieur Pamplemousse stared down at Il Blobbo as he absorbed what had just been said. He had been assuming all along that the two men had been looking for Caterina for their own immoral purposes. But if Uncle Caputo had charged them with Caterina's safe-keeping while she was away and they had also lost track of her, it put a whole new slant on things. The men would have been in exactly the same position as himself. They, too, would have been going in fear of their lives, and understandably so.

In all probability they would both have ended up suffering the same kind of fate as had the American, William Jackson – a classic case of its kind, demonstrating the extremes of revenge the Mafia took on those members who failed their bosses. People still talked about it.

William 'Action' Jackson, who had blotted his copybook with Mafia boss Sam Giancana, ended his days hanging from a steel meat hook in a Chicago meat-rendering plant, literally hacked and burned to death, slowly, deliberately and without mercy, by gang members wielding a variety of weapons; ice picks, knives, razors . . . a blowtorch.

Monsieur Pamplemousse stared at Il Blobbo. 'Think yourself lucky,' he said gruffly.

He almost wished now he hadn't mentioned the *Montmartrobus*. It would be a fitting punishment. Il Blobbo by name, ending up as a *blobbo* in the road.

'Aristide!' Doucette stared at her husband as he came back into the room. 'How could you? Attacking a poor defenceless man on crutches. Whatever came over you?'

'I was doing it on behalf of the family of a late attendant on the Palatino,' said Monsieur Pamplemousse. 'Also, a coachload of lathe workers from Nagihuku in Japan. It is unlike the Japanese not to finish off things properly, but that is the way the world is going, I fear.'

'There are times,' said Madame Pamplemousse, 'when I feel I shall never understand you properly.'

'It could have been worse.' Briefly and succinctly, and leaving out certain aspects which experience told might slow down rather than advance the story, Monsieur Pamplemousse brought Doucette up to date, ending with the sorry tale of William Jackson. When he had finished she gave a shudder.

'Such things!'

Monsieur Pamplemousse shrugged. Doucette didn't know the half of it.

Jackson's story hadn't ended there. Shot in the knees, an electric cattle prod stuffed up his rectum and water poured over it for good measure, he had somehow managed to survive for two whole days, setting a record which to date no one had been in a hurry to break.

Photographs of the grim event in its various stages had been distributed as a warning to others not to transgress. He would never forget seeing a copy at the time; even hardened members of the force had gone silent.

'Shouldn't you tell someone?' asked Madame Pamplemousse.

Monsieur Pamplemousse picked up the phone. Doucette was right as usual. There was no reason on earth now why he shouldn't come clean with Jacques.

'I was just about to ring you.' Jacques beat him to it. 'We've got a line on the two men. The short fat one owns a television store in Palermo. On the side he's a specialist in things electronic; phone bugging, safe-blowing . . .'

'. . . solar-powered burglar alarms?' said Monsieur Pamplemousse drily.

'You name it. The one you call Il Blobbo is known as Giuseppi "the Pin" – no prizes for guessing why. Both are known members of the Cosa Nostra. We'll pull them in as soon as we find them, but your guess is as good as mine as to what happens then. You know what it's like. The best we can probably do is make things difficult for them.'

'I don't think either will be bothering anyone for a while,' said Monsieur Pamplemousse. 'If you let me have a copy of the identikit picture and a medical dictionary I will make certain modifications.'

As quickly as possible he gave Jacques an edited version of all that he had told Doucette. He could always fill in the details later.

'Bang goes my dream apartment,' said Jacques when he had finished. 'I was planning to make you an offer when you moved out.'

'It's nice to know who your friends are,' said Monsieur Pamplemousse.

Madame Pamplemousse gave a final flourish of her duster as he put down the phone. 'Did I hear you say the girl has gone back home?'

Monsieur Pamplemousse looked at his watch. 'All being well, she should be in Rome by now.'

'She didn't stay very long. Although if she was how you described her, I imagine *Monsieur le Directeur* won't be sorry.'

'*Merde!*'

'Really, Aristide!' exclaimed Doucette. 'I don't know what has come over you this morning.'

Monsieur Leclercq! He had made one abortive attempt to telephone the Director from the Gare de Lyon the previous evening, but the number had been out of order. Since then he had been so embroiled with his own problems he had quite forgotten to try again.

'He left a message soon after I got in last night,' said Doucette. 'He said to tell you to use his other number next time you called. Ever since his telephone line was cut he's been having to make do with his mobile phone . . .'

'The Director's line was cut?' Monsieur Pamplemousse stared at his wife.

'Apparently it happened soon after you telephoned from the *gendarmerie* and he forgot to tell you the last time you spoke.'

'He forgot to tell me . . .' Monsieur Pamplemousse checked in his diary, then picked up the telephone and dialled. It solved another problem that had been bothering him. He could well understand Il Blobbo wanting to render the Director incommunicado with the outside world – it would have been one of the first things he would have done himself – but leaving him with a telephone had seemed to render the whole operation pointless. Clearly, he thought he had, and equally clearly he had reckoned without Monsieur Leclercq's addiction to gadgets.

'*Monsieur* . . .' But once again Monsieur Pamplemousse had to wait his turn. The Director was bubbling over with his own news.

'Pamplemousse . . . an extraordinary thing happened this morning. I was awakened by a loud explosion. I rushed to the window and was just in time to see pigeon feathers floating down out of the sky. It was an incredible sight –

there they were, silhouetted in the light from the rising sun. If only you had been here with your camera.

'What can it mean, Aristide? Do the Mafia have some new method of radio-control at their disposal? Or have they attached some fiendish device to the bird bath?'

'I think, *Monsieur*, it simply means you can come out now. If you go to the window again and look down, I suspect you may find your front door is no longer there.'

While the Director was absorbing this latest piece of information, Monsieur Pamplemousse seized his opportunity.

'Good news, *Monsieur*. Your *petite cousine* is safe. She is on her way home. You can breathe again. In fact, we can all breathe again.'

Quick to jump to the wrong conclusions in times of trouble, the Director was equally prompt in lavishing praise when events took a turn for the better.

Monsieur Pamplemousse wondered how long it would be before the Chief's mind started working in the same direction as his own. The answer came almost immediately.

'You must take Madame Pamplemousse out to celebrate, Aristide. Taillevant, perhaps, or Guy Savoy. I will make the necessary arrangements for this evening. If Chantal can get back to Paris in time we may even join you.'

'It is Sunday, *Monsieur*. They will be closed.'

'You are right. I have lost all track of time.' Monsieur Leclercq tried unsuccessfully to keep the note of disappointment from his voice.

'I did have somewhere slightly less exotic in mind, *Monsieur*.'

'Good. Good. Am I allowed to know where?'

'It is called Mamma Mia's. I believe the owner is a distant relative of Chantal's Uncle Caputo. You are welcome to join us there.'

'You have some unfinished business, Aristide?' The Director sounded slightly nervous again.

'No, *Monsieur*, simply some unfinished *ossobuco.*'

Pommes Frites pricked up his ears at the magic word. If it was anything like the *ossobuco* he had found in the back of his master's car the night before, he couldn't wait. Cold, it had been delicious- although he could have done without the foil – so what it would be like hot didn't bear thinking about! Gastric juices began to flow. Saliva accumulated. He could hardly wait.

'It sounds to me, Aristide,' said Madame Pamplemousse, 'very much as though you are about to make me an offer I cannot refuse.'

'That, *Couscous,*' said Monsieur Pamplemousse,'is one way of putting it. Although I think Pommes Frites would agree with me, it would be much nearer the truth if you simply said *ought* not.'